BEAR O

By

Steven A. McKay

Copyright © 2021

Book 4 in the

**WARRIOR DRUID OF BRITAIN
CHRONICLES**

LIST OF PLACES IN *BEAR OF BRITAIN*

Alauna – on the coast of present-day Cumbria
Alt Clota – Strathclyde
Branodunum – Brancaster, Norfolk
*Bryn Cleddyf -near Osbaston, Leicestershire
Caer Ebbas – Ebchester, County Durham
*Caer Lene – Laceby, NE Lincolnshire
Caer Lerion – called Ratae by the Romans – Leicester
*Cwrt Isel – just north of Leicester
Deva – Chester, Cheshire
Dun Breatann – Dumbarton, West Dunbartonshire
Elmet – Leeds
Garrianum – Burgh Castle, Norfolk
*Longhafan – Grimsby, Lincolnshire
Luguvalium – Carlisle
*Nant Beac – Near Bexwell, Norfolk
Othona – Bradwell-on-Sea, Essex
Powys – Powys, Wales
Rheged – Cumbria
Waithe – Waithe! East Lindsey, Lincolnshire

*Those marked with an asterisk were made up by the author.

CHAPTER ONE

Snow whirled in the wind around the slumbering army, making it difficult to walk and ensuring the soldiers gathered there stayed within their tents or close to the blazing fires that were dotted around, little pockets of warmth and light in the chill. Night had fallen quickly for it was early in January and Britannia was gripped in the unrelenting, icy arms of the harshest winter most could remember. Of course, the Saxons were used to the dark and the cold, particularly the men that formed this army, hailing as they did from Jutland, but even they had been bundled in thick furs on this night, sipping mead and playing tafl as best they could with numb fingers before retiring to their bedrolls for a few hours of shivering sleep.

Even the howling wind and bitter chill did not stop the usual routine of the warband, and muttering, sullen sentries were posted at regular intervals around the camp perimeter, while officers occasionally patrolled to make sure all was well and that the guards had not fallen asleep.

At the centre of the encampment stood the tallest, grandest tent. This one was circular, and the lack of snow on its sloping roof suggested a brazier was being tended through the night, offering some comfort to those resting inside. The pavilion was big enough for ten men to meet in if need be, although it only housed one warrior this night: Jarl Sæwine of Tornhem. He had command of this warband, forty or so of his countrymen ranging in age from sixteen to forty-eight, all seasoned fighters, even the very youngest who'd come to this island in the summer and earned their place at the jarl's table in brutal skirmishes with the native Britons.

Indeed, those battles had been fought with such ferocity, such unforgiving—and often sadistic—violence, that Jarl Sæwine's name had come to be hated and feared by the native people living here in Longhafan on the eastern coast of Britain. He was one of the Saxon *bretwalda* Hengist's most powerful chieftains, and the Britons thereabouts dreaded the return of spring, when Sæwine and

1

his son Leofdaeg would welcome more warriors from across the sea and once more bring fire and death to the local settlements.

If Jarl Sæwine survived that long.

Bellicus, druid of Dun Breatann reached out and grasped the arm of the long-haired warrior stepping carefully through the blanket of snow that lay ahead of them. The man turned, a frown on his scarred yet strikingly handsome face and jerked his head, silently demanding to know why his progress had been halted.

The druid, crouching so his near seven-foot frame wouldn't be spotted by the sentries, pointed into the darkness and the long-haired warrior turned, staring into the whirling snow for a moment until the light from a nearby fire reflected off the steel tip of a spear, revealing the presence of a Saxon guard not twenty feet away.

Without hesitation, the warrior raised a hand, bidding Bellicus wait while he slipped ahead, moving with a strange, incongruous grace through the thick snow, almost as if it was no more a hindrance than a summer meadow filled with wildflowers. In the blink of an eye, the Saxon sentry disappeared from sight, his dark presence swallowed by the hypnotic flakes of snow as if he'd never existed. A moment later the assassin returned and, without a word passing between them, they moved off again, towards the large central tent.

As they walked, the crunching from their footsteps masked by the whistling wind, Bellicus looked at the man ahead, believing he couldn't have picked a better companion for this task. When the druid first met the young warrior a few months ago he'd felt an instant kinship. Of course, he'd heard stories about the man who was the warlord Arthur's deadly champion, who hadn't? But Bellicus knew better than anyone that people did not usually match the exaggerated tales that were told about them.

Lancelot, however, did live up to his burgeoning legend.

With his long blond hair, high cheekbones and easy smile, women loved him and his battle scars. He was as hardy a warrior as anyone Bellicus had ever met though, deadly with a longsword but not averse to picking up a 'lesser' weapon like a hatchet, spear, or hammer, and dealing death to his Saxon foes with them in a variety of imaginative ways. His skill in battle was tempered by recklessness however, which accounted for the downward scar on his otherwise unblemished forehead. Earned during a raid on Hengist's forces in the southeast a year earlier, it had healed well enough, but would never disappear completely. Of course, that imperfection simply made him even more irresistible to the ladies.

When Arthur had first talked about the possibility of someone sneaking into Jarl Sæwine's camp and killing him while he slept, Lancelot immediately volunteered for what most expected would be a suicide mission. The man's confidence in his own abilities led him to believe even a forty-strong warband couldn't stop him though, and, amused and inspired by Lancelot's faith, Bellicus had offered to accompany him into the Saxon camp, much to his friend Duro's chagrin.

So, here they were, just the two of them in the middle of a snowstorm, surrounded by enemies who'd happily torture them to death if they were captured, edging their way ever closer to the circular tent in the middle of the camp. Bellicus felt almost naked without his faithful wardog, Cai, by his side, but this was no place for the hound. Their mission was simply to sneak past the guards, find a way into the jarl's tent, and kill him without the alarm being raised. Bellicus was happy to think of Cai safely resting back at camp with Duro beside a roaring fire. Indeed, the druid was beginning to wish he was there with them, so cold was the night.

Four steps ahead, Lancelot halted and raised his hand in warning. Immediately, Bellicus heard humming and realised they'd almost walked into a Saxon lookout who was crouching on the ground, blowing into his hands and softly singing to keep himself awake, if not quite alert.

As before, the wind covered Lancelot's movements and he managed to make it right up to the guard before the Saxon heard him coming. By then, of course, it was too late – Lancelot's right hand snaked out in a blur of motion and the dagger he held plunged deep into the sentry's back. Before a cry of pain or warning could escape his lips, Lancelot's left hand had clamped firmly over his mouth and, twice more, the dagger hammered in and out of the unfortunate man's body.

The shocking crimson stains on the pristine white ground were covered within moments, so heavy was the snowfall, and, when no shouts of alarm were raised, Lancelot moved on, leaving his latest victim where he lay. They were almost at their destination.

Heading towards the rear of the tent the two Britons stopped and crouched low in the shadows, pressing against the wet leather and listening intently. The wind whipped around them, covering any possible snoring or conversation within, so, with a shrug, Lancelot eased the tip of his knife into the material of the tent and sawed gently upwards, making an opening big enough for him to fit through. With a last grin at Bellicus, he poked his head into the Saxon jarl's tent and then the rest of him disappeared inside.

The druid waited with his long sword, Melltgwyn, in hand, and then he froze as a man suddenly came walking around the side of the tent towards him. Bellicus had seen Jarl Sæwine before, once, during a battle in which the Saxons were defeated but escaped without being completely wiped out, and then again earlier that day when he and Lancelot scouted this encampment.

This was the man staring back at him in surprise.

Although there were jokes told about how uncivilised and, well, stupid the barbarian Saxons were, the truth was, it took a clever man to become as successful a jarl as Sæwine. Bellicus knew this, but he also knew the importance a man's honour was to these invaders from Jutland, so the druid wasn't sure how the next few moments would play out.

Ultimately, Jarl Sæwine took in the enormous size of the warrior druid standing before him with naked blade in hand, and decided his continued existence on this earth was more important than dying an honourable warrior's death. Especially since he carried no weapon of his own having just got out of bed to empty his bladder.

So, he ran, stumbling and slipping in the snow, crying out to his men for aid.

"Shit," Bellicus muttered. He hadn't expected this, but their mission was to kill the jarl, so he chased the fleeing figure, mind racing as he wondered what in Dis Pater's name he'd do even if he did manage to catch Sæwine, now that the alarm had been raised.

And it certainly had been raised, as men shouted questions, demanding to know what was happening, and rousing their companions who were, somehow, still sleeping despite their jarl's panicked shouts.

Unfortunately for the Saxon nobleman, he decided to run back into his tent and gather his sword that he might face the enormous

Briton coming after him on a fairer footing. Bursting through the open door flaps of the leather tent that had been his home for months now, Jarl Sæwine ran straight into Lancelot.

Arthur's champion couldn't believe his luck as his target bounced off him. When Lancelot, whose eyes were accustomed to the darkened interior of the tent, realised who was before him he laughed shortly, eyes blazing, dodged the hurried punch Sæwine threw at him, and thrust his knife upwards, through the jarl's jaw, warm blood spurting down and across his hand and wrist. It was a short blade in comparison to Bellicus's sword, but long enough to kill Sæwine instantly.

The druid came in through the front entrance then, eyes taking in the scene before him, and with a satisfied nod, grasped Lancelot by the arm and pushed him towards the tear at the rear of the tent with its man-sized tear.

"Hurry, by the gods. Get out and start running! The bastards will be on us any moment."

Lancelot slipped easily through the opening in the material that his knife had made, while the druid chose another spot and pierced the thick material with Melltgwyn, dragging it up to make an escape hole of his own. But Bellicus's shoulders proved too wide and the heavy leather of the pavilion slowed his escape.

A young Saxon warrior came into the front of the tent at that moment, roaring in outrage as he saw the dead jarl on the ground. "Father?" he cried, staring down at the bloody figure on the ground, and Bellicus, peering back over his shoulder, recognised the grief-stricken soldier as Leofdaeg, son of the dead jarl. The Saxon looked up at them and, seeing the blood-stained knife in Lancelot's hand through the torn opening, pointed his own *seax* at the blond Briton, moving forward with the promise of vengeance in his light-blue eyes.

Two more Saxons burst into the tent behind him and, with a roar, Bellicus forced himself into the ripped leather, tearing it even further until, at last, he burst out of the tent, falling forward into the snow. His efforts were enough to pull the entire structure over, and it would have trapped him had Lancelot not been standing there, ready to grasp the druid by the arm and haul him to safety.

Howling, the Saxons inside the collapsed tent tried to use their own blades to cut holes in the material but it was no easy task with the weight on top of them and Bellicus and Lancelot were off and running towards the wooded area that stood a short distance to the east of the camp.

"We'd be better splitting up," Lancelot called over the wind, looking back and seeing Leofdaeg finally emerging into the night with at least a dozen men and a couple of snarling warrior women coming around the sides of the collapsed pavilion after them.

"What's the point in separating?" Bellicus replied. "We stay together, watch one another's backs if they manage to catch up to us. There's a chance one of us will get lost if we split up."

Lancelot might have been Arthur's right-hand man, his champion, and besides the Merlin his closest advisor, but Bellicus was well used to being in command himself, and Lancelot didn't argue as they forged their way through the thick snow towards the looming spectres of the leafless trees in the gloom ahead.

To their right a war-cry was shouted and, as fast as the speed of thought, Lancelot turned, spotted the charging Saxon sentry, and threw his knife, still crimson with the blood of Jarl Sæwine. It struck home in the chest of the roaring warrior who fell back in dismay although his thick winter furs had stopped the blade from piercing his heart. Still, it was enough to give the fugitives time to get nearer the trees without slowing.

An arrow zipped past, and then another, and Bellicus swore, but the Saxons were loosing their missiles hurriedly and in the dark, and their wild, unfocused shots merely served to make the druid and his companion run even faster.

Curses, threats, and promises of the agonies they'd suffer when they were captured followed almost as fast as the arrows had, but the Britons were at the trees now, at last.

"Where the hell are our horses?" Lancelot demanded, looking around and trying to get his bearings in the midst of the drifting, whirling snow. He wasn't smiling any more. "Gods, our tracks have been completely covered. We'll never find them in this…!"

"Darac!" The druid called softly and, a little way to their right, came the unmistakeable whinny of a horse. Now it was Bellicus's turn to grin as he led Lancelot towards the horses they'd pegged to the ground.

"You trained your mount to answer your call?" asked the blond warrior in open astonishment.

6

Bellicus nodded. "Horses are very clever," he said, reaching the big black that had been a loyal friend to him for years and jumping up onto its back. He dragged free the peg that tethered Darac to the snowy forest floor and kicked his heels in as the murderous cries of the Saxons came close behind.

More arrows tore through the air but once again the archers' aim was off and the two Britons picked up speed, their horses' hooves sending clods of snow flying in their wake.

"We'll meet again, you Waelisc scum!" screamed Leofdaeg behind them, using the Saxons' name for the native inhabitants of Britain. Impotent rage and grief carried his voice through the heavy snow. "You'll pay for your work this night, by Thunor, I swear it!"

"I thought you were supposed to be like a shadow," Bellicus called to Lancelot as they put distance between themselves and the furious, thwarted Leofdaeg. "A silent killer, who slips into a place and out again without anyone noticing." He glanced back and shook his head. "I'd say they noticed us."

"You're the one that demolished their tent," Lancelot retorted, but his voice was full of joy, and he again broke into the laugh that had become so familiar to Bellicus in the short time he'd known Arthur's champion.

Behind them, the Saxons could only watch as their quarry disappeared into the howling night.

CHAPTER TWO

"You ready to go, Bel?"

The druid started at the sound of his friend's voice and he realised he'd fallen asleep fully dressed, so exhausted had he been after his night with Lancelot. "Go?" he asked groggily. "Go where, Duro?"

The former Roman centurion looked down sympathetically at his tentmate and stroked the ears of Cai, Bellicus's massive wardog. "We're going to ambush those Saxons you raided last night. Didn't anyone tell you?"

The sounds of men breaking camp filtered through the soft leather of their tent and the druid grinned ruefully. "Aye, I did hear talk of that when I returned but I must have been more tired than I realised and the mugs of ale I downed with Merlin just before going to sleep can't have helped. Have I time to wash my face?"

Duro nodded. "Aye, but Arthur wants us to move soon. He's convinced the Saxons will look to avenge their jarl's death by destroying one of the nearby towns." He stamped his feet and rubbed his red hands to try and bring some warmth into them as Bellicus threw off his blanket and stood up.

"I must admit," the druid said, lifting a jug of water to rinse his face and shaved head, "that I really like Arthur's boldness and desire to act quickly and decisively when he sees an opening. Huh, guess I won't be having a wash." He showed Duro the upended jug, with not a drop of water spilling from it. "Frozen solid."

They went outside, Cai following eagerly, great muscles rippling as he moved a little way ahead of them and turned a patch of pristine white snow yellow.

"It's absolutely bitter," Duro noted, pulling woollen mittens onto his hands, one of which was missing the pinkie and ring fingers as a result of the Pictish King Drest's brutal torture not so long ago. Both he and Bellicus had been imprisoned in Drest's fortress at Dunnottar before escaping with the help of the beautiful young druidess, Ria, who'd become Bellicus's lover for a time. They were chased back home by the Pictish army which besieged Dun Breatann and might have taken control of the fortress if Duro hadn't realised Ria was a spy. Acting just in time, Queen Narina's

8

soldiers foiled the Picts' plan, smashing King Drest's army and taking his daughter, Aife, prisoner. Narina became, in effect, High Queen of all the lands north of Hadrianus's Wall and agreed to marry a Votadini prince named Ysfael before Bellicus and Duro led a warband south to join Arthur in his continuing war against the Saxons.

"I'll actually be glad once the fighting starts," the centurion said vehemently. "Since it'll warm me up a little!"

A rider charged towards the camp from the east, heading towards Arthur's tent and Bellicus led the way there himself. "That'll be one of the scouts," he said. "Bringing word of the Saxons' intended target perhaps."

"Morning, big man," a voice called, and they turned to see their young compatriot, and rowdy champion of the Votadini tribe, Eburus, warming himself by a fire. He'd travelled south with them after forming an unlikely friendship with both during the previous year's battles against the Picts. "What's happening? Are we moving out?"

"Soon, I'd guess," Bellicus replied. "We're just going to see Arthur now. Have our men ready to move, will you?"

Eburus grinned. Like Lancelot he was loud and brash and confident in his own abilities as a warrior. "They're all ready to go, don't worry, druid. Some of us have been up for hours you know."

"Aye, not many can sleep once you start talking, Eburus. You're a giant pain in the arse, lad." Duro's face was serious, but his eyes twinkled and, as he and Bellicus passed the guards and entered Arthur's tent they chuckled at the foul insult Eburus called after them.

"Ah, you're awake. Good." Arthur nodded to them politely although he seemed pensive as he directed them to sit on a couple of stools by the table in the middle of the tent.

Lancelot was there, looking as fresh and clean-cut as he had before the previous night's raid and Bellicus thought he could even smell lavender from the man, as though he'd washed in scented water recently. Also present were two local chieftains and, of course, the Merlin.

Nemias was his real name, but he was now more widely known as Merlin, the title given to the chief druid of all Britain. Cai headed straight for the white-bearded old High Druid and allowed

9

his muzzle to be stroked and a kiss to be planted on his head before padding back and flopping onto the floor at Bellicus's feet.

"I was just saying," Arthur told the newcomers, "That our scout reports the Saxons are moving south. He believes they're heading for Waithe. Which means they won't have as far to travel as I'd hoped. We should get moving now if you're all ready?" He looked around at the gathered lords who all nodded agreement. "Let's not waste any more time then. I'll lead with Lancelot and my personal guard. King Caradoc, these are your lands, you ride with me, if you would? Bellicus, you bring up the rear with your men, all right?"

The group split up, exiting into the dry, but freezing morning and hurrying off to get their men on the move.

"How far is Waithe, my lord?" Duro asked Arthur before they parted.

"Eight miles, give or take," the warlord replied as his horse was brought for him and he jumped nimbly up into the saddle with the grace of a natural rider. "It'll take us half the morning, I think, given the weather. When we're almost there I'll have Caradoc and Edern take their men to either side so we can flank the Saxons. If we move quickly we'll get there ahead of them, with time to setup an ambush."

With that, he raised his arm in salute, which Duro returned Roman legionary fashion, and rode off to take up his position at the forefront of the small army.

"Why do I get the impression Arthur isn't as confident about this ambush as he should be?" the centurion muttered as he and Bellicus walked quickly back to where Eburus was already marshalling the men into marching formation.

"Seems like he expected the Saxons to strike one of the villages closer to our position," the druid said. "That's why we camped here in the first place. I imagine he's worried the bastards will get to the village before us and destroy the place. That would be on Arthur's head, since he ordered Lancelot and me to take out their jarl."

"He's young," Duro noted, reaching his horse, which he called Pryderi, and mounting with rather less grace than Arthur had done. "He worries too much about what might go wrong. I expect once he loses a few battles he'll grow more pragmatic."

10

"Perhaps," Bellicus said, stroking Darac's nose before climbing into the big black's saddle. "But a leader who worries about the deaths of innocent villagers is not a bad thing, even if it might make him more cautious than he would otherwise be."

"Ready, Eburus?"

The blue-eyed Votadini warrior nodded. In Bellicus's company, he'd come down from Alt Clota with twenty of his Votadini kinsmen and a similar number of the druid's own Damnonii tribe. Only a handful of them were with the warband that day though, for the main body of Arthur's army had remained to the west, under the command of Arthur's cousin, Cador, and the redoubtable Kay.

"Aye," Eburus replied to Duro. "Like I keep telling you, centurion, we've been dying for a fight all morning. Let's do this!"

Some of the men shouted agreement, while others gave Eburus irritated glances. Clearly, he hadn't won them all over yet, and probably never would. He was just one of those people who polarised opinion, although, since Bellicus had taken him under his wing, as it were, the Votadini champion had become slightly less abrasive and loud. As strange as it seemed, Eburus just wanted to be liked, and it made him try too hard at times.

A horn sounded from the front of the warband and soon everyone was moving, trudging through the snow which lay thick outside the camp's perimeters. Thankfully, King Caradoc knew these, his own, lands, like the back of his hand and led them along the white-covered road at the front of his men who all carried round shields painted red making them easy to pick out in the warband, since Arthur's own companions and warriors had blue shields. Caradoc, a barrel-chested, clean-shaven man with bowl cut brown hair, and his son, Edern, both wore golden torcs around their necks and dressed in the Roman style. They seemed happy to have Arthur's men with them to clear the Saxons out of the settlements surrounding their hometown of Lindum.

Bellicus looked about, taking in the folk he'd chosen to throw his, and his men's, lot in with. Arthur, Warlord of Britain by agreement rather than by dint of royal blood or birth right, had eleven of his own guard with him, including Lancelot. Caradoc had twenty of his local warriors behind him, while Edern had fourteen. Bellicus, besides Duro and Eburus, had seven, plus Cai who was as dangerous in a battle as any man.

Almost sixty men, against the forty or so coming from the Saxon camp Bellicus and Lancelot had narrowly escaped from the previous night. It should be a straightforward victory – *if* they made it to Waithe before the vengeful enemy and had time to choose the ground they launched their ambuscade from.

Although it was freezing and the breaths of men and horses steamed in the air, it was no longer snowing and the sun was beginning to appear. The fog would lift eventually, Bellicus expected, but, for now, it muffled the sounds of their passage so the Saxons, even if they were nearby, should not hear them. Despite that, the men were subdued – winter was no time for war, it was a time for feasting in the lord's hall, telling stories, singing songs, and downing ale.

Every man there understood the importance of wiping out this particular Saxon warband, since their exploits were notorious, but, trudging along with sodden boots, dripping noses and numb fingers, the Briton warriors didn't feel much like singing joyous marching songs as they would in spring's full bloom. They did, however, look forward to the chance to spill the invaders' blood, and warm their own bones in the heat of battle.

When they'd only been walking for an hour or so they passed a man, one of Caradoc's local troopers, crouched in the snow, pale and shivering behind his red shield. He looked up at Bellicus and Duro shame-facedly as they passed, and the centurion couldn't help growling in disgust at the sight.

"What's the matter wi' you?" Eburus demanded of the man, and Bellicus rolled his eyes. The entire warband had passed the fellow without comment, but the Votadini had to involve himself. It wasn't mere curiosity, or nosiness, that drove him, the young warrior genuinely wanted to help the man, but all Eburus's words had done was draw attention to his plight.

"Nothing," the stationary soldier replied shortly, eyes flashing irritably. "Just move on."

Eburus frowned but the warband continued to march and he didn't want to lose his place in the line so, with a muttered, "Prick," in the local warrior's direction, he hurried on, leaving the man alone in the snow.

"What's his problem?" Eburus asked, looking up at Bellicus and Duro and jerking a thumb over his shoulder. "Are we just leaving him behind?"

"Aye, boy, we're leaving him behind," Duro said with a sigh. "Not everyone is as hardy as you. Did you not see him holding his foot? The cold's got to him and his king's ordered him to go home since he can't keep up with us." The centurion turned to Bellicus and shook his head. "It's not a good sign, is it, druid? I fear many of these so-called warriors won't have the balls to see off the Saxons."

Bellicus nodded at his friend's ominous words. He too had noticed the lack of discipline amongst the men of Lindum, and the way they carried themselves. They were more like farmers than hardened soldiers and that did not bode well when the enemy they faced were so well versed in the ways of war. He feared this was not only a problem for today, in these particular lands, but something they would find all throughout the southern tribes of Britain. The Romans had kept them safe, and they'd grown fat and weak in those peaceful generations, but the legions, and their protective influence, had left these shores over twenty years ago, believing Britannia not worth the cost, or trouble, anymore.

Still, Caradoc's men might not be fit for the task of beating back the Saxons, but Bellicus looked at his fellow Damnonii tribesmen and felt a surge of pride. They were used to battling Dalriadan and Pictish raiders; their martial skills were as finely honed as the swords and spears they carried.

At least *they* would be a match for the raiding sea-wolves.

Long before they reached Waithe it became clear they were too late. There was a chill mist in the air but anguished, agonized cries, and the smell of burning carried along the road to the Britons who didn't need their captains' prompting to hasten their pace.

"We'll ride on," Bellicus said to Duro. "Eburus, bring the men as fast as you can. Gods willing we'll reach the village before the Saxons kill everyone in it."

The druid kicked his heels into Darac and charged ahead, the infantry before them parting to let the big black through. Arthur and the other riders throughout the column were already out of sight in the mist, for they too had hurried ahead with hopes of halting the Saxons' murderous raid.

The icy air stung Bellicus's eyes but he ploughed on as fast as he dared in the thick snow, desperate to help the villagers while at the same time loath to put the horse at risk of losing its footing and possibly breaking a leg. Their destination was closer than they'd realised though, and the sounds of fighting suddenly seemed to be right in front of them as they charged through the pitiful village gates. Arthur had visited as many towns and settlements as he could during the summer and autumn, warning the people of the danger the Saxons posed and insisting walls and gates be erected. But not every place had skilled woodworkers, or spare time to build defences that would truly be up to the task of keeping out a horde of invaders.

In Waithe's case, it hadn't even taken a horde, just a moderately sized warband, to smash open the gates and storm the village. To their credit, the villagers must have had someone on watch and they'd managed to kill one of the Saxons with a thrown spear. The corpse lay in the snow with the polearm sticking out, a pained, surprised expression on the bearded face.

"We should dismount, Bel," shouted Duro. "The horses will only get in the way in the village."

The druid had already jumped down to the ground and unsheathed Melltgwyn before the centurion finished talking. A moment later they were both on foot, hurrying towards the centre of the small settlement, as a terrified, heart-wrenching cry filled the air.

CHAPTER THREE

"Please! Don't—"

The woman's voice was cut off abruptly and a man laughed as children wailed. Through the open door of a low hovel, Duro saw the pale, bare arse of a Saxon dropping his breeches and, without hesitation, the centurion ran inside and hacked his blade into the man's legs, just beneath his buttocks. There was a scream as the sword left two terrible, gaping red wounds in the white flesh and, as the Saxon collapsed, the pommel of Duro's weapon smashed into the back of his head.

Still, the Saxon wasn't finished. Dazedly scrabbling about the floor for his axe, he found it just as Duro's sword tore through his armour and deep into his ribs.

"Are you all right?"

The woman's clothes had been torn off below the waist and her grimy face was streaked with tears, but she appeared uninjured and nodded at the centurion as two small boys ran into her embrace, trying not to look at the dead would-be rapist.

"You're safe now," Duro said reassuringly. "Just stay here, out of the way, until the fighting stops."

"Come on," Bellicus called from the doorway. "We don't have time for talking. Cai – on guard." The powerful dog sat down on the threshold and the druid nodded. "He won't let anyone pass," he told the frightened lady. "He won't hurt you, or your children, though. Don't worry about that. He's a friendly giant to everyone except Saxons." He smiled but received only wide-eyed stares in response.

Patting Cai one last time, Bellicus and Duro moved on without him, both men relieved to notice the mist was lifting rapidly as the morning sun finally began to make its presence felt. A further relief was the appearance of Eburus and the rest of the foot soldiers. They charged into the village and joined druid and centurion as they headed towards the sounds of battle.

It didn't take long to reach the middle of the settlement and the men threw themselves with gusto into the battle. Well, most of them did. Bellicus took Duro by the arm and drew him off to the side.

"What are you doing?" the centurion demanded in confusion. "There's Saxons to be slaughtered."

Bellicus shook his head, intent on the fighting before them. "We're not needed, we have the greater numbers. Let's just stand and see how things go. Don't worry, if there's need of another two swords, we'll jump in."

So they stood and they watched. Both were happy to see their Damnonii friends and kinsmen giving a good account of themselves. They met the enemy without fear and were their equal, for the most part, in strength, savagery and enthusiasm for the battle.

The warriors with the red shields were, however, not faring so well. Caradoc and Edern's men, who all hailed from around these very lands and should, one would think, be the most eager to defend their compatriots here in Waithe, seemed like startled deer. Bellicus looked on in bemusement, wondering if this was the first time these men of Lindum had faced a Saxon warband, for the enemy's ferocity, and undeniable skill with their weapons appeared to have shocked them.

"Go and bolster their nerve," the druid said, and Duro gladly raced across, bawling orders and, in his best parade-ground voice, commanding the men with the red shields to hold them up and stand their ground against the whoresons from across the eastern sea. Their own leader, a tall young man with a dazed expression, did not question the centurion's sudden appearance, rather he seemed pleased to be absolved of his responsibility and glad to follow Duro's orders.

Arthur and Lancelot must have dispatched the foes who'd been engaging them, for Bellicus saw them rise above the battling men as they remounted and, like him, moved slightly away from the fighting which was almost over now.

"Kill them all," Lancelot roared, eyes blazing, and Bellicus noticed blood caking his philtrum and chin. He lived, but had not quite come through the battle unscathed, and he shouted once more, "Kill them all. Leave none alive!"

His command merely served to encourage the few remaining Saxons who, knowing they would be dead soon, threw every last scrap of energy into taking down as many of the hated Waelisc as possible. There was no attempt to smash through and escape into the countryside – the invaders accepted their fate and merely wanted to take as many souls with them to the feasting halls in the afterlife as they could.

Again, the red shields faltered and Bellicus ran forward, adding his own powerful voice to Duro's as they combined to try and rally the men against the handful of surviving enemy troopers. The tip of a sword narrowly missed his eye and the druid lunged forward, thrusting Melltgwyn as hard as he could towards the bearded man who was pushing against one of the red shields with a look of almost beatific savagery on his face. His sword hit home, scraping against bone and leaving the Saxon open mouthed in surprise at the sudden pain tearing through his torso. His legs gave way and he collapsed, dead.

From there the battle lasted only moments and, as Lancelot had commanded, not a single enemy was left alive. The Britons stood panting and tired, hot breaths steaming in the cold air as white-eyed jackdaws landed on nearby rooftops and waited for the men to disperse that they might fill their bellies with the soft flesh of the dead.

The druid looked up at Arthur who sat stony faced in his saddle, and knew that, despite their victory, the warlord was not happy. It was not Bellicus's place to give the orders for what should happen next, so he waited, along with everyone else, for Arthur's command.

At last, Lancelot took it upon himself to take charge since it seemed Arthur was lost in thought and the warband was growing restless. "You men," the handsome rider called, pointing to his right at a group of half a dozen warriors. "Help the villagers put out any fires. Check the whole settlement – it can sometimes take time for a smouldering roof to catch."

As they ran to do Lancelot's bidding, Arthur finally focused on the task at hand, looking directly at Bellicus and jerking his head towards the druid. "The danger isn't over. We should check around the village for any Saxons that might have escaped. Bel, you and Duro find your horses and spears and come with me. You too Bedwyr."

17

Soon, druid and centurion were mounted, suitably armed, and riding in linear formation through the snow with Arthur and Bedwyr, another of the warlord's trusted captains. Lancelot remained behind, with Cai by his side, to direct the warband in their efforts to restore Waithe to some semblance of normality.

"There," said the warlord, pointing at fresh tracks in the snow. "Two men came this way, running, if the length of their stride is any indicator."

Their eyes followed the trail which led towards a thick stand of sycamores, and Arthur forged ahead, calling over his shoulder as the others followed. "The trees there are densely packed, but they don't go very far. The Saxons will either be trapped or have to come out into the open again. Come on, let's get this over with."

The snow plumed around their mounts' hooves as they thundered towards the leafless trees, and, long before they reached them, they saw two figures appearing on the eastern side of the copse and running desperately to escape their pursuers.

"I told you," Arthur shouted, but there was no triumph or excitement in his voice, just a calm detachment as he prepared to end the threat of these particular invaders. "They've realised the trees offer little protection. Be careful, lads, they'll be desperate. Use your spears and keep out of sword range. If possible, whoever reaches them first, don't give them a chance to fight back."

The snow was thick here, and the ground uneven, and the Saxons struggled to move faster than a man would normally walk on a clear summer day, despite expending far more energy as they dragged their feet in and out of the powdery white blanket.

"They won't let us spear them in the back," Bedwyr predicted, and sure enough, the fleeing enemy turned, shouting at one another as they hefted their own weapons and faced the charging Britons.

"Front, back, they'll die just the same no matter which end the spear takes them," Arthur growled. "But let's be careful. No point in any of us, or our horses, dying here, when we have them at our mercy."

"Mercy?" Duro asked.

Arthur glanced at him, hearing the harsh tone in his question. "Don't worry, centurion, I was merely using a figure of speech. You and Bel ride to their rear. We'll come at them from both directions."

Bedwyr was looking at the Saxons who were holding their spears in front of them defensively. "I'm not so sure the horses will charge them down, Arthur," he cautioned. "Horses don't like spears. And I don't particularly like riding towards them myself."

The warlord reined in his mount and eyed Bedwyr curiously. "There's four of us, we're mounted, and we can't just let them escape," he said. "What do you suggest?"

Bellicus noticed Arthur did not seem angered, or even irritated, by his subordinate questioning his orders and thought it was a good sign. In the heat of battle it wouldn't be ideal, but here, with time to take stock and make sure their next move was a sensible one, the druid believed it a good trait for the commander to be willing to accept advice from another wise man.

Unfortunately, that man was not Bedwyr.

"I've no idea," the warrior from Powys admitted, smiling wryly as Duro snorted with laughter. "I just don't fancy riding straight at them – there's a good chance one of us will be speared."

"What about you, Roman?" Arthur demanded. "Your legions used cavalry. What would you suggest we do here?"

Duro frowned. "I was infantry, my lord. I can ride, but I'm no expert on fighting from the back of one of these beasts."

Arthur's eyes slid to Bellicus who grinned. "It seems we're in the unusual position where none of us have ever encountered a standoff like this before. And we've had too much time to think about it."

"True," Bedwyr nodded. "If we'd just ridden them down, chances are they'd both be dead, and we'd already be riding back to Waithe."

The Saxons, seeing the Britons' indecision, had turned and were attempting to run away through the snow once again.

"They won't want to lose their spears," Arthur said. "They won't throw them at us, since they're the one weapon they have that'll make our horses keep their distance."

"But we can afford to lose a couple of ours," Bellicus replied, narrowing his eyes as he sized up the fleeing enemy. "I'll take one of them down."

"And I'll take the other," Bedwyr put in before Duro could say anything, his tone suggesting he didn't want the northerners getting all the glory.

"All right," Arthur said, urging his horse forward again. "You two flank them, while Duro and I will ride directly towards them. Throw your spears before we reach them. Even if you miss, they'll be distracted, and we'll attack before they're ready for us again."

Bellicus was already riding hard to the west, while Bedwyr headed east and the other two continued in the tracks of the enemy. The gap between them narrowed quickly for the Saxons' legs were burning with fatigue while the horses were still relatively fresh and found the snow much less of a hindrance.

The druid got well ahead of the fugitives and then turned his horse so it was pounding back towards them. On the opposite flank, Bedwyr had done the same, and Bellicus watched the Saxons shouting in alarm to one another as they faced the prospect of being struck from three different sides rather than one. As he expected, they stopped running again and stood with spears held out, turning now and again to face the oncoming riders.

Although he was not trained in this kind of mounted attack, Bellicus was able to match Bedwyr's speed and angle of approach, and as he neared the wide-eyed, snarling enemy he hefted his spear and drew back his arm.

"Ready?" Bedwyr called, to shouts of agreement from both Arthur and the druid and then they were within range and Bellicus threw his spear.

The missile sped through the air, propelled by all the power in the druid's enormous arm, and he watched it fly, willing it to take the nearest Saxon in the side and end the man's battle without further trouble. He had not practised such a move, however, and he looked on in dismay as the spear sailed wide of its mark, punching into the snow to the side of the Saxons.

Bedwyr's aim proved only marginally better, his spear drawing cries of alarm from the enemy but, again, it failed to strike either of the men.

Arthur and Duro had not slowed their charge though, and, as the Saxons tried to turn and plant their spears in the ground in time to face the next threat, the warlord's thrown spear took the first of them right in the side of the face. The unfortunate warrior never even had time to cry out as he was thrown backwards onto the ground, limbs flailing, his head a ruined, red mess on the white snow.

The remaining Saxon screamed some unintelligible oath but was forced to use his spear to parry Duro's clumsy thrust, and then both centurion and Arthur were past, and riding away from him. Or at least that was their intention.

"Look out!" Arthur roared as Bedwyr's horse came into his path and the animals collided, drawing outraged braying from both beasts as the warlord was thrown from his saddle, headfirst onto the ground.

To the left, Duro brought his horse around as fast as he could, and Bellicus had drawn his sword to continue the fight, but the Saxon saw his chance and, with a fierce, lupine grin, came roaring towards the fallen warlord, slipping and sliding in the snow but unwilling to let it stop his progress now that he had a target in sight.

Bedwyr had regained control of his mount by now and pulled its head around to the right, urging it into a canter, facing the wrong way so he was unaware of the imminent threat to Arthur, simply wanting to put some distance between himself and the final spearman for now.

Arthur appeared unharmed, but his spear had fallen from his hand when he was thrown into the snow and his sword was still in its scabbard as the Saxon came relentlessly towards him, calling out in his own language with such a thick accent that none of the Britons could understand a single word.

Words. Bellicus's mind spun as he watched Arthur's doom approaching and knew there was no way he or Duro could reach the Saxon in time to stop him from plunging the tip of his spear into the warlord who was so important to the future of their lands.

Words.

Words, the druid knew, could hold as much power as any shield or spear. More!

"Woden!" The druid screamed the name of the Saxon god with every ounce of air in his lungs. "Thunor!" Again he cried out, naming another of the deities worshipped by the followers of Hengist.

Faster than any man could have thrown a spear, the words penetrated the charging Saxon's brain and, surprised, he turned towards the druid, momentarily halting his momentum towards the downed Briton warlord. For just a moment, the warrior stared

21

balefully at Bellicus, confused, before realising he was merely being stalled, and then, with renewed purpose, he turned back towards Arthur and hefted his spear.

Off to the side, thudding hooves muffled by the snow, Duro came back towards them and, in sheer desperation, threw his spear. He was no more used to launching such long missiles from horseback than Bellicus or Bedwyr, and his aim proved little better, but as the thick ash shaft of the weapon whistled past him, the Saxon ducked instinctively.

When he looked up again, Arthur was coming for him, having launched himself across the snow from his prone position, drawing his sword as he did so. The blade licked out and, as the warlord fell back onto the ground, the steel chopped deeply into the Saxon's unarmoured ankle.

It was not a powerful blow, but the sword was sharp, and it bit deeply into sinew and bone. The Saxon fell, mewling like a tortured animal as Arthur made it onto one knee and slammed the blade down onto the enemy's torso. The man shouted, and scrabbled to get up, but Arthur was rising while simultaneously hammering down, again and again, with his sword, destroying the mail link by link while crushing ribs and, eventually, silencing the Saxon forever.

The Britons came to stand over their vanquished foe, amazed that the four of them had struggled to defeat him and been within mere moments of losing their leader to his spear.

"Good thinking, Bel," Bedwyr murmured. "Shouting the names of his gods to distract him."

"He fought well," Bellicus replied, drawing the dead man's sword and placing it into his limp hand respectfully, in accordance with the Saxon belief that they would need the weapon in the afterlife. "And I think we have much to learn from this battle."

"Agreed," Arthur said, arching his back and rubbing his neck which ached from his tumble. "Starting with figuring out an easier way to kill an enemy from horseback!"

CHAPTER FOUR

Once the village of Waithe had been put to rights and the corpses of the Saxons plundered and dumped in the open country for animals to scavenge, Arthur's warband made camp a short distance away. Although it had been a relatively short battle, clearing up the mess in the settlement and tending to the wounded ate up all the hours of sunlight remaining and Bellicus was relieved when it was time to settle in for the night.

It hadn't snowed again, but the temperature was, if anything, even colder than it had been during the day and Bellicus was glad his druid's cloak was of good, thick material. Despite that, the battle fever had long worn off and he drew himself as close to the blazing fire outside Arthur's tent as he could get with the other men gathered around, placing an arm around Cai to share some of the mastiff's body heat.

Rocks had been set up close to the fire to heat, and now some of the lower ranked, younger warriors were wrapping them in cloth and carrying them into the warlord's tent. When they were finished, Arthur bade his closest advisors join him inside and Bellicus followed Duro through the flap and took a place on one of the folding stools that had been set up around a table in the centre of the tent.

The shelter was made from heavy leather and, combined with the heat from the stones and the few candles which were set on the table and on stands near the corners, the place was surprisingly cosy. The sight of overflowing ale mugs set at each man's place around the table made things even more welcoming and both druid and centurion half drained theirs as soon as they sat down. Sighs and grunts of appreciation filled the tent although Arthur, looking on, and Merlin, at his side, both appeared less pleased by their victory than Bellicus would have expected.

He glanced around the table at the other men gathered there: Lancelot, of course, along with Bedwyr, King Caradoc, and the latter's son, Edern. Eight in total, not counting Cai who'd found a place close to one of the hot stones and was contentedly licking one of his paws.

"Why the long face, Arthur?" Caradoc asked with a smile, raising his mug in salute to the man they'd all accepted as their war leader, if not their lord. "We kicked the shit out of the Saxon bastards and Waithe still stands. We should be celebrating harder than this. Anyone would think we lost, eh?" He downed the last of his ale and clumsily nudged Edern, making Bellicus suspect the man had already emptied a few mugs before this council had gathered.

"Aye, Waithe still stands," Bedwyr spoke up, but he shook his head, not sharing in Caradoc's pleasure. "But we lost a few men ourselves, and more villagers died than I'd have liked. I understand Arthur's reluctance to make merry."

Duro snorted mirthlessly, drawing glances from everyone in the tent. "I must admit, I'm a little surprised that you're happy about how the battle went," the centurion said evenly, eyes boring into Caradoc. "Your men were a disgrace."

"How dare you?" demanded the king, jumping to his feet and placing his hand on his sword hilt. "Who do you think you are?" He turned to look indignantly at Arthur whose expression remained unreadable. "Why is this fool here anyway? He's no lord, he's merely some ex-legionary with fancy armour."

Bellicus watched his friend, worried that he might react to Caradoc's words, but he needn't have feared for the centurion seemed more disgusted than enraged by the nobleman.

"He's here," Arthur said coolly, "because he's a friend of the druid and because he has more experience of war than most of us. The Romans didn't promote just anyone to centurion."

"More experience? Perhaps," Caradoc admitted, glaring once more at Duro. "But I'll not sit here and listen to him calling my warriors a disgrace. These are my lands, Roman—"

"Not for much longer," Bellicus broke in. "Unless you take heed. Now," he raised both hands, palms up, and dipped his head a little, "I admit, Duro's choice of words was rather harsh."

"Harsh?" Edern retorted, finally speaking up. "Aye, I'd say so."

"All right, I'm sure he meant no offence, but I also watched your men today and they were simply not up to the task of defending Waithe. No, listen to me!" He raised his voice, filling the enclosed space with its druid-trained power, noting Merlin smiling in the shadows as Caradoc blinked and sagged like a wineskin that had just had its contents drained out. "I'm not here to criticise you, or your preparations for this war that's upon us. Most men on this island of ours have not yet fully grasped the threat these sea-wolves pose, and that was evident today amongst your warriors."

"Sit, my lord," Arthur said softly. "We all must learn from today's events, if we're to stand any chance of holding onto what's ours. Listen to the druid, for he's one of the few who's had dealings with the Saxon commanders. He understands their capacity for violence and cruelty better than most."

Caradoc remained standing, staring murderously at both Duro and Bellicus, before finally Edern grasped his sleeve and pulled him down onto his stool once more. "Fine. Say your piece, druid," the king growled. "But remember, this land belongs to me, and I'll not listen to any more insults."

Bellicus nodded. "Of course, lord." There was no point embarrassing the man further – they would need his goodwill, and his men, in the future, no doubt.

Duro, too, knew when to play the diplomat, and he spoke up again now. "My apologies, lord, I'm a simple soldier. Sometimes I speak without thinking. Your men were invaluable today, as was your leadership."

"Indeed," Bellicus agreed, raising his half-full ale mug in salute to Caradoc as the others joined him. "You've seen for yourself now just how dangerous the Saxons can be, though. You will, I'm sure, recognise the fact that your men will need to train hard if they're to defeat the next warband that comes to your lands."

"Next time," Merlin put in, "you won't have Arthur or Bellicus's warriors and expertise to help you."

Caradoc blew out a heavy sigh and, from the hunted look in his eyes, Bellicus could tell the nobleman had known all along that he and his men were not up to the job today. Of course, he would never admit it, but the druid could read his expression and his posture well enough. When he spoke again the almost pleading tone of his voice merely reinforced Bellicus's opinion.

"What would you suggest, druid? It's true, we've never faced an enemy as vicious, or as well organised, as these Saxons, and maybe I do have things to learn about fighting them. I'm listening."

Bellicus smiled. This was a start.

For a while they sat, enjoying the warmth in the room as the frost grew thick on the ground outside, discussing ways for Caradoc to improve his settlements' defences and his warband's readiness for future battles. After a time the earlier anger and resentment faded and jokes and anecdotes were shared between the men. Duro even refilled Caradoc's mug himself, drawing a happy smile from the chief.

When the young warriors came in carrying freshly heated rocks to replace the ones which had now cooled, Caradoc got to his feet and, with a drink-fuelled grin, said good night to them all.

"I should go and speak to my own officers now," he said. "Thank them for their part in today's victory. Tomorrow, we'll begin the hard work. If the Saxons return, they'll not find me or my men wanting again, by the gods."

"I'll see you to the camp, father," Edern said, standing himself. "It's time I returned to my own men too."

With hearty farewells, the two noblemen left the warmth of the tent and made their way, none too quietly, back to their own camps.

"You really should learn to hold your counsel, centurion," Lancelot said with his now familiar crooked grin. "That old fool might have caused a lot of trouble after that insult of yours."

Merlin broke in sharply. "That 'old fool' might yet cause trouble, if he hears you calling him that." He turned then to Duro, eyes narrowed. "No harm's been done and, if anything, Caradoc and Edern now understand their position and the need for their men to toughen up. In future, however, it might be best to be more tactful."

"What now?" Bedwyr asked, not even trying to hide an enormous yawn. "Are we done for the night? I'm needing my bed."

Everyone looked to Arthur, but he shook his head. "Not just yet. I'm worried."

"About what?" Bellicus asked, although he had a fair idea what was playing on the warlord's mind and his suspicions were confirmed when Arthur replied.

"Cavalry."

Bedwyr shook his head in confusion. "Like I say, I'm tired. Cavalry? What about it?"

"We don't really have any," Arthur said.

"We do," Lancelot disagreed. "We have plenty of horses."

"Aye," Arthur said heatedly, getting up and pacing up and down the tent as the others looked on in bemusement. "We have horses, and riders, but we don't have true cavalry. Not like the Romans had." He gazed at Duro and received a nod of agreement.

"No-one has cavalry like the legions had," Duro said. "Not any more. A proper, well-trained, well-equipped cavalry unit takes a lot—a *lot*—of resources, my lord."

"Today opened my eyes to the fact we don't truly know how to fight from horseback," Arthur said, taking his stool once more. The earlier annoyance and unfocused energy had given way to a stony resolve. "We need to learn."

The men thought about his pronouncement, glancing at one another uncertainly, for such an undertaking would, as Duro had noted, consume a great deal of resources and time. On top of that, none of them gathered there in the tent had the knowledge or experience to teach warriors how to be a proper cavalry unit on a par with the old Roman *turmae*.

"I think this is a fine idea," Bellicus said slowly, reaching down to stroke Cai's ears. "But, well, do you have someone to lead this new, mounted warband, my lord? To train the riders?"

"I don't," Arthur admitted, and he was smiling now as the possibilities filled his mind. "But we'll find someone, a Roman officer like Duro perhaps, and we'll learn. We all know how to ride – we just need to train twenty or thirty men to operate in a group."

"Oh aye, it'll be easy," Merlin said somewhat sarcastically. Clearly this idea had not been suggested to the High Druid before this evening and it had put his nose out of joint not to be consulted, although, to be fair, it seemed the plan had only just come to their warlord in a flash of inspiration.

"It'll be worth the effort," Arthur said, and now he was like an excited child who'd been told his father was bringing him home a fantastic new toy to play with. "The Saxons will have no answer for it, we'll be able to cut them down like farmers harvesting wheat!"

"They'll eventually learn ways to deal with it," Lancelot cautioned, although he was smiling too, a natural response to his friend's infectious enthusiasm.

"Pah," Arthur waved a hand. "By that time we'll have driven them back across the sea to their own lands, or destroyed them utterly. Britain will be ours again and we can build from a position of strength to make sure we're ready for them if they ever return."

"All that, just from forming a cavalry unit?" Bedwyr, always more thoughtful and less impulsive than Arthur or Lancelot, asked.

"That'll just be the start," Arthur replied happily. "Once we learn how to utilise our horses to best effect, we'll begin using them more and more. Great oaks grow from small acorns, my friend."

"What say you, Bel?" Merlin looked at his fellow druid. "You've fought the sea-wolves a number of times now, you've seen how they are in battle. Do you think Arthur's plan worthwhile?"

Bellicus thought of his own warhorse, Darac, and knew how terrifying the beast could be – he'd seen the fear in enemy eyes as he charged towards them and they imagined the enormous weight of the animal smashing into their fragile flesh and bone, and he nodded. "I think it's worth a try. The Saxons respect and even love their horses, but they don't fight from them. If we had a unit of cavalry to smash the back of one of their warbands as our spearmen engaged them from the front, I think it would cause chaos and lead to a quick victory. At least," he said, as Arthur's eyes lit up at the picture being painted for him, "until, as Bedwyr says, they figure out ways to counter us. Caltrops, spear-lined pits, that sort of thing."

"But, by then," Arthur said, "we'll have learned new tactics of our own."

Bellicus smiled. He too was seeing the worth in this plan. Then a thought struck him as he remembered the battle he'd fought beside Arthur two years before, in Duncrieff. "Wait," he said. "You *had* cavalry when we fought the Saxons before. Chariots too. What happened to them?"

Arthur shook his head. "They weren't much use," he admitted ruefully. "Either of them. The chariots I only ever used as transport and to make an impression but, unless the ground was completely flat, they were precarious things to get around in. As for the 'cavalry'…"

"They performed well at Duncrieff, from what I recall," Bellicus said. "We won that fight handily enough, and the horses played their part."

"Aye," Arthur agreed. "But we didn't really understand how to utilise them or train them properly. Not long after Duncrieff we came up against another Saxon warband whose commander knew how to deal with our horses. The animals really don't like charging towards a wall of spears…" He sighed heavily. "We lost more than half of them that day and, well, I decided we should stick with infantry after that."

"Until now," Bedwyr said dourly, clearly not convinced about his friend's plan. Even the bold Lancelot seemed unsure.

"I think it's a good idea," Duro said. "If you can find someone how knows how to train them."

Merlin nodded. "I agree."

"It's settled then," the warlord practically shouted, raising his ale mug in salute to his friends and the success of their proposed cavalry unit. "In the morning we'll start looking for those of our people who know horses best, and use their skills to form the deadliest group of mounted warriors these lands have seen since the Romans!"

The men around the table lifted their own mugs and joined Arthur's toast with varying degrees of enthusiasm. Some were yet to be convinced that this entire scheme wouldn't prove to be a waste of time, but even Bedwyr managed a smile for it was hard to deny their leader's infectious optimism.

Bellicus turned to see Duro joining in with the salute, downing whatever ale was left in his mug. The druid hoped all the talk of the Romans would excite and inspire his friend, but he could see sadness in Duro's expression and guessed thoughts of the legions had brought back memories he'd rather have kept repressed. Memories of being young and carefree, of a time when he wasn't mourning the death of his wife, Alatucca, and hadn't suffered the things that had happened in the intervening years.

Bellicus looked away, knowing there was no point in allowing his friend's melancholy to infect him. Time would ease Duro's pain, and so would smashing the Saxons. The coming year would see a new strand emerging on fate's web, and Bellicus hoped he and Duro would both have a large part to play in its weaving.

CHAPTER FIVE

When his advisors had all filed out of the tent, Arthur remained seated, drink in hand, pondering the future and praying to the gods that he would be able to live up to the grand title Merlin had bestowed upon him: Bear of Britain.

The High Druid had been in Arthur's life for as long as he could remember and his thoughts drifted back across the years now, to those early days when he was but a child, learning how to survive in a world filled with uncertainty...

"Who were my parents?" Arthur, just fourteen years old at the time, asked the druid with the long, brown beard.

Merlin shook his head. "I don't know, my lad," was the reply.

That was *always* Merlin's reply to this particular question and, as ever, it frustrated the youngster. Arthur had spent his whole life, as far as he could remember, here in the household of Munatius, a nobleman of the Carvetii tribe in Rheged. Munatius was not his father, though, they looked nothing alike and the man had never claimed to be anything more than a foster parent to him.

Munatius was a widower, his wife Veldicca having died five years ago. Their only child was a son Cador, almost twenty years older than Arthur so, although they'd both grown up within the same household and liked one another a great deal, the age gap meant they'd never formed any real childhood bonds.

Arthur's best friends were the similarly aged Bedwyr and Kay, who came from Powys, and Lancelot, from Deva. The fathers of those boys, powerful noblemen, were all friends and business associates of Munatius and visited his home often. This meant that, although they lived many miles distant from one another, the lads were able to spend a lot of time together hunting, fishing and generally getting up to mischief as they grew up.

"My foster father is a nobleman," Arthur said petulantly. "And my friends' fathers are powerful noblemen too. But *who am I?*"

Merlin had been a constant presence in Arthur's life, but he did not live here in Rheged – he spent most of his time travelling about the country meeting his fellow druids and, in fact, that was why he was there that day. Arthur's usual tutor was a very old, white-bearded druid named Vindissus and he'd been teaching his charge how to speak basic Frisian that morning. Why, the youngster did not know, for he felt it a complete waste of time learning the tongue of some enemy people he hoped never to meet, but Vindissus often made him study strange topics.

Merlin had arrived to visit that morning and asked to speak with Arthur for a while. The High Druid always made time to see Arthur when he came to Rheged and this was another thing that confused him.

"Why do you bother with me, Merlin? You surely don't go visiting every young fellow in Britain. So, what makes me special?"

The druid smiled and nodded. "You're correct, Arthur," he said. "You are special, or at least I hope you will be, one day."

"Why?"

There was no petulance or anger in the youngster's voice, only curiosity.

"Because I've known you since the day you were born, Arthur," Merlin replied seriously. "I was there. And I've watched, and guided you, ever since." Seeing Arthur still frowning, he went on. "What I'm trying to say is: I know you. I know your potential, and I believe you're growing up to be just what I hoped you would when I asked Munatius to foster you, and Vindissus to mentor you."

Arthur thought about this, absorbing the words and their meaning. Before he could ask any more questions, ones which Merlin might not want to answer, the druid stood up and gestured towards the door.

"Come," he said. "I think it's time you left behind your childhood lessons. Vindissus has taught you well, but now you'll have a new mentor."

"Who?" Arthur asked as he stood and followed Merlin out into the courtyard.

"Me, of course."

From then on, Merlin spent much more time in Rheged, teaching Arthur much the same subjects and skills as Vindissus had, but to a much more advanced level. They would pore over old Roman writings on battle tactics and strategy, weaponry, fortifications, and all sorts of military subjects. At other times Merlin would show Arthur how to manipulate people using body language and inflections of his voice – 'druid tricks' as the youngster would term them somewhat distastefully, but he picked them up easily enough. Unlike languages, which he had no natural talent for. Many mornings he would curse the lessons Merlin would make him learn, wishing he had his foster brother Cador's aptitude for the Saxons' harsh tongue.

The lessons Arthur enjoyed the most, and the ones which surprised him the most too, were the hours spent with wooden sword and shield learning how to fight. Of course, the boy had always been given lessons like this, but Merlin's teachings went much further. Although the druid was wiry and ascetic-looking, he could fight like a gladiator, much to Arthur's shock.

"By the gods, druid, how did you do that?"

Merlin smiled down at his young charge who was lying flat on his back on the grass sparring ground off to the side of Manutius's villa. "Misdirection," he replied, reaching out to help Arthur up. "Look. You saw my eyes go this way, but my hand went that way. Come on, let's try again."

And so it went on, day after day, month after month, until Arthur's head seemed so crammed with knowledge and learning that he wondered it didn't pop with the pressure. Yet he grew taller and stronger, and more confident within himself the more time he spent in the High Druid's company.

Merlin did not think he would ever be the world's greatest swordsman, or the greatest ever general, or speak the language of the Saxons like a native – ha! – but Arthur was mastering all these subjects and more. In short, he was becoming a true leader.

"Today we'll find out just how much you've learned," Merlin told him one morning in early summer when Arthur was still but sixteen years old.

"What d'you mean?" asked the young man who was now taller than his tutor.

"There's Dalriadan raiders nearby," said the druid. "You've heard? Well, Munatius's men are going to hunt them down before they can steal any more of his sheep."

Arthur's eyes sparkled for he'd been in warbands like this before and always enjoyed the thrill of the chase and excitement of facing a man in battle, although the first time he'd been forced to kill an enemy warrior he'd gone off on his own and cried for most of the evening. That had been a harsh lesson, but one that had toughened him up more than any words of Merlin could have done, and the realities of battle – of life in a world that no longer enjoyed the protection of the legions – were no longer shocking to him.

"I've fought Dalriadans before," he said, a little confused. "You know that."

"Aye, so you have," Merlin replied nodding and fixing him with a level gaze. "But today you'll be *leading* the warband."

A cold shiver had passed through Arthur then, as if someone had thrown a bucket of ice-cold water on his bare back. He was only sixteen, after all, how could he be in charge of Munatius's seasoned warriors?

"This," said Merlin, eyes still boring into him as if searching for any sign of weakness or doubt, "is what you've been trained for. To lead. Will you do it?"

Arthur hesitated for just a moment longer, and then that icy sensation disappeared, replaced with pride and a sense of purpose like he'd never known before.

"Of course," he replied. "Come. Let's get our horses and join the men."

That afternoon was little more than a blur to Arthur. He'd led Munatius's men – farmers and labourers mostly but all with far greater battle experience than he had – across the western fields, where most reports placed the Dalriadan raiders. They came across them, chasing a shepherd and driving off his sheep, just after noon. Eight of them, red-haired, blue-eyed men, stripped to the waist to show off their muscular torsos and arms.

Arthur had commanded his companions to dismount, and then, in the centre of the shieldwall, he'd led them into battle. Merlin watched from horseback as the young man fought with courage and skill, calling out to the older warriors, encouraging them as if he'd been their captain for a decade or more.

This was no Battle of Edessa, with thousands upon thousands of soldiers being directed by mighty generals. It was a minor skirmish between two small forces of footmen, with no tactical skills involved. But it proved, to Merlin *and* Arthur, that he could take command of a warband and defeat an enemy bent on slaughtering them. For Arthur's men did win that battle, killing six of the raiders and allowing two to escape back to their own lands, to tell their kinsmen how dangerous it was to steal from the shepherds in Rheged.

After that, Bedwyr, Kay, and Lancelot seemed to visit even more often, and Arthur knew this was down to Merlin's influence. The druid often expounded the importance of trusted, loyal captains to any general and it seemed Arthur's friends were to be given these very roles.

"Am I to be a king, then?" he asked his mentor after a feast in Manutius's villa one evening two years after his first successful command. "With my three boon companions by my side?"

"Not a king," Merlin replied, eyes twinkling merrily. "A warlord."

"Why not a king?" Arthur asked. "Kings lead, don't they?"

"Aye, but Britain has dozens of kings, and not one wants to follow another. A warlord, though? A man who holds no power over them, but will defend their lands from the Saxon invaders while they stay safe and secure behind their own walls? That might be tempting, don't you think?"

That did indeed make perfect sense to Arthur.

"But," he asked, shaking his head, still not quite satisfied with what he was being told. "What if I'd died when I fought those Dalriadans? Or I fall off my horse and break my neck tomorrow? Or...any number of similar fates. All the time you've spent training me would be wasted, you'd have nothing to show for it. No warlord."

"There are others like you, Arthur," the druid had told him. "Young men and women, trained by druids, all across Britain and even some in Gaul. It's what my Order has always done and continues to do. It just so happens that you're in my care, and I believe you are exactly the man Britain needs. Or will be, eventually. But, if anything happened to you, one of those other youngsters would take your place." He smiled thoughtfully. "Indeed, my friend Qunavo is training a fellow in the far north, on the island of Iova. A prodigiously tall young student who shows a great deal of promise..." He shrugged. "But you have been chosen for this task, Arthur. You will be warlord. Fate has different things in store for those other men and women we're training."

This idea of the druids controlling things from behind the scenes was strange, and even a little disturbing, but Arthur could only go on his own experience. The druids he knew best, Vindissus and Merlin, were good people. Rather them directing the fate of the lands than some vindictive, mad emperor like Caligula, or Nero, whose bloody deeds old Vindissus had spent many lessons describing.

"You will be warlord," Merlin repeated levelly. "And your friends, Bedwyr, Kay, and Lancelot – who all have various strengths and talents – will be your captains."

Arthur accepted the druid's words, for, when Merlin made such a pronouncement it generally came true. He could think of worse ways to spend one's life – bringing peace to a land beset by invaders and raiders on all sides was a truly noble goal, and one Arthur would put everything he had into achieving.

And then, one day, when he'd proved himself and defeated Britain's enemies, maybe Merlin would answer that question Arthur had always wanted to know the answer to: *Who were my parents?*

There was a crashing noise outside as a servant dropped a plate he was carrying, and Arthur came back to the present with a jolt. Merlin's predictions had all come true so far, he thought, but, to this day, the High Druid still hadn't answered Arthur's question about his lineage.

The warlord suspected he'd never find out, but the older he got the less important it seemed. As long as he had his childhood friends by his side, what did it matter who his parents had been?

CHAPTER SIX

The arrow was released with a loud snap and Bellicus watched as it flew through the air with tremendous power. Unfortunately, its accuracy didn't match its speed, as the missile landed well wide of the intended target—a brown hare—and Duro cursed loudly as the little animal scurried away into the undergrowth along with its companions.

"Shit," the centurion cursed, lowering the bow and eyeing the druid miserably. "I'm never going to get the hang of this."

"It's fine, we'll get there. Besides, a man offers a bigger target," Bellicus replied but his words didn't soothe Duro's annoyance.

Since Arthur's decision to train a cavalry unit, some of the men, including Duro and Bellicus, had been trying to hone their mounted archery skills but finding it rather harder than expected. Bedwyr had suggested making their riders serve purely as heavy, shock troops, with long spears to slam into the enemy footmen or to hunt them down once routed, but Arthur thought that a waste. If possible, he wanted his cavalry to do those things as well as being effective from a distance by using bows and arrows.

Many of the soldiers were good at fighting with sword and spear from the saddle, *or* shooting a bow, but not many were naturally good at both, and it had proven harder than expected to find anyone who could teach those skills. When the Romans left Britannia they took the knowledge of many things with them, and this seemed to be another.

"I'm away back to camp," Duro said flatly, removing the string from his bow and securing both before riding towards, and past, Bellicus. "Coming?"

"No, you go on," the druid replied. "We still need to catch something for the pot, so I'll keep trying with the others. You go ahead, I'll see you in a while."

With a nod, Duro rode off, westwards, towards the low hills where Arthur's camp lay, basking in the spring sunshine.

"What's the matter with him?" Lancelot asked. "When you first joined us the centurion was good company. Now, he seems to take any minor setback to heart. He rarely laughs, druid, and he's not eating well."

Bellicus glared at the warrior riding beside him but bit back an angry retort. Lancelot was right, after all. Duro had retreated into himself lately and, now that it was pointed out to him, Bellicus had to admit the centurion appeared somewhat gaunt. When they first met a couple of years ago, Duro had been working as a baker in the northern town of Luguvalium and, although still tough, he'd undeniably been fat. The weight had dropped off him once he joined the druid's quest to rescue the abducted princess Catia and he'd worked hard to stay lean and fit since, but perhaps he was going too far in the opposite direction...

"Life has not been kind to him in recent times," Bellicus said. "I think he feels lost."

Lancelot appeared unmoved. "Life is hard on us all," he said levelly. "I know you're close to him, but he needs to pull himself together – his moods aren't good for morale around the camp."

Bellicus wasn't used to being given orders like this, but he knew Arthur's captain was right. He'd seen it himself in the past when one man's black mood soured an entire camp and turned men against one another. Little things like that could exacerbate existing tensions or even throw up entirely new ones.

"I'll have a word with him," the druid muttered. "Now, are we going to catch some damn hares today? I thought you were the finest warrior in Arthur's retinue?"

Lancelot laughed at that. "Aye, so the rumours say, but I've heard tales about you too, druid, and seen you in action. Impressive. Yet here we are, and neither of us has managed to bring down a single animal between us."

"Let's stop talking then," Bellicus said, raising his bow and nudging Darac into a walk in the direction of the budding bushes the hares had disappeared into. "And start hunting. First to shoot three gets the other's ale ration tonight!"

* * *

That night was a cold one again, for, although the pale yellow narcissus blooms had been joined in the meadows by snowdrops and other, more colourful, spring blooms, it was still bitter when the sun went down and the stars twinkled in the cloudless sky over the warband's encampment.

Both Bellicus and Lancelot had managed to bring back three hares each for the pot, although neither man had shot them all from horseback. In the end, they'd admitted defeat and gone after the scurrying animals on foot, which had proved more successful and meant the pottage the officers were served for their evening meal actually had some meat in it. Even Duro had been pleased at that.

Now, though, with their dinner finished and the men nearby telling jokes and tales around their crackling fires, the centurion's gloominess returned, and Bellicus wondered what he could do or say to help his friend deal with whatever dark thoughts seemed to be plaguing him lately. True, Bel was a druid, and he'd spent his life learning—gaining knowledge and wisdom that he might advise people from all social classes—but there were times like this when he felt that wasn't quite sufficient. Bellicus's wife hadn't been murdered by the Saxon, Horsa, and Bellicus hadn't been brutally tortured and kept in a tiny, pitch-black cell for weeks, almost losing his mind in the process. The druid was not yet thirty, and hadn't suffered the things Duro had, so how could he presume to tell the centurion how he should deal with his pain?

Especially when Duro hadn't asked for his advice.

"How did the mounted archery go today?"

Bellicus looked to the side and saw Arthur there. The warlord appeared happy, although his face fell slightly when Bellicus admitted he'd not managed to shoot a single hare from the saddle, and neither had Duro or Lancelot although some of the other men in their hunting party had been luckier.

"That's disappointing." Arthur took a place on the damp log Bellicus was using as a seat before the campfire. "Still, I won't get too downhearted about it. None of you have ever trained for this – gods, most of you aren't even skilled with a bow on foot." He stroked his short beard thoughtfully. "No, I'm sure we'll get better with practice, and we'll begin to move forward in great strides soon enough."

Bellicus wasn't so sure; he feared fighting from horseback as part of a large, co-ordinated unit was so different to their usual way of approaching a battle that it would take too much time, and too many mistakes, for it to ever be worthwhile. He held his peace though, since he'd agreed to support Arthur's efforts and he still had faith in the young warlord's tenacity and vision for the future of Britain. Besides, Merlin would not be slow in letting them know if the whole idea was proving to be a waste of time.

"I'm away to bed."

They peered through the flames at Duro, who got to his feet and nodded politely, if unenthusiastically, to them, adding a low, "Good night."

"'Night, centurion," Arthur responded cheerily then, when Duro disappeared into the tent he shared with Bellicus, the warlord turned to say something, but the druid's raised hand stopped him.

"I know, he's not the best of company right now. He's got a lot on his mind."

Arthur turned back to the fire, gazing into its flickering, dancing light. "I know how he feels."

There was no criticism or warning in his tone, unlike the conversation with Lancelot earlier, and Bellicus appreciated the warlord's understanding. Patience with one's subordinates was a skill the very best leaders possessed, and this just proved Arthur's wisdom even further in the druid's mind.

"You know," Arthur said, returning to their initial subject, "if we could get some cavalry units trained properly—say, four units of twenty-five riders—we could take the fight right to Hengist."

"Attack the Saxon Shore?" Bellicus asked uncertainly.

"Aye," Arthur said. "I mean, not the fortified part of it, the walls are still strong, and the bastards might have built new fortifications to supplement the original, Roman, ones. But we could draw them out into the open land there, or ambush them as they left to go raiding, hold them in place with our spearmen, and then use the cavalry to smash them."

His eyes twinkled in the firelight as he imagined this scenario playing out in his head, and Bellicus could understand why, for it was a powerful vision. But they were a long, long way from such a position of strength.

"As we saw in Longhafan, Hengist's forces are expanding out into the lands surrounding the Saxon Shore," the druid noted. "I'm not sure we'll be able to get our cavalry trained to the required standard in time to halt that expansion, my lord. Let's be honest, we don't really have a damn clue what we're doing when it comes to mounted warfare."

Arthur sighed and the hopeful light went out of his eyes as he turned to look out into the starlit countryside around the camp. "If only we had some old Roman officers in our army. I mean, Duro's advice is greatly appreciated – his training in the legions will be invaluable in the coming months. Just imagine if we had someone like Duro who'd been trained, not as an infantry officer, but in their cavalry."

"A decurion," Bellicus said.

"Is that what they were called?"

"A decurion was in charge of a unit of riders," Bellicus confirmed. "Or a *turma* as they knew it."

"Yes, now that you mention it, I remember Merlin telling me about that. Well, some of those decurions must surely have remained here when the legions left, like Duro did." The fire was back in Arthur's gaze now as he spoke to the druid. "All we have to do is find them and enlist them in the army. By Sulis, why didn't we do this years ago?"

The warlord was laughing now, as if his plan was already completed and, again, Bellicus felt a pang as he tried to dampen Arthur's enthusiasm.

"Let's not get too carried away, my lord," he said. "Who knows how long it'll take to find men like that? And then we have to persuade them to join us – bear in mind they'll be quite old by now."

"Duro isn't that old," Arthur retorted, waving his hand as if parrying an attack from an enemy.

"He was promoted when he was very young though. I think any decurions we find will be well into their fifties or sixties, and men of that age aren't always keen to return to the warlike days of their youth…That's assuming we can find any. Where do we start?"

Arthur immediately turned and looked towards the tent where Duro was presumably fast asleep, and now Bellicus couldn't help but return the warlord's smile.

"Your friend must know other ex-legionaries," said Arthur, rubbing has hands together either from glee or just to keep them warm as a bitter wind made the campfires all around flicker wildly.

"Aye, I'm sure he does," Bellicus agreed. "And maybe this job is exactly what he needs. It'll give him something to focus on again. Something important."

"All right," Arthur said, slapping the damp log cheerfully. "We'll talk to him in the morning and, before you know it, we'll have Hengist and his arsehole of a brother running for their ships and sailing back to Jutland as if Dis Pater himself was at their backs!"

With that, he stood up and began wandering about the camp, wishing the men a good night's rest, reminding those on guard duty of the importance of their task, and generally inspiring loyalty in everyone he encountered. Bellicus watched him go and knew Merlin had chosen this young warlord wisely – if anyone could wrest Britain back from the outstretched, grasping hand of Hengist, it was Arthur.

Bear of Britain right enough.

For the first time in days, the druid went into his tent and lay down to sleep with a light heart and happy anticipation for the coming day, when he could finally offer Duro a way out of his pit of melancholy.

He slipped into unconsciousness with happy images in his mind's eye of heroic Briton cavalry driving fleeing Saxon warriors before them, into the foaming, roiling, sea beside Garrianum.

CHAPTER SEVEN

The smile fell from Bellicus's face as he listened to Arthur talking the next morning.

They'd met in the warlord's tent with Bedwyr, Lancelot, and Merlin, and broken their fast together with buttered bread, a little cheese, and some warmed ale. The food and drink had given Bellicus a pleasant glow inside, but it was rapidly fading as he took in the warlord's words.

"So, will you go, Duro?"

The centurion looked at Arthur, and then to Bedwyr, and smiled. "If that's your wish, my lord, then of course I'll go. In fact, I know exactly where to start: right in my old home of Luguvalium. There's a retired legionary living there who keeps a stable. Or at least, there was, when I was last there. Sulinus his name is. Cranky old bastard, but he knows his horses, or so I was told, and I know he was with the cavalry so it's as good a place as any to try finding some old officers who can help us out."

"Excellent." Arthur nodded in satisfaction. "Bedwyr, you can pick two or three men to take with you. Any more than that will draw attention and make it harder to avoid any Saxons or bandits you might meet on the road. You might need to cover a lot of miles before you're able to recruit the men we're after."

"Very good, lord," Bedwyr replied. "How many officers are we looking for?"

Arthur shrugged. "One at least, to get us started. But if you can find one, perhaps he can lead us to more. They'll be quite elderly, remember, so it'd be best if we can get a few together and learn as much as possible from them before their age catches them up."

"As Arthur says," Merlin put in, "they'll be old, and probably quite comfortable. So, offer enough silver to persuade them taking a few weeks out of their retirement will be worthwhile."

"I'll leave that up to your own discretion," Arthur said, looking from Bedwyr to Duro. "But offer them whatever it takes to get them here, if you think they have the knowledge and skills we need. These men could be worth their weight in gold if they can help us drive Hengist and his hordes out of our lands for good."

Bedwyr stood up and Duro followed his lead. "If that's everything for now then, lord, we'll make ready to leave, and pick out the men to come with us."

"Thank you, Bedwyr," the warlord replied. "Is there anything anyone else wants to say before they head off?"

Bellicus cleared his throat, still surprised at the way the discussion had gone. "Er, I think you've forgotten something. Or someone. I assumed I'd be going on this mission."

"What for?" Merlin asked with genuine surprise. "Duro knows how to deal with his fellow legionaries better than you would, I'm sure. And Bedwyr and his men should be enough protection against any threats they might run into on the road."

"He's right, Bel," Arthur agreed. "There's really no need for you to accompany them. In fact, with your height, and the dog," he looked down at Cai, "you'd just draw even more attention to them. And let's not forget, Horsa and Hengist will have made sure every Saxon in Britain knows your description. They'll all be after your head to try and impress their *bretwalda*."

"On top of that," Merlin continued, "we need you to command the warriors you brought to join us. There's Picts, Votadini and Damnonii amongst them, and you're the one they look to for leadership. If you go riding off to Luguvalium and Lug knows where else, who'll keep the different tribes from fighting amongst themselves? And don't say—" he raised a hand imperiously as Bellicus opened his mouth "— Eburus. He's the one most likely to start them all battling with one another!"

Cai sensed his master's unhappiness and gave a soft whine. The druid met Duro's gaze and they looked at one another for a heartbeat before the centurion nodded and followed Bedwyr out of the tent and into the morning sunshine.

"Bel, you're the highest-ranking nobleman out of all those who came with you," Arthur said, and despite his relative youth, he spoke like a kindly father. "And it's highly likely that we're going to see more battles with the Saxons in the coming weeks. Your leadership and skill with a sword will be invaluable to us here."

"And men will be needed to travel around the nearby lands, meeting other great lords, seeking their men, horses and supplies for the coming battles," Merlin said. "Your presence and training will be useful for that too."

Bellicus felt a terrible pang of sadness to be separated from Duro when the centurion was struggling with the way his life was turning out, but he felt mollified by Arthur and Merlin's praise. He also felt slightly foolish for acting like a little boy who was losing his closest playmate. Still, Duro had become like an older brother to him in the time they'd known one another, and it felt strange to think of life without the centurion by his side to offer advice, and a strong right arm when it came to a fight.

"Of course, my lords," he said, smiling somewhat sheepishly and getting up. Cai followed suit, eyeing him expectantly as he said to Arthur. "I'll say my farewells to Duro, and then join Eburus and the rest of the men. We'll be moving south today, aye?"

"We will," Arthur confirmed. "Caradoc will travel home to Lindum, while his son, Edern, and half their men will come with us. Kay, Cador, and the rest of our army will join us near Caer Lerion in a few days or so." He touched his beard uncertainly. "I haven't decided what we'll do after that – it'll depend on what Hengist and his lackeys do."

"Very good, my lord," Bellicus said. "Me and my men will be ready to go when you are." He bowed his head and left with the great mastiff loping along at his back contentedly.

For a time, Arthur and Merlin sat in silence, sipping their drinks and listening to the bustle of the warband breaking camp in preparation to march. Eventually, the High Druid shook his head and smiled almost wistfully.

"I sometimes forget just how young so many of you men are," he said. "A great responsibility has been thrust onto the shoulders of the likes of you and Bellicus, Arthur. The gods have marked you for greatness but... I sometimes wish you'd had more time to simply *live*, in peace, before this was all forced upon us."

Arthur frowned. "I was born for this. And so was Bel. You druids teach that we live and then die and are reborn in another life. Well, perhaps we lived in peace during all our previous lives and are ready now for war." He shrugged. "Who can say? All I know is that I've been tasked with protecting Britain from those who want to destroy us and our way of life and take from us by force what we've spent generations building and rebuilding since the Romans left." He stood, emptied the last of his now-cold ale into his mouth, wiped his lips with the back of a hand and rested his palm on the rounded pommel of his sword. "Come on, we should get out and let the lads pack up the tent."

Merlin followed at his young protégé's back, breathing deeply of the fresh, if bitterly cold, air. "South then," he said, looking around with satisfaction as the warband made quick, efficient work of the camp teardown.

"Aye," Arthur confirmed. "To Caer Lerion."

"This should be an interesting trip then," Merlin said, and Arthur snorted with laughter.

"'Interesting'. Aye, that's one way to describe an audience with King Ceneu ap Coel…"

CHAPTER EIGHT

Five horsemen rode out of the camp around mid-morning. As Arthur and the rest of the warband headed south, Duro led Bedwyr and three other riders across the fields to the northeast, towards Luguvalium. The winter snows were gone, and it hadn't even rained for a while, allowing the horses to move a little faster than they might have done a few days earlier.

Bedwyr looked at Duro as they rode, noting a change in the centurion's demeanour. In the weeks since the men had come down from Alt Clota with Bellicus, Duro had been morose and uncommunicative. Sad, even. Bedwyr had known many warriors like that, for even the cheeriest of souls could lose their love of life when those close to them died, so he hadn't thought much of it. A centurion must surely have seen his share of death and suffering over the years after all. Arthur's captain was pleased to have such an experienced, well-trained man joining their warband, but he hadn't gone out of his way to seek the centurion's company, and the idea of travelling on this mission at his side hadn't been particularly pleasant.

Yet, as they crested the brow of a low hill and the sun cast their shadows off to the right, Duro looked ahead of them, and Bedwyr saw his face soften in a smile. It wasn't exactly the first time the warrior from Powys had seen the expression on Duro's face, but it seemed more natural, more heartfelt, than at any time since they'd known one another.

"You're glad to be away from the camp, eh?"

The centurion turned to look at Bedwyr uncertainly, almost as if he wasn't sure himself what he was feeling, and then he nodded. "Aye, it feels good to be on the road, without all the bustle of an army about us."

The other men with them continued riding down the hill and Duro followed, Bedwyr keeping pace at his side. "You don't like being among so many men? I'd have thought a Roman officer would be used to it. To thrive on it, even."

Duro shrugged. "My days in the legions are far behind me, my friend. I spent years living quietly as a baker, only recently being drawn back into the wider world. It feels strange to be part of an army now. Restrictive." He raised a hand and gestured at the wide, empty fields all around. "This…This is freedom."

"If you want to be free, why not just go home and back to your bakery?"

There was no harshness in Bedwyr's tone, no criticism, just curiosity.

Duro didn't reply immediately. Instead, he sighed, and the darkness seemed to return to his eyes as they reached a narrow brook and their mounts jumped nimbly across the clear, gurgling waters. "My life as a baker is gone as well," he said at last. "I've no idea where I belong anymore, but, for now, we have our orders from Arthur to complete, and that's enough. It'll give me something to channel my energy towards." His voice became a low growl and Bedwyr saw his clean-shaven jaw tighten as he went on. "I may not have a home these days, but I have a task: To see the Saxons driven from our lands and for that bastard Horsa to suffer an agonizing death. Preferably at my hand." He looked down without thinking and stared at his missing fingers, cut away by the Pictish king, Drest, and muttered, "I have a score to settle with the Lord of Dunnottar too."

They lapsed into silence and Bedwyr was happy to let it go at that. The terrain had become rocky here, more treacherous, and besides, they had many days riding together to look forward to. If the centurion wanted to tell him more about his life, so be it. If not, that was fine too. Bedwyr was not the type who needed constant conversation to pass the time.

They caught up with their companions, who'd been forced to slow their pace as the ground turned marshy and the horses found it more difficult to walk. One of the other riders, a tall but slim middle-aged man with a dark moustache, glanced back at them.

"How do we know this old decurion still lives in Luguvalium?" he asked. "Or even lives at all?"

"We don't, Aesibuas," Duro admitted. "I haven't been in my hometown for months, and even then, I didn't visit the stables. I didn't know Sulinus at all. But we have to start somewhere and Luguvalium is as good a place as any. If Sulinus is dead, we'll look elsewhere."

"D'you think some old Roman officer will be much use to us?" another man asked no-one in particular. "No offence meant, centurion. I just mean, well, the old fella was trained in a different time, with a different army and stuff. Things have moved on."

"That's exactly why we need someone who was there at the time, Rianorix," Bedwyr replied. "We *have* moved on, and forgotten how to train a proper cavalry unit. So, aye, if we can find him, I think the old decurion will be useful."

"Depends how old he actually is," the last of their companions, a lean, dark fellow called Catti said cheerily. "He might be too old to travel. Or he might have gone mad. Maybe he's gone blind. Or—"

"I suppose we'll find out when we get to Luguvalium," Bedwyr broke in, rolling his eyes. "Just you three keep a look out for enemy scouts, all right? We don't want to be killed before we even reach our destination."

"Yes, sir. Sorry, sir."

Bedwyr turned to Duro and shook his head in mock irritation, glad to see the centurion's earlier smile returning.

"I'm happy to know your men respect you," Duro said. "I reckon you'd have been a natural in the legions."

Bedwyr laughed shortly. "We'll see. If Arthur's plan works out like he hopes, we'll soon have a legion of our own."

Duro grinned but didn't feel the need to inform his new friend that a cavalry unit in the Roman army was called a *turma,* or that one such unit wouldn't come close to constituting a legion. Instead, they rode on, all five of them in silence, wondering how the coming days and weeks might turn out and if their mission would be a success.

* * *

When they finally came into Ceneu ap Coel's Kingdom of Caer Lerion Bellicus was glad to see winter banished, as trees sprouted buds and a giant queen bee, fresh from her hibernation, sailed drowsily across their path at one point, searching for a place to nest. The town itself, with its old stone walls and lookout towers, was situated in a valley, and the Roman roads in the area were mostly in decent condition. This was all good for the men's morale, as the going would be easier now after the frost-rimed fields and tracks further north.

Once, this had been a thriving Roman town, with an aqueduct, marketplace, and fine houses. Pottery, horn, metal and even glass industries expanded and, over time, a forum and a basilica were built. Most of it had been destroyed in a great fire though, and when the legions left it had not been rebuilt. Still, it was quite an impressive looking place, Bellicus thought as they rode towards it.

"What's this king like?" the druid asked as they rode past a group of sheep, warily eyed by the shepherd and his dog on a nearby ridge in case any of the warband tried to steal one of the valuable livestock.

"Ceneu," replied Merlin, "is a Christian, and doesn't like druids much."

Lancelot laughed humourlessly. "He doesn't like anyone much." He looked at Bellicus and shook his head. "Ceneu's an arsehole."

"Now, now," Arthur said, smiling himself to offset the rebuke. "Watch what you say here, Lancelot. Even the sheep have wagging tongues in Caer Lerion, it's said."

"The mark of a good ruler," Merlin said. "Ceneu's people are fiercely loyal to him, and any seditious talk will see the would-be rebels in irons before they can raise a hand against him."

Bellicus took in their words and looked at the shepherd who, although still watching their passage, was now walking towards a large farmhouse not far to the east. "A good ruler," he mused, "or a dictator whose people are held in his thrall by pure fear?"

"A bit of both, perhaps," Merlin said. "But you'll meet Ceneu soon enough and can make up your own mind on his character."

It had taken them the best part of six days to reach the outskirts of Caer Lerion, despite their steady pace, and the sun would soon be setting, so Arthur called back to his men for one last push, forcing them to march just a little faster. Word of their coming had preceded them, perhaps sent on by some messenger of the shepherds, and the small settlements they passed were quiet, with doors closed and windows shuttered. It was rare indeed to see so many unknown warriors travelling in these lands, and, understandably, the locals were wary. Arthur could no doubt use his charm to put their minds at rest and procure some meat and drink should the warband be forced to stop for the night, but the warlord did not want that. Not when they were so close to Ceneu ap Coel's fortress.

"The king will already know we're here," Lancelot said as they passed another seemingly deserted farm. "Why don't I ride on ahead and tell Ceneu who we are? If they think we're Saxons they might lay an ambush, and attack without giving us a chance to speak."

Arthur frowned. "Our shields are painted blue and have my bear on them. Ceneu will know who we are."

"Anyone can paint a shield," Merlin advised. "But the king knows Lancelot. His idea is a good one."

"Aye, Ceneu knows Lancelot," Arthur replied rather sharply. "And dislikes him almost as much as he dislikes druids."

"I never touched his daughter," Lancelot objected, rakish grin firmly in place now. "Despite her advances. I'm an honourable man, my lord. You know that."

Arthur merely shook his head, but Bellicus could see the amusement in his eyes as he looked at his blond captain. "Aye, all right. Ride on and ask Ceneu if he'll put us up for a time in his hall. We'll pay if he insists, but don't offer unless he demands it. A king should be ready to offer his visitors sustenance, but I suppose it is short notice, and there's quite a lot of us, although the main body of our men can camp outside the town."

With a nod, Lancelot kicked his heels into his mount's flanks and cantered along the road which was still damp from the recently melted snows.

"And don't tell him I'm here," Merlin shouted after him, "Or Bellicus!"

Lancelot raised a hand to show he'd heard, but soon disappeared into the distance as the warband marched steadily after him.

"Does this king really hate druids so much?" Bellicus asked Merlin. "Should I be hiding my staff before we meet him?"

"No, lad," Merlin replied. "He's not the ogre we've been making out. He is a recent convert to Christianity, and feels the need to proclaim his faith any chance he gets, so he'll insult us, and the old gods, but he won't harm us. Just don't rise to his bait and all will be well. You might even find you like him. Arthur does."

"Not you, or Lancelot, though?"

"I would rather there were no Christians in places of power," the grey bearded high druid said levelly, "and Ceneu knows it. There's no love lost between us, but I respect him as a good leader, for he's proven himself over a long lifetime." He looked along the road as if he could still make out Lancelot's diminishing form on the horizon. "As for our handsome friend, well, who knows what happened with him and Ceneu's daughter. He tells one story, the king tells another, and the princess denies everything." He shrugged. "Wars have been fought over less, but only Lancelot and the girl truly know what happened."

"*I* know," Arthur put in firmly. "Nothing happened. Ceneu's daughter tried to seduce Lancelot and he rejected her. That's all there is to it, but, of course, she wasn't pleased about the rejection and made a fuss. Her father got the wrong end of the stick and still hasn't forgiven us for that little escapade."

Bellicus thought about this, and about the stories he'd heard already about Lancelot and the myriad beautiful women in every corner of the land who were ever eager to lie with him. "He turned down the chance to bed this girl?" he asked. "You believe he really is that honourable?"

Arthur laughed shortly at that. "No, Bel, I don't think he's particularly honourable when it comes to women throwing themselves at him. If they're willing, so is he, usually."

"Then what makes you so sure he didn't lie with Ceneu's daughter?"

"You'll understand soon enough," Arthur replied, and would say no more on the matter as the hall belonging to Ceneu ap Coel came into sight just as the sun began to dip beneath the far horizon.

CHAPTER NINE

"It's not much of a fortress, is it?"

Bellicus smiled indulgently and turned to see a bleary-eyed Eburus. The Votadini champion was already quite drunk and thoroughly enjoying the feast King Ceneu had laid on, grudgingly, for the visitors. Arthur's earlier suggestion that the king was still angry at them because of Lancelot's treatment of his daughter proved correct. The old ruler wasn't pleased to see them, and if looks could kill, Lancelot would have been food for the crows, but Ceneu understood his responsibilities to guests. Even if he didn't like them much.

"I don't think there's all that much need of the high walls and towers here, my friend," Bellicus said, having to raise his voice to be heard in the noise of the festivities. "It's not like Dun Breatann, or Dun Edin, where invaders are always coming in on the water or from neighbouring lands. Caer Lerion is surrounded by allies nowadays and, before that, the Romans kept raiders at bay." He took in the high-ceilinged hall, attractive furnishings, tapestries on the walls and fresh reeds on the floor and nodded appreciatively. "This is a comfortable place. What more could Ceneu need?"

Eburus belched loudly. "With the Saxons wandering about as if they own all Britannia, I'd say those thick, high walls would be more useful if they were manned properly and not crumbling. More useful than some Roman tapestry anyway." He gestured disdainfully at an exquisite piece of art on the wall opposite them which showed a hunting scene. "That shit won't stop Hengist's sea-wolves when they come hammering at the doors."

Bellicus didn't reply. Eburus had a point and advising King Ceneu to strengthen his defences was one of the reasons Arthur had come here, but there was more to think about tonight. They'd been on the road with the warlord for a while now, fought battles along the way, and now Duro was off adventuring without the druid. Bellicus wanted to simply fill his belly with roasted meat and ale this night and enjoy the songs and stories and games the good folk of Caer Lerion might provide.

"You're the druid from up north, aren't you?"

The king sat down on the bench beside them and Bellicus bowed his head respectfully, seeing Arthur and Merlin watching from the high table at the far end of the hall.

"I am, lord. Bellicus of Dun Breatann." He raised his ale mug and grinned. "You have my gratitude for your warm welcome. After weeks on the road it's good to have fresh food and a roof overhead to keep the snow and rain off."

"You Merlin's successor?"

Bellicus almost drew back on his stool in surprise and only his years of training allowed him to hide his reaction. "No," he replied. "I have my own lands to look after in Alt Clota, where I serve Queen Narina and the Damnonii people."

"What are you doing here then, so far from your home? With this lot?"

Bellicus searched the king's face, looking for some clue to what lay behind his questions, but all he could see was a vague interest. There was no slyness or cunning in Ceneu's eyes and the druid guessed the old man was simply curious. "I met Arthur and the Merlin some time ago, and fought with them against a Saxon army at Duncrieff," he said, a smile lighting his face at the memory. "What a day that was! We'd feasted and sang the night before – everyone in Arthur's warband, dozens of us – all chanting the words to the old song, 'The Battle of Duncombe' and then, the next morning, we slaughtered the bastards. It was a great victory."

Ceneu nodded thoughtfully. "I've heard of that fight at Duncrieff," he admitted. "Didn't some elderly druid magically turn into a giant young warrior and defeat the Saxon champion in single-combat?"

Bellicus smiled enigmatically. "I seem to recall something like that happening, aye," was all he said in reply to the king's question though, before he went on. "Arthur's determination to see the invaders pushed back that day impressed me and, since Alt Clota is enjoying a rare period of relative peace right now, my queen agreed to send me south with some men to join him." He looked directly into King Ceneu's eyes now. "Defeating the Saxons is imperative if our lands, all our lands, my lord, are to remain in our possession."

Ceneu gazed back at him, seemingly unimpressed or uninterested in his pronouncement. Rather than answering, he stood up and jerked his head for Bellicus to follow suit.

"You're a heathen, of course, and I don't like what you druids stand for, but I know you're an intelligent man who understands the importance of history and culture. Come with me." He turned and walked off, past the dais upon which Arthur and Merlin sat. Usually, Lancelot, as the warlord's closest advisor and champion, would sit with them at the high table, but on this occasion Arthur had told his friend to sit with the rest of the men, so as not to antagonise their host. Ceneu led the way through a doorway into another part of the hall, Bellicus hurrying to catch up. Cai came too, scattering revellers in his wake, the hound's great size and baleful eyes making even those in Arthur's retinue shrink from him.

They went along a gloomy corridor lit only by the glow from the great hall behind them, and then into a large, spacious chamber. This was not dark at all; in fact, it was well lit with candles and lamps which, Bellicus guessed, had been lit especially for him. There was a wonderful nutty smell in the air and the druid knew at least one of the lamps was burning sesame oil. If Ceneu hoped to impress him, it had worked.

Like the great hall, this room boasted intricately woven tapestries depicting scenes from Roman and Christian mythology hanging on the walls. There were also life-sized busts of men and women, emperors, and gods and goddesses perhaps, beautifully sculpted by some long-dead artisan. There was even a satyr-like figure in one corner, which came up to Ceneu's waist and was complete with horns, hooved feet, and a set of pan pipes. The king might have been a Christian, but he clearly appreciated the culture and artwork of his pagan predecessors.

Cai sat down as Bellicus drank everything in with his eyes, marvelling at the workmanship of each different piece, before meeting Ceneu's gaze.

"Didn't expect the ruler of a regressive little kingdom like Caer Lerion to have treasures such as these, druid, did you?" He was smiling proudly, almost gloating at the effect of his room on the druid, and Bellicus felt distaste at the man's arrogance.

"I thought you were a Christian," he said, gesturing with his chin towards the satyr.

"I am," Ceneu agreed. "But I can appreciate the skill behind these things, be they heathen creations or not. Besides, look. You haven't noticed the crowning achievement of my little room." He pointed downwards, to the floor.

Bellicus looked and noticed that he was standing on a mosaic. His eyes had been drawn to the tapestries and sculptures when he came into the chamber, but now the druid realised each candle and torch had been placed strategically, so their light would fall on the mosaic in certain places.

It covered the entire floor, from wall to wall, and showed a number of scenes. There were dogs hunting deer, and men riding strange fantastical beasts which were presumably from some old tales even Bellicus with all his learning did not recognise. In the centre of it all was a round panel with the portrait of a clean-shaven man, and behind his head were the Greek letters chi and rho. The druid knew very well what that symbol meant, being the first two letters of the name of Christ.

"You see?" Ceneu said in wonder, bending to trace the lines of the chi-rho with his finger. "Of all the spectacular things in this room, this mosaic is the most incredible; the most valuable. And at its centre is Christ himself." The king stood up, making the sign of the cross with his right hand, before turning back to the druid with a triumphant, almost challenging look in his eyes. As if he was in some titanic battle with Bellicus, the representative of the old, pagan, gods.

"It's incredible," the druid admitted, for it truly was. "The knowledge, and skill, to create such a work of genius has long passed from our lands, my lord. How did you come across it?"

Ceneu beamed with pride, like a child who'd just shot his first hare and wanted to bask in the glory of it.

"It's been here for almost a hundred years," he said, bending again to take in the countless little blocks of stone, tile, pottery and even glass and marble which made up the mosaic. "Originally, this site was the villa of a Roman dignitary named Decimus Cornelius. He left when the legions did, and his house was rebuilt over the years by each succeeding lord and King of Caer Lerion." He looked up at the druid, towering above him. "Does your fortress of

Dun Breatann have anything that can match this? Of course not," he answered the question himself, not allowing Bellicus to reply. "You men of the north are renowned as hardy fighters – you have to be, to keep those damn Picts at bay, I suppose – but here, in the very heart of this great island, you'll find mighty warriors *and* high culture." He stood up and stretched his back out, staring at Bellicus as if to remind him who was the lord here, despite the great difference in heights. "Your gods are dying, druid. This mosaic is a symbol of that."

They looked at one another for a long time, until, at last, Ceneu turned away.

"I should know better than to outstare a druid," he laughed. "But for all your training, Bellicus of Dun Breatann, your ways are passing."

"All things come to an end," the druid replied coolly. "But I think your triumph is premature, my lord. I've seen your lands – we rode through them to get here after all – and I wasn't impressed."

Ceneu's eyes narrowed dangerously at this insult, but Bellicus was not put off.

"Your farms and steadings are ripe targets for raiders. Your people will be easy pickings for rapists and slavers and this?" He raised his arms to encompass Ceneu's fortress, then gestured with an open palm at the priceless mosaic floor. "All this will be torn from you and smashed to pieces by those who follow much older gods than your Christ."

Ceneu's hand fell to the long knife in his belt and he stepped back a pace. "You threaten me, druid? Here, in my own home?"

On the floor, Cai didn't move from his seated position, but he growled, low and deep in his great chest.

"I merely warn you, my lord," Bellicus replied stonily, not allowing himself to be distracted by his canine friend. "I speak not of my own people, but of the Saxons: Hengist, and his brother, Horsa."

The king's face relaxed, betraying the relief he felt, for it was obvious who would win in a fight between the pair of them in this treasure-filled room, had it come to that. "Pah," he spat, and his hand moved away from his knife as he walked towards the doorway leading back to the feasting hall. "Caer Lerion is

57

insulated from those rats by the kingdoms surrounding us. I don't fear them, or their bloodthirsty gods. Come, I think we deserve a drink, druid. I'll tell you what all the scenes in my mosaic depict, and hopefully those you travel with can keep their hands, and their cocks, to themselves while the rest of us drink."

He moved back along the darkened corridor, Bellicus trailing behind.

"A drink and a few tales," the druid said, making his voice light and ignoring the jibe about Lancelot. "That sounds good, lord king. Think on what I said about the Saxons, though. We thought we were safe in Alt Clota too. What chance was there of sea-wolves coming all the way into our lands, when they had so far to travel on foot, or by ship? And yet, they did attack us, and took our princess prisoner, all the way to the Saxon Shore and beyond."

Ceneu glanced over his shoulder at him, face grim, and then they were back in the hall with its hearth fire blazing brightly and ale-fuelled revellers bantering loudly, and the king led the druid to his high table on its dais, where Arthur and Merlin watched their return with open interest.

"As if one of your kind wasn't enough," Ceneu cried, shaking his head at Merlin in disgust. "I have to entertain – and feed! – this young giant as well tonight."

"King Ceneu," Arthur replied, frowning in surprise. "One of a druid's greatest skills is in entertaining people. Let Merlin or Bellicus spin a tale for your people, it's the least we can do to repay you for this feast."

Ceneu waved a hand dismissively. "Maybe later, although I'm not too keen on letting their kind fill my people's head with heathen stories and such. For now, Bellicus, take up your ale and let me tell you about my mosaic, as I promised. The rest of you – eat and be merry. Never let it be said the King of Caer Lerion wasn't a good host!"

For a time, Ceneu regaled Bellicus with what he believed was the story behind each of the four quadrants surrounding the central Christ figure of his floor mosaic. Without exception, they were older, Roman legends, such as the ancient hero, Bellerophon slaying a monster called Chimera but, although the druid found the subjects interesting, Ceneu was no master storyteller and the druid was glad when it was all over. Indeed, Bellicus's attention was mostly drawn to Eburus at the rear of the hall, who had a laughing girl with wonderful strawberry-blonde hair in his lap, pouring ale into his mouth while he fed her cuts of meat. The druid wondered where the king's daughter was, and if she'd avoid Lancelot or make a scene.

"Well, my throat is dry from talking," said Ceneu, not noticing his audience's apathy. "Why don't you or the Merlin entertain us all now? It's been many moons since my people listened to the lore of a druid."

Bellicus looked at the white bearded high druid and received a nod in return.

"Let me," said Merlin, and got to his feet, raising his arms wide and gazing out imperiously until the men and women gathered in the hall noticed and their drunken chatter faded entirely, leaving only the crackling of the fire and the torches in the silence. "Good folk of Caer Lerion," he said, and his voice, although he spoke rather than shouted, filled the hall right to its rafters. "Your king would have me tell you a tale, and I'll gladly oblige."

There were cheers at that for, although the people, like their lord, were mostly Christians, they loved the old tales and knew none were better at telling them than the druids.

"Before I tell you my story, though," Merlin went on, "I'd like to hear some of yours. Come, speak up – have any of you gathered here a tale to tell? Short ones, please!"

A few hands went up, and the high druid, eyes sparkling, looked at the people who would entertain their kith and kin as well as Arthur's warriors.

"You," he said at last, pointing at a red-haired young woman whose cheeks flushed red as every eye in the great hall turned to stare at her. "Let's hear your story," Merlin commanded, grinning widely. "Come, climb up on the table so we can see you."

She did as she was bade, her companions on either side clearing a space for her to stand, then, uncertainly at first, her voice grew in strength and confidence as she spoke. She asked if anyone there had heard of something which she called the "barguest", a fearsome spectral dog which roamed the hills surrounding Greenhow, the village she'd grown up in. Apparently, it wasn't a well-known legend in Caer Lerion, however, for only a few gathered there said they'd heard of this barguest.

"It had flaming red eyes, as big as the bottom of an ale-pot," she claimed, lifting up her own mug to illustrate the point and spilling its contents onto her neighbour, a pig-tailed man who cried out angrily, bringing peals of laughter from everyone looking on. "And teeth, as long and sharp as knives. It was no mortal dog, though, it was a demon, and it would roam the fields, killing sheep and even cattle in the night. Its howls could be heard for miles and brought great fear to all who heard them."

"Just sounds like a normal dog, or a wolf," someone called out derisively, and the woman turned in his direction, anger blazing in her eyes, although the crowd meant she couldn't see who spoke.

"That's what Bran the Butcher said too," she cried. "He took his big cleaver and promised to spend the night on the top of the hill where the barguest was said to have been seen the night before. He vowed he'd kill the thing and prove to everyone that it was just a normal beast."

"What happened?" King Ceneu demanded, thoroughly enjoying the girl's story.

"The men found him the next day, my lord," she said, eyes downcast respectfully as she addressed him directly. "Dead."

"So, the wolf got him," the man who'd called out before shouted.

"It was no wolf," the woman retorted, pointing to her own throat. "His windpipe was torn open, but not by any mortal animal. All over his body there were marks – *burn marks*, as if whatever had mauled him and ripped him apart had been on fire, although there was no sign of a blaze anywhere on the ground nearby." There was a horrified silence then, and wide-eyed, she finished by saying, "To this day, people in Greenhow hear the barguest howling at night, and some have seen its massive, spectral form on the hills and found their sheep drained of blood the next day. Not one soul has ever followed Bran the Butcher's example and tried to catch the barguest though…"

No-one spoke for a time as they took everything in, and then Merlin clapped in appreciation, followed by the king and the rest of the people.

"That was very good," Ceneu told her as she climbed somewhat sheepishly down from the table and accepted a fresh mug of ale from one of her neighbours. "Perhaps I should organize a hunting

60

trip for this 'barguest'. See if we can stop the beast once and for all; I think it would find my warriors harder to kill than a lone butcher. Now, Merlin, it's your turn now. I'm not as young as I once was, I'll need to retire soon, and I'd like to enjoy your talents before I go."

The people thumped their mugs on the table and the druid, who – with his long white beard and hair appeared quite elderly although Bellicus suspected he was only in his fifties – got to his feet and smiled.

"All right, lord king," he said, raising his voice to be heard over the din. "I'm not a youngster myself anymore, though, and I think it would be hard to top that young lady's tale." There were murmurs and grumbling at this, for everyone wanted to hear another story, but Merlin raised his hands in supplication. "Have pity on an old druid," he said. "Besides, if King Ceneu's hospitality will allow it, we'll still be here tomorrow and my friend, Bellicus, can spin a long, twisting tale for you."

That mollified the crowd, for the idea of feasting over two days was not something they were used to. The king looked amazed at Merlin's suggestion, and then furious, for laying on meat and drink for so many people was an expensive business, but the druid didn't give him a chance to protest.

"In Caer Ebbas," he cried, gesticulating theatrically with his right arm, "lived a nobleman of a long and distinguished line, named Venutius."

His audience quieted, some of them nodding for they knew Caer Ebbas, it being only a week's journey to the north.

"This nobleman had a son called Atined, who was lazy and enjoyed fighting, fornicating, and drinking wine more than he did an honest day's work. Honestly, who doesn't?" He grinned, drawing cheers from everyone there, apart from the king, who merely frowned, not wanting to encourage such un-Christian behaviour in his subjects. "Venutius despaired at his wayward son's behaviour, and then, when the boy was accused of raping and killing a farmer's daughter, it was enough to harden the old man's heart. When the lord's men came to arrest Atined, the young man fought them and escaped on his horse. As Venutius watched his son ride off into the forest, the old man cried out, disowning him and vowing, 'May my right arm burn away before I forgive you!'"

Merlin paused to sip his drink and some in the crowd followed suit, but none spoke. Bellicus watched in admiration, feeling the tale was rushed, and not a particularly good one so far, but noting the audience's rapt attention and understanding it was down to the high druid's skill.

"In time, the truth came out: Atined was innocent. Three men, in their cups in a local alehouse and believing they'd got away with it, bragged that they'd been the ones responsible for the rape and murder of the farmer's daughter. They were soon caught and hanged for their crime. Atined, however, did not return home and years later, Venutius lay on his deathbed, thinking about his life and the mistakes he'd made. 'I wish I could see my son again,' he told his servants. 'I would beg his forgiveness for accusing him of that terrible crime. He was a wayward youth, but I should have known he was not capable of such heinous acts as rape and murder, and waited to find the truth before judging so harshly.'

"Hearing this, one of the servants who'd been close to Atined sent word to a town a day's ride away, where he knew the young man had been living all these years. Sure enough, Atined returned home the next day, tall and strong and healthy, for he'd become a successful merchant with a wife and two smiling children of his own. Venutius cried tears of joy to see them all, and father and son made peace before the old man finally died."

Heads bowed respectfully then, and many of the listeners made the sign of the cross.

"There was much weeping and wailing in Caer Ebbas when the news of Venutius's death came out, for he'd been well loved by all who knew him. Preparations were made for the funeral and dozens gathered when the time came to say their farewells to the old man. His body had been laid out, ready to be buried, and the village druid performed the usual rites and said the usual words until, eventually, Atined approached for one final look at his father's body. That's when he noticed something odd and recalled Venutius's words that fateful night when Atined had ridden off and been disowned by his father: 'May my right arm burn away before I forgive him.'

"Lifting the shroud that wrapped the old man's body, Atined shrank back, crying out and making the sign against evil. For where Venutius's arm had once been, there was now nothing more than a blackened, burned, stump."

Thoughtful eyes stared back at Merlin as he finished his tale. It had not been an exciting one, there'd been no great battles or lofty deeds, but its themes of justice and forgiveness touched a chord in everyone listening and the druid was gratified to see husbands and wives reaching out to grasp one another's hands. "Sometimes we are all too quick to rush to judgement," he said, gazing pointedly at King Ceneu.

"Thank you, Merlin," the king said quietly, rising stiffly to his feet and returning Merlin's look steadily. He'd understood the druid's message well enough. "I had hoped for something a little more stirring, but your tale's message was a good one and I appreciate it." His earlier scowl returned then, and he looked at Arthur who had the sense not to smile as the king growled, "I never promised to pay for two nights of feasting, though, so if you're all staying for another day, you can pay for the meat and drink yourself, mighty warlord!"

And, with those parting words, King Ceneu ap Coel headed off to his bedchamber, his guests at the high table hiding smiles behind their ale mugs.

"An interesting story," Arthur said to Merlin as the noise level rose to its earlier almost deafening blare. "Bit obvious though, don't you think? You might have well just have said to Ceneu, 'Your daughter's a liar. Now, give us some men for our warband.'"

"If I'd done that, he'd have thrown us out, guests or not," Merlin replied. "This way, he can take the tale however he likes, without accusing me of besmirching the girl's name. Perhaps now he'll ask a few more questions and learn the truth of what happened between her and Lancelot."

Arthur nodded, but Bellicus, listening to them, hoped their opinion of Lancelot was right. He looked out at the men and women below their dais then and felt his heart sink.

Wandering out through the main doors into the night with a pretty, dark-haired woman in tow, was Lancelot who, it seemed, would never learn.

"Please tell me," said the druid, catching Arthur's attention, "that Lancelot hasn't just gone outside with Ceneu's daughter."

Arthur looked puzzled for a moment, then shook his head. "Ceneu's daughter? Velugna? Oh no, my friend, that wasn't the princess he went off with. Has no-one pointed Velugna out to you yet, Bel? No? Tall girl, long face, prominent teeth." Then, as if realising how unflattering his description was, he added, "She has beautiful strawberry-blonde hair."

Bellicus stared at him and then turned to peer into the shadows at the back of the hall where his men were seated. Eburus was gone, and so was the young lady with the striking hair that he'd had on his lap for much of the night.

CHAPTER TEN

The ride to Luguvalium was slower than Duro had hoped, since the ground was either treacherously hard or soft and muddy almost the entire way, thanks to the changeable weather. The last thing any of the five men wanted was to injure their mount so they took their time, thankful not to see any sign of enemies – Saxon or merely bandits – as they slowly drew closer to their destination.

"Arthur told me Luguvalium was hit by Horsa and his men not too long ago," the dark, lean rider called Catti said, not seeing Bedwyr shaking his head behind Duro. "Are we going to find the place in ruins?"

"No," the centurion replied, staring straight ahead at the horizon. "It was a while ago the Saxons attacked. The place has been mostly rebuilt since then. I passed through it with Bellicus and the other men from the north on our way down to meet Arthur and the rest of you and it looked…much as it always had. Besides, we won't be going to the town itself – Sulinus's stables are a mile or so away from there."

"Balls of iron on that Horsa," Rianorix said, and there was grudging admiration in his voice. "To raid a place this far from the safety of their camp in the southeast."

"They were looking for me," Duro replied and now the other riders noticed Bedwyr's lowered eyebrows and angry expression, but it was too late, the subject had been broached and the centurion spoke on in a tight, emotionless tone. "Horsa's men came through Luguvalium with the little princess they abducted from Alt Clota. I tried to rally the men there to stand against them. I managed to kill the Saxon leader, but my people didn't have the stomach for the fight and they – we – let them escape with the girl. Bellicus followed them soon after, I joined him, and we rescued the princess." The ghost of a smile tugged at the corners of his lips as he thought of Catia, and the way they'd stolen her from under the Saxons' noses, but then he sighed heavily as other, more painful memories flooded back. "Horsa rode to Luguvalium to catch us, but he made it there before us and ransacked the place."

The pain was evident in his voice and he kicked his heels into his mount's flanks, forging ahead of his companions who watched him go with quizzical looks.

"Is that it?" Rianorix asked. "The end of the story?"

"No," Bedwyr retorted irritably, berating himself mentally for not filling the others in about Duro's recent history and avoiding this awkward moment. "Horsa and his men killed the centurion's wife and I get the impression it wasn't an easy death."

"Oh, shit," Catti murmured. "Why didn't you tell us that before now?"

Bedwyr didn't answer but he was glad when, a short time later, the smoke from a number of fires appeared in the sky ahead and he knew they were almost at Luguvalium.

"Come on," he said, and urged his horse into a canter that brought him alongside the centurion. The other three came up at their backs and Bedwyr was glad to see Duro's face dry of any tears he might have shed, jaw set determinedly.

"Late afternoon," the centurion said. "Hopefully Sulinus will let us sleep in one of his barns but, if not, I'm sure I can find us somewhere in town." He forced a smile, but it did little to mask his obvious grief from Bedwyr. "At least we'll be dry if it rains, or snows."

"Maybe one of us should go on ahead," Aesibuas suggested. "You know what these people are like."

"'These people'?"

"Aye, centurion," Aesibuas nodded. "Farmer-types that live out in the wilds with their animals. One thing's for sure: he'll have about a dozen mangy dogs wandering about the place, ready to attack anyone that comes onto his land."

Duro laughed at that, nodding at the mental image his new companion had painted for them. Aesibuas was in his mid-thirties and more thoughtful, more serious, than the other riders Bedwyr had chosen to accompany them.

"Aye, true enough," the centurion admitted. "The sight of us riding towards his home might make him unleash his hounds and he'll have men, workers, living around the stables too. No point in stirring up trouble. All right." He looked at Bedwyr. "I'll ride ahead. The old boy might recognise me and, even if he doesn't,

I'm sure he'll know this." He tapped the centurion's helmet, with its front-to-back metal crest, on top of his head.

"Maybe not a good thing," Bedwyr said, smiling. "He might think he's seeing a ghost and attack you anyway."

"I'll take my chances," the centurion replied and, with a final wave, rode on ahead, towards the long, low buildings that were beginning to take shape in the fields not far ahead of them. The others followed, but at a slower pace, hands on their swords, ready to charge after Duro should it look like he needed their help.

As they watched him go, Rianorix lifted his hand to stroke his beard, a veritable birds' nest in varying shades of brown, ginger, and grey. "I wouldn't want to attack the centurion," he said. "Looks a right hard bastard. Although," he glanced across at Bedwyr. "He must be pretty old himself if he served in the legions."

"So?"

Rianorix shrugged. "I just think, you know, war is a young man's game. It seems like we're going to be relying on these old lads to beat the Saxons. Feels like we're doing things the wrong way around to me."

Bedwyr didn't reply for a time, watching Duro ride through the tall, open gates and into a long, fenced-off field which he assumed must be an exercise ground for the horses. "I understand what you're saying," he replied at last. "And, if it comes to it, I'd rather have twenty men under forty years of age beside me in a shieldwall than twenty greybeards. But," he pulled his cloak up around his neck as a cold breeze hit them from the east, "these old soldiers have knowledge and skills we don't have. Besides, Arthur's given us our orders, so we carry them out. That's it. Come on, it looks like someone's coming out to meet the centurion."

He led them on at a slightly faster pace as Duro shouted a greeting to a middle-aged, balding man, the sound of barking filling the countryside as a number of dogs appeared.

"Told you," Aesibuas muttered, tugging at one edge of his dark moustache. "Dogs. Always bloody loads of them in places like this."

No-one replied, but it seemed the hounds were friendly, or at least trained well enough not to immediately attack Duro for invading their territory. Two other men had walked out from the stable buildings as well by now, both carrying what looked like, at this distance, swords.

"They're well-armed," Bedwyr warned.

"Not surprising," Catti said. "If there's been a Saxon raid on the nearby town in recent months everyone living hereabouts will be wary of more. Especially an old soldier and his kinfolk."

Their approach had been noted, and two more stablehands came out into the exercise ground carrying polearms of some sort. In a low tone, Bedwyr commanded his men not to draw their swords unless a fight actually broke out, and then he reined in his mount at the gates, the others following his lead.

"All right, centurion?" he called, and Duro held up a hand in reply.

"Fine, Bedwyr. I'm just explaining to the manager who I am, and who you are. We're all friends here," he finished, looking down at the balding man who seemed to be in charge of the stable workers. The fellow didn't seem convinced by the centurion's words, and the continued barking and yelping of the dogs wasn't helping ease the tense atmosphere.

"Don't bother dismounting," the stable manager said, shaking his head up at Duro but calling loudly enough that Bedwyr and the others could hear. "Whatever you're selling, we don't want any."

"By Mithras, what's all this noise about?" A new voice cut across the equine exercise ground and a sixth man strode out from one of the buildings, heading straight towards the manager. "What's happening here, son?"

The newcomer looked like an older version of the manager, so Duro took his 'son' appellation to be a fact rather than a mere figure of speech. A little below average height, bald, clean-shaven and with skin like toughened old leather boots, the wiry old man stopped before Duro's horse and glared up at him.

"A centurion, eh? Where are you from?"

"Luguvalium. Victorious Sixth Legion."

For a moment, the old man stared at him, as if weighing the truthfulness of his words, then he said, "You're the fat baker."

Duro couldn't help but smile, although he sat straighter in his saddle as he replied, "I was. Not quite so fat now, though. You must be Sulinus. It's you we've come to speak with, decurion."

Sulinus looked out towards the gates where Bedwyr and the others waited, but he did not invite them to come into the practice ground. "What do you want, baker? We're busy here, and when I see five heavily armed men on my land it makes me nervous."

Duro didn't think he looked nervous at all. In fact, considering his age, Sulinus seemed remarkably fit and in control. "We want to hire you," he said. "To train riders." The old decurion appeared to be taken aback by this, which was understandable, Duro had to admit.

The yapping of the dogs still hadn't abated, in fact it had grown even louder as another small terrier had bravely sallied forth to join its larger companions and it was really starting to irritate the centurion. "May we speak inside, Sulinus?" he asked, wincing as a particularly loud bark assailed his left ear. "We've been riding for days and could do with a seat that doesn't move around the whole time."

Still, the decurion didn't seem inclined to offer these dangerous looking riders hospitality, but, at last, as the little white terrier took to barking directly at him and jumping against his legs, he relented. Irritably nudging the dog away with his foot, he nodded at Duro. "All right. My men will see to your horses." He turned then to his son, the stable manager. "I'll go and get some food and drink ready and stoke the fire. It's bloody freezing again. You bring them to me when they're all sorted."

He stalked off, rubbing his biceps to try and warm himself, and Duro, greatly relieved to have completed this first, crucial part of his mission, gestured for Bedwyr and the others to ride into the grounds as the workers, still eyeing them all warily, lowered their weapons and moved forward to grasp the animals' bridles.

The five riders from Arthur's warband dismounted and allowed the stablehands to take their horses off to be rubbed down and made comfortable, while Duro and Sulinus's middle-aged son waited for everything to be taken care of and Bedwyr to finally lead the others over to join them.

"My name is Rues," said the stable manager by way of introduction, but he did not move to grasp Duro's arm, apparently not quite ready to let down his guard and offer friendship. "Follow me."

The centurion led them after Rues as he made his way towards the same, homely building Sulinus had gone into.

"I'm Duro, and—"

"I know your name," Rues replied, cutting off the centurion mid-sentence. "I used to buy bread and honey cakes from you in town. You might not remember me – I had a lot more hair back then – but I remember you well enough. You were a good baker; I liked your cakes, and I was sorry when you left the town."

That was that in terms of conversation or niceties, as Rues lapsed into silence and pushed open a heavy door which took them into a large, comfortable room with a blazing fire against the far wall providing welcome warmth and light in the cold afternoon.

On each surface of this room—storage chests, windowsills, even a footstool—were carvings and figurines of horses and riders, many in battle and others depicted in the act of jumping or rearing. Only the large table which Sulinus was seated at was free of such ornamentation, instead being laid—much to Duro's delight—with three large jugs of ale, seven well-worn cups, a round, plain loaf of bread, some cheese, and a slab of yellow butter.

The centurion, mouth already watering at the sight of the food, took the proffered seat at the table, directly across from Sulinus. It hardly compared to one of Trimalchio's famous feasts, but the bread would fill their bellies and the ale would help ease the ache from their tired muscles after days of hard riding, and, when the centurion tasted the ale his smile grew even wider. It was dark and rich and very fresh, and he wasn't the only one of Arthur's emissaries to give a low groan of pleasure as it went down.

The bread was neither as fresh or as tasty as the ale, but, once it had been slathered in butter, Duro and his companions shared it with gusto. Sulinus and his son ate and drank little, choosing instead to watch the others patiently, until they were ready to talk.

"This is good ale," said Bedwyr with a smile.

"I know," Sulinus replied with one eyebrow lifted. "Now enough of the niceties. Let's get to business – you said you wanted me to train riders. What riders?"

"You've heard of Arthur?" said Bedwyr. "The warlord?"

Sulinus looked at him and ran a hand across his bald pate, scratching at a dry patch on the back. "Not a lot," he admitted.

"We don't hear much news from the outside world here, and I was never one to go hunting for gossip."

"I've heard of him, father," Rues said. "The Bear of Britain they call him. He fights the Saxons and seeks to unite all Britons against them."

"A noble cause," Sulinus noted, but his dry tone suggested he thought Arthur foolish or at least naïve. "I wish him luck. But it'll take more than some warlord – not even a king? – to stand against Hengist. Our legions recognised their threat and built great walls to keep them out all along the coast. Didn't work though, did it? The sea-wolves own those walls and fortresses now."

Bedwyr's face flushed angrily and Duro spoke up before the younger man could jump to his friend's defence.

"Arthur wants to train cavalry, and he's wise enough to know it'll take someone with great knowledge and experience to help him do it. I immediately thought of you. I don't believe we ever fought beside one another, but you have a fine reputation, so we've come to..."

"Enlist me?" Sulinus cackled, showing that he still retained at least a few of his teeth. "War is a young man's game."

"That's what I said," Rianorix agreed eagerly. "I don't see what some ancient old horseman can do for us either."

Now it was Sulinus's turn to look annoyed, and Rues almost imperceptibly leaned away from his father, as if expecting an explosion from the old man. Aesibuas upbraided Rianorix in a low hiss, but Sulinus's furious gaze turned to a dangerous smile.

"You're a rider?" the decurion asked, and Rianorix nodded. "A good one?"

"One of the best in Arthur's warband."

"Come outside, then. Show me."

Rianorix glanced at Bedwyr and Duro, but neither man said a word. They wanted to see what would happen next themselves. Rues was smiling too, and Rianorix seemed unsure what to do, but he was confident in his own abilities and so he stood now to follow Sulinus back out onto the exercise ground, the others following eagerly behind.

Catti and Aesibuas made low comments to one another about Sulinus, noting his bent back and the liver spots that dotted his hands and scalp, questioning his age, his temperament, and the futility of this entire mission, but Bedwyr remained silent, perhaps sharing their sentiments.

Duro was beginning to feel quite foolish for wasting their time coming here.

"Get your horse, then, boy," Sulinus ordered Rianorix, who was already walking towards the stables. The workers were still there, and one of them quickly hurried to fetch the animal Rianorix pointed out to him. Together, they put the saddle back on and made sure everything was safely buckled in place as, further along the row of stalls, Sulinus was readying his own mount.

They came out together, and Sulinus was given a leg-up by a groom while Rianorix nimbly jumped into his saddle without needing any help and said, with something of a smug look, "A race then, old man?"

The decurion nodded, muscles and veins popping out on his wiry arms as he guided his horse onto the exercise ground. "To the end and back."

Rues came forward as the horsemen lined up, side by side, and Catti shouted encouragement to Rianorix, exhorting him to show the old man how fast Arthur's riders were. By contrast, Rues and the rest of the stable hands said nothing and Duro was impressed by their calm professionalism in everything they'd done since he and his companions arrived at the property.

"Take your marks," Rues called, indicating a line on the ground for Rianorix to move forward to, then, "set, go!"

Sulinus's horse exploded forward, giving him an early lead, but Rianorix's beast, a dark brown stallion, was fast and managed to close the gap by the time they reached the turn at the far fence. Again, Sulinus's technique was superior to his opponent's and, as they raced back towards the spectators, the old man was in the lead once more. Rianorix shouted and kicked his heels into his mount, but it was no use and the elderly decurion crossed the finish line a heartbeat before him.

"It was close," Aesibuas commented as the riders slowed and turned their horses to walk back towards the onlookers.

"The horse my father's riding is a favourite of his," said Rues. "But it's not the fastest animal we own. Not even close."

Aesibuas digested that with a frown, and no-one commented, accepting Rues's word as the truth.

"Get us the javelins," Sulinus commanded as he reined in his horse at the starting line again. A stable hand sprinted to one of the buildings where a stack of wooden staves lay propped against the wall. He grabbed six of them and hurried back to hand three each to the decurion and Rianorix, who accepted the javelins uncertainly.

"What now?" he demanded, obviously annoyed at losing the race and wondering what was about to happen next.

"Three missiles apiece," replied Sulinus, holding his javelins in his right hand with practiced ease, reins in his left.

Now Duro noticed his saddle was designed a little differently to Rianorix's too, it having large horns at the front and rear and, thus, providing more support for the rider.

"Hit the targets," the old man was saying now, gesturing as the grooms were quickly dragging large circular boards made from wood and straw onto the ground. "Whoever hits the most, wins. You get extra points for hitting the targets in the centre, understand, lad?"

Rianorix nodded, and even managed a smile. He had been one of the few amongst Arthur's men who found this sort of mounted warfare came naturally to them, and, given how old his opponent was, believed he'd do well in this.

"First back gets an extra point as well," Sulinus said, and looked then to his son. "Start us off again, Rues."

"Take your marks," said the manager, not allowing Rianorix to finish his complaint about having to race as well as striking targets. "Set, go!"

Again, the decurion's horse seemed to go from standing completely still to moving at full gallop almost instantly, a feat that greatly impressed Duro and the others watching. Rianorix was left trying to catch up once more, but within moments the first of the targets were in front of them.

Duro watched Sulinus intently as the old man tightened his grip on the reins while hefting one of the javelins in his skinny right arm, not slowing his thundering horse at all, let fly. The missile struck home in the dead centre of the target with thump that sent pieces of straw skittering into the air.

Rianorix threw his first javelin, but his technique was nowhere near as polished as the decurion's, and neither was his aim, and it flew well wide of the mark.

On the horses galloped, with Sulinus building even more of a lead as he grasped his next javelin, loosed, and raced past as it too hit home in the centre of the shuddering target.

Rianorix threw his second javelin and this time he did hit the target, but the missile merely grazed the top of it and spun wildly off to the right, drawing a loud oath from the young rider who kicked his heels angrily into his horse, desperately trying to catch up with his opponent who was a long way ahead by now.

Sulinus came to the end of the training ground and turned his horse in a tight, graceful arc, before his horse pounded back towards the spectators. The decurion hefted his final javelin, gazed at a target fast approaching on his right, and let fly. Like the others, this missile struck the circular, straw covered board near the very centre, and Sulinus whooped in pleasure.

Behind him, Rianorix had made the turn so Duro could see his face as he tried his best to catch up with the decurion, but, with one last javelin to throw, and failing miserably with his previous two attempts, his face grew firm and determined as he closed in on his last target, slowing markedly to steady himself. With a frustrated shout, he threw the weapon and watched it fly right over the round board, strike the ground, and slide along until it came to a stop.

Sulinus had already crossed the finish line by now, and, knowing he was well beaten, Rianorix allowed his horse to slow to a canter, and then a walk, coming back to Duro and the others with an angry frown on his bearded face.

"You must practice that every day," he said as Sulinus turned and walked his own mount back to join the others.

The old man grinned, shaking his head. "First time I've tried it in..." he looked thoughtfully at Rues.

"Weeks," supplied his son. "At least."

"Aye, probably," Sulinus agreed, and the triumph had left his expression as he became coolly serious again. "Didn't do very well at all, lad, did you?"

Rianorix pursed his lips but didn't reply. What could he say? The decurion was right, he'd performed terribly. In a real battle there was as much chance he'd have injured his own men as the enemy. He wasn't happy to be made a fool of, however, like most young warriors.

"You look like you want to knock me right out of my saddle," Sulinus said.

Rianorix still didn't say anything, but the glower he gave the old man spoke volumes.

"Why don't you give it a try then?"

Duro stepped forward, mouth open to put an end to the display of Sulinus's display of expert horsemanship, but the decurion turned to glare at him and Duro stopped. These were Sulinus's stables, and the old man was the officer in charge of this exercise. The centurion nodded and stepped back, hoping he was reading the situation correctly, and Rianorix wasn't about to get badly hurt.

By the gods, this old man was a hard case! And yet...he *was* at least sixty, whereas Rianorix was in his early twenties, tall and lithe, and knew how to wield a sword. It would be an interesting match-up, but Duro couldn't imagine Sulinus continuing his run of victories with this event.

A groom came over carrying long, thin sticks, handing one each to Sulinus and Rianorix, who took it with a bemused frown and swung it through the air. It bent but didn't break.

"Aye," the decurion nodded at him. "It'll hurt like hell, but it won't break any bones. Much safer than using a heavy wooden practice sword. Put that on though, no point in ruining that pretty face of yours."

Rianorix took the helmet another stable-hand offered him – he had one of his own with his pack, but it was a proper, iron battle helm, whereas this one was a light, leather affair, designed exactly for this type of mock battle. Sulinus was given one too. They tied them in place, took the shields the grooms handed them, and eyed one another coolly.

"Ready, boy?"

"How do we decide who wins?" Rianorix asked. "Surely we don't just beat one another to bloody strips with these things until one gives in? That won't be me, just so you know, but I don't really want to hurt you, grandfather."

Sulinus laughed shortly and kicked his horse into a walk towards the centre of the practice ground. "Oh, I think we'll know when it's over," he called, and his voice was strong and confident.

CHAPTER ELEVEN

Duro feared this whole thing was about to get out of hand as Sulinus and Rianorix faced off. Still, they were getting a good demonstration of the decurion's skills and what he might offer to Arthur's cavalry and Rianorix looked like he knew how to handle himself. It would be a fight worth watching, no doubt about that.

The combatants walked their horses warily around the ground, watching one another and getting used to the feel of their 'sword' and shield, and then the decurion gave a shout and his mount suddenly exploded forward, as it had done at the start of the races. Rianorix brought up his willow wand and easily parried Sulinus's, but, somehow, the decurion's horse dodged nimbly forward, and Rianorix found himself facing in the wrong direction as Sulinus's willow wand whipped out and hit him a stinging blow on the back of the head.

The leather helmet saved the skin from breaking, but the pain was intense and Rianorix roared as Sulinus smiled and walked his horse calmly away a short distance, allowing the younger man a moment to gather his wits about him again.

Rather than wasting time, Rianorix kicked his mount and charged directly at Sulinus, slashing wildly at the older man as they came within range of one another. The decurion batted away each attack, but Duro could see this kind of exertion was taking a lot out of the old man.

Suddenly, Sulinus's horse moved forward, but turned left immediately, circling Rianorix so the decurion was at his back again and, again, he whipped the young man's helmet with his stick. There was a ringing crack as it struck, and another cry of pain but, as Rianorix tried to land a blow of his own, Sulinus's mount easily skipped away out of range.

"That's got to hurt like a bastard," Catti muttered, grimacing as Rianorix rubbed the back of his skull.

"The old man's horse moves like lightning," Aesibuas said. "I've never seen a beast so nimble, have you, centurion?"

Duro shook his head. "I don't think so. Maybe years ago, but I didn't take much interest in the cavalry. I had other things to deal with in the army."

"Well, Rianorix will have to do something special if he's going to beat the fellow."

As they spoke, the riders came together again, and a similar passage of moves played out, but this time, when Sulinus jinked around to the back of him, Rianorix used his shield to parry the old man's attack, and then he lashed out himself. The decurion was off balance, but, somehow, was able to lean back without falling out of his saddle and bring up his own shield so Rianorix's willow wand slapped ineffectually against the wooden boards.

Sulinus moved away, opening a wide gap between them, and Rianorix took the opportunity to rub the back of his head again, teeth gritted.

"You had enough yet, lad?" the decurion asked, and there was no hint of triumph or gloating in his voice. He'd proven his superiority over the younger man and felt no need to humiliate, or hurt, him any further.

Rianorix looked thoroughly embarrassed, and Duro thought he might charge furiously at the decurion, possibly even throw himself out of his saddle in an attempt to unhorse his elderly opponent. But Rianorix was not a stupid man and accepted the fact that Sulinus was simply a better rider than he was – there was no shame in it. The decurion had been trained by the Romans after all, and spent his life learning how to fight from the saddle.

"Aye, fair enough, grandfather. I yield. I hope you've got plenty more ale, though. I need something to dull the pain in my head!"

Duro let out a low sigh of relief, and noticed Bedwyr and the other two beside them did the same. Clearly, he hadn't been the only one fearful of how this would all turn out. Indeed, the only people who didn't seem at all worried were Rues and the stablehands, who'd acted calmly and professionally throughout. It was testament to Sulinus's operation here and Duro knew they must persuade the old decurion to join Arthur's army. He was exactly the type of man they needed.

The riders came to join them and dismounted, with Sulinus once again needing assistance onto the ground. His horse was like an extension of his body, Duro thought, but without its support he was still an elderly man, and the way he limped towards his house proved it. He'd ridden with confidence and skill, and handily beat young Rianorix in every contest, but the physical exertion had plainly left Sulinus exhausted and suffering from aches and pains he did his best to mask.

As was always the way with warriors, or younger men in general, Duro thought, Sulinus tried to hide his discomfort from the rest of them, and moved stiffly towards the comfortable building in which they'd shared their frugal meal earlier. He seemed too tired even to gesture for the others to follow him, but he muttered something to Rues, and he relayed the message to Duro.

"Come on," he said. "My father will talk with you in the house."

Bedwyr spoke, looking up at the rapidly darkening sky with a frown. "Can we count on your hospitality for the night? Even just a place for us in one of these outbuildings? We have our own provisions—"

"I'm sure it won't be a problem, lord," the stable manager replied, nodding. "There's plenty of space for you all, and the buildings are quite weatherproof so you should be comfortable enough. Come, though, we can discuss that later."

The grooms had already disappeared from the exercise ground with the two horses and again Duro was struck by their quiet professionalism. He wondered how the stable paid for its upkeep, for so many mouths to feed – human and equine – was an expensive business. As they walked back into Sulinus's living quarters, the centurion thought he saw a way to approach this next conversation with the old decurion and his son.

Sulinus was already in the main room when the others reached it, and his wiry arms were lifting an amphora from a side table. Duro surreptitiously watched him filling a cup with what looked like wine, some of it spilling as Sulinus's hands were shaking so much. The decurion muttered irritably at the wasted drink but put down the amphora and grasped the nearly-full cup, downing it in two quick gulps before moving across to join the others at the table. He was pale but happy enough, and the colour soon returned to his features as the wine warmed him from within and the fire – which Rues prodded back into full, flickering life – soon made the room cosy again.

"Pour some ale for our guests, son," Sulinus said to Rues, who did so without a word.

"That was some display you put on," Duro said to the old man who accepted the praise with a tight smile. "Clearly you haven't lost your touch since you left the legions."

"Not all of us left the army and spent the years eating honey cakes, centurion," Sulinus noted. "I might not be a soldier anymore, but I still know how to fight."

"Clearly," Rianorix grumbled ruefully, although he was smiling as he took another sip of his ale.

"You'll be wanting to spend the night here no doubt," Sulinus said, changing the subject and continuing before anyone could reply. "Rues, why don't you show those three," he gestured with his fingers towards Catti, Aesibuas and Rianorix, "to the guest quarters. Not you two." This to Duro and Bedwyr. "I'll listen to what you have to say regarding the warlord, Arthur, but, as you can see, I have a good life here, and responsibilities. Rues is the manager, but I still take a lot to do with the daily running of the stables."

Rues downed the last of his ale and looked at the three riders he was to lead to their beds for the night. "You can take the bread," he said to Rianorix, pointing to the remainder of the loaf they'd been sharing earlier. "It's not much but I'll have one of the servants bring you meat and some jugs of drinking water. That'll do you until morning, I expect."

Rianorix lifted the loaf with a murmur of thanks to Sulinus, who was watching him with eyes that sparkled from more than just the wine he'd drank, and then the four men strode off to the guest area, which was in the adjoining building behind the stalls their horses were housed in.

The room was quiet for a time, as Sulinus stared into the fire, lost in thought. Duro and Bedwyr allowed him his reverie, although the centurion worried the old man might fall asleep, given how tired he must be and how cosy the room was now. Indeed, he feared he might nod off himself if no-one continued the conversation.

"So," the decurion said at last, forcing his attention away from the dancing red flames and eyeing Duro with no hint of drowsiness or inebriation. "Arthur wants me to train cavalry for him."

It was Bedwyr who spoke, and Duro let him, since Bedwyr was Arthur's captain and the one charged with negotiating the details of Sulinus's enlistment. "He does," the man from Powys confirmed. "Obviously, we have horses, and we have riders, but, like the Saxons, we don't use them in battle. At the moment we ride for transport, or for scouting, or sending messages. Men like Rianorix are excellent at all of those, but, as you proved today, using a horse as a tool of war is something else entirely. Your skills would be extremely valuable to us. To Arthur."

"And he'd be willing to pay handsomely for my services?" Sulinus's face was impassive now, a mask of parade ground coolness.

"Aye," Bedwyr agreed. "Bearing in mind he's not a king himself, however, so the pay will be generous but not drawn from an unlimited well. And we are looking at enlisting one or two more retired cavalry officers like yourself for this task."

Duro watched the decurion as he was given that information, and he noted the old man didn't seem as bothered about the pay as much the fact there would be other officers working alongside him.

Bedwyr had seen Sulinus's narrowed eyes too and tried to reassure him. "You'll be given a rank high enough to make your voice heard, don't worry. We just don't want our whole operation falling to pieces should something happen to you. It makes sense to bring in two or three men with your particular skills, if we can find them." He spread his hands and smiled. "Besides, even if we do manage to enlist more cavalry officers, it could be Arthur thinks you're the most experienced, and the most knowledgeable, and grants you overall control of the training regime. It'll depend on who else we can find."

"I think," Duro put in, "that we've seen enough in our short time here to say you'll be welcomed with open arms in Arthur's army and given the position you deserve. If I may ask, how do you earn a living just now? I mean this place must take a lot to keep running."

"I have a good reputation, centurion," Sulinus replied, stretching his hands out towards the fire to warm them. "The noblemen all around these lands send their horses to me to be trained, and they pay me well in silver, or goods."

Duro nodded. "You don't need money," he said, taking Sulinus's point, "but think of the opportunity we're offering you."

"Pah," the decurion waved a hand dismissively and reached for the cloak that hung over the back of his chair. "Opportunity. Opportunity to do what? Spend what's left of my days trying to show young fools how to ride?" He pulled on the woollen garment, instantly appearing even older than before. "War is a game for men much younger than me, centurion."

"Maybe," Bedwyr conceded. "But the Saxons are bringing that war to everyone, young or old. D'you think Hengist will leave your stables alone? A prize like this? You know what his brother did to Luguvalium, don't you?"

"I heard," Sulinus admitted. "But even Saxons will need my services."

"Hengist, and particularly Horsa, take what they want," Duro said. "They don't pay fairly for that which they can take for free."

Sulinus frowned. "I've heard of towns and villages to the south, who've taken in the Saxons readily enough, and now everyone there lives together quite happily."

"That's true," Bedwyr said. "Not all of the men coming across the western sea are warlike savages. Some of them just want to settle here and live in peace. But Hengist and Horsa are not like that. To them, war and killing is how they earn their place in the afterlife and, if it comes to it, whose side do you think those peaceful Saxons you mentioned will take? Mark my words, Sulinus, if Arthur can't defeat the sea-wolves your comfortable life here won't last long."

Silence returned then, as all three men pondered the future.

"I'm old," the decurion finally admitted with a heavy sigh. "I've no desire to watch the invaders burn down everything we've built in these lands since the legions left. It was hard enough for the people trying to come to terms with that." He shook his head sadly. "I only wish I was younger and had more to offer."

"You have exactly what we need to defeat them," Bedwyr said vehemently. "Your knowledge can help us beat the bastards once and for all."

Sulinus looked at him, impressed by his enthusiasm, but not quite convinced. "I think you, and Arthur, are placing too much importance on the power of cavalry," he said, and then shrugged.

81

"I am tempted by your offer though. It's a comfortable life here, admittedly, but..." He stood up and walked slowly to one corner of the room, lifting a small bronze statue of a horse and squinting at it lovingly. "I was given this by my old commander, as a reward for the part my *turma* played in quelling a Selgovae uprising along the Wall. I miss those days." He looked at Duro. "I expect you did too. That's why you're not a baker anymore."

"Something like that," the centurion admitted. "We're not asking you to fight in Arthur's army, though. Just to help us train it. Show the youngsters how to ride, and how to throw a javelin from horseback, and how to charge a shieldwall without the horses breaking and fleeing in panic before they can do their job."

"We'll need men to take care of the horses too," Bedwyr put in, sensing Sulinus was close to joining them and adding one last worm to the hook. "You can bring your son, Rues, and your grooms as well if you like. Or leave them all here to keep operating the stable, it's up to you."

Sulinus walked back to the table and sat down, still holding the bronze statue in his right hand. "Arthur isn't a king," he said. "He's a warlord, who wanders the land fighting battles, correct?"

"That's what he's been doing recently, aye," Bedwyr agreed. "That, and trying to add more men to his army."

"So, I would have to travel with him."

Bedwyr nodded. "I'm afraid so."

"Where is he just now?"

"Caer Lerion," Duro said. "About—"

"I know where it is," Sulinus broke in irritably. "Ceneu ap Coel is the king there. He's no friend to the followers of Mithras. If you were to roll up your sleeve, centurion, would I see the tattoo of a bull on your arm? Aye, I thought so. How does the Christian king look upon a warlord, and warriors, who don't follow his nailed god?"

"Ceneu might wish everyone was a Christian," Bedwyr replied dismissively. "But he fears the Saxon's gods, and what they drive the likes of Horsa to do, much more than Mithras or the others who were here even before the Romans arrived."

"Then you think we have a chance of winning this war? Speak truthfully, now."

"I think Arthur can defeat Hengist's hordes even without cavalry," Bedwyr said and the pride he held for his commander was evident. "He's the greatest battle leader we could have asked for. Adding your skills to the mix will just make us even stronger."

Sulinus gazed at them for a short time, and then looked down, into his cup, as if weighing up whether to refill it again or not. He chose not to, instead rising to his feet and pulling the collar of his cloak up around his neck. "I'll sleep on it," he said. "We can talk again in the morning. Have another cup of ale, lads. I'm off to bed but I'll send a servant in a little while to clear up and show you to your sleeping quarters."

They could hear him making his way in the dark to wherever his bed chamber was, and then silence. Neither Duro nor Bedwyr made a move for the ale jug, for it was late and both men wanted to be up, fresh and clear-headed, in the morning.

"What do you make of him?" Bedwyr asked quietly as they waited for the servant to show them to their own quarters for the night. "I mean, from the perspective of a former Roman officer yourself."

Duro didn't have to think about the question for long. He'd been silently appraising the decurion from the moment they met. "I'm very impressed by him," he said. "He has the air of command, of authority about him, that all the best officers need. You can see it in the way his stablehands work, quietly and efficiently, with minimal direction."

"Agreed," Bedwyr said. "I can imagine him at the front of a cavalry unit, helmet and armour gleaming and immaculate, riders following his every movement on the exercise ground instinctively."

Duro pictured that, nodding in approval as his mental image moved on and showed him a young Sulinus, leading his men in a charge downhill, a trumpet blaring as the enemy turned in alarm to see the mass of horses bearing down on them. He had no idea if it was a real memory, of an event that he had really witnessed when he was serving with the legions, or if it was just his imagination, but it served to illustrate what Sulinus might offer Arthur's warband.

Such a charge, against an army entirely unused to cavalry being deployed in that way, could be devastating. It was an exciting prospect.

"The only issue," Bedwyr was saying, disturbing Duro from his sleepy reverie, "is his age. Not just his physical ability to travel and to lead training manoeuvres, but his desire and drive to do so. Can a man in his sixties push himself to deal with a squad of young, mouthy, recruits every day? A man who's already done his part serving in the legions?"

They sat enjoying the warmth of the fire and pondering these questions, until footsteps could be heard coming from the rear of the house. The door opened and a young woman's head appeared around it, blue eyes peering at them.

"Are you finished your supper, my lords?" she asked, politely but without the subservience of a slave, and Duro guessed the girl was some relation of Sulinus. Possibly Rues's daughter.

Bedwyr looked at the centurion and they stood, smiling at the young girl who stepped further into the room now. "We are, lass," said Arthur's captain.

"Follow me then," she said, and took them out, into the night. A crescent moon hung in a cloudless sky and the men shivered, missing the warmth of the fire, but soon enough they were in the stables, greeting Catti, Aesibuas, and Rianorix.

"Do you need anything else, my lords?" the girl asked, and Bedwyr thanked her, saying no, they had everything they needed, and she left them with a slight bow and headed off to clear away the empty cups they'd left in the main house.

"Not bad quarters, eh?" Catti asked, looking about him. He was already in a cot with his blanket and cloak over him. Only a single rushlight provided illumination and the door and shutters were closed to keep out the worst of the cold, but it was enough for Bedwyr and the centurion to find their own cots and blankets and bed down for the night.

"Perhaps," Bedwyr suggested once the light was extinguished and they were all comfortably drifting off to sleep, "when our cavalry units are in operation, and the Saxons beaten, we could have Sulinus train any new units here. Maybe even have a whole string of stables like this, training horses and men all throughout the countryside, right down to the fortress of King Conomor in Duntagell!"

Duro smiled in the darkness, appreciating the enthusiasm he could hear in the young officer's voice as he thought about the possibilities such a future would bring.

"What d'ye think lads?"

Catti and Rianorix drowsily agreed with their captain's suggestion, as did Duro, but, when Aesibuas's gentle snore filled the bedchamber they took it as a cue to get some sleep. Hopefully the morrow would see Sulinus agreeing to join them, and then Arthur's cavalry dream could start to become reality.

CHAPTER TWELVE

"I knew it was a mistake to offer you hospitality, you bastard! Your men just can't keep their hands to themselves, can they? Well, I'll cut the cock off this one, and make sure he never does anything like this again."

Bellicus awoke to the sound of shouting and tried to shake off the grogginess that a night's drinking and feasting was wont to bring. He'd fallen asleep on a bench in King Ceneu's great hall, along with the rest of Arthur's men, and a few locals. Cai was already alert by the druid's side, ears twitching, nose sniffing, as the massive wardog's senses checked their surroundings for danger. He was used to shouting, but he could tell as well as any man that trouble was brewing.

Now Bellicus recognised a second voice, answering the first.

"Lord King," Arthur was shouting too as he responded to Ceneu's furious accusations and threats. "You're jumping to conclusions *again*, just as you did on my last visit here. Calm down, man, and deal with this rationally—"

"Don't you give orders to me, you landless young whoreson," Ceneu roared, turning his scarlet face as he sensed the approach of the giant warrior druid. "And you can keep out of this as well, heathen scum!"

Bellicus frowned but kept his temper in check, knowing from bitter experience that attacking a king in his own hall could lead to far more trouble than it was worth. Still, he was a nobleman too, and deserved more respect than Ceneu was offering him, so he drew himself up to his full, imposing, height and stood just a little bit too close to the king than was polite, before addressing Arthur.

"What's happening, my lord? What's he shouting about?"

"My daughter's been raped, that's what I'm shouting about, druid!"

Behind Ceneu now came four warriors, his personal guard, all with swords drawn, their naked steel glinting in the flickering lights of the candles and rushlights that hadn't yet burned themselves out.

Arthur looked at Bellicus and, from his eyes, the druid could tell that there was some truth to the King of Caer Lerion's

86

accusation. His heart sank as he recalled who the princess had slipped out into the night with during the feasting: Eburus.

Shit! He knew it was a mistake to bring the hot-headed young fool along, he'd been nothing but trouble since the moment the druid had met him. And yet, Princess Velugna had been smiling when she led the Eburus out through the door earlier, and, really, was the Votadini the type to do something as heinous as what Ceneu was suggesting? Bellicus wouldn't have thought so – the young man was a loudmouth who enjoyed being the centre of attention as much as he enjoyed a good fight, but he'd not seemed the type to misuse women. Still, a bellyful of ale had turned more honourable men than Eburus into mindless savages so... Bellicus looked about the hall for Merlin, knowing he would be a useful peacekeeper, but perhaps it was best that the high druid wasn't here, given Ceneu's dislike for the old ways.

Arthur might not have been a king, but he had enough men gathered around him in the hall to give him confidence should it come to a fight, and the temperament not to be frightened or cowed by a situation as volatile as this.

"If one of my men has committed a crime against the princess," said the warlord, looking earnestly into Ceneu's eyes, "we'll deal with him. You have my word on that." He too cast about for Merlin then, not seeing the white-bearded druid, went on, "Can we speak with your daughter, Lord King? Find out exactly what happened?"

"I've already told you, she's been raped," Ceneu retorted angrily. "And I've sent men out to find the man responsible for it. There'll be no need for a trial when they find him, you have *my* word on that."

Arthur frowned but knew it would be futile to argue with the king when he was in such an understandably emotional state. Instead, he nodded. "These are your lands, and your laws, my lord, and we will, of course, abide by whatever justice you decide to mete out but, if I may, I would speak with Princess Velugna and hear the facts from her."

Bellicus's gripped his staff, sensing the conflict within King Ceneu who was enraged and in no mood to allow some interloper to involve himself in Caer Lerion's justice system. Arthur had been granted powers by many of the kings of the Britons, but those powers were in relation to leading an army of disparate tribesmen against the common, Saxon, enemy. He had no say in how a king like Ceneu should govern his own lands.

Still, Arthur had half a dozen warriors right here in the hall and that automatically granted a man some kind of leverage in a situation like this.

"Fine," the king growled. "Come with me, I'll take you to her."

"Bellicus comes too," Arthur said firmly, "since Merlin seems to have disappeared. Bel, like all his Order, is trained to store things in his memory accurately. I want your daughter's words to be noted properly, so they aren't misinterpreted."

Ceneu looked up at the druid, then shrugged and stormed off towards the door. Arthur, Bellicus, and Cai followed, along with the king's guards as they went out, squinting, into the morning light.

They headed for the rear of the building, to a smaller section with a lower roof: The royal family's dwelling. Ceneu didn't speak as they walked, but Merlin had already told Bellicus about the situation in Caer Lerion when they were on the road here. The king had been married for years to a woman called Banna, and they had one surviving, adult, child, Velugna. Just a few months ago, Banna had died so, since Velugna had never been married herself, only the king, the princess and their servants now lived here in the house Ceneu was leading Arthur and the druid into.

His guards remained at the entrance although there were another two stony-faced, grizzled warriors stood outside the chamber the king took them to. They saluted him, but he ignored them and pushed open the door, peering inside and nodding, presumably as his daughter gave him silent permission to enter.

Gesturing for them to follow, Ceneu went into the room and knelt by Velugna's bedside. Arthur stood in silence and Bellicus took the chance to finally get a good look at the king's daughter, since before now he'd only seen her in passing in the gloomy, smoky great hall the previous evening.

She was in her early twenties with long, strawberry blonde hair which she clearly took good care of, but as the druid looked at her face, he understood why Arthur had said Lancelot would not have bedded her. His rakish champion had a particular type he went for when it came to women, and one thing they all had in common was that they were always beautiful. Bellicus would not describe the princess using that word – her face was plain, her eyes a little too close together, nose upturned and just a little bit too long. For all that, Bellicus had seen her walking through the hall the previous day and noticed her confident gait and long, lithe legs. Perhaps she did not match up to Lancelot's standards, but the druid could see why Eburus had been drawn to her.

Reminded of the brash, young Votadini warrior, Bellicus felt a renewed surge of anger and disappointment at his crime, and he gripped his staff tighter, vowing to make sure justice was done. Raping any woman was unforgivable, never mind the daughter of a king – their host! – and Eburus would pay for it, even if it might bring trouble with the Votadini tribe and their own ruler, Cunedda. That thought brought another reminder, this time of Narina's marriage to Ysfael, and Bellicus felt a surge of anguish, but it was not the time to be focusing on anything other than the young woman lying on the bed and her pain.

"How are you feeling?" Ceneu was asking the princess and he fidgeted with his hands awkwardly, as if he wanted to reach out and embrace her but didn't think it would be well received.

"I'll survive," Velugna replied in a voice that seemed to come from far away. "I'm not the first woman to suffer like this, and I won't be the last, I'm sure."

"Well, don't worry," the king said. "I've sent out men to capture the bastard that did this to you. If he tries to fight them off, they'll make short work of him. I'd rather he was brought back here though, that we might hang the scum!"

Velugna looked surprised. "You know who raped me?"

"Of course," King Ceneu replied. "The man you left the feast with." He rounded on Arthur, pointing an accusatory finger at the warlord. "One of *his* men; the big northern oaf with the hair like yours."

"Eburus?" Now Velugna was frowning and pushed herself up onto an elbow as she reached out to grip her father's arm tightly. Painfully, from the look on Ceneu's face. "What have you done?" she demanded angrily.

"What?" confused himself now, and embarrassed by her treatment of him in front of the visiting warlord and druid, Ceneu wrenched his arm free and glared at the girl. "You told me he raped you."

"I did *not!*" Velugna shouted, standing up and looking for her clothes. "I told you I was raped, not that it was Eburus who did it."

"Trust me," Ceneu replied, his voice calmer now, almost soothing as he tried to placate his daughter. "I saw the young fool grinning at his companions in the hall last night, when he came in to fetch more ale after taking you outside. I know the look he had on his face. I can always tell when a man's had his way with a woman."

Shaking her head in disbelief, Velugna found her skirt and pulled it on over her underclothes, not caring who could see her. Despite her ordeal, she was quite masterful and Bellicus couldn't help but admire her. "Eburus *did* lie with me, father," she said. "But I initiated it. I'm a grown woman, by Christ, and sometimes I like to be with a man! To feel..." She trailed off sadly and lifted her tunic over her head, dragging it down and roughly pulling out any wrinkles.

"Then get married," Ceneu said softly. "You're well past the age—"

"I don't want to get married to one of those idiots you keep bringing to meet me," she retorted. "But, if I'm not married, it means I can't lie with anyone, doesn't it? That's what our God, our Bible, tell us."

"It is," the king confirmed. "But you don't seem to be living by its teachings, Velugna."

Arthur cleared his throat and Bellicus was glad. The argument between Ceneu and the princess could be continued later, when they were alone and in a calmer frame of mind. For now, the warlord had to know what was happening with Eburus.

"My lady," he said respectfully. "You say it wasn't Eburus who..."

"Raped me," Velugna replied, meeting his gaze. "You can say it, Arthur."

It was at a moment like this that Bellicus was made fully aware of how young and inexperienced Arthur actually was in matters like this. He might be a masterful tactician and leader of men, which explained why Merlin had chosen him to be the Warlord of

Britain, but when it came to dealing with the problems of individuals, he had to rely on older, or at least, wiser heads.

"Tell us what actually happened, if you would, lady," Bellicus asked, to Arthur's obvious relief.

Velugna had a long knife in her hand now, the kind used as a tool for hunting, or for war, not some eating implement, and she tied its leather sheath to a loop on her belt. This, and her height and athletic build, made her appear quite formidable, but, as she recounted her experience of the previous night, her anguish and anxiety were painfully obvious.

"I enjoyed Eburus's company. We drank together and I eventually suggested we go outside to the barn."

King Ceneu looked mortified at this but held his peace as the princess continued, looking directly at him.

"He's a kind and gentle man," she said, and Bellicus had to mask his amazement at that. "Well, he was with me anyway," she qualified, smiling just a little. "No doubt he's a monster when it comes to a battle. But we spoke together and appreciated one another's company and then, we'd both had a lot to drink, especially Eburus, and we fell asleep out there. Together." She took a deep breath and a distant look came into her eyes before her earlier anger bubbled to the surface once again. "I woke up with someone on top of me. It took me a moment to remember where I was, and then it all came back, and I opened my mouth to tell Eburus to get the hell off me. I was amazed that he wanted to do it again but then I realised he was still lying, snoring, at my side." There was a cold fury in her voice as she went on now, grasping the hilt of her knife spasmodically. "I turned to look up at the man on top of me and he pressed his hand over my mouth so I couldn't speak. And then he started..." Tears glistened on her cheeks and her hand was still at last. "He was so heavy, and he pressed down on my face with his hand the whole time so I thought he might suffocate me. But it only took him a few moments, thank God."

The men remained silent, but Ceneu also had tears in his eyes as he listened to his daughter recount this terrible experience.

"I could see his teeth in the darkness – he was smiling down at me once he finished. I tried to turn away, so I didn't have to see him, and that's when I felt the edge of a blade pressing against my neck. It must have been there the whole time." She reached up and pulled down the collar of her tunic, revealing a livid red welt below her ear. It did not look like the weapon had broken the skin, but it proved the truth of Velugna's words, had anyone there doubted them. "Then he leaned down and told me he'd kill me, and Eburus, if I screamed." She shook her head as if astonished. "When he walked out of the barn...You'd think my first thought would be to raise the alarm. To wake Eburus and tell him what had happened and find the bastard. But I didn't. I felt dead inside. I just lay there for a long time until the sun came up and Eburus woke up."

"You told him then?" Bellicus asked in a low voice.

"Not at first," she replied. "He was smiling, despite his hangover, and making jokes, until he noticed I was crying. And then I told him."

"And he went after the rapist," Bellicus said, knowing he'd have done the same as Eburus.

She looked at the druid and nodded and, again, there was an awkward silence until Ceneu stepped in beside Velugna and took her in an embrace. She hid her face in his heavy fur cloak and sobs wracked her body as Arthur and Bellicus exchanged impotent glances. Eventually she stepped back, almost embarrassed to have shown any weakness before them and the druid once more was greatly impressed by her strength.

"I assume," Arthur asked hesitantly, "that, if Eburus went after your attacker, you had some idea where he should begin his search?"

"Oh, I did, my lord," Velugna replied levelly, wiping her face dry and drawing herself straight again. "It might have been almost pitch black, but I recognised the filthy bastard's voice."

Ceneu's face flared with vicious wrath and he practically shouted, "Who?"

"Nynniaw."

Bellicus was looking at the king and noticed the man blanch visibly as he heard the name and asked his daughter levelly, "Are you sure?"

"It was him," Velugna confirmed. "I could see his missing teeth in the dark, and I heard it when he spoke. The gap makes him speak in a distinctive way. I noticed him watching me in the hall during the feast but thought little of it; he's always looking at women as if they were pieces of meat laid out for him on a trencher."

"You know this Nynniaw?" Arthur asked the king.

"Oh, aye, everyone knows him," Ceneu nodded thoughtfully. "He's what we might call 'moon-touched'. An excellent warrior to have on your side, but he's a law unto himself."

Arthur simply looked at him, as did Bellicus, and the king took this as a criticism.

"He's never done anything like this before, as far as I know," he shouted. "Usually, he just likes to start fights, but he always pays reparations for the damage he causes and, like I say, he's useful to have alongside you in a battle. You say the Saxons are coming? Well, Caer Lerion needs men like Nynniaw to defend our lands against them. Fight fire with fire."

"And Eburus knows where to find this man?"

Velugna nodded at the druid's question. "I told him where Nynniaw's farm is before I was thinking clearly. He left without another word."

"Alone?" Arthur asked, a worried frown on his youthful face.

Velugna shrugged and looked at them with a similar, anxious expression. "I don't know. He went out of the barn and I haven't seen or heard any more since."

"Right," the warlord said, taking command of the situation at last. "I think we've got enough of the story to know we have to find Eburus as soon as possible. Lord King, you sent men after him?"

"Aye," Ceneu admitted sheepishly. "He was seen heading off to the west. I had some of my guards go after him with dogs."

"Then they're well ahead of us," Arthur said, already heading towards the door. "Come, Bellicus. If we ride hard we might yet reach them before they kill an innocent man."

Ceneu opened his mouth to say something, but Velugna broke in first.

"I'm coming with you. Don't even think of refusing, druid. I'm a princess, and these are my lands, and I can ride as well as any man."

The king nodded. "That's true."

"Let's go then," Arthur said, stepping aside as Cai, understanding they were on the move again, nudged past him and stood by the door expectantly. "We've wasted enough time as it is."

There was no mention of Ceneu coming, perhaps because his days of riding to battle were behind him, but he hurried after them as they made for the stables, pleading with Velugna to be careful and to stay back from any fighting. Her face was cold and emotionless however, and she didn't reply.

Bellicus watched her mount her gelding with ease and thought he wouldn't want to be Nynniaw if she got to him before Eburus. Or after, come to think of it.

"You know the way?" Arthur called to her, and she nodded although not entirely confidently.

"I know where Bryn Cleddyf is," she called, walking her horse out onto the main thoroughfare, where the morning traffic was already quite heavy as people went about their business. "I've never been to the farm before, but I've passed it on occasion and it's the only steading in that area, so we'll not miss it. Come on, it's about ten or eleven miles away I'd guess."

"Shouldn't we bring more men?" Bellicus asked Arthur as they mounted up and followed the princess, Cai pacing them. "If this Nynniaw has sons or friends or whatever, we could be riding straight into a battle for our lives."

Arthur shrugged. "Ceneu's warriors are already on their way, I expect we can count on them to take our side if it comes to a fight. And Eburus will be with us."

"If he still lives," Bellicus growled, shaking his head at Ceneu's hasty decision to send men hunting the Votadini champion before he had all the facts at his disposal. "I don't think they'll give Eburus much chance to plead his innocence if they catch up with him before us."

The people bustling about the town made way for the horses and soon enough the three riders were through the gates and in the open countryside, heading east at a fast pace. Of course, even Cai couldn't keep up with a horse at full gallop, but the riders did not push their mounts too hard since the ground was uneven and they wanted to keep an eye out for signs of Eburus, or his pursuers, who might very well have veered off course since none of them really knew where they were going.

There was no chat between them as they travelled, for there seemed little to say. Bellicus expected a man accused of rape in Caer Lerion would be given a chance to defend himself before any sentence was passed but, in this case, he didn't believe it would come to that. Whether Eburus reached Nynniaw's farm first or not, it looked to the druid like Velugna was riding to meet her rapist for one reason only: to kill him.

Bellicus had no problem with that. Rapists were in a class with murderers and deserved to be dealt with ruthlessly. He just prayed to Lug that they were looking for the right man – already that day someone had been falsely accused of the crime and, truthfully, the evidence against this Nynniaw was not entirely compelling. Velugna admitted herself that she'd drunk a lot, woken up groggy and unaware of where she was, and then been unable to see much other than her attacker's teeth thanks to how dark it was in the barn. The point about the man's speech impediment wasn't even that damning, since so many people, especially warriors, had missing front teeth.

The druid could see that Velugna was utterly convinced this Nynniaw was her rapist, but, until Bellicus had a chance to question the man himself, he would keep an open mind.

And then, if it turned out Nynniaw *was* the perpetrator, Dis, god of the underworld, was welcome to him.

CHAPTER THIRTEEN

Eburus had been walking at a fair pace for quite a while now, but he felt neither tired nor dissuaded from his task. The unfamiliar journey might have given other men time to reflect, for their fury to cool, their common sense to tell them going alone into a steading that could be swarming with armed men – even if they were simple farmers – may not be the best idea.

But Eburus wasn't like most men. He was young and fit and the greatest fighter of the Votadini tribe – their champion! He was also headstrong and acted on instinct, just as he had the day he'd met Bellicus for the first time and attacked him in front of both their armies. He'd ended up on his back with a broken nose that day, but it had been a learning experience. He would not be so foolhardy again.

He would take his time and scout this man Nynniaw's farm before he charged in, sword in hand, to avenge Velugna's rape.

His mind wasn't completely devoid of thoughts as he walked – he reflected on the fate that had thrown him together with, first, Bellicus the warrior-druid, and then the warlord, Arthur. Both of those men held immense power and influence, and both were true leaders, even if they were, like him, still in their twenties.

Arthur and Bellicus had seen more battles than he had, but even they had never been part of an army that had sacked a town or city; had not seen how victorious warriors sometimes behave in those situations. Eburus was even less experienced than they were when it came to war, so although he'd been told about it, he'd never seen a comrade, filled with battle-lust and the glory of victory, sacking a settlement and taking anything, and anyone, he found there for himself. Never had he personally known a woman who had been the victim of rape.

When he looked into Velugna's eyes that morning the emotions had been clear to him. Shock, devastation, pain, disbelief, even – incredibly – guilt. There had been no need to ask her how she felt because it was all written there on her face. The face which had been smiling and so lovely to him just a few short hours before. In response to his questions she had whispered Nynniaw's name and his crime, and rage had overtaken him.

He'd stormed straight out of the barn and searched the buildings nearby, starting with King Ceneu's great hall, but he'd not found his quarry. Returning to Velugna, she had, dazedly, almost as if she wasn't quite sure where she was, told him which direction Nynniaw's farm lay, and, with a last, apologetic glance, Eburus headed east.

Like the princess, a maelstrom of emotions whirled around inside Eburus's head as he tried to make sense of everything. Aye, he felt fury and a desire to see justice done, but he also felt like it was his fault. He had lay there in the hay, sleeping, as Velugna was assaulted right next to him. What kind of warrior did that make him? Not much of one. And, of course, those thoughts made him feel even guiltier, for this was not about *his* pain, or…

He tried to move his mind away, onto matters he could understand: finding his quarry, and gutting the bastard.

Ahead, at the foot of a low hill populated with still-leafless grey trees, buildings came into sight, blue smoke from cooking fires spiralling up into the leaden sky, carrying the scent of bacon to Eburus. The thought of Nynniaw tucking into a hearty breakfast made the Votadini warrior even angrier and he moved faster while crouching low and hugging whatever foliage he could find as he approached the small settlement.

He could see the heads of small figures poking above fences and guessed it was boys or girls feeding hogs or fowl in their pens, and that made him frown, for he had no wish to slaughter Nynniaw in front of children, especially if they were the man's own. He cursed himself for his eagerness to come after the rapist without thinking it through properly, or seeking aid from his companions in the warband. It was broad daylight now, by Taranis, and here he was trying to sneak into a man's house, in a place he didn't know, with the gods knew how many armed enemies waiting to stand in his way!

He could hear the children shouting to one another now, their high voices full of energy and enthusiasm, and he stopped behind a juniper bush to try and get some idea of where he should be aiming for. The animal pens, with their attendant children, were on the left, attached to what Eburus guessed, from the ramshackle nature of it, must be a barn for housing larger animals and their food during the winter months. On the far right were some small houses in rather better condition than the barn, and he could see a couple of women outside, chattering and working at some task, laundering clothes perhaps; it was hard to tell at this distance.

In the middle was the largest of all the buildings, and this one surely belonged to the most important person in the steading – Nynniaw. Eburus pictured the man, satiated, still addled with drink, lying in his bed, sour breath stinking out the room as he snored and drooled and assumed he was safe despite his earlier crime.

Yet there seemed no way for Eburus to get inside and make him pay for what he'd done. He should have waited until night fell since he would surely be spotted coming towards the farm if he continued on his way – there simply wasn't enough undergrowth to hide behind, and the land leading towards the place was almost completely flat.

In the middle distance he could see the white forms of sheep, and a man with a dog watching over them, and knew that the fields behind the buildings must also be populated with men working in them. The young warrior had no idea what farmers did at this time of year—planted seeds, tilled the soil, spread horse shit about the place, whatever—but he knew they worked hard and were out in the fields all day. They would see him coming and, whether they were trained fighters or not, they would be fit, hard men and they'd not hesitate to attack an intruder. Especially one as tall, broad-shouldered, and obviously dangerous as Eburus.

And a farm like this would undoubtedly have more than just sheepdogs, for vermin would be everywhere and need to be controlled. As he thought this, the Votadini warrior spotted a white terrier sprinting across the courtyard, its little legs pumping, barking at something Eburus couldn't see from this distance.

Cursing, he wished Bellicus was with him. Maybe the druid could call down a magical mist or some other distraction that would allow Eburus to reach the farmhouse undetected. But the druid was back in Caer Lerion and knew nothing of this. He was on his own.

And that meant he was as well turning back and doing what he should have done in the first place: telling King Ceneu and Arthur what had happened and coming back here with a proper force of warriors.

The knowledge that he'd failed Velugna again lay heavy on him, but there was nothing else to do and, slapping his hand on the ground in impotent rage, he made to stand up and then stopped.

The atmosphere had changed, growing suddenly colder, and he looked up, noticing an enormous bank of grey cloud moving fast from the east, quickly swallowing the sun. The temperature was already dropping and now Eburus pulled up his hood as heavy drops of rain fell, growing in ferocity with every moment. He grinned, and thanked the gods out loud as he started moving towards the steading again, knowing this was just the chance he needed to get inside Nynniaw's house.

"Who needs a druid?" he muttered, noting the women grabbing up armfuls of laundry and making for shelter, while the children feeding the livestock were laughing and screaming as they too headed for cover. Crouching low, Eburus quickly headed for the farm, aiming for the right so that he could get behind the buildings there, and work his way to the back of the big, main farmhouse.

As he went, he realised suddenly that he was trespassing on another man's land. Of course, Nynniaw was a criminal and Eburus was there to mete out justice, but what if he was met by other residents of the farm? If he killed anyone, he'd be classed as a murderer, no better than the man he was there to see. The other folk living and working here didn't know him, and would be perfectly within their rights to try and kill him if they spotted him.

He had to be wary, and try not to hurt anyone except Nynniaw. With that in mind he spotted a long-handled broom propped against a hedge a little further ahead and, when he reached it, he grabbed it up and snapped the head off it with his foot. Inspecting it, he could see the wood was firm, not rotten at all, and thick enough to make a good, hopefully non-lethal weapon, if he was careful.

The rain showed no signs of letting up, coming down in great sheets now that battered noisily off roofs and made massive puddles all over the courtyard. It truly was the ideal cover Eburus thought as he slipped carefully past the houses which the washer-women had been working outside before the storm hit. There were windows at the back of the dwellings, but all had been shuttered so there was no chance of anyone inside noticing him sneaking along. When he reached the end of the building he stopped and peered around the corner to make sure no-one was about. Facing him was a small wooden structure with a sloping roof and Eburus immediately recognised it, his left hand dropping to his sword hilt, ready to pull that weapon free rather than resorting to the 'staff' he'd made from the broom. Bright eyes watched him from the arched opening in the kennel and he froze, but the dog made no sound, or any move to approach him. Either it was too old to care about him, too used to strangers visiting – which seemed unlikely – or it was chained up and knew it was fruitless to try and catch him.

He smiled reassuringly at it, fervently praying to Cernunnos that it wouldn't bark and raise the alarm, but it simply gazed balefully at him until he started to move once more, eventually leaving it behind as he came at last to the side of the main farmhouse.

Making his way towards the back of the building he stopped at the corner of the rear wall and listened. Hearing nothing except the continuous hammering of rain on mud and thatched roofs, he grasped his staff firmly and stepped around, eyes scanning the land. There were small fields here, running right up to where the ground sloped upwards into the thinly wooded forest, but, as hoped, there was no-one working there. The fields appeared freshly dug, as if ready to receive seeds for the coming year's harvest, but the downpour had halted work and chased the workers indoors for now.

"What are you doing here, you big ugly bastard?"

The voice was so unexpected that Eburus couldn't help but start back in surprise, and mentally kicked himself when he saw a man staring suspiciously at him by the back wall of the farmhouse. He was wearing a long leather cloak that was so wet and drab in colour that he'd blended in with his surroundings. They were almost close enough to touch one another and Eburus sized the fellow up, glad to see he was much smaller and older than himself, but he held a narrow-bladed shovel in his right hand and brought it up now. The movement wasn't exactly threatening, more defensive than anything else, but Eburus could see the man's initial curiosity at his appearance quickly turning to alarm.

"I'm looking for work," the Votadini warrior replied, smiling, and then he lashed out with his makeshift staff. Eburus was a

100

naturally gifted fighter, and his attack was much too fast for the man to parry. The broom handle smashed against the side of his face and the power left his legs. He slid down against the wall, raising a hand to try and ward off further blows, but Eburus brought his staff down on the top of the man's hooded head, then repeated the movement twice more.

"Thank you," Eburus murmured to the gods as he inspected his weapon, glad to see the wood was still intact. So too was his victim, who lay unconscious but alive in the mud. For a moment, the young warrior wondered whether he should find some rope and tie the farmer up, but he didn't want to waste time and besides, the man would be in no fit state to fight when he came to.

He stepped over the prone figure and walked on, towards the door he could see halfway along the building. From the road approaching the steading Eburus had thought this farmhouse was smaller than it actually was, for, although the façade was not particularly long, the building had been built in more of a square shape than a rectangle. So, unless there was only one, great room inside, he might have to search for a time before finding Nynniaw. Assuming the rapist was even here.

Again, the sheer madness of his mission struck Eburus, but he couldn't back out now. He was there, and he'd see what there was to find within the large farmhouse. He was at the door by this time and pressed his ear against it. The rain was lessening in ferocity already, the heavy drops making much less noise as they landed, but, even so, he couldn't tell if there was any sound of movement within the house.

If he went inside there would be no turning back, and the occupants would try to kill him while, without drawing his sword and attacking innocent people on their own land, all he had to defend himself was a broom handle. Which was also too long to swing indoors, if the place was divided into smaller rooms. He knew he'd made a grave error in coming here, but when he remembered Velugna's tear-stained face the fury swelled inside him again and he didn't even bother lifting the latch on the door to see if it would open.

Stepping back, he kicked the wood as hard as possible. The door was thick, and sturdy, and it shuddered beneath his blow, but it held. Again, understanding he was now past the point of return, he hammered his boot against the wood and this time the door exploded inwards as the iron latch shattered. Without hesitation he ducked inside, looking around for enemies in the gloom.

It was almost pitch-black within the house and, to Eburus's annoyance, it was not just one big room which would have been much easier to search, but instead split into multiple smaller chambers by partition walls. He'd expected this however, and there was nothing for it but to begin looking in each room for his quarry. How exactly he would know Nynniaw he wasn't sure, but it was much too late to worry about that.

Smiling at his own foolishness, he started on the left, poking his head into each room. He was able to form a mental impression of the house's layout as he went: the back door he'd entered through led straight to another at the front of the building, and this hallway was intersected by another running to the left and right, forming a cross shape. Off these arms lay each of the individual rooms, perhaps eight of them, but maybe more, maybe less.

The first two he looked in were mere storerooms, filled with junk which Eburus could see no reason for the occupants to hold onto and he swiftly moved on, to the next pair of rooms on the opposite arm of the cross-shaped hallway. These both contained sleeping pallets, and stank of stale beer and piss, suggesting people lived, or at least slept, here, but there was no-one there now.

Outside, the rain had stopped and the sun was already out, casting its yellow light into the house via the back door which Eburus had left shattered and open. The warmth would be working its life-giving magic on the seeds the farmers were planting, but it seemed to have had a similar nurturing effect on the man that had been so brutally knocked unconscious by the young warrior. Eburus could hear him outside, groaning loudly, and then vomiting and mumbling to himself in a plaintive, angry voice.

"Shit, I better hurry up," muttered the Votadini champion, hurrying along the right arm of the hallway and looking into the first of the rooms he came to there.

A woman was in the corner, cradling a baby and staring at him with wide, terrified eyes. This threw Eburus completely and, for a moment, he had no idea how to react. At last, he growled, "Nynniaw?" and she pointed a tremulous, wavering finger towards the room on the opposite side of the hall.

"Please don't hurt us," she begged, and Eburus shook his head vigorously.

"Of course, I won't," he replied softly. "You don't have to fear me, lass. I'm no rapist, unlike your man there." He smiled, hoping it would be reassuring, but seeing the woman flinch he nodded and stepped out of the room. Listening outside the chamber she'd indicated, he heard the unmistakable sound of snoring and, joined by it now, the voices of men heading towards the farmhouse, asking the downed farmer out the back what was wrong with him.

He didn't need the broom handle now, its usefulness was past, so he dropped it with a clatter onto the floor, drew his sword, and kicked the door leading into Nynniaw's chamber. This one didn't require a second blow to open. The latch wasn't even on, yet, despite the terrific bang it made as it bounced off the wall, the man lying on the bed barely flinched.

Eburus looked at him and knew this was who he'd come to find, for he recognised him from the previous night's feasting in Caer Lerion.

Nynniaw was asleep, sour breath rasping from the back of his throat through missing teeth. The stench in the room was overpowering, both from the man on the bed and the wooden bucket of piss lying on the stained floor next to him.

There were outraged shouts outside now, and Eburus glanced back over his shoulder. The woman still sat crouched in the other room with her baby, gazing at him in terror and he wondered if she was afraid of him, or the man on the bed before him. He reached down and placed a hand around Nynniaw's throat, then pressed down. At last, the man reacted, eyes flickering open in shock and fear, but his expression quickly changed to anger when his drink-addled brain allowed him to understand where he was.

"What—"

Eburus pressed down even harder, forcing Nynniaw's neck and head into the straw mattress, cutting off his question with a strangled gasp.

"Shut up, or I'll ram my sword between your legs and shove it so far up it'll come out your fucking mouth."

Confused, and weak, Nynniaw's body went limp but still Eburus choked him, only letting go when he was sure most of the fight had gone out of his victim. Then he let go, and grasped the front of Nynniaw's tunic, using it to propel the man to his feet. He was choking though, and Eburus had to hold him upright, pushing him, stumbling, out into the hall.

Still, the woman made no move in the other room, simply watched him go, and he knew he didn't have to worry about her attacking him.

He thought about going out the back, where he'd come in, but Nynniaw's fellow farmers, kinsmen perhaps, would surely come after him and give him no chance to speak before they attacked. So, instead, he pushed his captive out the front door, just as the shapes of two burly men approached the entrance, blocking out the sun. They stepped back when they saw Eburus with the tip of his blade at Nynniaw's throat.

"What's going on?" the foremost of the pair demanded, shaking a gleaming sword at Eburus as he spoke. The man wore good quality leather armour and the Votadini warrior knew these were no mere farmers. When he heard even more men approaching, he knew he'd made a bigger mistake in coming here than he'd already suspected.

Nynniaw was not some simple tiller of soil, rearing a few sheep and pigs for the markets. Yes, this was a working farm, but the two men facing him, and the others hurrying towards them, were soldiers, and that meant Nynniaw was a lord.

Eburus cursed himself for walking into such a dangerous place with only his sword for protection. He should have known Velugna's rapist was not some simple farmer – the girl surely didn't know the names of all such men within her father's kingdom, after all. Yet she'd known this man.

"I'm one of Warlord Arthur's men," he said, trying to speak as clearly as possible, without his naturally thick Votadini accent. It didn't fool them.

"No, you're not," said the man at the front. "You're a Pict or something, I can tell from your speech." This idea seemed to startle the soldier and he looked around at the other men coming towards them. "Raise the alarm," he shouted. "We're under attack by Picts! There must be more of the bastards about!"

"I *am* with Arthur," Eburus shouted, and he shook his prisoner viciously as he spoke, making Nynniaw's teeth rattle but, when he tried to twist out of the big Votadini's grip, Eburus hammered his knee into his kidney, blasting the fight from him again, if only for a while. "The warlord is in Caer Lerion, visiting your king. Ceneu himself sent me here to arrest this man for the crime of rape."

The warriors facing him, half a dozen of them now, plus the farmer he'd battered unconscious during the downpour out the back, gazed at him in astonishment for a moment, and then, to Eburus's amazement, they burst out laughing.

"Rape?" one of them cried, and he too held a decent sword in his hand. He even wore an iron helmet. "Ceneu knows better than to interfere with us for something like that. He'd never prove it, and we're too valuable to him. He needs us to defend the border here on the eastern side of his lands."

"Why would the king send one man, alone, here anyway?" another demanded, but there was no mirth in this one's voice. Only anger and impatience. "And a stranger at that?"

Eburus could see he was getting nowhere with the crowd of men, so he pressed the edge of his blade against Nynniaw's neck and was rewarded with a line of crimson trickling down the man's rough, stubbled skin.

"Whatever you believe," he said through gritted teeth. "I'm taking this one with me, and if you try to stop us, I'll gladly take his head off his shoulders."

Nynniaw groaned and retched, spilling watery vomit down the front of his cloak. He squeezed his eyes shut as if trying to block out a spasm of pain or nausea, and then, squinting, he looked up at Eburus who was half-a-head taller than him.

"I recognise you now," he said, with a grimace that might almost have been a smile on his lips. "You're the big bastard that lay snoring while me and the princess had some fun. Lucky girl, eh? To be ploughed by two handsome men in the one night!"

Eburus's right fist lashed out, snapping Nynniaw's head back and probably breaking his nose. The man retched again, blood and bile now staining his horribly moist lips.

"You think you can just walk all the way back to Caer Lerion with him?" one of the soldiers demanded angrily. "While we stand here and let you?"

"Aye," Eburus retorted, walking slowly backwards, dragging Nynniaw by the collar as he went. "Because, like I say, if you try to stop me, I'll kill this ugly bastard, and all of you as well. My name is Eburus," he growled, eyes shining with pride. "And I am Champion of the Votadini tribe."

"Well I'm Senorix, and I don't give a shit who you are," the man said, eyes narrowed. "You're a young fool, and I'm going to spill your guts the second you slip or lose your footing."

Eburus was not stupid, just rash and headstrong, and he knew very well how difficult his journey back to Caer Lerion was going to be, so, rather than wasting time trading words with Nynniaw's kinsmen he walked faster, squeezing the material of his captive's collar to make him move.

The warriors, joined now by other occupants of the steading – men, women and children – followed him and he wondered if he should just walk until he found some trees, then kill Nynniaw and try to escape into the undergrowth. It wasn't much of a plan, but, on his own, he could see no other way to survive for much longer. Senorix or one of the other farm folk would attack him eventually and he'd be forced to slaughter his prisoner, and that would be the end of it all, for, despite his earlier bravado, there was no way Eburus could defeat so many enemies alone.

The sound of barking came to him and he cursed, wondering if someone had released the dog he'd seen in the kennel, but then he realised the noise was coming from the west, towards Caer Lerion. Squeezing even tighter on Nynniaw's collar, he squinted and made out men in the distance.

Who were they? More allies of his captive? Or hunters who just happened to be in the area? If they were not inhabitants of this steading there was a chance they were no friends of Nynniaw since he was obviously not a man of great character. Perhaps they would help Eburus take the rapist back to meet the king's justice! It seemed unlikely, but it was the only way the Votadini warrior could see of making it out of this ridiculous situation in one piece and he continued walking, angling his steps to take him directly into the path of the approaching hunters.

He watched Nynniaw, and the farmers as they followed, growing ever closer to the approaching, barking hounds. From the worried glances and muttered, anxious conversations, he guessed the men coming towards them were likely not friends to the inhabitants of the steading. That gave him heart, especially when he recognised two of the approaching hunters as men who'd been amongst King Ceneu's retinue in Caer Lerion the day before.

Velugna must have told her father what had happened, and he'd sent his men to arrest Nynniaw. Eburus was saved!

"You've had it now," he grinned, giving his captive a quick, satisfying punch in the back of the head. "That's the king's men. Raping his daughter wasn't the smartest thing you've ever done, was it?"

Nynniaw didn't reply. His skin was an unhealthy shade of grey, either from fear or his hangover, or a combination of both, and his expression suggested he might throw up again at any moment.

The men with the dogs were almost upon them now, and Eburus grinned, counting seven of them.

"There he is," the hunt leader, a portly man with a thin moustache, said over the barking of his dog as they closed on Eburus and Nynniaw. "Take him."

"I've already done the hard work for you, lads," the Votadini warrior called, looking back to the angry farmers and warriors who were still following him, although at a greater distance now. "But it's good to see you anyway. You're just in time. I was worried these bastards would rush me long before I made it back to Caer Lerion." He looked down, directly into Nynniaw's face and, speaking savagely, said, "I'm going to enjoy watching you suffer for what you did to the princess."

He heard the heavy footsteps of Ceneu's hunters closing in on them and lowered his sword while releasing the pressure on his captive's cloak, and then, astonished, Eburus realised he was on the ground and there was a terrible pain in his head.

CHAPTER FOURTEEN

"Take him." The words seemed muffled, as if he was hearing them from underwater, and he felt hands grasp him and roughly begin to drag him up. "You'll pay for what you did, Votadini scum." Somehow, he was still holding his sword and, when someone tried to take it from him, he lashed out, feeling it bite home and hearing an outraged cry of pain.

"Kill him!" Nynniaw shouted eagerly, almost desperately. He had to be as confused as Eburus as to what was happening, but obviously saw this as his opportunity to get revenge on the big northern warrior who'd been making his life hell since the moment he'd woken up that day. "Kill him before he kills you! Help them, boys!" This last command was screamed at the farmers and soldiers from his own steading and they charged forward, overjoyed to get the chance to hack apart the arrogant fool who'd brazenly come to their home as if he was invincible.

Eburus knew very well that he wasn't invincible – the bright spots of light that were filling his vision confirmed that, along with the weak feeling that wanted him to just collapse onto the road instead of fighting to remain on his feet. Giving in to his body's weakness would mean certain, and violent, death so he tried to lift his sword before him, but there was no strength left in his arm and the blade felt like it had been encased in a slab of rock.

Nynniaw's fist hit him on the chin and he stumbled back, struggling to breathe, as the men and women all around him closed in again, the hunting dogs barking and howling in a terrific, ear-piercing cacophony.

What a mess he'd made of this! He couldn't think straight, and a heavy, gleeful kick from Nynniaw didn't help, but it seemed like he, Eburus, had been blamed for raping Princess Velugna – they were going to kill him in retaliation, and the piece of filth who had actually committed the crime would get away with it. And there was nothing Eburus could do. His sword was gone now, to the gods knew where, and Dis Pater's dark embrace was closing around him.

"Get back! Get fucking back, all of you!"

Eburus wondered if he was already dead for he recognised the voice that was calling out, seemingly across miles of countryside but he could retain consciousness no longer and, with a choking sob, gave in to the black wave that was engulfing him.

Three horses came barrelling along the road, and yet another dog, but this one was much, much bigger than the hunting animals Ceneu's trackers had brought with them.

Nynniaw was bending low, not caring who the riders were, just knowing he had to make sure the bearded Votadini didn't ever wake up and cause more trouble for him. He quickly patted his hands along the fallen man's body, eventually finding the dagger that was tucked inside Eburus's woollen sock and pulling it free.

With the single-minded focus that a hangover occasionally brings, Nynniaw moved up to the prone Votadini's chest and raised his hand to plunge the dagger down, into the heart. The world around him did not exist in that moment, all that mattered was his task.

The massive weight of Cai slammed into him and he screamed in terror and agony as the mastiff's jaws clamped brutally around his forearm.

"You idiots," shouted a woman on horseback, gesturing to King Ceneu's hunters. "Get those farmers back, well away from the Votadini." She looked at Nynniaw's men, eyes blazing like fire. "If they've killed Eburus…"

"Cai!" Bellicus called to his dog and it responded immediately, letting go of the howling Nynniaw, whose arm was bleeding but, surprisingly, mostly intact.

Velugna jumped down from her horse and knelt by Eburus, staring at him, looking for signs of life. Everyone remained quiet as Arthur and Bellicus walked their mounts forward, to the side of Ceneu's confused hunters who were facing Nynniaw's people. Both sides watched each other warily but little was said as they waited to see what the princess would do next.

She stroked the Votadini warrior's beard tenderly, no emotion showing on her long face until, at last, Eburus groaned very softly, so softly it was almost imperceptible. Then his brow furrowed, and his head moved as he began to swim slowly back to consciousness, and Velugna smiled.

"You're alive," the princess murmured, reaching down to grasp his hand reassuringly.

"Wish I wasn't," Eburus replied. "My head's pounding like a blacksmith's anvil."

"That'll pass. The main thing is you're all right."

"If any man as daft as Eburus can ever be described as 'all right'," Bellicus said, smiling in relief himself.

"Has anyone got a skin of ale? I don't know how much more excitement I can take without getting a drink down me." All eyes turned to Nynniaw. He was still on the ground but had pushed himself up to a sitting position and was cradling his torn arm. Far from looking sheepish or frightened or any other emotion a captured criminal might be expected to show, Nynniaw was grinning as if he hadn't a care in the world.

Bellicus wondered if it was mere bravado, or if he genuinely expected King Ceneu to let him off with some trifling punishment or, perhaps, do nothing to the rapist at all. It was a notoriously difficult crime to prove after all and, if Nynniaw's warband was important enough to Caer Lerion's defence, maybe the king would—

The druid's attention wavered, and he watched as if in a trance as Princess Velugna stepped across from Eburus to Nynniaw and, producing her dagger, knelt in a quick, fluid motion, and plunged the blade deep into her rapist's stomach.

He screamed, all trace of arrogance or smugness gone in that instant, and his arms flailed to ward off further blows, but Velugna was done. For now, at least. She stood and stared coldly down at the terrified man, then looked up at his soldiers, as if challenging them to come and attack her.

Bellicus and Arthur both shifted their horses, just a little, to make sure the men from Nynniaw's steading didn't forget they were there.

"Help me," Nynniaw pleaded, staring up at Arthur on his horse, then, seeing no pity in the warlord's eyes, his head moved and his gaze darted from one man to another in the watching crowd. "Help me, the crazy bitch has stabbed me! Help me, Lovernisca," he snarled at the woman Eburus had seen with the baby in the farmhouse. "Or by God you'll be sorry later on when I get you in the house."

"Don't move," Velugna commanded. "We're taking him back to Caer Lerion," She continued imperiously, her tone leaving no room for argument. "To face my father's justice."

"If he survives long enough," Senorix shouted, his face a mask of impotent rage. "You've stuck him in the guts, you stupid whore. That's not something men survive easily, and especially without treatment from a healer."

Velugna's mouth opened but, before she could reply to the man's disrespectful words, Bellicus slipped down from his saddle and unclipped his eagle-topped staff of office from it, then walked silently across to the red-faced man, ignoring his companions.

Senorix blanched visibly as he took in the great size of the druid, and the dog at his side with the reddened muzzle, but he couldn't move, or back away for fear of being branded a coward.

"Do none of you have any respect for your princess?" Bellicus asked in a low, dangerous voice.

"Respect?" Senorix asked in surprise. "She just stabbed our lord in the stomach, you big northern bastard. Why should I show her, or you, any respect?" His words seemed to give him confidence, as did the murmured agreement from his friends behind him. "In fact, you lot are on our lands, so I think we're quite within our rights to force you off them, eh, lads?"

Bellicus hadn't expected this reaction, but he did see Senorix's sword coming up and he reacted instinctively, twirling the end of his staff so the butt hit the farmer in the left arm. It was a glancing blow, but it knocked Senorix off balance, and allowed the druid a moment to turn his staff and smash the other end, the one with the heavy bronze eagle, into his opponent's face.

Cai, of course, took this as his cue, and once again launched himself forward, locking his jaws around Senorix's shoulder and viciously shaking the man who let out a tortured scream.

The speed of the whole thing, and the ease with which their leaders had been dispatched, gave pause to the rest of the farm-folk and allowed Arthur, Velugna, and the rest of King Ceneu's men to form a line alongside the druid. The hunting dogs, maddened by the scent of blood and sight of Cai still mauling the screaming man on the ground, were yapping and pulling at their leashes to be set free that they might join in with the excitement.

"You can return to your homes," Arthur called over the sounds of Senorix's cries. "And live. King Ceneu will deal with this as he sees fit. Or you can fight us, and die here." He held his arms wide, as if daring Nynniaw's people to try their luck. "Choose, fast, before I tire of waiting and let the dogs loose."

Some of the farmers, men and women, including the nervous girl with the now-squalling babe, had already moved back, well away from the soldiers at the front who Bellicus was now able to count.

"Two dead, or dying," the druid said in his rich, powerful voice. "And seven of you left. Cai, here!"

The dog instantly left Senorix who was still alive but in no state to fight any time soon and, behind them, almost forgotten, Nynniaw was still begging piteously for someone to help him, to see to his wound, to bring him wine or ale.

"Shut up, fool," Velugna shouted, and battle fury was burning fiercely in her stare now. "Or I'll come over there and ram my blade into your guts again!"

"You're outnumbered," Arthur said levelly now that things were finally growing quiet again. Eburus too was up on his feet having retched, but he was well enough to stand beside Velugna and hold his sword once more.

The farmers facing them were quite well armed, and obviously had some professional pride or they'd already have given up and retreated back to the safety of the farm buildings, but they were not stupid. Quite possibly, Bellicus thought, looking at them as they took in the sight of their dying leader, they didn't even like Nynniaw much. Certainly, they were not about to throw away their lives for him.

"Come on," one of them said, stepping back, and sliding his sword into its scabbard. "There's no point in the rest of us getting hurt. Nothing we can do for Nynniaw now anyway, he's done. Can't survive an injury like that."

It seemed to be true, for the stabbed man was sweating and his face a hideous pallor, while his cries had stopped completely now as he tried to simply keep drawing in breath after gasping breath. When he saw his comrades sheathing their blades, looping axes into belts, and retreating, he gave one plaintive, weak cry, then closed his eyes and his head fell back onto the road.

Senorix was still alive, and holding his shoulder, watching Cai nervously. Arthur pointed his sword at the man and said to Velugna, "What do we do with this one, my lady?"

She shrugged. "He was just defending his lord, and his lands. Leave him." Her look settled on Bellicus then. "You move fast for such a big man, and your dog is even more brutal than you."

The druid accepted her words with a nod and then he walked over to Nynniaw, kneeling to inspect the wound Velugna had inflicted on him. Even if he was to stitch it shut and apply a cleansing poultice – which he could do, since he had most of the necessary ingredients for it within the many pockets sewn into his dark robe – it would not save the man. The girl's thrust had been too deep, and too well-placed, to undo its deadly work.

"Did you rape her?" he asked.

Nynniaw's eyelids flickered and his jaw clenched as if he would reply but it was too much effort. Bellicus watched as the spirit fled from the man's body, and he cursed.

"No need for your anger, druid," Eburus said. "He already confessed his crime to me, in front of his men. Velugna was justified in killing him."

The princess didn't seem to care about any legal issues she might face for dispensing her own form of summary justice, she was standing at Nynniaw's feet and spoke to the druid now.

"Help me lift him onto my horse, Bel," she said, bending and grasping his feet. Within moments the corpse was securely lashed in place behind her saddle cloth and she was mounted and ready to return home.

"D'ye think your beast will take the weight of both of us?" Eburus asked Bellicus sheepishly. "I'm not really fit to be walking all the way back to Caer Lerion."

"No," the druid laughed, slapping his young friend on the back and bending down to form a step with his hands. "Darac is strong, but I'd not ask him to carry the pair of us. You can ride, I'll walk. Climb up, and, Eburus?"

"Aye?" the Votadini asked, placing his foot on Bellicus's hands and hauling himself clumsily atop the big black.

"Next time you want to go off on an adventure like this," the druid said, more sternly, "ask permission first. You're part of an army and you have commanding officers to follow."

113

"That would be Bellicus and me," Arthur put in, and he was visibly angry at Eburus. "You could have been killed, you fool. We all could. We're lucky it's ended so well."

"I wouldn't be so sure of that, my lord," one of King Ceneu's hunters said in a worried tone. "I don't think it's over yet."

The man was looking into the field on their right, where a dozen or more figures were approaching, the sun occasionally glinting off metal. Spear points, polished helmets, chain mail – all the accoutrements of war.

"Soldiers," Bellicus said grimly, and he turned back to look at Nynniaw's farm. The men there had already started to walk along the road towards them again, in tight formation. The lupine grin on Senorix's bloodied face told the druid all he needed to know. They were about to be attacked on two sides, and they were outnumbered by more than two to one.

"What should we do?" the hunter who'd first noticed the approach of the soldiers asked in a frightened voice, and Bellicus could think of no better advice than what Arthur had offered.

"Ready your weapons," growled the warlord. "And pray."

CHAPTER FIFTEEN

"Ow, by Jupiter, my old bones aren't thanking me for our little display yesterday." Sulinus walked slowly into the main room of his house and taken his seat at the head of the breakfast table, but he was limping, and in obvious pain.

"Are you all right, decurion?" Duro asked, and received a dismissive wave in reply.

"Pushed yourself too hard didn't you, father?" Rues said reproachfully. "Showing off."

Sulinus grinned, blunt teeth showing as he reached for the loaf sitting out for everyone to help themselves. "Had to show our guests how a real horseman rides, didn't I?" He tore off some bread and dropped it into the bowl his son shoved across to him, then splashed milk over it to make it soft.

Duro, Bedwyr and the others had already been awake when the young girl came to collect them, roused by the sounds of the grooms in the adjoining room getting ready for their working day. She had brought water for them to quickly wash their faces, and then led them back here before disappearing after a quick nod and smile from Rues. They hadn't been slow in filling their bellies, ever mindful, as soldiers on a mission always are, of the wisdom in eating, like sleeping, whenever the opportunity arose, for who knew when the next chance to do either might arise?

Duro could not read their elderly host at all; had no inkling whether the man was going to agree to join Arthur's army or decide to see out his final years here, in his own comfortable pocket of Britain. Sulinus was, despite his aches and pains, in a jovial mood, but what that meant the centurion couldn't say.

He didn't have long to find out.

"When do you want to leave?"

Bedwyr looked up from his plate of bread and frowned at Duro. Was the old fellow kicking them out already?

"Er...we can be off just as soon as we finish here," the centurion replied, a little confused. Sulinus had been bluff and perhaps even somewhat arrogant since they'd arrived the day before, but he had, until now, not grudged them hospitality. It seemed strange that he was sending them away so hurriedly now.

The decurion shook his head and slapped the table, sending knives and other utensils jumping into the air. "What?" he demanded. "I'll need more time than that to pack."

Even Rues seemed surprised by this, but Bedwyr was grinning and Duro felt his own spirits rise greatly now that he knew they'd succeeded in at least the first part of their mission to create a cavalry force made up of well-trained Britons to fight under Arthur's command.

"Take as long as you need," Bedwyr laughed. "We're very happy to have you on board, decurion."

"Aye," Rianorix agreed. "It wasn't much fun being embarrassed by you yesterday, but your skills and experience will be a massive help to us."

The others from Arthur's warband added their own thanks and voiced their pleasure at Sulinus's announcement. The only person who didn't seem too happy was Rues, who pushed away his bowl of salted porridge and stared coolly at his father. Sulinus affected not to notice and ate lustily until Bedwyr stood up and bid his men, including Duro, follow him back to the stable where they would gather their belongings and make ready to leave. The decurion promised to pack as quickly as he was able then join them in the yard when he was all ready to go.

As Bedwyr led his companions outside, Duro could hear Rues behind them, arguing with his father. The centurion understood the man's misgivings – Sulinus was getting on in years after all, and possibly not quite fit for long distance travelling – but Duro fervently hoped Rues would not succeed in making his father change his mind. Breeding and training horses for noblemen was a fine occupation, but it wasn't comparable to the excitement and sense of accomplishment training a crack cavalry unit could bring. Not to mention possibly saving the Britons from the marauding sea-wolves.

He wondered how true that was, and remembered the Saxons who had, so he'd heard, managed to live comfortably alongside Britons in southern villages quite happily. That didn't matter to Duro though – the Saxons had kidnapped a little girl to use her in a human sacrifice, attacked his own village and murdered his wife and friends. If Sulinus could help him wipe Hengist's followers from the face of the earth, Duro would assist him in any way possible.

"This has gone well," Bedwyr stated when the grooms brought their horses out, looking happier and healthier than ever, and they began loading their saddlebags onto the animals. "We'll escort Sulinus back to Arthur and they can get started training those the old man wants in his unit. Then…" He took an apple from his pocket – there was a bag of them in a corner of the stable – and fed it to his horse as he looked at Duro. "Where to next? Do you have any ideas where we might find more old Roman cavalry officers?"

"Not really," the centurion admitted. "I mean we could ride to settlements along the great wall and ask the people if they know of any old soldiers, but I'm hoping Sulinus might give us some advice." He tightened the buckles on his horse's reins and found them already well secured by the grooms. "The decurion may know where some of his old comrades are living now."

As they spoke, Sulinus appeared into the sunshine, smiling. Rues was nowhere to be seen but it looked like the old man's mind was made up and no amount of arguing would dissuade him from joining up with Arthur.

"We're just about ready to go," Bedwyr said, seeing Rianorix, Aesibuas and Catti all packed and prepared for the ride back west to join with the rest of their comrades in the warlord's army. "Do you need any help?" The question was asked out of politeness, for Bedwyr was sure the stablehands would be able to provide Sulinus with any assistance he required but the decurion nodded.

"Aye, actually. I've got some things I want to take with me, and my horse can't carry them all himself, big as he is. Now, come here, and let's see."

Bedwyr and Duro shared a glance then walked across to follow Sulinus through a door they'd not seen opened before. It led into a storeroom with small windows high up which allowed light to shine in and reveal the items stacked and piled across almost every available inch of space.

Duro gaped, and a smile tugged at the edges of his mouth as a wave of nostalgia swept over him. "By Mithras, did you empty the stores completely at your last posting? I haven't seen weapons like this in years." He reached out and took up a javelin, picturing in his mind's eye a volley of them cutting through the air during some forgotten—until now—battle he'd been part of, and the joy that had filled him when he'd heard the screams of the enemy cut down by them. It felt very strange to be reminiscing happily about something so horrific, but those missiles from the cavalry units had decimated the Gauls that day and allowed Duro's legion to win without taking many casualties.

"When the legions sailed away," Sulinus said, "they left much behind. Not just men like us who'd outlived their usefulness, centurion, but equipment and weapons too. Most of this," he gestured about the packed room, "came from the stables at Banna. Left behind to rot or be plundered by the locals." He shrugged. "The stuff was valuable! So, I took what I could, just in case it ever came in useful. It never has, until now."

Bedwyr was frowning as he eyed the old javelins in their long quivers, the odd-looking saddles with protruding horns in each corner, and other equipment he didn't recognise. "Forgive me," he said, "but, although there's enough here to fill the room, it's not enough to arm an entire cavalry unit. And that's assuming it's even still in good order, given the fact it's been lying about for, well, years." He frowned at the decurion. "I don't see how we can fit all this on our horses either. Not without a cart—"

"Don't be stupid, boy," Sulinus growled, shaking his head and lifting the quiver of javelins Duro had been looking at. "We're not taking it all. But this—" he shook the quiver and the missiles inside rattled loudly, suggesting the wooden shafts were not rotten at all, despite their age "—is exactly what we need to kill Saxon spearmen. Do you have any of these? No, I didn't think so." He placed the quiver against the doorframe and lifted one of the strange saddles, rubbing his hand almost lovingly across the wood of one of the upright horns. "And you won't have any of these, I'm sure of that. I saw what you and your men were sitting on when you turned up here yesterday. Bloody useless in a fight. But these?" He grinned, displaying the saddle for the bemused Bedwyr. "These are worth their weight in gold to a horseman in battle."

"You want us to take some of this stuff so our blacksmiths and saddlers can make replicas and outfit an entire unit." Duro said, taking up an oval shield bearing a fading design of eagle's wings and a lightning bolt. He smiled again for this image had been a common sight during his legion days and, like the javelins, it brought back almost painfully vivid memories.

"The centurion has the idea," Sulinus confirmed, head cocked as he peered at Bedwyr as if the younger man was an idiot. "So, you take the saddle out and ask one of the grooms to put it on my horse. Take one each, there's enough here and you'll find them useful I'm sure. You, Duro, take that quiver of javelins. Again, my grooms will show you how to attach them to the horses. Send in the other three of your men and I'll see what else I've got that's worth taking. Hurry up then, what are you standing there for? Go!"

Under the decurion's expert direction there was soon a large collection of equipment sitting in the yard beside the horses.

"What are we supposed to do with all this?" Catti asked, running a hand through his dark hair. "Carry it all in our arms all the way back to Arthur?"

Sulinus grinned and looked at Duro. "Are they all this stupid, centurion?" he demanded, then they watched as a groom bent down, lifted the quiver of javelins and looped it across the rear horn on the right of Sulinus's own saddle.

Aesibuas in particular seemed interested in the new equipment, lifting things and pondering their usefulness before looping a quiver onto his own saddle, clearly impressed by the simplicity of it.

"Then this," Sulinus said, as if speaking to children, lifted one of the oval shields and hooked that around the opposite horn of his saddle. "See? That leaves your hands free to guide your mount. The rest of it," he pointed at some other items which weren't designed to fit on the cavalry saddles, "can go in packs which you can strap to your back. It's not ideal, but it'll let us move much faster than taking a cart."

It didn't take long at all to get everything sorted and ready to travel, and the five men from Arthur's warband helped one another to mount up. Normally they could do it themselves, but with the new, horned saddles, additional gear, and no training in the technique required, they needed aid. Last of all was Bedwyr and he was assisted by one of the grooms.

Sulinus watched, a look of disgust on his face, but he was smiling in satisfaction when they were ready. "I need to say my goodbyes to Rues and the girl," he told them. "You boys can wait here for a moment, I'll not be long."

He limped away and Rianorix, smiling, said to no-one in particular. "'The girl'. Doesn't seem the affectionate type, old Sulinus, does he?"

Duro looked up at the sky, wondering if they'd have a dry day for their journey. "Don't be so sure of that," he said, deciding it would be chilly but not wet until late afternoon. "Aye, the decurion's a blunt old sod, but the way his son tried to get him to stay here makes me think he's better company than you might expect."

His words were backed up soon after, when Sulinus came outside again and headed for his horse. Rues, and the young girl, appeared in the doorway, watching him.

"You be careful, grandfather," the girl called. "I want to see you back here in one piece, d'you hear me?"

Sulinus grinned and, with some help from one of the stablehands, climbed up into his saddle. "Don't worry about me, Licinia," he replied. "I'm not stupid enough to go into battle anymore. I'll leave that to these fools." Jerking a thumb over his shoulder at Duro and the others, the old man went on. "I'm just going to impart some of my vast experience and wisdom to Arthur's riders, and then I'll come home a wealthy man. They've promised me lots of silver for this, and I'll leave it all to you and your dad." He winked at the girl and she laughed before running across and grasping his hand. They looked at one another with affection, and Rues came to join them, stroking Sulinus's horse on the flank absentmindedly.

"She's right, father," said the stable manager, looking up imperiously, as if he was the patriarch of their family. "You be careful. You're not a young Roman officer now, and the Saxons are vicious from what we've heard. Teach the warlord's soldiers what you can, then have them escort you home. We'll make sure everything here runs smoothly while you're away."

Sulinus smiled and even patted his son on the hand, then Rues and Licinia stood back and the old man glanced round at Bedwyr. "Let's get going then," he said, gently tapping his horse with his heels to make it walk towards the open front gates. "I'm looking forward to watching you men trying to use those javelins hanging

120

off your saddles. Should be a right good laugh, if young Rianorix's display yesterday was anything to go by."

Rianorix opened his mouth to reply, but Bedwyr spoke up.

"Uh-uh, my lad. Sulinus will be your commanding officer soon enough and should be spoken to with respect. So, whatever you're about to call him, I'd think twice."

Rianorix did think about it, then chose to follow his superior's advice and remained silent, just shaking his head in amusement as they passed through the gates and onto the open road, leaving the stables behind.

"What made you decide to join us?" Bedwyr asked as Sulinus turned to wave one last time at his son and granddaughter.

The decurion shrugged. "I don't like the stories I've heard about what the Saxons are doing," he said, gazing about and breathing in the fresh air. "If I can help to stop them raping and pillaging, well…It's a soldier's duty, isn't it? The thought of them turning up at my home, with Licinia there…"

The men all muttered agreement with his words and Duro felt light in his saddle as they picked up speed, despite the fact the muscles in his backside weren't used to the strange contours of the new seat. He suspected he'd be aching badly long before the sun reached its zenith but it didn't seem to matter. He was well on his way to completing the first phase of his mission and it felt good.

He couldn't bring his wife back, but at least this journey had given him something to focus on. And, he thought, smiling to himself, a decurion did not technically outrank a centurion, so Sulinus might insult the younger riders all the way back to Arthur's camp, wherever it was now, but Duro could tell him to piss off without any qualms!

121

CHAPTER SIXTEEN

"Nynniaw's people must have sent a messenger," Velugna said in disgust as they watched the soldiers approaching from the northeast. "Those are more of his men – you can tell by their green and black shields. Gods, one of them even has a banner, look!"

Arthur was shaking his head, trying to take everything in. "Are they really ready to attack—to kill—you? You're the daughter of their king, by Taranis! I know Nynniaw was willing to assault you, but that was the drunken act of one man who probably thought he could get away with it. But this? This is something else entirely."

The princess must have been thinking along the same lines as the warlord and she gripped the long knife at her side as she came to the inevitable conclusion. "They're going to kill us all and leave no trace. Feed our bodies to their pigs, or burn them, I don't know. But wipe away all trace of us, so when more of my father's men come looking for us there'll be nothing left of us to find."

The soldiers in the field were on foot but closing the gap between them steadily, while, on the road behind them, Senorix was leading his own warriors towards them at a pace that would bring both their forces together at the same time and force Arthur and his companions to face attacks on two sides.

"Velugna, you have to ride to Caer Lerion and tell the king what's happened," Bellicus said. "You go with her, Arthur, and you too, Eburus – you're injured and won't be much use in this battle. The rest of us will have to take our chances."

The hunting dogs had sensed the fear in their handlers now and were yapping and whining nervously, which wasn't helping anyone's nerves as the jaws of the vice formed by Nynniaw's men closed together upon them inexorably.

"I'm not riding off and leaving you to die, druid," Arthur retorted angrily, almost as if he'd been called a coward although that was obviously not what Bellicus had meant.

"Neither am I," Velugna added fiercely and Eburus echoed their words although his pallid complexion suggested he wouldn't be much use in the coming fight.

"Look," the druid said, firmly and forcefully. "One of you has to tell Ceneu what's been going on here or our deaths will never be avenged. Your father will spend the rest of his days wondering what happened to you, Velugna. That kind of pain will send a man to an early grave, trust me."

The girl's face was a mask of conflicting emotions. "I can't run and leave you all to die," she shouted. "We're all here because of me. If I'd never told anyone what Nynniaw had done—"

"None of this is your fault," Arthur interjected. "The crime was his, and he's faced justice for it. But you are a princess, and you have a horse so can escape back to Caer Lerion. So, go now, before the fighting starts!"

She sat in her saddle in silence, indecision and pride restraining her from kicking her heels in and galloping to safety.

"We should all run," someone said, barely audible over the noise of the dogs, and Bellicus turned to see who'd spoken.

"We'll be caught," the druid said, scanning the faces of the hunters and finally alighting on a young, beardless lad of about seventeen who seemed, despite his age, less frightened than any of his comrades.

"We should all run," the boy repeated. "I know a place we can hide."

Startled by this revelation, everyone turned to stare at the youngster whose face became scarlet beneath their scrutiny. "It's true," he said, looking at the ground. "I grew up near here. There's a place not far off that we can all fit in while someone goes to Caer Lerion for help."

Arthur was watching the oncoming enemy forces. They weren't far off, and their numbers were easily visible now. "Fourteen in the new group," he informed Bellicus from his vantage point atop his horse. "And seven coming from the farm. Twenty-one in total. Whatever we're doing, we should do it now. Are you men," he looked at the hunters Ceneu had sent to capture Eburus, "capable of running back to town with us?"

Two of them nodded, but the other three seemed uncertain. "We've just hurried all the way here, my lord," said one of them. "Running for much of the time. I don't know if I can do it again without a rest. It's too far." His words were backed up by nervous murmurs from the others and Arthur nodded, knowing he couldn't just ride away and leave them. Nynniaw's soldiers would surely slaughter them all.

"Fair enough," said the warlord. "Outrunning them is out of the question then. Druid. What say you?"

"Velugna," Bellicus said, looking up at the princess. "You and Eburus ride to Caer Lerion." He held up a hand to stop any arguments and looked at the hunters. They were all fairly young, but their leader was a little older and plumper than the others, and his foot was bleeding, injured in the scuffle with Eburus. He would be the one that might slow the rest down. "You," the druid pointed at the fellow who looked nervously back at him. "You take Arthur's horse and go with your princess and the Votadini back to town."

"What about my dog?" the man said, stroking the top of his hound's head.

"Let it go," Bellicus replied. "All of you, let your dogs go, they'll only give us away if we're trying to hide and they're too small to be much use fighting armoured soldiers. They should be able to make their own way home."

"Are you sending your dog away?" the hunt leader asked somewhat petulantly, and Bellicus glared at him.

"My dog will stay with me, like he always does," growled the druid. "I'd rather have him by my side than you, once the fighting starts."

A couple of the hunters bent then to remove the leashes from their animals, shooing them away in the direction of Caer Lerion and being rewarded with confused barking. The rest of the men were less willing to send their loyal friends off into the wild, but Arthur had dismounted and spoke harshly to them.

"Do as the druid says," he commanded. "Hurry up, the more time you waste the closer our enemies get." The hunters reluctantly moved to do as they were told, but still one man looked uncertain and almost defiant, until Arthur took out his dagger and slashed through the leash tethering dog to man. "Go! Shoo!" The warlord shouted and stamped his feet and the dogs moved back but still didn't seem eager to leave their masters.

"Where's this hiding place?" Bellicus asked the young hunter. He gestured towards Velugna high atop her horse. "Give her a rough idea, so she knows where to find us when she comes back."

The boy looked to the south but was thankfully smart enough not to point and give their approaching enemies an indication of where they'd be going. "I'm not sure exactly but…" He looked about at the topography of the land, trying to get his bearings and remember where the place he'd spoken of was located. "I'd say it's about two miles away from here. To the south."

Velugna frowned. "The haunted ruins?" she asked, making the sign of the cross.

"Aye, my lady," the boy replied. "You know them?"

"Of course," she replied. "It's a good place to hide since people are afraid to go near it." Her gaze fell on Arthur and Bellicus then. "I know exactly where you're going. We'll get back to Caer Lerion as quickly as possible and bring help. Just you stay alive until then and, Bellicus, the place is ill-omened. You might want to ask your gods for protection before you step foot inside its boundaries. God go with you all."

"I'm sorry, Bel," Eburus said. "For all of this."

"Get going," the druid replied, trying to smile reassuringly but Nynniaw's men were not far away now and had quickened their pace as they began to understand that those on the horses might be leaving their companions to their fate. "Just take good care of Darac. If he breaks a leg because of you, I'll kick your arse all the way to the Otherlands myself."

The portly hunter had been helped onto Arthur's horse and it was plain he'd never ridden before, but Velugna brought her mount alongside the man and helped him get going, telling him how to hold the reins and keep from sliding out of the saddle. Then they began moving, the horses' powerful strides taking them quickly away towards Caer Lerion even though they couldn't reach a full gallop when only Velugna was an experienced rider. The mounted hunter called out, "here!" to those dogs who were still hanging about and when one followed, so did the rest, the whole party streaming away to the west.

"Right," Arthur said, turning to the young lad who seemed to have more confidence now that their course was set. "Lead on."

"Yes, my lord," came the reply and the hunter turned to the south and strode forward.

Arthur, Bellicus and the remaining five hunters followed their companion who was setting a good pace. The druid looked back and saw both sets of pursuers hurrying after them, but the men with the shields were weighed down by their gear and couldn't hope to match their speed. The others, the ones led by Senorix at the farm, had lighter armour and no shields and they were keeping up, if not actively closing the distance between them.

Bellicus did not know these lands at all but, unfortunately, they were very flat. With no valleys or hills to hide in he could only hope these so-called 'haunted ruins' they were heading for had some kind of cave or tunnel system, or at the very least, walls they might attempt to defend with their lesser numbers.

Arthur must have been thinking along the same lines. "What's your name, lad?" he called to the hunter leading them.

"Cocca, my lord," was the reply and Bellicus looked at the boy as they went. He had brown hair that came down to cover his ears but looked as if someone had placed a bowl on his head and cut around it with a blunt knife. It wasn't the most flattering hairstyle the druid had ever seen, and combined with his short limbs and pronounced overbite, gave him something of an oafish air. Yet the boy was energetic and had intelligence in his eyes and Bellicus suspected he was destined, one day, to reach a higher office than the rest of his fellow hunters.

"What are these ruins you're taking us to like?" Arthur asked Cocca. "Stone walls we can defend? Tunnels?"

"It's an ancient Roman temple, my lord," the boy replied, not at all out of breath. "The roof is mostly gone, and the walls are all broken down with many of the stones taken away, but there's a chamber underneath we can hide in."

Arthur looked at Bellicus, frowning uncertainly, but their course was set, and there was nothing else they could do now. Stopping to fight a pitched battle would only hasten their demise. They had to hope this ruined temple would offer some protection although it was more than likely that their bloodthirsty pursuers would be at least as familiar with the place as Cocca or Velugna.

"When were you last there, boy?" one of the other hunters asked, and, although his legs were much longer than Cocca's, he was quite out of breath and obviously feeling the effects of having walked there from Caer Lerion and now being forced to run for his life over rain-slick terrain that might trip and injure one of them at any moment.

Cocca's brow furrowed as he pondered the question, then he said, "Seven or eight years ago. I was about ten years old at the time."

The older hunter wasn't too pleased by that answer. "So, the place might be nothing but rubble by now?" he demanded, a note of hysteria in his voice. "We could tire ourselves out running there, only to find the locals have taken all the stones off for their own building projects!"

"Calm yourself," Arthur ordered, his voice firm and steady as they went down a shallow slope, careful not to lose their footing. "We don't have many options, so we go with this and hope the gods are with us." He slipped but managed to right himself before he fell onto his backside. "There's a good chance we're going to have to fight for our lives at some point before all this is done," he told them. "So, prepare yourselves for it."

Bellicus was impressed by the warlord's command of the situation. His words were not unnecessarily harsh or aggressive, and his delivery of them seemed to have given the hunters a firmer resolve, for their backs straightened and their strides became longer as they continued the run towards the haunted ruins. Another glance back told the druid they had managed to widen the gap between themselves and their pursuers, and a look at Cai, whose eyes were shining with the thrill of the race, made him smile.

"What's so funny?" Arthur asked, noticing the incongruous expression, but Bellicus just grinned even more. Sometimes it took the threat of death to make the wonder of life really resonate within a man.

They jogged on in silence, preserving their energy. A couple of times they had to stop to let one of the hunters catch their breath, and this meant the distance between themselves and their pursuers never grew too wide. The heavily armoured spearmen coming after them were well out of sight now, obviously reluctant to take off their mail and leave behind their shields when such equipment was valuable, even if it was highly unlikely to be stolen out here in the middle of nowhere. The rest of Nynniaw's men remained fairly close behind however, or Bellicus might have suggested they just head towards Caer Lerion. Maybe that's what they should have done in the first place, he thought, but it was too late for that now.

"There," Cocca suddenly burst out with obvious relief. He was pointing a little way to their right and Bellicus could see the heavily weathered remains of what must have been an impressive and imposing temple to the Roman gods, surrounded by the remnants of smaller structures.

They modified their course, running with renewed vigour now that they could see their destination and happy to see that some of the buildings would offer basic protection from their enemies' weapons, if only for a short time. Seven of them against twenty-one would be a rout on open ground, but with stone walls to hide behind the defenders would have a much better chance of survival. Or at least be able to kill a few more of the attackers than they could have done on the road to the farm, where they'd have been easily encircled.

"Wait," Arthur called, stopping and, hands on aching thighs as he gasped in deep breaths, examined the ruins. The others followed his lead, only Cai taking the opportunity to sit on the grass which was still sodden from the earlier downpour.

"It's just like I remember," Cocca said, gazing at the place with a nostalgic smile.

"Good job, lad," Arthur said, nodding. "I'm glad you were with us. This place will suit our needs nicely, eh, Bel?"

The druid grunted agreement. The old temple had once towered above the dozen or so buildings that surrounded it, but its mighty columns were gone, along with much of the roof and some sections of wall. As such, Bellicus looked at the other structures—most likely used originally as kitchens, granary, bakery, storehouses and the like—and wondered if they'd be better making one of those the base for their stand against Nynniaw's soldiers. He turned again, happy to see Senorix had realised where they were and decided to wait on the fourteen spearmen catching up with his smaller force.

The attack would come, but not for a little while yet.

"We should go down and take a look," he said to Arthur. "What looks like a sturdy wall from up here might be a crumbling piece of rubble up close."

"But…"

Arthur stared at the hunter who'd spoken. "But what?"

128

"The spirits," replied the man, eyes wide in fear as he looked at the ancient temple with its lichen-encrusted stones and clinging ivy doing its best to tear the whole structure into the earth with the patience of æons.

The warlord looked amazed and glanced back over his shoulder at the men following them. "Spirits?" he demanded. "I think the very real, more immediate, danger of having a spear rammed up your arse should be the thing at the front of your mind right now."

Bellicus touched the frightened hunter on the shoulder and smiled at him. "You don't have to worry about spirits." He tapped the bronze eagle atop his staff. "I'm a druid. No ghosts or devils will bother us while I'm around. In fact..." He crouched close to the ground and lifted a rock thoughtfully. "Our pursuers will know the legends about this place. Perhaps we can use it to our own advantage." He rose again and met Arthur's gaze. "My lord, if you could take the hunters down to the ruins and decide where you want us to make our defence, I'll quickly scout the grounds and see if I can find anything that might come in useful."

Arthur nodded. "Aye, all right," he said. "But be quick, Bel. It won't take long for the spearmen to catch up with their comrades and then there'll be no stopping them coming down here for us. We need to be ready for them."

Bellicus watched them go, Arthur leading with a confidence that inspired calm in the anxious hunters, then the druid ruffled Cai's ears and hurried down towards the ruined temple.

He dearly wished it was a different day, with no enraged warriors coming to slaughter them, that he might spend some time really looking around this incredible old site. Clearly the place had seen much over the years and been a centre of worship and learning for generations of Romano-Britons. Possibly its origins stretched even further back in time, to a period before the legions arrived on these shores, and the ancient gods of the druids had held full sway over the people here.

Stopping to allow himself just a brief moment, he closed his eyes before the remnants of the temple's main entrance, and simply breathed in the air. He could hear Arthur talking to Ceneu's hunters, suggesting one building's defensive qualities over another's, but he put them aside and, for a few heartbeats, it seemed like he'd gone back in time, seeing in his mind's eye the temple as it was in its glory days. Solemn men and women, ascetic types, wandered around him, chatting softly although he could not hear the actual words. His spirit seemed to soar high overhead, allowing him to look down on the whole complex and view it in all its glory.

With a start, he opened his eyes and stared at the drab ruins in front of him and knew, somehow, that he had to go inside. It didn't matter that death was stalking them in the form of Nynniaw's spearmen – Bellicus felt compelled to go into the ruined temple and, when a feeling like this came over him, he knew better than to fight it.

"Bel, come over!" Arthur called from one of the nearby buildings which was in better repair than the rest. "I think this'll be the best place to defend. Look, the walls are intact and there's only this one door, so we won't have to worry about attacks from behind."

The druid raised a hand and waved. "Give me a moment," he replied, eyes fixed on the temple interior which was shrouded in shadow despite there being not much roof left to speak of. "I just want to check something."

He stepped forward, wondering what it was that had pricked his senses, and felt the hairs rise on the back of his neck. Bellicus, as a druid, knew better than most when the connection between our world and the Otherlands was at its most tenuous, and he also knew there could be danger in such places of power, but he gripped his staff tighter and, with the reassuring presence of Cai by his side, went into the ruined temple, fearful but excited although he couldn't quite say why.

His initial feeling was simple disappointment when he reached the centre of the building. It had consisted originally of one large room, with other, smaller ones leading off at the far end. These would have been places for the priests and priestesses to change into their ceremonial clothing, to prepare any items they might need for the public ritual, and even, in some cases, to conceal themselves while they spoke, literally, through eldritch masks set into the wall.

But, as Bellicus stood there, a cold breeze blowing the accumulated leaves and other detritus of the decades about him, there seemed nothing of the old magic left in the place. It was just another mouldering collection of stones and rotting wood and bronze. He started, noticing the bizarre face staring back at him, then he moved across to examine it more closely, smiling in wonder at it.

"Sulis preserve us," came a hushed voice behind him and Arthur walked into the building with none of the reverence Bellicus had displayed. "What is *that* thing?"

The druid grinned. "A god," he replied, reaching out to touch the cool metal which the face was made from. "Look," pointing at the mouth, "there's even a moving tongue. I can't believe this is still here! You'd think it would have been looted years ago."

Arthur came up to stand next to him, squinting critically at the sightless face set into the wall. "Are you joking?" he demanded. "Who would want to touch this? It's probably cursed. It's certainly hideous. What kind of deity looked like this? Gods below, no wonder the Romans claimed your predecessors made a habit of performing ritual human sacrifice."

Bellicus wasn't really listening, he was too fascinated with the bronze mask and picturing how it would have been used by the temple's long departed occupants. "Aye, it's truly a thing of beauty," he said, oblivious to the look of confusion on Arthur's face at the pronouncement.

The warlord shook his head. "Whatever, Bel. We can look at the crazy thing in more detail once we survive the battle that'll be upon us any moment now. Are you coming to join us in the building over there?"

Bellicus tore his eyes away from the bronze deity but didn't follow Arthur's pointing finger. Instead, he led Cai through the door that lay a little to the left of the mask. "Let me just see what else is in here," he said, then broke off with a startled, "oh."

"What now?" Arthur demanded, coming through the door himself, irritated at the druid's delay while their doom was fast approaching. He looked down at the stairs which seemed to have stopped Bellicus in his tracks. "Come on, man," the warlord said, and for the first time there was an emphasis, a distinct command, in his tone. He was in charge here, and wanted the druid to know it.

Bellicus either didn't notice, or ignored it, moving quickly down the rough stone steps which bowed in the middle suggesting they'd seen much use over the generations.

"We don't have time for this, damn it!" Arthur called, angry now. He was not at all used to having his wishes ignored, even by the Merlin who tended to humour the young warlord in most things. "Get back up here, now, Damnonii fool, or I'll leave you to face the spearmen with just your dog by your side."

Bellicus's disembodied voice floated up from the gloom below. "It's a Mithraeum."

Arthur brows knitted together. "Do you not realise what's happening, druid?" he called down the stairs. "Or where we are?"

Bellicus's shaven head suddenly reappeared, still smiling, but now his eyes were sparkling with excitement, and he grasped Arthur by the upper arms, staring at him while Cai looked on curiously. "Go and bring the men," he said. "We'll make our stand here, in the Mithraeum."

The warlord felt his irritation close to bubbling over into full-blown rage at this obtuse mystic's bizarre behaviour but there was something in Bellicus's expression that gave him pause. "Here?" was all he said.

"Here," Bellicus nodded enthusiastically. "Assuming our enemies fear this place and the spirits it holds, this is the best possible place we could be."

Arthur grunted. "What about if our own men fear this place and its spirits? And I include myself in that, druid."

Bellicus merely grinned wider and turned to head back down into the Mithraeum. "Go and get the men. And ask if any of them have flint and steel."

Arthur's frown deepened. "What? Are we going to start a fire down there?" he asked, bemused but interested despite himself.

No answer came from the stygian depths at the bottom of the uninviting stairs, and, with a sigh, Arthur, Bear of Britain, did as he was told and ran back outside to fetch the five hunters who formed the rest of their 'army'. Whether they would be fighting spearmen, or ghosts, Arthur wasn't sure, but it seemed he had little choice but to trust to the will of the gods, and their representative here on earth: Bellicus.

CHAPTER SEVENTEEN

Cocca came down the stairs, slowly, obviously fearful of what he might find at the bottom, in the echoing darkness. "My lord?" he called, softly, almost inaudibly. "Druid?"

"Aye."

The voice came from right beside him and Cocca nearly jumped out of his skin, yelping like a dog whose paw had been trodden upon. "Here," the young hunter said, holding something out towards the voice. His eyes still hadn't quite adjusted to the gloom, but he could make out the massive bulk of the druid even so. "The flint and steel you asked for."

A spark flared, lighting Bellicus's face. "It's all right," he said, smiling as a child would when he was about to play a prank on some friends. "I found some in the back". The spark flared again, and eventually, after a few attempts, the dried mushrooms the druid was using for kindling caught light. A candle appeared in his hand and, as the wick burst into flame, the unmistakeable, unpleasant smell of tallow seemed to fill the already musty chamber. "Use that candle to light a few more of them – not too many – and place them in the alcoves on the walls."

At the top of the stairs they could hear Arthur talking to the men, ordering this one to hide behind the doorway and that one to be ready in another position, but Cocca did as he was told and lifted an armful of candles from where the druid had placed them. Then he lit one and gingerly carried it across the wall, using its feeble glow to find one of the little niches Bellicus had mentioned. He put the candle in it, then used its flame to light another and moved on to find the next alcove.

"Forgive me, my lord," he said, eyes fixed on the floor so he wouldn't trip over some unseen obstacle. "But shouldn't we be preparing for a fight?"

"We are," Bellicus replied, continuing to light candles on the opposite side of the chamber. "But we have to even things up a little, since they outnumber us so heavily."

"By lighting candles?" Cocca was young and curious enough to vocalise questions older men would be reluctant to ask. "I don't understand, my lord."

For his plan to work, the hunters, and Arthur, had to appreciate what they were doing, so as they worked their way towards the far end of the Mithraeum, finishing by lighting candles around the statue of the god slaying the bull, Bellicus explained everything to Cocca. The lad appeared unconvinced, and Bellicus wasn't sure himself if they'd have been better just continuing to try and outrun their pursuers, but his instincts had led him down here and he could only pray the god so many Roman soldiers had once followed would aid them.

He thought of Duro then, wishing his friend was with them, for the centurion was always useful in a fight. He had a tattoo of a bull on his bicep, being a follower of Mithras, rare nowadays, and Bellicus knew the centurion would have loved to visit this old shrine. There was evidence that the place had still seen use quite recently, which was why the tallow candles were there and other treasures had not been looted. Stories of strange rituals still being conducted here would have keep nosy locals away, especially if they were followers of the Christ, like their king.

With any luck, the spearmen coming for them would be deeply superstitious and this little piece of theatre Bellicus was planning would put their nerves on edge and make the battle less of a foregone conclusion. The alternative did not bear thinking about.

Arthur came down into the Mithraeum, looked about at the candles with a perplexed look, and told them the spearmen were in sight. Nynniaw's two forces had joined and were now coming towards the temple complex.

"Whatever your idea is," the warlord said to Bellicus, "I hope it works. Now, what do you want us to do?"

"I would like you," replied the druid, with that ever-present smile, "to let me be a god."

Arthur looked from him, to Cocca standing by the statue of Mithras plunging his dagger into the unfortunate bull's neck, and wondered if they had all gone insane, or just the druid.

* * *

The sun had disappeared behind the clouds which never seemed far away in this part of the world and the wind was picking up again as Nynniaw's spearmen, led by his second-in-command,

134

Senorix, approached the haunted ruins. The chill that usually presaged a downpour was not present so the warrior hoped it would at least stay dry while they killed the men from Caer Lerion.

Senorix was, at thirty-three, ten years younger than his lord, Nynniaw, and, despite his thick black moustache and eyebrows, he appeared older thanks to his bald head. He'd been Nynniaw's trusted friend and confidante for the past five years and they'd enjoyed much together in that time, building their warband and enjoying the fruits of the successful farmlands Nynniaw owned. Although Senorix was not interested in forcing himself on women, preferring the company of those who actually wanted to lie with him, he did not think any worse of his lord for doing so. It was a nobleman's right to take what he wanted after all. So, it hadn't been too much of a shock when the big northerner had accused Nynniaw of raping the princess. Of course, Senorix thought it an incredibly foolish thing to do – there were plenty of better-looking women in Caer Lerion the man might have taken without fear of repercussions – but so what? Drunk men did stupid things and always would. You couldn't just go around murdering them for it, especially when that weak old fool, King Ceneu, had allowed them to behave as they liked for years.

When he saw Velugna plunging her blade into Nynniaw, Senorix had been outraged. She might have been a king's daughter, but she was a mere woman! The death of his friend had been truly upsetting, and he would make Velugna's companions pay for it now. She might have ridden off to safety, but she too would be made to suffer for what she'd done. A message had to be sent, not just that the people of Bryn Cleddyf were not to be pushed around, but that he, Senorix, was not a man to be crossed. For he was now the lord of this steading.

He grimaced, gingerly poking his tongue into the bloody hole where the druid's staff had knocked out a tooth, but then he brightened as he thought of the young wife Nynniaw left behind. Senorix had always thought she would be a pleasant bedfellow and now she was his by right. Once the men in the old temple were dead he'd head back to the farm, drink himself silly, and enjoy his new woman. She would not refuse him, he knew, she was far too docile and would do anything to make sure her baby was safe. Rejecting the advances of her dead husband's successor would be unwise, and the girl was no fool. Aye, she would welcome him home with open legs and he would let her carry on living in the big house with Nynniaw's babe.

"I hate this place," one of his men muttered as they approached the derelict buildings that constituted the ancient temple. "Everyone knows it's haunted."

Senorix could feel the hairs rise on his arms as they made their way closer to the ill-omened place and he replied angrily, to mask his own anxiety as much as anything else. "Old wives' tales," he said. "That's why the fools have come here. They think we'll be too frightened to follow them. Ha." Glancing about he gestured with jerks of his chin at some of the other men. "Look how many of us there are, and since Brice's spearmen have joined us with their shields and armour, we can't lose. No matter how many ghosts haunt those ruins."

Brice, the man in charge of the soldiers who'd come from the fields to join their fellows, was of average height and build, with nothing remarkable about him. He was a competent fighter, however, as were his men, all of whom had years of experience in seeing off brigands and livestock thieves.

Senorix noticed him touching the cross he wore on a thong around his neck and sighed. Some of the men followed the new Christian teachings, while others, like himself, were loyal to the old gods. It didn't matter though, for all of them, no matter their choice of deity, were deeply superstitious and, if given a choice, would have avoided the temple.

"We'll hunt them down like rats," he promised. "As quickly as possible, all right? No playing with them; just get the job done, and away from this place. If we're fast we can make it back to the steading before full night falls."

They plodded on without making any response to his words, for although he was respected and even feared by the men, the battle fever had not yet kicked in and, indeed, most of them had no real heart for this fight. But Senorix was their new lord, and it was their duty to avenge Nynniaw's slaying, so, on they went, stolid and stoic if not exactly enthusiastic.

"What the hell is that?"

There was palpable fear in the man's voice and Senorix followed the pointing finger to see an enormous, hooded figure standing at the entrance to the temple.

"It's one of the ghosts," someone suggested, bringing up his shield before him as if the willow boards would be able to turn any attack from the wraith.

They had all stopped walking and, in fact, Brice's men had formed themselves into a shieldwall without any audible command. It seemed ludicrous to Senorix, but he knew better than to mock his soldiers. No man appreciated his beliefs being laughed at.

"It's not a ghost," the new lord said in relief as he finally understood what he was seeing. "It's just the druid that came to the farm with Velugna."

"A druid?" Brice demanded. "But he's huge!"

Senorix shrugged and started walking again, assuming the others would follow his lead. "Aye, he's a big bastard, and he's got a massive dog with him somewhere, like I told you earlier, mauled my shoulder pretty good. But we have spears and anyway, you're a Christian. Why should you fear a druid?"

"I'm not afraid of a druid," Brice retorted, teeth bared. "I'm just pointing out how big he is."

"Bigger they are the harder they fall," one of the men muttered, drawing nods from a few of his companions but, again, their line halted as the hooded figure lifted its arms wide and looked up at them.

"He's going to do something."

"He's going to do something bad to us!"

There were frightened murmurs all along the line and, once more, weapons and shields were lifted protectively.

"Shut the fuck up!" Senorix raged. "He's just one man, not some god. Listen to yourselves, acting like a bunch of little girls when they see a—"

"In the name of Mithras," called the druid, his voice clear and powerful, washing over the gathered soldiers like an icy wave and silencing Senorix instantly. "Come to me and suffer for all eternity." The dark figure pointed at Brice. "Your weak Christ has no power here." He dropped his hands to his side and a strange laugh escaped his lips. "Welcome to Hell."

With that, he turned and disappeared inside the temple, swallowed in the dark shadows that lay behind the doorway which gaped at them like an open wound.

"I don't like this," the man next to Senorix mumbled, and regretted it immediately, as the lord's fist lashed out, striking him in the side of the face.

"He is just a man," Senorix ground out, emphasising every word. "And there are no ghosts here, only frightened men from Caer Lerion, and a druid trying to scare us with tricks." He glared at his men and they looked back at him, not convinced, but too proud to walk away. "I owe him for smashing me in the face with his staff earlier. Come on, let's get down there and kill the whole bloody lot of 'em."

He stepped forward, leading from the front as he felt a good commander should do, but was brought up short by yet another whimpering cry from one of his men.

"What is it now?"

"Look," Brice said, pointing at the thick grass just in front of them.

Senorix did look, and saw a skull staring back at him from empty eye sockets. A sheep's skull.

"There's more of them," another man said, and so there was. Four more sun-bleached skulls lay in a line before them.

"The druid's put them there," Senorix said, kicking the closest of the sinister heads and sending it rolling away. "Ignore them."

He walked on, knowing they were being played by the druid but unable to feel anything other than discomfort at the way things were going. His men were dealing with things even worse than he was, muttering about bad omens and being afraid of no mortal man, but ghosts and demons were something else entirely. He ignored their talk, content enough that they were at least continuing to follow him.

"Movement. There!" Brice hissed, staring at one of the auxiliary buildings off to their right. "You want me to take some men and check it? My lord," he added, understanding who was truly in charge of his fate now that Nynniaw was dead.

Senorix looked at the building but could not see anyone there. Should he divide his warband? They knew the druid was in the temple, but that didn't mean the rest of their prey was. If there were enemy warriors in that building, there could not be more than six of them.

"Aye," he finally decided. "Take seven men with you, Brice, and sweep all the ruins down that side. I'll take seven to the left and search the buildings there, while the rest can guard the temple door and make sure none escape from inside."

Brice nodded and gestured to the men closest to him, hurrying off to the right while Senorix did the same, moving swiftly away to the left, weapons drawn confidently.

All the men in Senorix's warband had grown up within thirty miles of this place, but none of them had ever really visited it before. The old stories about ghosts, along with a natural lack of curiosity and need to spend time doing worthwhile things like planting crops and tilling fields, meant not one of them knew much about the haunted ruins. Senorix didn't think it would be a problem, however, for the place was not exactly a maze – it was laid out quite simply in fact, with small, mostly demolished buildings and rubble strewn about.

He pointed into one of the few structures that still retained its roof, and followed one of his men inside, sword up, ready for an attack that never came. The little building was empty and there was nowhere for anyone to conceal themselves, so he nodded and led the way back outside, moving on to the next possible hiding place for the druid's companions. It was obvious they'd find no-one here – their enemies were inside the temple, skulking like children hiding from a beating.

They stopped as one then, hearing a strange, yet familiar sound. Senorix couldn't quite place it, but it only lasted a moment, then there was a cracking noise followed by angry shouts.

"What was that?" he shouted back in the direction of the men he'd posted at the temple entrance. In reply, there was another of those unusual noises, like a whirring which grew in speed and pitch, accompanied by more shouts and then another crack although this time it sounded like something striking hollow wood. "Come on," Senorix shouted, running back the way they'd came, finally realising what the whirring noise was: a sling. It was a sound he heard often, but amplified and modified by the acoustics of the temple, it had taken him a moment to recognise it.

The trooper on the receiving end of the sling had not been given time to understand what he was facing. The stone bullet had caught him unawares, smashing the front of his skull and killing him instantly. His body lay on the ground, unmoving, while the other men who were supposed to be guarding the temple entrance had scattered and now peered out from behind ruined walls. Thankfully for them, the second of the slinger's attacks had struck a shield rather than a man, so their numbers were only depleted by one. The advantage was still very much in Senorix's favour.

"It's a feint," Brice said as he, like Senorix, ran back and found shelter in front of the temple. "They want us here so they can set up an ambush in one of the other buildings, or so they can escape."

Senorix spat, eyeing the shattered forehead of the warrior lying on the grass before them. "Don't be stupid," he said. "There's only what, seven of them? How can they lay a trap with so few men? They just want to deplete our numbers as much as possible before we storm the temple."

"What do we do then?"

"Rush them," someone suggested. "Shields up, and just charge."

Senorix was nodding. "I agree. It's the last thing the druid wants. Enough of his sheep skulls and threats – we go in there and use our better weapons and numbers to kill them." He looked around, smiling at his men. "Mithras was a god of war, was he not? I think he'll be happy to accept the sacrifice of seven men within his temple, don't you?"

Some of the men, the Christians, made the sign of the cross, pale-faced and nervous, and that decided things for Senorix. The longer they procrastinated, the more frightened they would all get.

"Ready your weapons," he commanded, staring at the temple doors. "We're going in."

"All at once?" Brice asked.

Senorix nodded. "I'm no coward, you all know that. But it makes sense for those wearing armour to make entry first. Give your spears to the rest of us, they're no use in an enclosed space like the temple entrance."

This was quickly done, and soon those men lucky enough to have chain- or scale-mail were holding swords and shields, while Senorix's unarmoured farmers were carrying the borrowed spears.

"Right," he said, nodding in satisfaction. "Brice, you lead the way, keep your shields up in case that slinger is still waiting. Clear the entrance hall, then we'll join you, supporting you with the spears when we move into the larger interior."

"Have you been in here before?"

"No," Senorix admitted. "But I've been in other temples like this. They usually all have a similar layout."

Brice grunted uncertainly but offered no argument. He was a simple, effective soldier who did as he was told, which was why Nynniaw had given him command of the small unit of spearmen.

"Let's go then."

Brice stood up and started moving at a fast walk towards the temple, shield held up to protect his face. The men with armour followed and Senorix watched in satisfaction, knowing they must all want to run—to narrow the distance between themselves and their target as soon as possible, before a slinger's bullet could steal their life—but they held their discipline and maintained Brice's steady pace.

No attack came from the temple's doorway and Senorix barked an order to the remaining men and they all stepped out from their cover and hurried after their comrades who had already made it to the temple.

Brice's soldiers stood on either side of the doors, listening and peering into the shadows for some sign of defenders, but, seeing no-one, the bearded Christian slipped inside. No sounds of fighting issued forth from the ancient place of worship and Senorix felt grim satisfaction as Brice took his troopers deeper into the building.

The entrance hall was theirs.

"Spears ready, lads," Senorix growled. "This is it."

Suddenly, he jumped back in shock, unable to prevent a cry bursting from his lips. His men stared at him in amazement as he waved his sword towards the wall.

"It moved," he shouted. "It's speaking! The god is speaking!"

Those of his men who hadn't yet moved on from the entrance hall looked at what their leader was gesturing towards. A bronze mask was set into the wall, shaped like a face, although not quite a human face, it was merely an oval with eyes and a mouth and more than one of the warriors shuddered as they looked at it for there was something incredibly sinister in its aspect.

"What are you talking about?" one of the farmers asked, angry at Senorix for frightening them even more than they already were. "It's just a stupid mask. It's not talking."

Senorix was staring at the mouth, and the tongue which he'd seen moving. It was completely still now, and he forced himself to breathe, to calm down and complete the mission they were set on. He must have imagined the thing talking. There had been no words after all – or at least, none that he had heard.

"It must have been the wind," he said, trying to laugh, to reassure his men, but no sound came, for, as he looked at it, the mask's tongue moved again, the curved, accursed sliver of metal, rising and falling, and this time there *were* words.

"*Turn back fools,*" a hideous, metallic voice issued forth from the wall. "*Turn back, or die.*"

The warrior nearest the thing struck out with his sword, sending sparks flying onto the mouldering flagstones beneath them. It made barely a dent in the bronze, however, and a hair-raising laugh came from the thing.

"It's a trick!" Senorix screamed as the sounds of fighting came to them from within the temple. "It's just a trick of the druid's! Advance, our comrades need our spears! Advance!"

He watched, astounded, as one man seemed to interpret his command in the exact opposite direction it was intended, running back out of the temple, apparently deciding he'd rather be known forever as a coward than going further into the haunted ruins.

Senorix lowered his spear to make sure no-one else could leave, and screamed again, "Advance," using the weapon's shaft to push his men forward, into the darkness on the other side of the door leading deeper into the temple. The blood was pounding in his veins now, and his missing tooth and chewed shoulder were completely forgotten in his fear and battle-lust.

"Steps leading down, my lord," the foremost warrior shouted, but by now Senorix was through and into the great, sprawling space of the old building himself. There was no sign of the rest of his men in the light that filled the roofless chamber, but the sounds of a battle, including the terrifying sound of an enraged dog tearing at someone's flesh and the agonized screams that followed emanated from the stairwell off to the right.

"Move, then!" Senorix cried, hurling himself down the stairs, heedless of the others in his rage and desperation to help Brice face the men from Caer Lerion who were causing so much more trouble for him than their meagre numbers had ever suggested. Well, he was done tiptoeing around this accursed ruin. Damn the ghosts and damn the gods and their talking masks – it was time to kill Arthur, Ceneu's men, and that fucking druid with his crazy dog!

CHAPTER EIGHTEEN

Bellicus had watched in amusement as he'd manipulated the handle attached to the tongue in the bronze mask and Senorix almost soiled himself in fright. The mask, not of Mithras, but some elder god even Bellicus's druids had probably forgotten by now, was quite crudely made, but ingeniously designed. There was a little slot for him to look through from the other side of the wall, and the handle to move the tongue, but there was also a space to talk into and, much to his delight, it was somehow filtered – perhaps by a system of mesh or other sound-altering material – so that, when his voice issued from it, it had a bizarre and otherworldly timbre to it. Quite inhuman, and, as he could see, quite terrifying to Senorix and his men who had not at all expected to hear it.

And then Arthur and the others had attacked the forward party of armoured swordsmen downstairs in the Mithraeum and, in his haste to get into the fight, Senorix hadn't even thought to see if some mortal hand had been guiding the mask's motion. The new lord of Bryn Cleddyf led his men right past the little alcove Bellicus was hiding in without even trying the door. Which was just as well, since the lock had been smashed long ages before, probably by brave looters or curious, and fearless, children.

His sword, Melltgwyn, was already in his right hand and he stepped out into the passageway now, just as the last of Senorix's men went by. With brutal force he rammed the point of the weapon into the back of the final warrior in the enemy group, and the unfortunate man gasped in pain, then, choking, fell forward.

The next man in line felt his comrade's arms striking his lower legs and turned round angrily, wondering what the idiot was playing at. Before he could ask, Bellicus's bloody sword punched upwards, into his jaw and out the top of his skull. At the same time, the druid stamped down on the face of the first man who was scrabbling to pull the dagger from his belt, to strike out at his killer before he expired.

The sounds of fighting in the Mithraeum had stopped now, replaced by angry, outraged shouts, and Bellicus ran back to the main temple entrance, knowing he was dead if he was discovered up here alone.

If the gods were on their side, Arthur and the others might have killed three or four of the enemy downstairs and, with the two he'd dispatched himself, and the slinger's kill, that would leave Senorix with perhaps fourteen troopers. It wasn't enough, he thought, not yet. They were still outnumbered two to one by their opponents, but it was a start, and it would hopefully give the enemy pause when it came to renewing the fight.

Arthur would have retreated into the chambers at the far end of the Mithraeum by now and be safely barricaded with Cai and the hunters behind the stone walls and thick doors there. It would hold Senorix off for a time, for his farmers would have to find something—a fallen tree trunk or the like—to batter their way into the sanctuary.

Bellicus halted before he went outside, listening for sounds of pursuit. The air inside the temple, even with its lack of a complete roof, was stifling and oppressive and the cool breeze coming in through the entrance was inviting. No-one seemed to be coming after him though, and he wondered if he should maybe go return to the alcove behind the mask and look for an opportunity to pick off another one or two of the enemy soldiers. The shouting seemed to have stopped now, leaving only silence at the bottom of the stairwell behind him and the druid wondered what was happening.

He didn't have to wait long to find out.

The fusty air of the Mithraeum, almost tomb-like before, now rose from the stairwell with a new scent—one that made Bellicus's blood run cold. Smoke. Senorix had decided not to waste time finding a battering ram, the fool was going to try and burn Arthur and the rest alive! Cai was down there, by the gods…

The druid's mind spun. Should he head down the steps and attack the men there? Perhaps he would get lucky and find Senorix himself right at the bottom of the stairwell and be able to take him captive; force him to extinguish the flames before the smoke and heat did their deadly work. What else could he do? It was possible the fire would not take hold, since there was no real supply of air down in the gloomy Mithraeum, and setting alight to such thick doors would not be easy but…

145

Bellicus thought of the dark, windowless chamber Arthur and the others would be in right now. It would not take much smoke to fill it and suffocate them all.

He would have to try and kill all fourteen of the warriors who stood between him and Cai and the others, even if it was absolutely suicidal.

He looked up at the sky, noting absently that a gentle rain was falling from the lowering clouds again, and then he set his jaw and turned back towards the stairwell.

Just as he heard the movement from outside the temple doors behind him, he remembered with dismay that there weren't fourteen enemy soldiers downstairs. One of them had run off and…

He spun, bringing up Melltgwyn instinctively. There was a clatter and his own blade was knocked down, slicing deeply into his left bicep and making him roar as fire lanced along the crimson gash. Then he felt a boot hammering between his legs, and his teeth clattered together as something smashed into his chin.

He collapsed onto the flagstones, the smell of burning wood in his nostrils and terrible pain flooding throughout his body until it all faded away and he knew no more.

* * *

"What are we going to do?"

The hunter's voice was cracking from fear and from inhaling the smoke that had begun to drift under the door and Arthur felt, bizarrely, like laughing. To die like this, trapped in an underground temple to some Roman god only a few people still cared about, surrounded by men he didn't know and a whining dog who'd killed more of the enemy soldiers than any of the hunters had managed. It was not how he'd imagined his end. Arthur, Bear of Britain, Warlord. The Merlin had claimed to have seen great things for Arthur, and convinced him that he was the man to unite the disparate, decadent tribes of Britain against the ferocious Saxon hordes.

He coughed, knowing it was only a matter of time until he inhaled so much smoke that even if Bellicus somehow opened the doors and helped them escape from the Mithraeum, it would be too late. The damage would be done and there'd be no way for their bodies to recover. He had seen it before, in the aftermath of raids, and it was not a pleasant way to pass into the Otherlands.

"We have to get out," he said. "The druid must have been killed, and there's no-one else coming to help us."

"They'll tear us to ribbons as soon as we open the doors," Cocca said, and Arthur was impressed again by the steadiness in the lad's voice. Of all the hunters, Cocca was the youngest, least experienced, yet the one who'd fought with the most bravery and now faced their doom the most stolidly.

"Aye, no doubt," the warlord replied, nodding in the darkness. "But we'll die like men and, gods willing, take some of those bastards with us. Are you all ready?"

Only Cocca replied and even that was barely more than a murmur.

"Are you ready?" Arthur demanded again, more forcefully. "Or are you going to just lie down and let the smoke slowly suffocate you?"

Cai let out a pitiful yowl and Arthur's rage grew, flaring, like a blacksmith's forge would when air was forced into it from the bellows. "Are you ready?" he roared, then, past the point of caring whether the hunters would follow him or not, he leaned down, pulled the druid's great mastiff into an embrace and bared his teeth. "Good boy," he muttered. "Let's get 'em."

He stood up and lifted the heavy wooden beam that barred the door, knowing, from the heat, that the fire their tormentors had laid outside was finally beginning to catch hold. The doors opened outwards though so they would hopefully push aside whatever kindling was there, leaving the floor clear as Arthur led his little warband out and probably onto the spears of Senorix's soldiers.

"Cocca, take the other door. Now…Push!"

Together, they shoved as hard as they could, the weight of the doors easily shoving aside the burning debris placed there. Their eyes quickly grew accustomed to the light from the smouldering fires and the few candles which hadn't yet burned out, but the smoke was dense and, as a result, not a single enemy soldier was waiting to cut them down.

"They're upstairs," Arthur said, covering his nose and mouth with his sleeve and stroking Cai's coat reassuringly so the dog

147

wouldn't simply bolt up the steps onto the blades assuredly arrayed there. "Come on, get behind me, and hurry. Try not to breathe too much of this stuff in."

Whatever had been used for the fire, it hadn't burned fiercely, but it did give off a lot of smoke and the men coughed and gagged as they ran for the stairs and the cool, clean air that was promised there. Arthur led the way, Cai at his side, Cocca directly behind, the others trailing, wanting to escape the fumes but fearful of the doom that awaited them above.

At the top of the stairwell they saw two enemy soldiers lying dead and Arthur eyed them with grim satisfaction. Bellicus had managed to cull at least a couple from the enemy's numbers. It meant little, for Senorix's victory was not in question, but it was good to know the likeable big druid had died with his sword in hand.

Now it was Arthur's turn to do the same. He could see their enemies lined up outside, at the entrance to the temple, waiting for them.

CHAPTER NINENTEEN

Senorix still wasn't sure what to believe. It was true that his man, Elpin, had managed to capture the druid who'd been such an irritation. Gods, Elpin had even managed to grievously injure the giant and it was possible the fellow would never open his eyes again for he remained unconscious and was losing blood from the wound in his arm. It hadn't helped that Brice and a couple of the other lads had dragged the druid upright and laid him out, spread-eagled, over the low wall Senorix and the others had used earlier as cover from the slinger.

But Elpin had been so much of a coward that he'd run away, out of the temple once the fighting had started in earnest. How could he have found his balls so quickly, and so effectively, to take on the druid and actually beat him?

Right then, it wasn't important. Senorix would question Elpin properly later, when they were safely back at the steading with bread, beer, and meat. For now, it was enough to watch the warlord, Arthur's, face as he came stumbling out of the smoke-filled temple and spotted his friend draped across the wall. It was enough to see Arthur trying to hold back the terrifying wardog who wanted to run to his stricken master.

And it would be more than enough to slaughter these fools and finally put an end to the day's long chase.

"Spears at the ready," Senorix called, laughing joyously. "Move forward and leave no one alive!"

* * *

"We can't win," one of the hunters exclaimed, and Arthur suspected the man was actually crying. Instead of hating him for it, the warlord only felt pity. These were not soldiers by his side; they had not expected to be chased across the countryside and end up spitted on the end of a spear when they'd woken up this morning. Damn it, they didn't even have shields to hide behind. But fate was inexorable, as someone – probably Merlin – had once said to him, and Arthur quickly grasped the distraught hunter's arm.

"There's always hope," he said, squeezing the man's bicep and nodding encouragingly. "Until your soul leaves your body and travels to the Otherlands, there is always hope. So, raise your sword and do your best to survive for as long as possible. Yes?" He smiled and looked at the rest of his pitiful 'warband'. "The more of these bastards you can kill, the more chance there is the gods will look favourably upon us and grant us all another day of life."

"Here they come," Cocca growled, although there was hardly any need for his observation as Senorix's warriors were screaming warcries as they raced towards them in a terrible wave of leather and iron.

"Ready," Arthur called, surprising even himself by how calm he sounded. He still grasped Cai's collar and, thankfully, the hound seemed to know how to follow orders for he'd ceased straining to reach Bellicus and now waited for Arthur to release him. The warlord would not want to be on the end of the massive dog's teeth once the fighting started again. At his side, the hunter who'd been crying suddenly threw down his sword and ran in the opposite direction, towards the side of the ruined temple. Now Arthur did curse the man. It was one thing to be frightened, quite another to leave your comrades to their fate while you tried to save your own skin.

"Brace!" he shouted, praying that the rest of his men wouldn't follow their companion's lead, but by then it was too late anyway. Senorix was so close that Arthur could see the saliva in his mouth as he roared with the joy of battle and the promise of the coming slaughter. There could be no escape.

Then, on the crest of the hill which they'd all come down earlier, Arthur saw a rider, their mount's hooves clattering into one of the sheep's skulls the druid had left there.

"Look," Arthur shouted, pointing with the tip of his sword.

Senorix must have realised the smile on the warlord's face was no sham; no simple trick to distract his enemies. He slowed, glancing quickly back over his shoulder, and his own wolfish grin morphed into an "oh" of disbelief.

Horses were streaming across the brow of the low hill, riding directly for them. Senorix did not recognise the bear motif emblazoned on the riders' blue shields, but he knew the newcomers were no friends of his, and, from the number of them, he did not fancy his chances of defeating them all.

"Retreat!" he screamed, holding out his arms to slow his men. "Brice! Retreat! Retreat!"

Senorix looked all around and then, coming to a decision in that moment, started running towards the little temple outbuildings away to the left of the main structure, shouting at the top of his lungs for his men to follow.

Brice, and all the rest of Senorix's warriors, had sensed the sudden shift in the atmosphere and slowed their charge, stopping short just four or five spear-lengths away from Arthur's tiny force.

"Where are you going?" the bearded spearman shouted at his departing leader's back. "What's happening, Senorix?"

"Look behind you," Arthur called in reply, laughing even harder when he saw the dismay on Brice's face as he understood the dire trouble that had just found them.

"Shit," came the spearman's very audible response, before he too called for the retreat and, with a last venomous look at the grinning warlord, ran after Senorix, followed by the rest of their men.

"I told you there was always hope, didn't I?" Arthur said, looking at Cocca and the others who'd stood bravely beside him. Now he released Cai, allowing the dog to streak across the grass towards Bellicus who had still not moved this whole time.

Velugna rode towards him, and Lancelot was with her. For once the handsome warrior did not have a smile on his face, instead he looked furious.

"What are you doing away out here, Arthur?" he demanded. "And why didn't you take me with you when you came on this fool's errand?"

"We'll talk about it later," the warlord replied, hurrying after Cai. "In the meantime, see these brave hunters are given something to drink. We all swallowed a lot of smoke." He coughed as if to emphasise his point, reaching Bellicus's side.

"What about those spearmen?" Lancelot shouted. "Should we pursue them?"

"No," Arthur replied distractedly as he examined the unmoving druid. "We know where their homes are. They'll have to return there at some point. Have the men lined up in a shieldwall though, just in case the whoresons decide to attack again. I'm glad you turned up when you did. Did Merlin come with you?"

In answer the white-bearded mystic rode up beside him and jumped down with an ease that was at odds with his aged appearance. "Aye," he said, moving towards Bellicus. "Is he alive?"

Arthur shrugged. "It's hard to tell, looks like he's lost a lot of blood. See what you can do for him. Come away, Cai, come on, good boy."

The mastiff was licking the dried blood from Bellicus's nerveless fingers but allowed himself to be pulled back as Merlin fished inside his robe for a bandage to bind the wound on the giant druid's arm which continued to ooze crimson.

"By Sulis, this doesn't look good at all," the old sage muttered as he hastily, but expertly, tended to Bellicus's wound.

"Deep?" Arthur asked, looking on with Cai who whined plaintively but sensed the men with him were trying to help his master.

"Not really," Merlin replied. "But it's been bleeding for a while, as you can see."

Velugna came to join him, shaking her head and muttering about this all being her fault.

Lancelot had already ordered their men to dismount and line up in a shieldwall. Now he watched Merlin and then kicked his heels into his horse and galloped away in the direction Senorix's troopers had taken. Arthur opened his mouth to order him not to engage them but, although his captain was headstrong and generally overconfident in his abilities, the warlord didn't think even he would take on a whole warband by himself.

Bellicus didn't make a sound or a movement as Merlin tended to him, and Arthur felt the rage rising within him as he took in the knowledge that his new friend might never wake up. All this, for what? So that a man could empty his balls. It was almost unbelievable. Arthur had come to Caer Lerion simply to try and recruit soldiers for his army – an army whose enemy was the foreign invader who came from across the eastern sea. Yet he found himself here, in the middle of nowhere, having come within a hair's breadth of being killed by one of his own countrymen.

152

He slumped down onto his haunches and shook his head sadly, praying to the gods that Bellicus would show some signs of life. What if they did raise a mighty army and drive off the Saxons? It wouldn't put an end to his people's suffering. There would still be rapists and murderers amongst the Britons. What was the point in it all?

Dazed, and with a lump in his throat, he barely registered the approach of Merlin, only snapping out of his reverie when the High Druid touched him lightly on the arm.

They looked at one another and, as if reading his thoughts, Merlin said, "This is the way of the world, Arthur. Either we give in and just lie down to die, or we do what we can to make things better."

"How? How can I make this—" he gestured angrily towards Bellicus, Velugna gently wiping his brow with a piece of wet cloth "—*better?*"

"A blacksmith makes his world better by crafting useful items, which he sells to earn food for his family and supplies to make more items. A fisherman catches as many fish as he can for the same reasons."

"That makes the world worse for the fish he catches," Arthur retorted and felt like a child, being given lessons by his old tutor once again.

"Are you a man, or a fish?" Merlin asked coolly. "You're supposed to be a warlord."

Again, they eyed one another, both sensing this was an important moment, the outcome of which could decide the very fate of Britain. "We must do what we can in the time the gods have allotted for us in this life, Arthur. Decide what is most important to you, and then put every fibre of your being into it. Be the Bear of Britain, or...do not." He shrugged. "There is no right or wrong choice, my friend."

Arthur turned away, watching the distant speck that was Lancelot riding back towards them. *Bear of Britain*. He had always felt silly when Merlin called him that. Such a grand title, but one he did not feel he had earned. How could he have? He had not seen thirty summers and, although his men were fiercely loyal to him, he had no royal blood and no lands of his own. Merlin always said the title was meant to inspire the people, to give them a symbol of hope to look up to. Now Arthur could see it was also something for *him* to aspire to.

Something for him to earn.

Lancelot came charging up to them, a look of disgust on his face. "They've changed course. Looks like they're heading north. No stomach for a fight now that the numbers are more evenly matched."

"They're just going to return to their homes," Arthur said. "And hope Ceneu leaves it at that since the princess has dealt with the man who raped her."

Lancelot waved a hand, as if he was bored of this whole thing. "Well, let's get back to Caer Lerion and finish what we went there for in the first place. Justice, of a sort, has been served." He walked his horse past them, to the men still forming a shieldwall and commanded them to mount up once again.

Merlin looked at Arthur, and the warlord stared back for a moment and then nodded. "The Saxons aren't our only enemies," he said, heading towards the riderless horse that Lancelot had brought for him. "Do what you can for Bel, Merlin. I'll leave the hunters with you; they can help you get a fire going and collect water if you need it." He climbed into the saddle with some difficulty for he was close to exhaustion.

"Are we just leaving Merlin and the druid here while we return to Caer Lerion?" Lancelot asked, brow furrowed. "And the princess? I can see Bellicus is badly wounded but—"

"We're not going to Caer Lerion," Arthur broke in. "Not yet anyway."

His captain stared at him, and then that familiar rakish smile spread across his face as he understood what Arthur was saying. "Are you sure about this?" he asked, though, concern replacing his delight. "You've had a long day from what Velugna told us. I can lead the men myself and see this finished."

"Oh, I've no doubts about that, Lancelot," the warlord said. "But I want to see this thing through. Come, they're on foot and already exhausted after marching about these lands all day. We'll get ahead of them and see what they do then." With a final nod to Merlin and young Cocca, who returned the gesture with such gravitas that Arthur couldn't help grinning, they rode up the slope, northwards.

"What in hell's been happening?" Lancelot asked as their mounts' powerful strides carried them easily up the hill and towards Senorix's retreating farmers and spearmen. "Did you set fire to a temple?"

Arthur told him everything that had gone on that day, from the point they'd first come upon Eburus and Nynniaw. Lancelot listened over the thudding of hooves, frowning the entire time.

"You might have asked me along," the blond captain grumbled at the end of the story, which Arthur had rather hurried since they were rapidly gaining on their quarry. "I didn't realise you were such good friends with the big Damnonii druid."

Arthur looked sharply at Lancelot. "Are you jealous, old friend?" he asked incredulously, receiving a muttered oath in response. "Trust me, if I'd known we'd end up here, I'd have brought you and the whole damn warband with me. It was just supposed to be a quick ride to find Eburus and back to Caer Lerion, but the gods enjoy finding ways to make things complicated, don't they? How did you get here so quickly anyway?"

"I saw Ceneu in town and he told me where you'd gone. I gathered some men and we rode out, meeting Eburus and Velugna on the road. Just as well, eh?"

They were almost upon Senorix's group by now, the fleeing men turning as they walked, looking back fearfully as the horsemen closed in.

"We'll split into two sections," Arthur said. "You lead the second and remain at the back of Senorix while I take mine on ahead. Dismount when in position and form a shieldwall. When you see me charging, you hit them from the rear, all right?"

Lancelot nodded, grim and supremely confident, or so it seemed to Arthur at least. Perhaps his friend felt the same churning in his stomach as he himself did every time he went into battle. Somehow, he found it hard to believe Lancelot ever felt anxious, but perhaps he was just good at hiding it. Arthur, on the other hand, licked his lips for his throat was dry from both the thought of the approaching fight and the smoke he'd inhaled in the ruined temple.

"Here." Lancelot noticed his discomfort and took his own waterskin from its place in his saddle bag, tossing it across to his leader. "They're forming up."

Arthur nodded, waved farewell to Lancelot and pointed to half of the men following them, splitting them down the middle. "You all follow me. The others, go with Lancelot."

He rode on, unstoppering the skin and taking a long, delicious swallow of the water. It was cold and soothed his parched throat and he would have liked to finish the lot but the idea of fighting with all that liquid sloshing about inside his belly was not a nice one, so he reluctantly put the skin away. He and his detachment were already past the watching enemy spearmen who'd stopped walking and formed into a kind of rough circular formation, weapons pointing outwards like the spines of a hedgehog.

Suspecting they did not have any archers or slingers since they'd not used them at the temple, Arthur still erred on the side of caution, turning and reining in his mount at a fair distance from Senorix and his warriors. If they did launch missiles at them, Arthur's men would at least have a few moments to raise their shields.

Lancelot's group was already behind the enemy, and they quickly dismounted and moved into fighting formation. Arthur, still atop his horse, looked at the opposing forces and smiled proudly. Senorix's men wore a wide variety of clothing and armour, from simple farmer's tunics to leather or chainmail vests, iron helmets and grubby cloaks. The colours were dull and drab and those who carried shields had painted them in various colours.

Facing them, Lancelot's men, like the ones accompanying Arthur, carried round shields made of linden, all stained blue and white with one or two bear motifs painted on them in the same colours. All the men carried similar gear, and it was all in good repair, the last of the day's sunlight striking polished buckles and blades and making the line of warriors seem like one, great, unified entity, rather than a collection of disparate tafl pieces.

It was a shame all of Senorix's soldiers would be dead shortly, for they would have carried tales of this day, of how impressive Arthur's forces looked, far and wide, growing with every retelling. That was not to be, however.

Dismounting, Arthur pegged the animal's reins to the ground and lifted the shield from its place on the saddle. It would be better to tie the beast to a tree or similar, fixed object, but the horses were used to the noises of battle and, hopefully, wouldn't run off when the fighting started. The warlord blew out a long breath, wondering how Duro was getting on recruiting the old cavalry officers who might have shown them how to smash these farmers from the saddle. Another day, gods willing. For now, he walked forward, his men shadowing him, spears or swords drawn, shields up, helmets making their faces appear quite sinister in the red sunset.

Senorix's men shuffled nervously in their loose formation and Arthur could see the back of the one named Brice's head, facing towards Lancelot's slowly closing warriors. They would have to fight on two sides and, like Arthur's warband, had sent the two highest ranking soldiers to lead from the front.

"What do you want from us?" Senorix shouted, red-faced and sweating as the young warlord strode confidently towards them betraying no hint of any fatigue from the long day's tribulations. "Surely it's enough that you killed our lord, and in his own lands too? Why are you following us?"

Arthur's troopers came up behind him and locked shields. He walked along the line and back, eyeing each one of Senorix's men who would meet his gaze before he said scathingly, "Your *lord* was a rapist, and you, well you sought to murder your King, Ceneu's men, along with myself and the Druid of Dun Breatann. Nynniaw has already faced justice for his crimes, as you shall now."

Senorix opened his mouth to reply, but Arthur carried on, not giving him a chance to frame a sentence. "You pursued us, including Princess Velugna, with the intention of slaughtering us all."

"We have a right to drive enemies out of our lands," Brice called back over his shoulder, and, with his spear and armour he looked more of a warrior than Senorix in his simple attire.

"You went a step further than that," Arthur retorted angrily. "Do you know who I am? Arthur, Warlord of the Britons by authority of your own King and all the other kings of these lands! Yet you tried to burn me alive in the temple back there! You left one of the gods' own representatives – a druid! – draped across a wall to die." He stopped pacing and opened his arms, with their shield and sword, wide. "Yet you ask what we want from you? I want you to feel my blade in your guts, Senorix, you cowardly scum. Lancelot!"

His call rang out over the heads of the enemy spearmen and Lancelot's reply came firm and steady.

"Ready, my lord."

Arthur took one final, lingering look up at the sky, drinking in the beauty of the setting sun and the long shadows its rays cast across the land, and then he stepped back into the embrace of his shieldwall. The time for words was over; it was time to kill.

CHAPTER TWENTY

Elpin felt the same desire to run that he'd experienced during their attack on the temple. That had worked out well for him, since he'd been able to catch the giant enemy druid unawares and attack him from behind before he took a blow himself, but he knew there was nowhere to hide this time. They were in open countryside and their pursuers had horses so, although he could move fast, he couldn't outrun a horse.

He looked around at his companions, noting the fear in all their eyes. Elpin wasn't the only one who was terrified of dying there. Even Senorix and Brice were perspiring heavily and continuously wiping the sweat from their hands onto their clothes so they could grasp their spears more firmly.

His gaze momentarily locked on Senorix's and Elpin was sure the nobleman's lip curled in disdain as they looked at one another. *He knows*, Elpin thought. *He knows I ran away from the fight, and he knows I was lucky to catch the druid by surprise.*

If that was true, Elpin's life would not be worth living, even if they did somehow survive this battle. Senorix would make sure everyone knew he was a coward, and he would be shunned at best. Beaten and even killed at worst. And for what? Why should they lay down their lives to avenge the death of Nynniaw, a rapist and drunken bully? That was the real reason he'd run in the temple – he did not believe in what they were here to fight for. Elpin was a farmer, he'd never wanted to be a warrior, especially if that meant standing in a field surrounded by those quiet, terrifying men with their blue shields and cold eyes.

They were walking forward now, those enemy soldiers. Elpin's panic rose, not helped in the least by the muttered, whining prayers of many of his nearby fellows and the sound of one man vomiting. The blood-red sunset cast sinister shadows over the troopers led by the blond-haired, high-cheekboned enemy nobleman and the colour seemed to Elpin like an omen. A presaging of the wave of blood that would spurt from his body beneath the plunging, tearing spears of—

"Wait!" He amazed himself by finding the strength to power his legs forward, towards the warlord who'd given his name as Arthur.

"Wait! This isn't my fight, it's his." He pointed back, over his shoulder at the astonished Senorix. "Most of us are simple farmers, not soldiers," Elpin hurried on, almost tripping over the words in his haste to spit them out before someone – on either side – launched a spear at him. "Why not settle your quarrel between yourselves in single combat? Surely we don't all have to die?"

The man's voice was plaintive but strong and indignant. Arthur looked from him to his leader, Senorix, noting the defiant stance and grim, yet unafraid expression on the enemy lord's face, despite the blood and bruising from Bellicus's earlier staff strike.

Single combat was always an option, but Arthur was not fond of using it as a way to settle the outcome of a battle – he was no coward, and he knew how to use a sword, but there would always be someone bigger, faster and better than him, especially in his exhausted state. He didn't believe Senorix was that man, despite the farmer's arrogant glare, but why should Arthur give up his massive advantage? He had the numbers, better trained and equipped men, and had the enemy hemmed in on two sides.

"Are you afraid?" It wasn't Elpin who spoke up this time. Arthur could see it was the spearman, Brice, who'd apparently also decided this would be a good way to survive this confrontation. "Too cowardly to fight Senorix, eh? And yet you style yourself as a 'lord of war'. Pah."

Senorix's expression had changed now, as more of his own men called for single combat instead of a pitched battle. Saving their own hides at, possibly, the expense of their new leader. But Senorix was not about to lose face and reject the suggestion, so he puffed out his chest and glared even more fiercely at Arthur.

A smile tugged at the warlord's lips. These farmers were beaten already, as evidenced by their desperate desire to avoid the promised battle. If there had been any doubt before, it was gone now, wiped away by the last rays of the falling sun.

"I'm Arthur's champion, and I'll fight in his stead."

Somehow, Lancelot had made his way past the enemy formation without Arthur even noticing him until he spoke up, proving to the warlord just how tired and blunted his senses were after everything he'd been through that day. His words were true – this is exactly what a champion did. Otherwise kings, many of them old men, would be forced to take on young challengers every day. Of course, it impressed soldiers when their leader fought on his own behalf, but Arthur's men already knew and loved him. They were not loyal to him because he was the fiercest man in Britain, but because he knew how to win battles. How to lead.

"Do you have a champion, Senorix?"

The farmers' chief eyed Lancelot and apparently saw nothing to fear. It wouldn't be the first time the blond warrior's lean frame and almost effeminate facial features, apart from the scar on his forehead, had made an opponent underestimate him.

"I fight my own battles," Senorix shouted, rolling his neck and working his limbs to loosen the muscles. "Let's get this over with. And when I beat that little girl you call a 'champion', Arthur, we'll return home unmolested. Then, when we get there—" he spun and pointed the tip of his sword at his own comrade, Elpin, "—I'll gut you, and use your skull as a drinking vessel!"

Lancelot, bored by all the chatter, nodded to Arthur and walked forward to begin the contest.

Arthur, noting the unhappy faces amongst Senorix's followers – it wasn't just Elpin who appeared frightened of their new leader – saw an opportunity. He had come to Caer Lerion to enlist men in his warband after all. He called out, looking at each face in the enemy crowd.

"Trust me, Lancelot will win. But in that case, I expect Brice there," he gestured with a flick of his head at the sullen spearman, "will just take over, and life at your steading will continue as before. I suspect that life is not a particularly pleasant one for most of you."

There were nervous glances along the line and eyes turned downwards to the ground and Arthur knew his intuition had been right. Bryn Cleddyf was not a happy place and Brice would not make things any better, judging by the resigned faces he saw amongst the farmers.

"Let Lancelot despatch Senorix, and then any of you who wish can join my warband."

Heads came up at his words, hope flaring in the eyes that stared at him. They had the same look as his hunters had when Lancelot and Velugna led the riders to their rescue a short time ago. Before any of them could pledge themselves to him, Senorix stepped forward, towards Lancelot, swinging his sword and hefting his

161

shield as if it weighed little more than a feather although it was clear he wasn't as strong as he wished to seem.

"Enough of this nonsense," the bald warrior roared, moustache bristling. "Are we going to fight like men or chatter like women?"

"It was a woman that slaughtered your lord Nynniaw," Lancelot replied, smiling.

Shouting with rage, Senorix charged towards his opponent, perhaps hoping brute force and speed would be enough to end the fight quickly. His sword swung and clattered against the linden of Lancelot's round shield, but the wood held and only a few splinters were sent flying by the blade. Senorix was undaunted and struck again and again and, to those who were farmers and untutored in the martial arts, it seemed like Lancelot was being driven back, worn down by a more ruthless opponent.

Arthur knew better. Senorix landed blow after blow but each one struck the shield. Lancelot was simply walking around in a wide circle, batting aside the attacks almost effortlessly while the continuous, brutal assault was quickly tiring the already fatigued Senorix whose own shield was weighing heavily thanks to Cai's earlier attack on his shoulder.

Another strike and another clatter of iron against wood and Senorix, furious, spun away with his sword held high, as if asking the gods what more he should do. Before he could turn back, Lancelot stepped nimbly forward and kicked out, hitting Senorix in the back of his knee. As the man fell, Lancelot's sword snaked out, the edge of the blade slicing into Senorix's pale, bald head. There was a sickening thud as the unfortunate farmers' lord was hammered sideways, a horrific bleeding wound in the side of his skull.

Yet, somehow, Senorix managed to stand up. He was dazed and apparently astonished, almost as if he had no idea what had happened to him. Reaching up with his sword hand, his fingers touched the gaping wound and came away and he stared at the blood while, behind him, his men winced at the sight of it.

"Should have worn a helmet," Lancelot said, still smiling. "That's going to leave a scar, and you've no hair to hide it. Then again," his smile became a grin and he pointed at his own forehead, "some women *love* a good scar. I'm guessing a man as

162

hideous as you could do with any help he can get, eh? Especially with that missing tooth."

Senorix charged forward, this time slamming his shield against Lancelot's, and then his sword, hammering with both alternately. It was an unskilled approach, but it was difficult to defend against and, at last, Senorix's shield knocked Lancelot's backwards, into Arthur's champion's face. Striking just above the eyeline, it stunned him, but Senorix had tired himself out and stepped back to catch a breath, unaware of the chance he had to at least land a thrust or a slash with his long sword.

The smile was not as wide on Lancelot's mouth now. He tossed down his shield and made a few lithe practice sweeps with his sword, becoming accustomed to the ability to move more freely. "Hurry up then," he said, sounding bored. "Come, let me kill you that we might all be about our business."

Senorix was touching the terrible gash in his head, fingers probing the bloody lips that Lancelot's sword had carved open and now it seemed he finally understood the severity of the injury, and the fact that, if it was to be survivable, it would need tended to very soon.

Again, the combatants closed on one another and Senorix was taking a different tack this time, no longer just charging and lunging wildly. He held his shield up and took a controlled swing at his opponent but Lancelot was much faster than he was. Arthur's champion easily parried the attack then reversed his sword's movement, thrusting the tip with incredible power and precision into Senorix's side. The cuirass the farmer had earlier taken from one of his own spearmen absorbed some of the force, so the blade didn't penetrate much more than a finger's length, but Lancelot quickly drew it out and hammered his left fist into his enemy's chin.

Senorix rocked back and everyone there held their breath for Lancelot had not pressed his advantage. Somehow he'd been able to tell there was no need.

Nynniaw's successor, Lord of Bryn Cleddyf for a mere handful of hours, dropped his shield onto the grass with a thud and then slumped down onto the grass as if all the energy had instantly drained from him.

"What're you doing Senorix?" Brice shouted. "Get up, man! This isn't over yet."

"You're wasting your breath," Lancelot replied. "He's already dead."

Everyone looked at the prone figure on the ground, searching for some sign of movement, listening for some sound, some cry that would prove the blond warrior's words were premature, but the horrific headwound Senorix had suffered had finally caught up with him. Lancelot was amazed the man had fought on for so long, thinking of the chickens he'd seen with their heads removed, running about as if their bodies hadn't yet got the message that they were dead.

"Who's next then? You?"

Brice visibly blanched at Lancelot's pointing sword. He was a decent fighter and an experienced spearman with half a dozen battles under his belt, but the idea of facing Arthur's champion alone, especially after witnessing the man dispatch Senorix with such ease, did not appeal to Brice. He shook his head.

Arthur, greatly relieved at Lancelot's victory, spoke up, directing his words to Elpin, who was obviously relieved that his own leader was dead. "You and your companions are free to return to your homes, as we agreed. Any who wish to join my warband, come forward now. You'll be well trained, well fed, and enjoy the camaraderie of Britain's finest warriors." He smiled and swept his hand around to encompass his men. "Or, you can go back to being a farmer, with men like that," he nodded at the sour-faced Brice, "controlling your lives. Make your choice now."

At first, no-one moved, but then Elpin, without a glance at the furious Brice, stepped forward and stood before the warlord. "I'm not a mighty warrior, my lord," he said to Arthur. "But I'll join you. There's nothing for me at Bryn Cleddyf now – no wife, no family – and my life won't be worth much if I go back there so, if you'll have me, I'll follow you."

"He's the one that attacked your druid," Brice shouted furiously, pointing at Elpin. "You still want him to join you?"

The farmer blanched at the accusation, staring at Arthur as if he expected to be cut down for what he'd done to Bellicus. Indeed, the warlord's face did darken, but he shook his head and reached out to grip Elpin by the shoulder.

"We were fighting one another at that point," he said. "You can't be blamed for striking down an enemy. The fact you managed to somehow best the druid just proves you'd be a useful addition to my army."

Hearing this, another six men walked out of the enemy line and came to stand beside Elpin who was greatly bolstered by their presence and asked Arthur, "Do we kneel, my lord, or swear an oath or something...?"

"I'm no king," Arthur replied, smiling and grasping the man's wrist in the age-old warrior's welcome. "You don't kneel to me. As for oaths – that's for another time." He looked at them all, nodding as if he liked what he saw. "Join your new comrades, you're more than welcome among my warband."

The seven men – four armoured spearmen and three farmers – bowed their heads respectfully as they filed past and were accepted into the shieldwall behind Arthur.

"The rest of you," growled the warlord, rubbing a hand over his eyes as fatigue threatened to overwhelm him, "go home."

As before, Lancelot had moved positions without anyone seeming to notice him and mounted his horse. As Brice silently led his followers in their unhappy trudge back to Bryn Cleddyf, Lancelot rode beside them, no longer smiling, instead appearing every inch the conquering hero.

"Remember this day," he called to the defeated farmers and spearmen who'd chosen not to come over to Arthur's side. "If ever you're tempted to force yourself on a woman, remember the fates of Nynniaw and Senorix, and remember the wisdom and mercy of Arthur, Bear of Britain, who spared your worthless lives."

Brice could not refrain from spitting on the grass but made no audible remark as he walked off with his men, slump-shouldered and glaring venomously at Elpin and the other defectors.

Arthur's two forces merged into one again, the warriors retrieving their horses and climbing up into the saddles with a mixture of relief and disappointment. A fight was always guaranteed to get the blood flowing in a man's veins, but at least they were all alive to face another day. The new additions to the party were, if small enough, allowed to climb up behind another rider, or told to continue on foot as they headed back to fetch Merlin and the others.

When the hunters spotted them coming Cocca's face lit up like that of a puppy when its master returns, but Bellicus was still unconscious and an unhealthy pallor, while Velugna looked completely drained. She'd been through more than any of them that day after all, Arthur thought.

Merlin had not been idle during their absence, directing the hunters to collect long branches and fashioning a stretcher for Bellicus using the druid's own voluminous cloak. Now they, along with those of Senorix's men who'd joined up with Arthur, were tasked with carrying the injured druid back to Caer Lerion, taking turns to let one another have a rest when needed. Cai padded along at the side, whining softly every so often and looking at Bellicus from large, hopeful eyes.

"You think Brice will seize control of Bryn Cleddyf now?" Arthur asked Velugna as they headed for the town.

"Undoubtedly," the princess replied.

"Maybe your father will have a better relationship with him than he did with Nynniaw."

"As soon as this war with Hengist is over," Velugna said in a grim voice, "I'll be demanding my father gives me twenty men and I'll ride to Bryn Cleddyf and take control of it for Caer Lerion once and for all. I love the king, but he's getting old and too settled in his Christian ways. It's time we reasserted ourselves as the dominant family in these lands. Brice can stand aside or face the same fate as Nynniaw."

Arthur and Lancelot listened to her words and the icy tone she used to grind them out and shared a glance. *I'd not want to be in Brice's shoes when Velugna comes looking for him*, mused the warlord, and with a wry shake of his head thought he wouldn't like to be King Ceneu either. His amusement faded quickly though, as their horses picked up speed and made for Caer Lerion and Arthur thought of Bellicus, grey and unmoving as blood seeped from his wounds.

Duro would be rejoining them soon, and the centurion would not be at all happy with Arthur if he allowed the druid to die.

CHAPTER TWENTY-ONE

"Is he…"

"Dead?" Merlin replied, and the old mystic was so pale he might have been referring to himself. He looked down at the pallet Bellicus was lying on and shook his head. "No, he lives, for now. But his wound became infected, and the blight spread through his body. His connection to this world is dangerously weak, and the longer the fever lasts…"

Duro stared at his friend and felt a wave of anger washing over him. He'd rejoined Arthur's warband here in Caer Lerion with Sulinus in tow and, for the first time in months, felt happy to be alive again. Waking in the morning, with spring slowly heading towards the glorious heat of summer, was not something to be apathetic about, or even feared – it was to be embraced! And then he'd asked where Bellicus was and been led here to this stuffy bedchamber within King Ceneu's own house and the old fears were rising within him again.

He'd genuinely believed he was over the black melancholy that had slowly wormed its way into his soul since his wife had been murdered by Horsa's Saxons. Despite the great friendship he had with Bellicus – they were like brothers now – the giant druid was a constant reminder of the bad things had befallen Duro recently. He shuddered as he thought again of the dark cell in Dunnottar in which he'd been imprisoned, beaten, and lost two fingers thanks to King Drest's tortures. Bellicus had been there with him, or rather *beneath* him, in the cell below, and they'd escaped together, just as they'd escaped other trials.

It had been strangely liberating to leave the druid's side for the first time in the long months since they'd first met one another while searching for Princess Catia. Strangely pleasant not to see that reminder every day of the world's wickedness.

Of course, now that he looked upon the feverish Bellicus, so young and as true a friend as a man could ever wish for, Duro felt terribly ashamed of his feelings. Nothing that had befallen him was Bel's fault. The lad did not deserve Duro's resentment, no matter how unintended or unconscious it was.

Making an effort to push aside the darkness fogging his brain, Duro channelled his hatred towards Horsa and vowed to do all he could to help Bellicus. Cai, who was lying on the floor beside his master, stood up, stretched out his great body, then sat and placed his head in the centurion's lap.

"Can I do anything?" Duro asked Merlin, still staring at Bellicus as he rubbed Cai's ears, praying to Mithras that the druid would open his eyes and everything would be all right again. "I could go to the market and get you a chicken, or a sheep to sacrifice. I remember Bel once sacrificed a pigeon and it, well…" He trailed off, feeling as if he was rambling and telling a story that had already been told a thousand times. "It seemed to work."

Merlin could easily see how upset Duro was, and he produced a fatherly smile. Truth be told, he was only about ten years older than the centurion, but his white beard and mannerisms made the gap appear greater. Duro responded to the High Druid's expression, seeming to take heart from it and sitting taller and straighter, almost as if he was about to head off to battle.

"I've already performed the correct healing rituals," Merlin said. "And his wound has been well cared for." He glanced down at Bellicus's massively muscled bicep and the clean, fresh bandage that was around it. "Now we just have to wait and hope his spirit can defeat the evil that's found its way inside him."

Duro nodded and a grim smile threatened to become a wide grin as he took in the Merlin's words. "The lad has the stoutest spirit of any man I've ever come across. Maybe things aren't as bleak as I'd thought when I first came in here and saw him."

Stroking the end of his lengthy beard, Merlin shrugged. "It's in the lap of Sulis Minerva now. You could visit her shrine if you want? It's outside the town boundary, to the south." He rolled his eyes in disgust. "King Ceneu, a Christ follower, wanted to destroy it but decided to just have it moved away from its original position beside the old bathhouse to avoid offending the few people in Caer Lerion who still have ties with the old ways. Take the dog with you, leave an offering, and ask Sulis to give strength to Bel. Other than that – eat, have a cup of ale. You look like you could do with it." He watched as the centurion stood to go, Cai standing also and added as an afterthought. "If you were to come across any samolus plants on your travels they might come in handy. I've made some potent healing tonics with their leaves in the past but haven't been able to find any lately. You know them?" Duro looked blank and the old druid chuckled. "They should be flowering about now, little white cup-shaped blooms with five petals. They grow about this high."

Duro nodded uncertainly and said, "I'll keep an eye out for them." He raised a hand in the Roman officers' salute, smiled, and ducked beneath the doorframe, whistling for Cai to follow as he made his way to the great hall where he'd promised to meet Arthur and deliver his report on the mission to Luguvalium.

Bedwyr was already there, stuffing his mouth with cheese and freshly roasted beef having already told Arthur how the mission had turned out. Sulinus had gone off with Lancelot and Kay to meet and informally inspect the men that might form his new cavalry detachment.

"Duro!" The warlord got to his feet and received him gladly when he came into the hall. Almost sheepishly, the centurion thought, and the reason for that soon became clear when he said, "I'm so sorry about Bel."

"He's a druid," Duro replied, pleasantly surprised by Arthur's obvious remorse at what had happened to Bellicus. "But he's also a warrior. Like any of us, he knows he might be killed or injured when he goes into a fight. I'm sure he'll be fine."

Arthur's brow furrowed at that and Duro wondered if Merlin had been hiding the true extent of Bel's condition from him. The warlord rallied almost instantly, however, and he ushered Duro to the table he was sharing with Bedwyr as Cai found a patch of warm sunlight to lie in. "Sit, centurion," Arthur said. "Eat and drink as much as you like. Ceneu has been extra hospitable since, well, since Bel was injured and the princess..." He tailed off. "Never mind, that can all wait. For now, relax and fill your belly. Bedwyr was just telling me how impressed he's been by Sulinus. Our first obstacle to having an efficient, deadly cavalry unit has been cleared it seems."

Duro didn't feel overly hungry since the sight of the sickly druid had ruined his appetite, but he knew how important it was to eat when given the opportunity, so he took a piece of bread and munched half-heartedly on it. "Sulinus will be a fine man to train your riders," he said, mid-chew. "But he's too old to command them in battle, he admits as much himself."

"What do we do then?"

Bedwyr answered, having already filled his belly and having only an ale left to nurse. "Either hope one of our own horsemen have the necessary skills and Sulinus can pick him out and coach him to lead, or we find another, younger, former decurion."

"Which probably won't be easy," Duro said, not even noticing how fresh and soft his bread was as he gulped it down. "Younger cavalry officers would have sailed off with the rest of the legions when they left Britain, unless they were invalided out, like me. Finding one will be hard, if not impossible."

"Then we must persuade Sulinus," Arthur mused, watching Bedwyr and Duro for their reactions. Neither man appeared convinced. It seemed they would have to look within their own warband for a suitable young decurion. As if it wasn't going to be hard enough training men to fight on horseback, now someone would need to learn a whole set of extra skills. He smiled and refilled his ale mug halfway. "Things will work out; they have a way of doing so."

Duro could only admire Arthur's optimism and believed he could feel it rubbing off on himself, or perhaps it was merely having a full belly that was inspiring him to get out and be about his business, whatever that might be.

They chatted together for a little while longer, Duro filling in Arthur on his thoughts on Sulinus and how they might progress, while the warlord recounted the events that had led to Bellicus's current sickness.

"That bloody idiot Eburus," Duro growled when he heard the tale. "I knew it was a mistake to bring him along, he's always causing bother. You'll have heard what happened at our first meeting with him, when Bellicus put him on his arse?"

Arthur nodded and leaned back on his stool, stroking his neat beard, a habit that made him appear oddly younger than his years. "Aye, it was a stupid thing to do, going to the farm," the warlord agreed. "But to be fair, Lancelot says the same about me, Bel, and Princess Velugna riding out after him and the hunters. I haven't heard the end of it in the days since! We all do what we think's right in any given moment, eh? And Eburus didn't realise what he was walking into, he thought he'd just find the one man – Nynniaw, the rapist – and make him pay for his crime. It was an honourable, courageous thing to do, in all honesty."

"It was headstrong and bloody stupid, my lord," the centurion retorted, before softening his tone and allowing himself to smile. "But that's Eburus, I suppose. He's a good lad underneath his bluster and loud mouth. Don't tell him I said that, though, or he'll take it as an excuse to act like an arsehole even more."

Arthur and Bedwyr both smiled and Duro stood.

"If there's nothing else you need me to do just now," the centurion said to Arthur, "I'd like to find an offering to take to Sulis Minerva on Bel's behalf."

The warlord agreed that was a good idea and suggested he ask Ceneu about taking one of the king's fowl from the coop attached to the kitchens, but Duro demurred. Merlin had undoubtedly already done that.

He left then, calling on Cai who was by his side instantly, and walking out into the early afternoon sunshine, appreciating its warmth after the coolness of the hall's interior. A gentle breeze seemed to guide him south, in the direction Merlin had told him the shrine to Sulis was located and, when he left the town's boundary – a sturdy but low palisade wall with a gatehouse manned by a bored looking pair of soldiers – he eventually spotted the tell-tale dip in the grass that marked a stream. He headed for that, knowing water was sacred to the goddess and it didn't take long before he found the shrine.

Cai bounded ahead, sniffing contentedly at the ground, licking patches he found interesting and leaving his scent in numerous places, leg cocked, head high, sniffing the air. Duro was happy he'd brought the faithful hound along with him – Cai would not wish to be parted from Bellicus for long, but the sweet open countryside was a nice change from the druid's stuffy sickroom. It would do the dog good and Duro appreciated the extra security the great mastiff brought for, although these lands were mostly safe, there were outcasts and brigands in every corner of Britain and it was always sensible to be prepared for trouble.

It would be a very brave robber who'd try his luck against the centurion when he had the massive wardog by his side. That thought brought memories of Bellicus's other hound, Eolas, rushing back. That one had been killed in a fight with Horsa too.

Before his pleasant mood turned sour again Duro forced himself to blank out those memories of brave Eolas and instead focus on the so-called shrine to Sulis that he now stood before.

"Is that it?" he muttered in disgust, taking in the pitiful sight. There was an altar stone, the one taken from the town surely, and someone had started to erect a shelter over it but had only managed to complete half the roof thus far. There were a few offerings placed around – garlands of flowers, a small pile of salt, old coins, even a fresh-looking pastry – suggesting the place did see some traffic and the Christ-cult hadn't completely taken a hold of Caer Lerion just yet. He crouched to look at the altar itself, a block of shaped stone with words carved into it:

DEAE SULI
CRISPUS CORNELIUS MEMNOR
HARUSPEX
DONO DEDIT

"For the goddess Sulis, Crispus Cornelius Memnor, haruspex, gave this gift." Duro wondered how old it was and pictured it in its original position within a more respectable temple or shrine to the goddess. That stone must have seen many people over the generations; been touched by many hands seeking favour or healing or just giving thanks for the good things in their lives.

And now it sat here, on the bank of a stream in the countryside, with only a half-finished little shelter to protect it from the elements. Duro felt profoundly depressed at the state of the world, and the old ways being shunted aside. Then a notion struck him, and his mood lifted as he thought, *But at least the old gods are refusing to be ignored, and still finding places like this where people can venerate them.*

"Cai," he said lightly, planning on telling the dog to take a position somewhere close beside him while he communed with the goddess. The dog was already lying on the grass though, eyeing him almost sarcastically, as if he'd read the centurion's mind. "On guard," Duro laughed, grinning at his silent protector, and sitting down himself before the stone altar.

Once upon a time, twenty years ago, he'd have crossed his legs but, although he was still well-muscled and fit, he wasn't as supple as back in those halcyon days with the army. He stared at the grey block of stone before him, not really sure what to do next. Although he was a follower of Mithras and bore the bull tattoo on his arm, he had never really been the type to sit and try to 'talk' with the gods the way Bellicus did. He'd had a little altar at home, and he and his wife would give offerings like wheat, wine and fruit to the household gods, but that was different. Here, in the peace of the countryside, he felt like simply leaving Sulis a honey cake and wandering back to town wasn't enough.

Bellicus was seriously ill, and the goddess's favour would surely not be so easily bought.

He closed his eyes and sat for a while. Nothing happened. Part of him expected, or hoped, he would slip into a trance and see some revelation, but it seemed more likely that he'd just fall asleep. He wished Bellicus was there to tell him what in Hades he should be doing – who'd have thought it could be so hard to pray?

He realised his thoughts were drifting and remembered the druid telling him that stilling one's mind – halting the swirling thoughts that constantly run through our heads every waking moment of our lives – was the key to making a connection with the otherworld. That was easy for Bel to say, of course, since he'd spent years being instructed by the druids on the island of Iova. The only training Duro had been given was…

He took a breath, amazed at just how hard it was to still his thoughts even for a moment. Then, when he thought he was getting the hang of it, he realised thinking even *that* was proof he hadn't properly silenced his mind!

Again, he tried and this time he didn't get irritated by the memories and daydreams that persistently distracted him. After a time, he felt utterly relaxed, as if he was sitting on a chair or comfortable lectus of the type he'd seen in his commanding officers' quarters. He did not feel sleepy anymore, merely supremely relaxed and at peace with the world and the trees and the streams and wildlife surrounding him. The realisation almost jolted him out of his reverie, but he concentrated on his breathing, feeling his chest expanding and contracting, and then, without knowing why, he imagined himself walking in a place very similar to this.

He was moving purposefully, past trees bursting with summer foliage, the green leaves and grass vibrant in the sunshine. A stream wound its way past him, waters reflecting the bright sun and burbling in a way Duro found reassuring. A fallen log had been placed on the bank as a makeshift bridge to the other side and he stepped easily across it, finding himself in a clearing. There was a campfire crackling merrily away, skewered meat roasting above it and sending mouth-watering smells wafting all around him.

And then he saw her. At first, he believed it was Sulis Minerva herself, but then he realised it was not the goddess. It was his wife, Alatucca.

When he came to his cheeks were streaked with tears but he felt oddly…rejuvenated. He'd come here to the shrine in order to seek the goddess's help for Bellicus, but it was he who felt stronger. He looked at Cai who returned his gaze, as alert as ever, and wondered if he'd been dreaming. If so, it had been a particularly lucid dream, like nothing he'd ever experienced before. It wasn't like the visions he'd had as a prisoner in Dunnottar's tiny cell – that had been a bleak and terrifying time when even the friendly characters that populated his fevered mind seemed foreboding and strange. This had been different.

He'd spoken to Alatucca!

Was it really her? He stared at the altar stone, part of him believing it *had* been his wife's shade he'd communed with, while another, more rational – the grizzled soldier – told him it had all been in his imagination.

One thing he was absolutely certain of was his state of mind: he felt stronger, mentally, than he had for weeks or even months. Something at this shrine had worked its magic upon him. Reaching out, he touched the altar, feeling the cold roughness, tracing the lettering carved into it with his fingertips. Had the stone retained the energy of hundreds of petitioners over the decades, allowing him to draw upon that healing force when he'd been in his dreamlike state?

Duro knew Bellicus could speak with beings in the otherworld, and even call upon the gods for aid – he'd seen it himself. Had some of the druid's powers rubbed off on him?

Cai whined softly and dropped his head onto his paws, watching some insect flying lazily past, and Duro stood, pleased not to feel the aches and pains he'd felt in his muscles when he'd first met Bellicus. Back then he'd been overweight and unfit but now he was lean and almost as light on his feet as he'd been as a legionary. Almost. He grinned at Cai, "Come on, big lad. Let's go."

The dog was on his feet in an instant but, with a clumsiness that was quite uncharacteristic, he barged into Duro, making the centurion's foot slip on the damp bank of the stream. Down the man went, boot landing in the water, a curse on his lips. Cai stood watching him though, tongue lolling, tail wagging, and Duro couldn't help but laugh.

"Stupid beast," he grumbled and moved to get back up but, as he did so, something caught his eye in the shimmering waters. A small, white flower. Instantly, Duro recognised it as the plant Merlin had asked him to look out for and, as he pulled some free, shaking the water from the green leaves, he said to himself, "Dockweed. If he'd just have called it by its right name, instead of that fancy one, I'd have known exactly what he meant. Well done, Cai!"

He carefully tucked the plant into a fold of his tunic and then, with one final bow of his head to Sulis's shrine and a silent farewell to Alatucca, they started the walk back towards Caer Lerion.

CHAPTER TWENTY-TWO

"No, you bloody arsehole! Have you never thrown a javelin before? Smooth, idiot, smooth!" Sulinus turned to Arthur and shook his head as the warlord tried to hide his smile. "Your men are terrible riders, my lord, you know that?"

"That's why we need you, decurion," Arthur replied. "I know my infantry can stand against an enemy of similar size but when it comes to attacking from horseback, well, we don't really have a clue." He patted the older man on the back encouragingly. "I can see you know what you're about though. You'll have these lads riding like the Roman *turmae* of old before too long."

Sulinus grunted, accepting the praise with the air of someone who knows it's warranted. "Some of them aren't too bad," he admitted, turning to Bedwyr. "The three that came to my stables with you and the centurion have potential. But the likes of that one." He shook his head again and pointed at the rider who'd made such a mess of his previous javelin throw, missing the straw target by quite some margin and almost striking one of his comrades. "I doubt he'll ever come good. Throws with the power and grace of a man older than me. Oh, by Jupiter!" Without another word the decurion stomped off towards the line of horsemen riding in a circle and taking turns to try and hit the targets on the practice field, roaring furiously at someone who'd managed to fall out of his saddle, nearly breaking his neck.

Arthur finally allowed himself to grin and turned to Bedwyr who stood by his side. "You did well persuading him to join us," he said. "He really knows his stuff, and the men either respect him or are too frightened to challenge him when he upbraids them for not performing as they should. Look."

They watched as Sulinus stood over the fallen man, shouting at him for being clumsy and explaining how, if he fell out of his saddle on a real battlefield, he'd likely be dragged along, screaming, by his horse, until he was either trampled or skewered by an enemy while he was utterly helpless. The downed rider was scarlet with embarrassment and humiliation, but he looked at the decurion from hooded eyes and accepted his dressing down in silence. The man was no green youngster; he was in his thirties and had seen many battles – on foot – either as part of his own lord's warband or, more recently, in Arthur's army. But he'd volunteered to join the new cavalry unit and he was obviously eager to learn from the decurion so, swallowing his pride with an obvious effort, he took Sulinus's insults and listened to the old man's advice in silence before finally getting up and retrieving his horse. Arthur and Bedwyr watched approvingly as he rubbed his neck where he must have been hurt in the fall but quickly rejoined the circling riders as they continued the target practice.

Sulinus looked on but it wasn't long before he was shouting again, telling one man to keep his aim up, another to use the horns on his saddle to brace his backside as he threw the javelin, and a third that his mother must be thoroughly ashamed of him.

"Aye, he'll have them working together as a unit within a few weeks, I'm sure," Bedwyr said, believing he could already see an improvement in the riders' cohesion and throwing in the few days since Sulinus took over their training. "Will that be soon enough?" he asked Arthur, wincing as two horses came together and Sulinus told the riders what he thought of them. "Have you heard anything from our scouts on the Saxon Shore?"

Arthur's smile faded in an instant. "Aye. With the return of spring Hengist's forces are moving out again. Just smaller warbands so far, hitting the towns near Garrianum. Well, the ones that haven't already been burned to the ground or abandoned. And even in the winter there were more of the bastards coming from Jutland or wherever and spreading out across our lands, settling where the local lords would let them. Or were too frightened to oppose them." He shook his head and Bedwyr thought the warlord more despondent than he could ever remember. "They're slowly taking control, my friend," he admitted, and this shocked Bedwyr who'd suspected it was true for some time but didn't think he'd hear Arthur admitting it.

"What are we going to do about it?"

Arthur shrugged. "Whatever we can." He fell silent and Bedwyr had the uneasy feeling his leader had been about to suggest they couldn't win the war. Thankfully he did not.

"This cavalry unit will just be the first," Bedwyr said and there was an iron edge to his voice which made Arthur's jaw set and his shoulders rise again. "Sulinus will turn these clumsy fools into the deadliest force Britain has seen for decades, mark my words, Arthur. And then we'll train another unit, and another, and when Hengist finally meets us in the open we'll crush him like the crawling insect he is."

They looked at one another and Arthur seemed to draw fresh resolve from his captain's determined expression.

"All right, I think I've seen enough for one morning." Sulinus was walking towards them again and, although he still looked disgusted by his new unit's performance, there was a glint in his eye that suggested he might secretly be quite happy with how things were progressing. "Take a rest, lads," he called over his shoulder to the relieved riders. "Get something to eat. Ease your aching arses. But, by the gods, I better see some improvement in your throwing come the afternoon!" He strode across to them, bent with age and a hard life but unmistakeably sprightlier than when Bedwyr first met him.

"How are they dealing with those new saddles?" Arthur asked him as they met again and started walking towards the wooden cabin that had been built to provide protection from the elements for the cavalry's food and drink supplies and also any visiting dignitaries like the warlord and his friend.

"Oh, they'll get used to them eventually," Sulinus said, dropping onto a pile of sacks and wiping sweat from his glistening pate. "They're uncomfortable at first but once your muscle memory takes over you can make manoeuvres that someone in a normal saddle simply can't match. You might do me a favour, though, and see that saddler in town. He was supposed to deliver another five saddles yesterday but I'm still waiting. If I don't have the equipment—"

Arthur held up a hand, frowning. "Say no more, decurion." His voice was hard, cold. "I'll have a word with the man. I won't have this training held up because a saddler's too lazy to do the work we paid him for."

"To be fair," Bedwyr said. "It's a strange design for someone to try and copy when they've been used to making much simpler saddles."

"He shouldn't have agreed to our timeframe then," Arthur replied and Sulinus nodded approvingly.

178

"You're right, my lord," the decurion agreed. "It's one thing to be late delivering a plough to a farmer, quite another when we're in the business of fighting off sea-wolves."

"True," Bedwyr conceded. "But if we're needing things like that in such haste, next time we should find more than one person to deliver them."

Arthur smiled and patted his friend and advisor on the back, saying to Sulinus, "This is why I value Bedwyr so highly. And why he'll be in charge of seeing you get all the supplies you need in future, decurion."

Bedwyr's face fell but Arthur's grin was infectious and he held his peace as Sulinus began telling them a little more about how he hoped the new unit's training would go over the coming weeks.

"I'll be needing someone to lead them," the old legionary pointed out. "D'you have anyone in mind for the role?"

"I thought we'd leave that up to you to decide," Arthur said, shrugging slightly.

"Are there any noblemen amongst that lot?" Sulinus pointed to the riders who were now milling about, chewing bread and drinking from cups of water collected that morning from the nearby stream.

Arthur shook his head. "Not really, but it doesn't matter. Of course, if some local lord brings us troops he'll expect to lead them, that's fair enough. But this new cavalry detachment will be led by the best person for the job, whether they're of noble birth or not. You choose who you think is best suited to the role, Sulinus."

The decurion nodded again. "They'll have to be good riders as well as good leaders. I've noticed a couple of the lads who might be decent candidates. I'll keep an eye on them and let you know. We'll need a standard bearer eventually as well, and that's possibly an even more demanding role, given how heavy all their equipment is." He laughed softly, reminiscing about past battles in his mind's eye. "Oh no, I never envied my standard bearers. I think Rianorix might be the man for that job."

Bedwyr smiled, remembering how easily Sulinus had beaten Rianorix in their contests back at the decurion's stables. The younger rider certainly had the temperament to carry a standard though, and, with Sulinus's tutelage, hopefully he'd learn the skills as well.

They sat in silence for a time, watching the riders mingling with one another, rubbing tired buttocks, laughing about their successes and failures on the practice ground, and generally getting to know one another. These men had been culled from Arthur's warband, but they were from all over Britain. One was from Dumnonia in the south, for example, three were from Isca, two from Gwynedd, and one was even from Alt Clota. Arthur had asked for volunteers for the new unit and Sulinus had then been tasked with choosing who he thought were the most promising candidates, then they'd come together here for the decurion to forge into something that might put the fear of Thunor into their enemies.

"So, are you going to fight the way the Romans did?"

Arthur turned to Sulinus, surprised by the question. "No," he said. "What gave you that idea?"

"Well," the decurion said, "you've got me training your cavalry, and the centurion, Duro, training your infantry. Seemed a logical conclusion to come to."

Bedwyr shook his head. "It's a nice idea. The thought of leading a hundred legionaries against Hengist's spearmen is appealing but simply unworkable."

"Agreed," Arthur put in. "The Romans had a standing army, with each man being paid wages from a central treasury. They had a command structure in place, a hierarchy built up over generations." Somewhat sadly, he held his hands up and jerked his head towards the riders still wandering about eating and drinking. "We lead a collection of men taken from various tribes, with various loyalties, various levels and methods of training under their belts...No, the days of the legions are gone. Here in Britain at any rate." He brightened then, taking a sip of his drink, eyes sparkling over the rim of the cup. "Perhaps one day I can lead such an army of Britons but, for now, we must make do with what we have and try to use our troops to the best advantage."

"Duro is helping us train the infantry," Bedwyr said, clarifying Sulinus's original question. "But it's under our authority, using our methods. He understands how to get the best out of the raw recruits although his experience is, like yours, invaluable."

"And he has a very loud voice," Arthur remarked with a wry grin. "Comes in handy when you're trying to teach men how to kill, but also how not to kill their own comrades."

Sulinus's eyes misted over as he looked back through the years to his youth. "The legions were never perfect by any means," he muttered, almost to himself, making Arthur and Bedwyr lean in to hear. "But by the gods they knew how to mould a man into a proper soldier."

"And that, decurion," said Arthur lightly, "is your job with these men. Good luck!" He stood up and stretched out his hand, grasping Sulinus's wrist as the old warrior did likewise in return. "Again, if there's anything you need, just let Bedwyr know."

"I'll go to the saddler's right now," Bedwyr promised. "Kick him up the arse and make sure you get your saddles as soon as possible."

Sulinus nodded, saluted in the old Roman style, and turned away. They watched him go as he wandered back to his men, hunched over but almost crackling with energy and purpose as he commanded the riders to mount up.

The warlord and his captain headed for their own horses and rode to Caer Lerion with a great sense of satisfaction and belief that their vision for a Britain free of marauding invaders was one large step closer.

CHAPTER TWENTY-THREE

"How are you, centurion? I have to say, it's good to see you looking happier these days."

Duro glanced up sharply at the Merlin's words, wondering if there was some rebuke in them. Did the old man think he should be sad all the time because Bellicus was still battling his fever? But there was no judgement or criticism in the mystic's eyes. Instead, he merely looked exhausted.

"Aye, I feel...reborn almost," Duro agreed. "I've even taken out my flute again, trying to learn how to play it with two missing fingers. Since I visited the shrine to Sulis Minerva I've felt rejuvenated somehow."

Merlin's eyebrows rose. "Well, she is a goddess of healing."

"She seems to have healed me," the centurion said, before turning to look at the silent druid on the pallet between them. "I wish she would heal him too."

"Be patient," Merlin said softly. "I used the samolus plant you brought for me – made a healing elixir with its leaves and gave it to our sickly friend. Powerful magic, Duro, powerful indeed but...It's up to him now."

They examined Bellicus, taking in the loss of weight and muscle mass and the growth of hair on his head and face, and wondered if he would ever fully wake again. He'd been in this room for two weeks now, occasionally coming to some form of wakefulness and accepting water or even a little broth, but he gave the impression he had no idea where, or even who, he was. Duro was still frightened his friend would die, as he surely would soon enough without eating proper meals, but the prospect no longer made the centurion feel a black, crushing depression. For a long time it had just been Duro, Bellicus and Cai. Of course, there were other people, other friends around them like Eburus and, back in Alt Clota, the loyal guard captain, Gavo, but centurion and druid shared a bond of friendship that was born of the experiences they'd been through together. The idea of losing that...

He'd expected to be sent off to find more old cavalry officers, but Arthur had decided Sulinus must be enough for now and, instead, wanted the latest recruits to the army to be trained as quickly, and as intensively as possible. Duro was asked if he could do it and he agreed, while warning Arthur it had been many years since he'd been involved in drilling raw legionaries. Those old ways had come easily back to him though, and it felt good to see the men, including Elpin and the others who'd joined them after the fight at the haunted ruins, starting to come together as a cohesive unit.

Similarly, his growing friendship with Arthur's captains such as Lancelot, Kay, and Bedwyr in particular, chased away the worst of the loneliness he felt at Bellicus's absence. Life within the structured confines of a working army brought a welcome, familiar sense of camaraderie that he'd once missed but eventually got over thanks to his wife Alatucca. With her gone it was almost a relief to be a soldier again, especially after what he'd experienced at Sulis's shrine.

At his feet, Cai shifted, stretching out on the floor and taking up much of it. Duro smiled and reached down to pat the dog's back leg. Cai eyed him silently, thumped his tail on the floor a couple of times, then drifted off to sleep again.

"The Saxons are moving," Merlin said, looking away from Bellicus to watch Duro's reaction. "We've had reports of a large force pushing out westwards from Garrianum. The weather's better, spring has sprung, and, as ever, that will mean war to the likes of Hengist. That's why our army's still camped outside Caer Lerion. No point moving anywhere else until we decide where to meet this coming threat from the east. Thankfully King Ceneu's been more hospitable than I expected."

Duro scowled but he'd been expecting the Saxons' return all through the winter months. Perhaps this year would finally be the Britons' chance to smash the invaders for good. "Will I be travelling with Arthur and the army when you go to meet Hengist?" he wondered.

Merlin shook his head. "When we march in the next couple of days you'll be tasked with riding off and *persuading* some, shall we say, stubborn, lords to send us more men. If we're to operate with a cavalry unit from now on, well, we must have more infantrymen to make up for the ones in training as riders."

The centurion took this in, wondering how he would be expected to force men to do something they didn't want to when they were in their own lands and surrounded by their household guards. He also didn't think Bedwyr would be allowed to come with him on this mission since he was one of Arthur's closest friends and advisors and had taken his new role in command of the army's logistics very seriously, so who would go with him? That familiar old black, despairing mood that he thought banished for ever threatened to settle around his shoulders like a mantle at the prospect of riding around unfamiliar lands, in unwelcome company, on a task he wasn't even sure he was equipped to carry out. *Gods, give me strength...*

"You're not going anywhere on your own."

Both Duro and Merlin's heads snapped around and they stared in amazement. Bellicus looked back at them from rheumy, unfocused eyes. "I need a drink," he croaked, before his head slumped back onto the pallet and he groaned. "What's that bitter taste in my mouth? Dockweed?"

Cai was already on his feet, eyes shining with joy, but he sensed it would not be welcomed if he were to jump on top of his master. Instead, he contented himself with whining and dropping his head beside Bellicus's hand. Duro felt tears welling up as his friend's fingers reached out and weakly stroked Cai's soft fur.

Merlin had already held a cup of water to his brother druid's mouth; much of the liquid spilled down Bellicus's chin but some was swallowed gratefully before, sighing tiredly, he relaxed again.

"Well, if you're coming with me," Duro said gruffly, hoping his voice wouldn't crack, "you'd better hurry up and get dressed. We've got a long road ahead of us, druid." Then he looked at the floor and offered a silent, heartfelt prayer of thanks to Sulis Minerva, and Alatucca.

* * *

Sulinus was shouting encouragement to his men as a bank of grey clouds threatened to unleash their contents on the training ground and make the riders' drills that morning even harder. Bellicus was visiting with Duro having walked there as part of his recovery from the infected arm wound. He was lucky and he knew it – a similar infection had killed Loarn mac Eirc, king of Dalriada, after all – but he was so weak it was frustrating. For a young man as fit and heavily muscled as Bellicus had been, it was humbling to find himself out of breath after walking even a short distance, legs aching and light-headed. He could see the shock on men's faces, members of Arthur's warband who'd known him before his recent injury. They could hardly believe he was able to move at all, given how gaunt and pale he was, but he was determined to get back to his old self as soon as possible. The men's pitying stares were not pleasant, but they merely served as further inspiration to regain his fitness.

Sulinus noticed their approach and came to meet them, commanding his men to continue what they were doing. He looked up at Bellicus who, despite his weight loss was still a towering figure, and frowned. "You must be the druid," he said. "You need a haircut. Looks like a bird's built a nest on your head."

Duro burst out laughing at the unexpected remark and Bellicus joined in although he retorted, "At least I've still got hair, you baldy old fool," and Sulinus ruefully rubbed his shining, sunburned pate and shrugged.

"Aye," he admitted, "the birds' stopped nesting on my head a long time ago. I'm glad you're back on your feet, druid. I've heard a lot about you. Duro's been worried you might die."

"Oh, really?" Bellicus turned to his friend who waved the suggestion away as if it was ridiculous.

"He told me you were clean shaven though," Sulinus continued. "And that you shaved your head. I only recognised you thanks to your height."

"No-one shaved me when I was unwell," the druid said, touching his new hair which, in truth, had only a couple of weeks growth so wasn't exactly long. Longer than it had been in at least fifteen years, admittedly. "I've decided to let it all grow until the day I feel like my old self again. That's very impressive," he said, changing the subject and staring at the cavalrymen going through their practise routines on the training ground.

That day's task was mounting and dismounting full size wooden horses, but what was so remarkable was the speed and ease with which the riders were able to do this, and also the fact they were wearing their full, heavy kit. To an unskilled horseman, as Bellicus and Duro were in comparison to true cavalrymen, getting on and off a horses could be a clumsy affair. Yet Sulinus's recruits, fully armed, were making it look very easy. Even Aesibuas, Catti and Rianorix were performing much better than Duro would ever have expected after riding in their company himself.

The decurion amazed them further when he said, "That's nothing. Soon enough I'll move them onto real horses. I want them able to mount when their animals are running." He looked at Bellicus who seemed unsure if he was being made fun of. "I'm not joking," Sulinus assured him. "Roman cavalrymen were expected to be able to do that, and more. Someone once said, I forget his name, some philosopher or other – Vegetius, that's it! – he said training and discipline had declined in our infantry over the years while the cavalry improved. He was right."

Duro snorted but Sulinus went on, ignoring him and pointing at his trainees.

"Soon enough, druid, I'll have them mounting running horses, in full armour, with drawn swords in their hands. And then we'll move onto riding basics: things like jumping, turning in circles, and starting and stopping quickly. All basic manoeuvres, but absolutely essential in battle. These are the things that turn a rabble of men on horseback into a true cavalry unit." He folded his arms and watched the men training with a look of paternal pride on his lined face.

"I can see why Arthur is so excited about this new part of his army," Bellicus said thoughtfully, still watching the trainees in admiration. He'd been taught to ride as a youngster, and he had a close bond with his horse, Darac, but he could only dream of doing most of the things Sulinus was describing. The mental image of thirty or so men all moving in formation, as one, stirred his own heart the way it must have stirred Arthur's when he'd first decided to push ahead with this scheme.

"The Saxons will not have a clue what's happening when we hit them for the first time," said the decurion, grinning with savage glee. "I've seen it before when an army isn't used to facing skilled cavalry and haven't developed tactics to deal with it." He nodded his head as if seeing the future in his mind's eye. "Hengist's in for a shock, lads, you wait and see."

They chatted a little more and then Duro and Bellicus said they'd see Sulinus later that day for an ale, when he returned to

Caer Lerion. His men were, for now, billeted outside the town but they'd eventually be sleeping beside their horses to help create that all-important bond between mount and rider.

"Sorry, Duro," said Bellicus after they'd been walking back towards town for what seemed an age.

The centurion smiled and patted his friend on the back encouragingly. "Take your time, Bel," he said patiently. "Soon you'll be strong again, and running back and forwards along this road."

They rested often, Bellicus consuming a fair amount of food which they'd brought in their packs, and, when they reached Caer Lerion once more there was a sense of real achievement for both men. The druid was truly on the path to recovery.

As they headed towards Ceneu's hall, a young man approached them. Neither recognised him, and, from his nervous, even frightened demeanour, they were both surprised when he stopped in front of them, barring their way.

Duro's hand was already on his spatha's hilt and Cai was eyeing the man suspiciously but, clasping his hands before him as if in prayer, the fellow said, in a rush of words, "My lord, it was me, Elpin, who attacked you at the haunted ruins. I'm so sorry." Then he stared at Bellicus as if he expected a lightning bolt, or perhaps the druid's fist, to strike him down.

The druid returned his gaze for long moments, allowing Elpin to stew, and then he growled, "You almost killed me."

Mortified, the young farmer nodded, apologising again for his actions but, at last Bellicus smiled and held his hands up to silence him.

"Forget it, Elpin," the druid said. "I'm on the mend now and, from what we heard, you were instrumental in saving many lives that day. And now you fight on our side." He held out his hand and the relieved farmer took it, looking uncertainly at Duro as if they were toying with him and might lash out at any moment. "What's done is done," Bellicus said. "The gods spared us both. Now, come. Join us for an ale."

"Thank you, my lord," Elpin replied, standing aside to let them enter the king's hall. "But I must get back to the training grounds – the lord Lancelot is going to teach us how to use a sword in a shieldwall this afternoon. I...I'm so glad you survived."

"So am I," Bellicus said with a wave and a wry smile, passing and heading into the building, as the dazed Elpin hurried away to rejoin the rest of his comrades.

The hall was wonderfully cool as the men were sweating from their travels that morning and both were looking forward to resting for a time.

"When do you think you'll be able to spar again?" Duro asked as they gestured for a serving girl to bring them drinks. "I don't want to push you too fast, but if you're to build fitness and muscle mass, sparring is a good way to do it."

The druid glanced at his friend, an incredulous look on his gaunt face. "Spar? Are you mad?" He accepted a cup of ale from the servant with a nod of thanks then continued when she'd returned to her earlier task of replacing the straw on the hall floor. "I'm as weak as a kitten thanks to that farmer out there. I'd not be much of an opponent."

Duro waved his words away with a dismissive tut. "I'm not talking about fighting Eburus or me to the death in some gladiatorial arena, Bel. We'll take it easy and build you up slowly. You don't want to let your muscles atrophy much more or you'll never be as strong as you used to be."

Bellicus pondered his words as he supped his ale. He was a healer himself, that was one of a druid's most important duties, and he knew Duro's advice was good, but…Damn, he felt so tired after their trip to see Sulinus's cavalry! It shocked him just how weak he felt given how strong he usually was. If he could barely walk two or three miles without feeling like he'd scaled the great mountain of Ben Laomainn near his home in Alt Clota, how could he even contemplate picking up one of the double weighted wooden practice swords?

"Look," Duro said, understanding his reluctance. "I know it's hard trying to regain fitness – think back to how I looked when we first met. A fat baker that Horsa and his Saxons laughed at because they didn't think I was a threat. And you didn't think I'd be much use to you either, so you refused my offer to travel with you in your search for Princess Catia." He shook his head, grimacing as he thought back to his days trailing Bellicus through the countryside, pushing himself to stay close to the druid while exercising every night in an attempt to lose his excess bulk and somehow fit into his old centurion's uniform without bursting out of it. "That journey almost killed me but…" He leaned back and patted his stomach proudly. "It was worth it."

Bellicus smiled. "Aye, the Saxons didn't know what hit them when you exploded out of the dark like a wraith."

"Well then," the centurion said, gazing levelly at him. "Push yourself. Otherwise you'll be no use to me on this new mission Arthur wants to send me on."

They drank the rest of their ales in thoughtful silence and then, when the last drop had been downed, Bellicus pushed back his stool and stood up somewhat stiffly. "All right," he said. "I'll spar with you. But let me have a nap first, I honestly feel like I could sleep for a week."

"You already did," Duro replied sternly, before softening his tone and his frown. "But it's a start, I suppose. Fine, you go and have a rest, grandfather. I'll wake you before the evening meal is served and we can spar for a little while before joining the others for our food. I'll make a soldier out of you yet, Bellicus of Dun Breatann."

CHAPTER TWENTY-FOUR

"Seriously? I can't use that." The druid drew himself up to his full height and his outrage was clear as Duro handed him a child's practice sword, rather than the usual double-weighted one warriors used. "It's ridiculous!"

The centurion shook his head with the patient air of a father talking to a stubborn toddler. "Don't be an idiot, Bel," he said. "Before your nap you didn't think you would be up to sparring; now you want to go straight at it with the same gear you'd have used before your injury and sickness? Take the child's weapon. Take it! Good. Now, we'll start with this one and see how you go. If it's a waste of time we'll move you onto something bigger."

A young man and woman, locals, walked past on their way to the town centre, and, when the man saw the little sword in the giant druid's hand he called some insult which made his lady companion laugh and Bel shook his head, not feeling his mood improve any when he noticed Duro's lips also twitching in amusement. Bellicus was too well trained in the druid ways to let his irritation show on his face, but he did launch an attack on his friend without giving any warning.

Duro was using the usual, heavier practise sword, and it clattered against the druid's lighter one, drawing a yelp of pain from Bellicus who stepped back, rubbing his right bicep and grimacing. "That hurt more than I expected it would," he grumbled.

"Well, you've lost a lot of muscle mass all over," Duro replied. "You need to take it easy until you start to build those great arms of yours back up. Now, come on, let's work on your movement rather than your strength. Use your skill, not brute force."

Taking his older friend's advice on board, Bellicus came on again, aiming his strikes and parries with more care.

Too much care for the centurion's liking. "Relax, Bel," he growled. "You're thinking too much. I've seen you in battle, going into a trance and fighting as if you can sense what your opponent will do next. Let me see some of that." He swung a blow and the druid parried, but it was a clumsy deflection and brought another grunt of pain from Bellicus.

"I only go into that kind of trance if I'm in real danger," he said, warily watching Duro's sword as the centurion feinted and then lunged again. "Besides, the point isn't to beat you, is it? It's to build my strength up again. So, shut up and fight!"

They did, and, eventually, some form of rhythm was achieved, where both men were moving well, striking and parrying instinctively as their muscle memory took over and their years of combat experience guided their movements almost automatically. It didn't continue for very long, however, as Bellicus was soon drenched in sweat despite the fact it was overcast and not particularly warm that afternoon. He was also breathing heavily and clearly in some discomfort.

Duro kept the fight going for a little while longer, pushing Bellicus just past his current limits, and then he called a stop to it, smiling in encouragement as he did so. The druid gladly lowered his little sword and bent over, hands on his thighs as he drew in lungfuls of air like a man rescued from drowning.

"I'm in worse shape than I realised," he said between gulps. "But at least everything still seems to work." He continued to suck in air until, eventually, he straightened again and managed a smile. "I'm going to regret this little workout later but it's a start. A few more days of this and I'll be well on the mend."

Duro placed the swords back in their racks at the side of the practise ground and felt some personal satisfaction in his own current fitness, as he was not sweating or breathing hard at all. Quite some change from, as he'd noted earlier, the excess weight he'd been carrying when he first met Bellicus. It was something to be rightly proud of. "Do you know what else is good for rebuilding strength?" he asked as the pair started to walk back to the great hall.

"Aye," Bellicus nodded. "Plenty of good, rich ale, and freshly roasted meat."

"Definitely," the centurion agreed enthusiastically. "And maybe you should get some more exercise tonight after the feast, in that sick bed of yours. There's plenty of willing women in Caer Lerion, you know. Look," he nodded towards three ladies washing clothes in a great wooden bath a little way off the road. All were openly admiring them, particularly the tall, young druid and, when Duro looked back he could see them giggling and nudging one another.

Bellicus pushed a hand through his new thatch of hair and laughed. "Maybe I shouldn't bother shaving this," he said. "If the ladies like it. Maybe I will find someone to share my bed with – it's been a while. Not since Ria, in fact."

"Ah, Ria." Duro shook his head in admiration as he recalled the dark-haired druidess who had been Bellicus's woman for a short time but had ultimately betrayed them before disappearing from Dun Breatann just before her Pictish friends mounted an unsuccessful raid on the fortress. "She was quite the beauty," the centurion finished.

Thoughts of home made Bellicus feel slightly anxious, for, during his fever he'd suffered worrying dreams which he couldn't now fully remember. He knew they were about Narina and Catia, though, and hoped all was well back in Dun Breatann.

But they were in Caer Lerion now and the druid glanced at his friend, thought about his next words, and then, softly, he said. "Maybe it's time you allowed yourself to be with a woman again too, Duro." He wasn't sure how the centurion would react, and half expected an angry retort, but Bellicus had noticed a change in his companion's manner over the past few days. As if Duro was finally coming to terms with everything that had befallen him recently.

To Bellicus's relief, Duro shrugged thoughtfully and said, simply, "Maybe. One day."

No more needed to be said. The healing process had begun for both men, but it would take time and Bellicus knew Duro's "one day" really meant "but not today."

* * *

The hall was filled again that night, and the people were happy to be inside for, although summer was finally upon them, it was pouring with rain outside. A storm had blown in during the afternoon and only grown worse as night fell. Velugna and Eburus, who'd formed quite a bond after their recent ordeal, had taken seats within the hall early and saved space for Bellicus and Duro although the young couple only seemed interested in one another.

Bellicus saw the centurion peering up at the roof now as a rumble of thunder pealed directly overhead. Part of the druid

192

wished he could look out and see the lightning and torrents of rain drenching the town, but he feared catching a chill while he was still recovering from his fever.

"What are you looking at?" he asked. "You worried the roof might collapse?"

Duro shook his head and turned his eyes down to the table, finding his ale and swallowing a good mouthful. "No," he said. "Just looking for leaks. Can't see many – King Ceneu has this place nicely weatherproofed." He wiped his lips and grinned happily as he placed his drink back on the bench. "Not much better in life than being in a cosy hall with good friends, good meat and ale, and a roof to keep off the worst of a thunderstorm. Eat up. Get your strength back." He pushed a trencher laden with bread and roasted meat across to the druid who took a slice of beef and tore the fat from the side which he held out to Cai who was waiting for scraps beneath the bench.

"Aye, Caer Lerion is a hospitable town, compared to some," Bellicus agreed, catching the eye of the king and nodding in greeting. "I wonder what the entertainment will be tonight."

They didn't have long to wait for the answer to that. Someone, one of Ceneu's counsellors apparently, had questioned what gave Arthur the right to lead the army of the Britons and, rather than simply explaining to him, the king asked Merlin to tell the tale. The High Druid readily agreed, for he liked nothing better than a chance to build Arthur's legend and solidify his place as warlord of all the disparate peoples of the surrounding lands.

Of course, the gathered townsfolk, and those of Arthur's army of sufficient rank to be invited to the feast, such as Edern, and Sulinus, didn't know about this, but they expected to be entertained and, when Merlin got to his feet to address them a ripple of anticipation ran around the hall. Bellicus noticed the hunter who'd led them to the haunted ruins, Cocca, wearing a new silver arm-ring and sitting amongst the revellers, eyes already shining from too much ale. It pleased the druid to know the young man could only be there as a result of a recent promotion, undoubtedly thanks to his valour in the fight against Nynniaw.

Despite the storm it was a warm, muggy evening and the cooking fire only made things worse, so the doors and windows were open as far as possible without allowing too much of the downpour to blow inside. A flash of lightning filled those openings now, revealing the surrounding buildings outside, shining and slick with the rain and Duro's eyes sparkled, enjoying every moment of his night.

"Having fun, old friend?" Bellicus asked, turning away from Cocca to address Duro.

"I am," replied the centurion. "And I have a feeling that things are about to get even more enjoyable."

Merlin waited as the revellers grew silent in readiness for whatever he was going to say. He had his staff in his hand and Bellicus admired it in the flickering firelight. Unlike his own ash staff of office, with its heavy bronze eagle on top, Merlin's was made of oak and of simpler design. Its rich colour was enough to draw the eye though, and its excellent craftmanship was obvious, even to those at the furthest corners of the great hall.

"It all began," said Merlin without preamble, "with the sword in the stone."

There were mutterings from all and knowing nods from those who'd already heard rumours of the tale. It was, in truth, something the High Druid had told many times over the past few years, and it had inevitably grown with the telling. Bellicus was familiar with it, but he was as interested as anyone to hear the story from Merlin's own lips, especially in this setting which seemed charged with magic or, at least, anticipation.

"Since the Romans left our shores," the High Druid said, pacing in front of the table on the raised dais which he, along with Arthur and King Ceneu, were using for the feast, "these lands have struggled to find peace. Security. Freedom from invaders from all sides, be they Picts, Dalriadans, Hibernians, Jutes, Angles, Saxons...Our enemies seem numberless and relentless, and our lack of a single High King has always been an issue."

There were some murmurs at this, both in agreement and otherwise, for some still did not like the idea of being ruled by some king who might never have set foot in Caer Lerion.

Undeterred, Merlin went on. "There is strength in numbers, of course, and so those in my Order, Druids, suggested a warlord might be a palatable solution to the problem. A man who could lead an army built upon warriors from every land in Britain." He raised a hand and gestured as he listed these places which would be expected to provide fit soldiers for this hypothetical army. "Alt Clota, Dumnonia, Powys, and so on, including, of course, Caer Lerion, which has, for generations, been known as a town filled with hardy fighters."

This brought a chorus of happy agreement and mugs were thumped on benches, sending dogs scurrying in the rushes underneath, lapping at the spilled ale.

"The kings and queens and great lords of Britain accepted our proposal, agreeing to provide a portion of their own warbands to join with this new, combined army of Britons. But..." He paused and looked about at the listening men and women. "Who should lead such a mighty force? Giving a king control of the biggest army in the land could lead to temptation. Lead them to think they might use their warriors to take over the lands of their nearest neighbour. And then the next nearest, and so on. This was, of course, no idle fantasy – Roman generals such as Julius Caesar had used their armies to march on Rome and seize control of the empire after all. So, who could be trusted to take charge of our army of Britons?"

Everyone was looking at Arthur, knowing what the answer to Merlin's question was, but interested to hear his reasons. It was true the warlord was young, lean and had a general air of competency and command about him, but so did many other men in the hall that night. What marked this Arthur as special?

"Who could choose this warlord," Merlin asked, raising his arms as he gazed out on the people gathered before him, "but the gods themselves?"

More muttering, and King Ceneu was frowning, being a follower of Christ, not the old deities like Taranis and Belenus. This tale was far too intriguing to be interrupted however, and Merlin continued before anyone could decry his gods.

"There had been a sword," he said, "magically embedded, point first, in a great lump of stone for...Well, no-one knows how long exactly. Æons, undoubtedly."

"Who put it there?" someone near the king's table asked respectfully, curiosity getting the best of them.

Merlin pursed his lips and shook his head slightly. "One old legend says Cernunnos himself thrust the blade into the stone many hundreds of years ago. Another claims it was Sulis Minerva.

One even states it was some disciple of the Christ," he frowned thoughtfully, as if trying to remember this saint's name although Bellicus knew his fellow druid recalled the man's name perfectly well. "Joseph of, where was it? Arimathea, that's it, yes. Joseph of Arimathea."

"I've heard of him," a man in the very centre of the many benches called out, and more of the locals claimed that, yes, they too knew of this follower of their martyred God. A very holy man, it was said. Bellicus smiled, understanding how clever this story of Merlin's was, to make it appeal to those who worshipped both the old gods and the new.

"One thread that runs through all of the old legends, however," the High Druid said, raising his chin and stroking his flowing white beard, "is the claim that this sword could only be drawn from the stone by the rightful warlord of Britain. Note," he said, raising a hand before this could be questioned, "I said *warlord*, not *king*. The person to draw the sword would be chaste, and pure, and have no ambitions of personal glory. No." He shook his head gravely and made a slashing motion with his right hand. "Whoever could draw free the sword – claim it for their own – would win no riches, or lands, or glory for themselves. They would be a servant of Britain, and all who would live here in peace."

Again, eyes were focused on Arthur who appeared very noble with his neatly trimmed beard and long brown hair which was slightly receding despite still being in his twenties. He certainly looked the part of one born to lead. He had an aura of confidence, of self-belief, which impressed everyone gathered there that night and added gravitas to the old druid's story.

"Many tried to draw the sword free from the stone," Merlin told them, and his tone was that of a man recounting something he knew everyone must have heard about before, as if this part of the tale was well-known throughout Caer Lerion. It wasn't, of course, but no-one admitted their ignorance, and many nodded as if they knew very well what he was talking about. "Over the years some even attempted to force the blade from its stone prison – without success, obviously, for brute strength can never overcome magic."

Merlin's eyes swept across the room, meeting Bellicus's for a moment, and both men smiled knowingly before the High Druid went on with his story.

"Even I can't say how many decades passed with the sword gripped in that stone embrace. The magic that placed it there stopped it from rusting, but it seemed none would ever be able to claim it and take up their place as rightful warlord of Britain. Until the Beltane feast of five years ago…" He stopped and turned his back on the hall to take a drink from his cup which lay on King Ceneu's table.

Bellicus watched the people, admiring his brother druid's storytelling skill – Merlin, like an expert fisherman, truly had his audience hooked.

"Is this all true?" the centurion whispered, but Bellicus merely shrugged.

"I assume so," he said, and then fell silent as Merlin took up his tale once more.

"The Beltane celebration of five years ago was held not too far from here, in Elmet," the High Druid told them, and there were nods for all knew the place and some had even been there. "King Ceneu himself attended."

"I did," the king admitted as Merlin glanced in his direction. "In the days before I was baptised in the One True Faith. I used to enjoy such occasions."

"Indeed," cried Merlin. "As well as feasting, there were foot races, wrestling, archery and sword-fighting competitions." He was using his whole body to act out these various pastimes and the audience were grinning at his lithe, and often amusing, movements. "Many great lords attended that particular Beltane celebration, and several of my own order. And we were all lucky, for we saw history being made that day." His eyes were shining as he gazed out, not at the crowd gathered there that night, but into the past he was describing. A log in the fire cracked and split open in a shower of sparks making many in the hall flinch, but Merlin didn't even seem to notice its loud report. "It had become a tradition," he said matter-of-factly, "for anyone of note visiting Elmet to try and draw the sword from its stone prison. That Beltane morning was no different, as lords and ladies grasped the ancient, leather-wrapped grip, and used every drop of their strength to dry and drag the blade free. All who tried envisioned themselves raising the miraculous blade aloft and claiming their rightful place as the protector of Britain." He lifted his own staff overhead, staring up into the smoky rafters, then smiled and addressed a wide-eyed, burly warrior seated in front of him. "They all failed of course. Until Arthur tried."

He laughed shortly, then walked back to retake his seat at the king's table. He sipped from his cup and lifted some meat from a trencher which he ate thoughtfully before licking the juices from his fingers. He seemed to have finished his tale and it took a while before someone called out, a little peevishly, "Is that it?"

Merlin gazed into the gloomy rear of the hall from whence the shout had come then lifted another slice of meat and popped it into his mouth. "Well, yes. Arthur pulled the sword from the stone in full view of a dozen kings and noblemen, not least your own lord."

Ceneu nodded but Bellicus could tell the king was not entirely pleased. He had a suspicious look in his eyes, as if he suspected more than the gods – or even his new One True God – had a part in Arthur's claiming of the sword that day half a decade past. Bellicus felt a smile pull at the edges of his mouth, for he agreed with Ceneu in believing Merlin knew a lot more about this magical event than he was admitting.

The great lords and ladies had accepted it at that Beltane celebration though, and they, along with the druids that had been there, spread the word, so it was now enshrined in the lore of the land, whatever the truth might have been.

Who in that hall could doubt Arthur's status as warlord of Britain now?

Still, the people wanted an exciting end to the story, and Merlin surely knew it.

"This all seems like heathen mummery to me," a voice cried out from the very centre of the revellers. "Caer Lerion is a Christian town."

Merlin's face grew dark, eyebrows coming together as he sought out the source of the voice. "Heathen, Christian, I tell you all the gods recognise Arthur as the rightful Warlord of Britain. You doubt my word?"

His tone was low, dangerous, but the man in the crowd would not back down. "Hard to believe a tale like yours without seeing proof."

Merlin spun and stared at Arthur. "Give me your sword, please, my lord."

198

He held out his hand and Arthur stood up, drawing his blade from its sheath and passing it pommel-first to the druid without saying a word.

"Your name?"

The man in the audience stood up and he appeared surprisingly confident despite so many eyes being on him. This was his home, though, and these were his kith and kin gathered here for this feast. "Bran," he said in a firm, unwavering tone.

"You think you might have been the one to draw the sword from the stone, Bran?" Merlin held up Arthur's weapon, the firelight glinting off it to reveal its exquisite workmanship. In this position it reminded one of the cross Christians were so fond of venerating and Bellicus guessed that was Merlin's intent.

Bran shook his head. "No. I'm not some great lord. I'm just a simple carpenter." He shrugged. "Maybe God would have chosen me that day, though – a Christian, rather than Arthur, who still follows your Old Ways."

A few people, Christians Bellicus surmised, muttered agreement at this, feeling like Bran's logic made perfect sense. Although drawing the sword had not made Arthur a king, he wielded power and influence, wore fine clothes and weaponry – his position was one many people coveted.

Merlin gazed coolly out over the heads of the feasting townsfolk and then his eyes blazed with fury. "Let's see then, shall we?" he said and although he did not shout his voice rang out, filling every corner of King Ceneu's mighty hall. Without another word, he grasped the pommel and grip of Arthur's sword in both hands and plunged it down into the wooden floor of the dais with all his might.

Even the strongest warrior should have only been able to drive the sword a finger's width or so into the sturdy pine boards in this manner yet, to everyone's surprise, the sharp point bit deeply into the wood and, when Merlin let it go a good quarter of the blade was stuck fast.

"Come up, then, Bran of Caer Lerion, carpenter and would-be Warlord of Britain! Ask your Christ to grant you the strength to draw the sword and claim your rightful place at the head of our combined army."

For the first time, Bran seemed uncertain and nervous. He remained seated, licking his lips and fidgeting with his ale mug, but those around him – Christian or not – shouted encouragement. They wanted to see the carpenter at least attempt to take the sword. How hard could it be after all? And Bran was a strong man thanks to his work, with powerful arms and shoulders. Maybe he would be able to claim the magic sword and what would happen then?

"Go on, Bran," called the revellers. "Take it!"

The lure of the prize was too much for him and he stood up, wiping sweating palms on his leggings. "Lord King…?"

Ceneu was as interested to find out what would happen next as anyone else in the hall and eagerly waved his subject forward. In truth, it had always rankled with the king that some unknown youngster with no royal lineage had been given the title of Warlord and, should Bran fail to claim the sword here, perhaps Ceneu could have another try…

Bellicus could see all this very clearly on the king's face and, looking about, it was mirrored on many other faces in the hall. He wondered what Merlin was doing. To put so much effort into solidifying Arthur's position over the past few years, only to throw it into jeopardy should some carpenter who'd probably never even left Caer Lerion in his life could pull the sword from the pine boards…It seemed incredibly foolish of the High Druid.

Of course, Bellicus knew Merlin was anything but a fool and, like everyone else, he wondered how things would play out as Bran stepped onto the dais before Merlin, Ceneu, and Arthur.

The carpenter seemed to be regretting his decision to heckle Merlin now, but the druid pointed at the blade protruding from the dais's floor and barked, "Draw it then, if you can!"

Once more wiping the perspiration from his palms, Bran stepped forward, grasped the sword by its grip and pulled. Muscles corded in his forearms and biceps, and his jaw tightened as he put everything he had into his attempt.

The sword did not budge, even after one final, desperate pull.

Sweating and beaten, Bran stood up, arching his back for his spine ached from his exertions.

"Your God does not seem to be on your side, my friend," Merlin said with no trace of mockery. "You may return to your place."

Mollified and even mortified, Bran, eyes downcast, stepped off the dais and walked back to his bench, downing his ale and gruffly demanding a refill from a serving girl as Merlin looked imperiously around the hall.

"Anyone else care to try, or are we—"

"I'll try, druid."

Merlin turned but King Ceneu was already beside him. He'd moved before the druid even had a chance to finish his invitation.

"You already tried once, my lord," Merlin said, shrugging. "And failed. But this is your hall." He stepped away from the stuck sword and clasped his hands to watch the king's attempt.

Ceneu did not immediately take a hold of the sword's grip. Instead, he looked around at the folk gathered in his great hall – each one of them taking advantage of his hospitality, eating his food and drinking his ale – and spread his arms wide.

"My people," he said. "Arthur here has proven himself to be a decent man and a capable warlord." He turned and nodded respectfully, receiving a response in kind from the younger man. "I've been happy to have him here in my lands during recent times. But…" He pointed behind him, at the cross on the wall above the dais. "It seems to me that God has given us a chance to take the place of a heathen. To have a follower of Christ as Warlord of Britain would…" He shook his head as if overcome at the possibilities to do his God's work.

Bellicus, of course, could see through this, and probably many of the people there also knew Ceneu wanted to expand his own power by taking this title from Arthur, despite the fact Merlin had already said the Warlord of Britain should specifically not be a king, or tied to any one land. Still, the High Druid seemed content to let Ceneu try.

The king lowered his head and began to solemnly intone the words of a prayer, his followers joining in, voices combining in a sonorous drone which Bellicus found quite relaxing yet strangely at odds with his idea of how one should commune with the gods. He could see why this new religion was growing so fast: it was easy. Anyone could do this, at any time, with no prior planning, no meditation, no real effort. Just recite words effortlessly learned and that was you in touch with 'God'.

To Bellicus it was laughable, yet at the same time frightening. There was little, perhaps no thought put into this prayer the people were mumbling along to, but he could see a fervour in their eyes, almost a blissful look. It was enticing and actually gave the druid a newfound respect for Christianity as a whole. Perhaps the druids should learn from this new religion, if it wasn't too late.

At last, King Ceneu finished his prayer and, drawing himself up and puffing out his chest, he reached down, called out, "God, help me!" and pulled with all his might at the sword embedded in the pine floorboards that formed the dais his table rested upon.

There was a collective indrawing of breath as the people of Caer Lerion fortunate enough to be at the feast that night watched their leader filled with the righteous power of God, pull, and pull until his face was scarlet with the effort. At one point it seemed there was just a slight movement, a little give, and Ceneu's face lit up with triumph, but a moment later he was still standing there, tugging at a sword that remained stuck fast in its wooden prison.

"Damn you, druid!" Ceneu finally admitted defeat with poor grace, letting go of the sword and flailing his arms like a spoiled child having a tantrum. He stormed back to his seat and, like the carpenter, Bran, before him, downed two cups of ale in quick succession.

Merlin allowed all this to sink in for a few moments, nodding ever so slightly as his piercing gaze swept around the room from Ceneu to Bellicus and all around the breathless revellers before, at last, he was looking at Arthur.

"Warlord," he said, in a voice that rang with power. "Reclaim your blade."

Grim of face but steady of step, Arthur rose up from his place next to the beaten king and came around the bench to stand next to the white-bearded High Druid. They stood facing one another in silence for a heartbeat, and then Arthur reached out with his right hand and, with seemingly very little effort, pulled his sword from the floor.

There were gasps and cries of amazement and even raucous cheering throughout the hall as he raised it aloft, letting all gathered there see its blade reflecting the orange-yellow glow of the hearth, and then he pushed it back into its sheath and, with a final nod to Merlin, returned to his seat.

"How?" Duro demanded, eyes shining with amazement, an expression which was mirrored all through the room at that moment. "How in Mithras' name is it possible?"

"How is it possible?" Merlin cried, overhearing the centurion's words somehow in the uproar and fastening on them like a tenacious dog with a bone. "Quite simply, lords and ladies," he said, holding his arms aloft until the people grew quiet, "the gods, or One True God if you prefer, have once again given their blessing to the man they would see as Warlord." He threw his arm back, pointing with his open hand at the young, bearded man sitting next to the scowling King Ceneu. "Arthur, Bear of Britain!"

The carpenter, Bran, was first to raise his ale mug in salute and call out, "the Bear of Britain!" with good grace. Seeing this, others followed his lead and even the king eventually joined in.

Taking his cue, Arthur stood up and smiled beatifically at the people calling his name. Merlin had completely won them over with his display and they were perfectly happy to accept Arthur as their warlord. In truth, they'd not been too bothered about it before but now they were utterly convinced of his divine right to lead the army of Britons and Bellicus knew word of this night's events would quickly spread, like a flame on a clump of dried mushrooms, throughout the countryside.

Arthur's legend was growing, and that was always a good thing when one needed to inspire the loyalty of the people.

"Thank you," said the warlord, meeting the eyes of the people and bowing respectfully to them, almost like a friend, rather than a powerful nobleman or a king looking down on his subjects. He was well aware of his status and the folk gathered there appreciated his humility in this moment. "My friends, I did not seek the title of Warlord, but the Merlin and other great men of these lands believed I should be given the honour. The gods seemed to agree. My first, and main task, is to destroy Hengist and his Saxon hordes." He slammed a hand down on the bench, making King Ceneu's expensive glass ale cup jump alarmingly. "I have vowed to drive them back into the sea and, with your support, it can be a reality. Death to Hengist!"

He lifted his drink and held it up as Bran, Bellicus, Duro, Ceneu and everyone else in the hall took up the chant.

"Death to Hengist! Death to Hengist! Death to Hengist!"

It was a fine way to end the evening's entertainment and Bellicus, too stuffed with meat and ale to be bothered moving, dropped his head onto the bench and allowed sleep to overtake him.

* * *

When he awoke the feast was over and the dark of night could be seen through the un-shuttered windows. Duro was dozing beside him, and Cai, as ever, was content at his feet. King Ceneu, Merlin, and Arthur were all gone, leaving the table on the dais empty. Bellicus guessed it must be the middle of the night and, still sleepy, decided to lay his head back down on the bench and make the most of the silence.

Then he heard a gentle thump, followed by a scraping that pierced the still of the night. No-one stirred, however, and Bellicus looked at the king's table, where the sound seemed to have come from. There was no movement, but then there was another, more prolonged scraping, as of wood rubbing against wood and the now alert druid dropped a hand to Melltgwyn at his side and made ready to wake Cai.

The fire had been allowed to burn low in the hearth and there was little light within the hall so it was with some astonishment that Bellicus saw a child suddenly appear as if from nowhere. One moment there was nothing, and then, as if by some strange magic, a boy stood silhouetted beside the king's table. Then the diminutive figure crouched low and there was a low grunting and then the child stood up again and moved with a kind of shambling gait, almost a waddle, towards the side door.

Bellicus stared, mind still fuzzy from sleep and the drink he'd imbibed during the feast, wondering what in the world he was seeing. As the small figure approached the hearth, the extra light revealed a broad set of shoulders and the druid realised he was not watching a child, but a small man and, from the way he was walking, he was carrying something heavy.

A breeze wafted through the hall, making the hairs on the back of Bellicus's neck rise and he shivered at the icy sensation. "By Cernunnos," he whispered as he watched the bizarre scene play out. "What's going on?"

Now, with the figure directly in front of the low fire its orange glow revealed more detail. Although the man's face was turned away from the light, hiding his features, the object he carried could be seen, glittering strangely in his muscular arms.

It was a rock of some kind. A rather large and clearly heavy rock.

What could it mean?

And then, as the little shambling shadow neared the door, it came close to one of the benches and, as Bellicus looked on, the iron, eating knife of some other sleeping reveller suddenly shot through the air and stuck, with a dull, metallic clatter, against the rock. The little man didn't bother to stop, if anything he moved even faster, finally reaching the door which was lying open to let in the cool night air and disappearing outside.

Bellicus's hand was still gripping his sheathed sword and he looked down to see if Cai had been a witness to any of this. The giant dog was still sleeping, as was everyone else in the hall, including Duro, who suddenly snorted loudly, choked a little, and then his breathing returned to normal and he slept on, oblivious.

The druid let go of his sword and smiled. As he lowered his head onto the table and the pillow made by the crook of his arm, he knew the gods had woken him from his slumber at just the right moment. A story came to mind, one an old Roman called Pliny had told about a shepherd named Magnes, whose iron-nailed shoes became stuck to an unusual rock formation through some weird, almost magical attraction. Was there something similar at play here?

But Bellicus was tired, and still weak from his injury, and he knew there was no danger from the little man with the heavy stone load, so sleep soon overcame him again. When he awoke in the morning, the druid felt more alive than he had in days.

CHAPTER TWENTY-FIVE

Ideally, they would have had more time to prepare. For Bellicus to fully build himself back up and feel like his old self once again. Arthur had great need of more men as soon as possible however and, as a result, the druid and his centurion companion were on the road together once more. Cai was, of course, with them, loping along beside Bellicus's big black, Darac, and Duro's mount, Pryderi.

Eburus, although still spending much of his time with Princess Velugna, would have liked to come with them, but Arthur wanted a man of his physical prowess and martial skill within his ranks when it came time to face the Saxons. Besides, the warlord and Bellicus both feared the headstrong young champion could be a liability on what was supposed to be a diplomatic mission for druid and centurion. So Merlin had given the pair a list of nobles – minor warlords and kings mainly of smaller lands surrounding Caer Lerion – who'd 'forgotten' to send men to join Arthur's army in the spring as had been agreed.

At least, it had been agreed between Arthur and the more powerful rulers of the various Briton factions and tribes, but perhaps some of them had not passed the command down to their neighbours and subordinates. Kings like Vortigern in northern Cymry, and Uriens of Rheged, had supplied men without too much prompting, for it made sense, even to those on the western coast of the island, to try and stave off the raiding warriors known generally by the catch-all term 'Saxons'. Other British kings, such as Constans in the far south, had hopefully sent men who simply hadn't arrived yet.

But there were some chieftains who'd failed to supply their quota of men this year and, with it being into summer now, Arthur knew he must send messengers to remind them of their obligations.

"How long will this mission take do you think?" Duro wondered as they rode along the road leading north. "We'll have to be as fast as possible or it'll be pointless. Even if we manage to persuade every one of the lords on Merlin's list, by the time they send soldiers to join Arthur the war will be over for winter, unless we get round them all quickly."

"Agreed," Bellicus said, watching as four magpies – two adults and two youngsters with smaller, fluttering wings and high-pitched calls – searched a nearby field for worms. "We won't have time to enjoy each chief's hospitality, assuming they feel like extending such niceties to us." He rubbed his eyes and thought of the long list Arthur and the High Druid had tasked them with visiting. "Gods willing, we can be round all of these in a month or so."

"Really?" Duro sounded surprised but then he didn't really have much knowledge of Britain's geography, especially compared to Bellicus who'd learned all about it during his early years with the druids.

"Aye," Bellicus affirmed. "We're not going from one end of the island to the other. Merlin's list only really includes the lands around Caer Lerion. We'll even be able to visit two or three of the names on the list in a single day if we ride hard."

"And you know where we're going?"

"Aye, I know well enough where the larger settlements are. For the smaller places, we'll ask for directions." He shrugged. "As long as we get around the main chiefs, who have the most men to provide, I don't think we need worry too much about missing some of the smaller places if they're too difficult to find."

A month. Bellicus had been happy to accompany his friend on this journey for it wasn't like the last quest they'd been sent on together, to kill the king of Dalriada. That had seen them visiting enemy lands, filled with men who would have killed them instantly had they known who they were. The towns and villages they'd be visiting in the coming weeks were all ostensibly friendly, ruled by men who'd already agreed to help Arthur, or at least their own kings had.

No, this mission should be safe and simple and see them back amongst Arthur's forces, fit and healthy, by the height of the summer.

Their first stop was in a small settlement called Caer Bach, and things went smoothly enough. They arrived mid-morning, spoke to the local lord, and he somewhat sheepishly apologised for his tardiness then promised to send what men he could spare to Arthur. The village barely held a dozen small houses so Bellicus and Duro both felt there wouldn't be much of an army going from here to join the warlord, but every man would be gladly welcomed. If every small village supplied even just two or three men it would soon become a considerable warband and possibly mean the difference between defeating Hengist's hordes or being completely overrun.

Druid, centurion, and dog were quickly on the road again, cloaks stowed away and sleeves rolled up as the riders made the most of the sunshine and aimed to turn their rather pasty white skin a little browner.

"Where next?" Duro asked, shading his eyes as he looked about at a land bursting with life. A stream snaked through the greenery, sunlight sparkling from its gently rippling surface and two figures could be seen on the bank, poles in hand as they attempted to catch some fish for their supper that night. The centurion had eaten some bread and blue cheese in Caer Bach but he still felt his mouth watering at the thought of the fishermen's catch – bream swam in these parts, a favourite of Duro's, who could almost smell it roasting on a spit over a campfire. Gods, he loved days like this!

"Thinking about your stomach again?" Bellicus asked with a wry grin, once again seeming to read his friend's mind, a habit the centurion had once found disconcerting but now accepted as the normal way of things. "Our next stop is a place called," he took out the scrap of parchment Merlin had given him and read off the second name on the list: "Cwrt Isel. Not too far. I'm sure if you ask nicely the lord there will cook a plate of bream for you."

As it turned out, Elffin, chieftain of Cwrt Isel, was already spit-roasting some fish as there was a feast in the town that day, for no other reason than it was sunny, and Elffin felt like enjoying himself.

Cwrt Isel was a small hamlet with around sixty inhabitants, and it looked prosperous enough at first glance. When Bellicus and Duro arrived there, they noted many of the houses had their walls and doors recently stained, the roofs freshly thatched and the main gates, although open, appeared sturdy. When one looked a little closer, however, it was apparent that the newly stained wooden houses were rotting in places and, although the gates were strong, sections of the timber wall surrounding the place had fallen down in the winter storms and never been repaired. The sight of many people feasting in the middle of the day when they should have been working only added to the impression of decadence.

"I can see why the chief here didn't send any of his men," Duro muttered as they dismounted at a stable which seemed to have no one there to take care of their horses. "They're all too busy enjoying themselves."

Bellicus looked around, hoping to see a boy coming to look after the animals, but no-one appeared. "It's not my place to tell folk how to run their settlements," he said. "But if the Saxons were to turn up here the place would be a smouldering ruin in the blink of an eye. Let's hope the lord at least lets us share in his feast."

"Why wouldn't he?" Duro wondered as they set about rubbing their horses down themselves and Cai lapped noisily at a trough of water. "We're representatives of Arthur. You're a druid."

"Exactly," Bellicus said, nodding towards the table set up on the grass in the centre of the town. The lord was obvious from his place at the head of that table, but beside him sat a rotund, bald man, wearing a white linen tunic with darker, patterned bands around the sleeves and, even from that distance the wooden cross hanging around his neck was visible, it was so large.

"A priest, or a bishop," Duro noted. "This is another Christian place." He patted his horse and set down the grooming brush where he'd found it. "I can't see it being an issue. Merlin wouldn't have sent us here if the lord was hostile to druids. Would he?"

The bishop was staring at them now, laughing at some joke of the lord's, cup in hand.

"I don't know," Bellicus replied. "Maybe Merlin thinks we can handle the bishop if he causes trouble. Perhaps he thought it would be amusing to send us into an…uncomfortable situation."

"Or perhaps he wanted to remind the people in this town that Arthur is their warlord and worthy of their respect even if he, and most of his followers, worship the elder gods. Who better to command respect than a mighty centurion and his druid companion?" He grinned and patted his lean belly. "Come on, you're worrying over nothing. Let's go and join in the feast, I'm sure the Lord Elffin will welcome a couple more revellers."

Duro's optimism faded along with his smile as they approached the long table on the grassy town centre and the twenty or so gathered townsfolk ceased laughing and chattering. The bishop whispered something to the lord, pointing at Bellicus's eagle-topped staff, and both their faces grew dark as the newcomers strode towards them.

Elffin did not rise to greet the travellers. He didn't even speak, he simply glared at them, as if their presence irritated him. The bishop fingered his cross as he eyed Bellicus with obvious disapproval.

Anger rose in the druid but he held it in check, sharing a look with Duro and then scanning the silent gathering before turning back to the lord and returning the man's black expression.

Elffin was a large man, that much was obvious even seated as he was. His shoulders were much wider than the rotund bishop's and his head was higher than any of the other men at the table. He had the look of a warrior, but Bellicus could also see the spark of intelligence behind his eyes as they stared at one another. Elffin was not a man to be easily cowed.

The druid had spent many hours perfecting his stare though, gazing into an old bronze mirror in his youth until he'd perfected it. It was always an advantage to be able to stare down an opponent, a psychological victory before any verbal or even physical attacks were thrown. Elffin held Bellicus's glare for a time, but eventually the lord blinked and looked away as his eyes tired and grew dry. As he opened his mouth to speak, and undoubtedly attempt to belittle the druid and regain some sense of authority over the situation, Bellicus broke in.

"Is this how you welcome guests, my Lord Elffin? Your hospitality's a disgrace; you should be embarrassed."

"What d'you want here, druid?" the bishop demanded. "Your kind isn't welcome in Cwrt Isel."

"Bishop Adelphius is right," the chief agreed. "This is a Christian village. We have no need for whatever druid potions you're here to sell us, so be on your way before my men chase you."

"Your men?" Duro interjected before Elffin finished speaking. "Would that be the men you promised to send to Arthur, Warlord of Britain? Those men I see sitting about feasting when they should be travelling to join the army that stands against the Saxons and the inevitable destruction of this town? Is that the men you mean?" His voice was rich and powerful, honed on the training grounds of the legions in his youth and brought back to full strength in recent days as he helped drill the recruits in Arthur's army and Elffin blanched as he took in the centurion's words.

"You're here on behalf of the warlord?"

"Aye," Bellicus confirmed, allowing his anger to show now. "And we're hungry and thirsty so are you going to invite us to your feast, or do we return to Arthur and tell him what a stinking shit-hole Cwrt Isel is?"

That didn't go down at all well with the locals, some of them even rising to their feet as if ready to start brawling with the giant, but still-weakened, druid. Cai bared his teeth, hackles rising, and that was enough to stop anyone from actually leaving their place at the feasting tables.

"Enough!" Elffin roared, using his hands to command his people to take their seats again before returning his stare to Bellicus. His demeanour was more welcoming now although not quite friendly. Instead, he had the air of a man who simply wanted to get through an unpleasant, but unavoidable, experience, like a trip to a healer to have a rotten tooth pulled. Necessary, but hardly enjoyable. "Come, sit at my table, guests," he said, looking to his left and waving away the two men sitting next to him. They offered no argument but gave druid and centurion venomous glances as they gave up their places.

Bellicus took a cup of ale from a serving girl but, despite his earlier declaration of hunger, refused the food she offered. Duro took some charred bream from her with a smile, eating the tasty flesh and sharing some leftover scraps with Cai who eagerly wolfed it down.

The townsfolk looked on glumly but after a time they went back to their feasting in the sunshine, forgetting for now about the insult the druid had bestowed on their home.

Before Elffin could offer an excuse for why he hadn't sent any men to join the army of gathering Britons, the bishop spoke up, suggesting to Bellicus that the clergyman had a lot of authority in the town if he could speak so freely even before his lord.

"We can't spare men to send to your pagan warlord," said the bald fellow primly and definitively. "We need them all here."

"For what?" Duro demanded. He was beginning to enjoy this role as Arthur's emissary. There might not be an army physically with him, but these minor noblemen still feared its existence. "It seems to me your people spend more time enjoying themselves," the centurion said, "than working. How can you justify yourself?" This last was directed at Elffin, as Duro had not come here to deal with a churchman.

Frowning, the chief shook his head. "We don't spend every day feasting," he protested. "Are you mad? This was a rare opportunity for our people to enjoy the sunshine. God knows, we see it seldom enough." He raised his hand and swept it around to encompass the houses closest to them. "Look, are you blind? The buildings in my settlement are all freshly painted for the summer. That didn't happen by itself."

Duro stood up and walked across to the nearest of the houses Elffin had gestured towards. He looked at the door frame, nodding his head, then kicked it. A small shower of damp wood exploded at his boot's touch and he turned back to the outraged chief. "You've the treated the wood so it looks nice, I'll grant you that," the centurion said. "But the stuff is rotten beneath its fresh coating." He pointed then to one of the fallen palisade wall sections. "Do you think that will stop the Saxons when they come hunting for plunder, and slaves, and men to slaughter?" The townspeople were angry again, but Duro addressed them, spreading his arms wide as he continued. "I *know* what the Saxons do to a town – I've seen it. They wrecked my home, Luguvalium, and murdered my wife. I don't want to see the bastards do the same to any more settlements. You people need to wake up and realise how big a threat the sea-wolves are!"

His words, spoken passionately, did strike home with those sober enough to take them in and he returned to his seat beside Bellicus with a grim expression, lifting up his ale and sipping it very slowly.

The druid could see his friend's hand shaking with emotion and he faced Elffin once more. "Duro speaks the truth," he said. "This is why you, and every other nobleman in the area, must send as many men as you can spare to join Arthur—"

"Arthur's a pagan," the bishop interrupted, looking down at his embroidered sleeves as if the druid was of so little importance that he need not meet his eye. "We don't bow to the wishes of a man who worships false gods. It shows he has bad judgement in all things. Hengist and your Arthur can let their heathen savages slaughter one another, and leave the world free for those of us who follow Christ."

Before Bellicus could reply, Elffin raised a hand to halt the inevitable angry retort and said, with a look at Duro, "I accept your testimony, centurion. I believe your words are true."

Bellicus nodded, pleased that they were finally getting somewhere, but his heart sank when he met the lord's eyes and saw, not sincerity but cunning. His fears were confirmed when the chief continued.

"Since you say the Saxons are such an imminent threat to us all, I must make every effort to repair our defences." He jerked his chin at the collapsed wall. "That needs raised again, along with the others that have come down. And we must see to our doors, strengthening the rotten wood you so helpfully pointed out, centurion. If the Saxons manage to breach our walls, well, we must have secure homes to seek refuge in, eh?"

"I'd say that's a good idea," Duro agreed.

"It'll be a lot of work," Elffin said, shaking his head ruefully but a small, sly smile was pulling at the edges of his mouth. "It'll take a lot of men and, as you can see," he looked about the place, "our hamlet is not a large one. If I'm to oversee this rebuilding project I'm going to need every man I can muster which means, I'm afraid…"

"That we won't be able to send a single one to your heathen warlord," the bishop finished triumphantly.

Some of the other revellers had been listening to this exchange and, overjoyed by their leaders' cleverness, laughed, cheered, and hammered their cups and mugs on the tables. Neither Bellicus nor Duro joined in with the merriment.

Sighing, the druid said, to no-one in particular, "I'm sick of trying to explain to people what the Saxons will do to them if we don't stop them before they grow too strong. Are you ready Duro? We might as well move onto the next settlement and see if their lord has more intelligence than this lackwit."

This brought more laughs, this time of disbelief and expectation. The townsfolk knew Elffin was not a man to take such an insult without offering something back – hopefully some good old fashioned physical violence. The jowly bishop was also

213

watching, mouth practically watering in anticipation at the thought of a pagan druid being put in his place.

Duro loosened his spatha in its sheath and, with an inward, yet excited sigh, prepared for the inevitable fight.

CHAPTER TWENTY-SIX

Elffin got to his feet, ignoring the low growl that came from the dog at Bellicus's feet. Cai could sense the threat just as easily as anyone else, but the lord didn't seem worried by the great mastiff which Duro felt was a bad sign. The man must be a fearsome warrior if he felt no trepidation at the sound of the monstrous dog's warning, not to mention the druid himself.

Of course, Bellicus was a shadow of his usual self, and, as Elffin faced up to the druid, Duro wished his friend hadn't spoken so harshly. The Lord of Cwrt Isel was a head shorter than Bellicus but his shoulders were nearly as broad and his arms were heavily muscled. He also had the stance and composure of a born fighter, not to mention dozens of his own people to back him up.

"You come to my town," said the chief in a low, dangerous voice, "and call me a lackwit in front of my people?" He shook his head as if astonished by the turn of events. "Are you so arrogant, druid, that you believe you can ride around the country, visiting places you've not been invited to and are not welcome, and threaten and insult noblemen like me? What gives you the right?"

Now this surprised Duro. He'd expected Elffin to attack Bellicus with his fists and hoped rather than expected the druid to win the fight, but this? He actually felt some sympathy with the chief. Framed in words such as he'd used, his point of view seemed completely fair.

"The right?" Bellicus replied, pushing his shoulders back to tower over the lord. "You act as if we've somehow wronged you, Elffin, but it was you who pledged men to Arthur's cause. What kind of a leader are you if you can break an oath so easily? You've treated us – travellers – with contempt from the moment we arrived, going against the ancient traditions of hospitality and general decency." He turned to the bishop then. "Is this how Christians behave? Isn't one of your own teachings, 'treat others as you wish to be treated yourself'?"

"What do you know of my religion?" the clergyman spat, but Bellicus broke in, voice rising, filled with power and strength.

"I probably know more about Christianity than you do, fool," he hissed, pointing at his head and staring at the bishop as he recited, *"'Hear this, you stupid and senseless people! You have eyes, but you cannot see. You have ears, but you cannot hear.'* Jeremiah, chapter five, verse twenty-one. Now sit in silence, and try to use your eyes and ears while adults speak!"

To the townsfolk's astonishment, Bishop Adelphius did sit, a look of shock on his face, as if he had no control over his limbs. No-one had ever known the churchman to be cowed by anyone – he always had to get the last word in any argument and never accepted he was wrong so... To see him sitting, mute, like a scolded child, amazed those watching.

"Farewell, then, Lord Elffin of Cwrt Isel," Bellicus growled, "henceforth known throughout Britain as Elffin the Oath-Breaker. Be warned, though: one day, either the Saxon *bretwalda*, Hengist, or our own warlord, Arthur, shall be the true power in all these lands. Know that you will be seen as no friend by either, or by my own Damnonii people." He turned smouldering eyes on all gathered there. "Enjoy your feast, people of Cwrt Isel. Your days of sunshine and merriment will be over soon enough, thanks to your Lord's foolishness. I, Bellicus of Dun Breatann, have foreseen it."

These last words were spoken slowly, with heavy emphasis, and Bellicus raised his hands to the sky as he finished. Duro wondered what his friend was doing until he felt something on his own hand and looked down to see a droplet of water.

Bellicus nodded to him and walked away from the feast, Cai trotting behind him, centurion following with his hand on his sword hilt just in case there was any further trouble. As they went, the rain began to fall, almost as if the druid had called it down himself to put an end to the revelry.

"He made it rain!" someone shouted fearfully, and others took up the call as the thunderheads unleashed their contents, depositing a solid downpour upon the previously sunny field and sending folk running for shelter. Duro looked back to see the only ones remaining at their table were Elffin and Bishop Adelphius, who were watching them go with expressions as dark as the clouds overhead.

"It might be pouring down," the centurion said as they reached the stables and their waiting horses, "but I think we should be back on our travels as quickly as possible."

Bellicus grinned as he made Darac ready to ride. "That was fun, eh? Feels good to be back on the road with you, old friend."

Duro muttered bleakly, "Aye. Life's always fun when you're around, druid." But he couldn't help smiling as they mounted up and headed at a canter through the town and back onto the northwards road.

* * *

The war had begun. Or, more accurately, it had started again, for it had merely paused during winter when the roads were mostly impassable and men looked to their halls for entertainment during the darkest days of the year, rather than to the battlefield. This year was destined to be different, however, as Arthur was beginning to realise.

"Over two hundred of them?" The warlord's brow creased as he took in the Merlin's words. "That's a much larger army than usual – what are they up to?"

Merlin tilted his head thoughtfully. "My guess would be that Hengist has grown tired of being confined to the Saxon Shore and decided this summer is the time to make his move for the rest of the lands surrounding his forts. Or his advisors have become impatient and told him to hasten the pace of their invasion. Either way, the fact our scouts and spies have reported such a large body of men moving eastwards suggests trouble for us."

Arthur took this in, his frown deepening for the druid was merely confirming his own suspicions: The Saxons believed they finally had the numbers to take control of central Britain, and there was every chance their army, already large, would gather even more recruits as they travelled.

"This is not good news," Arthur said. "I'd hoped to have a few cavalry units trained and fully operational when this time came."

Bedwyr muttered an oath, but Lancelot did not seem overly perturbed by the Saxon threat.

"So, we meet them in battle and crush them," the blond champion shrugged. "Isn't that what we planned to do all along?

These are *our* lands – we know them better than the sea-wolves. We can choose the best place to attack their army, take full advantage of the terrain, and wipe them out for good."

Arthur smiled. His friend's optimism was almost childlike at times, and he loved him for it, but he did not see Hengist as a fool. The *bretwalda* wouldn't be so easily penned in and destroyed. Besides, the Saxons had been in Britain for a while now, they knew the lands surrounding their own forts as well as, or better perhaps, than any of Arthur's captains. And the invaders' numbers had swelled with every passing month and year, as more men came from Jutland, Frisia, Saxony and various areas in Germania to find their fortune in the land the Romans had left all but defenceless two decades or so ago.

It was an alarming thought, but Arthur had to consider the possibility that, by the time they met in battle, Hengist's full army might number as much as three hundred and, on top of that, the Saxon *bretwalda* would likely have some plan on how to utilise such a vast force of Wotan-worshipping fiends. Maybe the Saxon warlord would simply use his troopers like a battering ram, employing little subtlety or tactical finesse to try and smash the Britons into submission, which would be bad enough, but Arthur respected his opposite number's intelligence.

This coming summer's fighting would be the toughest he'd had to face so far, and he feared he might not be up to the task. If only they'd had enough time to train two or three cavalry units, rather than the single *turma* of thirty riders Sulinus had managed to bring up to speed so far.

"Our numbers are swelling every day," Merlin noted, breaking Arthur from his uncharacteristically gloomy reverie. "More men come from the lands all over the country to join us." His white beard parted as his teeth flashed in a grin. "We even took in four young infantrymen from Cwrt Isel this morning."

Arthur looked at him in surprise. "We did? I'd never have thought that cantankerous turd Elffin would ever send anyone. Especially with his hateful bishop pouring poison into his ear every day."

Merlin laughed. "Exactly! Taranis knows what Bellicus and Duro said to them, but it must have greatly worried them, to allow so many of their men to come and join us."

"That's good," Bedwyr said. "The druid and his centurion friend could add an extra thirty or forty men to our ranks if their mission continues to be as successful as it's been so far."

"And it'll save us ever having to visit the likes of Elffin to punish him for breaking his oath to aid us in this war," Arthur agreed. "The gods only know if we'd ever have a chance to do that anyway, now that the Saxons are coming for us."

"True," Merlin growled. "Any lords who break their pledge to us must be punished for it. If we're to beat the Saxons, and actually keep them at bay in the years to come, our allies need to be counted on to help us. It's the only way Britain will flourish over the hard decades to come."

"Let's hope there's not too many places we have to visit to deliver retribution once we defeat Hengist," Arthur sighed. "It's one thing to fight an enemy intent on taking your lands, quite another to raise arms against your own people." He gazed thoughtfully out through the opening of the great tent he was using as his base of operations during this phase of assimilating, training and drilling his ever-growing army, and decided they'd been stuck inside in the stifling heat for long enough. "Come on," he said, pushing himself up to his feet. "Let's go and see how Sulinus is getting on. It always cheers me up to see the gruff old fellow putting his riders through their paces."

The others gladly agreed, for they too enjoyed the decurion's company and appreciated his skills, which were so different to their own. As they approached the large training ground with its finally completed wooden fence encircling it a loud voice could be heard, encouraging the riders brusquely.

"That doesn't sound like the old man," Lancelot said.

Bedwyr nodded. "It's not. Sulinus chose his duplicarius, that's who you can hear shouting."

"Duplicarius?" Lancelot muttered with a frown. "Is that what the Romans called a decurion's second-in-command? Bloody stupid name, we really need to come up with our own ranks, Arthur. We might be learning from them, but we're not Romans ourselves."

Arthur simply shrugged. "Sulinus can do as he likes as far as I'm concerned. If he wants to call it a duplicarius that's up to him.

Aye, going forward we might look at it but, for now, I just want a working cavalry unit before we meet the Saxons in battle."

Lancelot took this in and then asked who'd been chosen for the promotion.

"Aesibuas," Bedwyr replied, then continued, guessing Lancelot didn't immediately recognise who the name. "He came with me and Duro to enlist the old man. Black moustache. Serious type. Sulinus says he's a natural leader."

They reached the circular training ground, known as a *gyrus* by the Romans, with its fence which was built high enough that the horses could not see over it, focusing their attention fully on the task at hand. Arthur led the way, climbing atop a viewing platform where they spotted Sulinus, sitting on a camp chair, watching as twenty or so of his men went through their routines, with Aesibuas leading them on his fine white mare.

The new duplicarius sat in his horned saddle with confidence and the bearing of a man who took no nonsense. On mere looks, he appeared a fine choice to be Sulinus's second.

"I don't see bows," Lancelot said, casting his eyes around the training ground and the riders' kit. He'd been helping drill the infantry and not taken much to do with the cavalry but he'd assumed the new unit would be used to provide long range support as mounted archers.

Arthur disabused him of the notion. "Perhaps in future we'll be able to train more riders as bowmen but, with only one unit at this stage, we didn't have time to train them to the required standard in different disciplines. Shooting a bow from horseback is a skill that needs a lot of practice."

Sulinus grunted agreement. "These men were not, for the most part, great riders. A lot of my time has been spent getting them used to simple manoeuvres, and then teaching them to throw javelins, or fight with sword and shield, without falling out of their saddles. Asking them to also learn how to shoot a bow? It would be too much." He stood up and rested his hands on the fence as he glanced over his shoulder at Lancelot. "Better to have one unit trained well in a couple of disciplines, than a unit that can do many different things badly, eh, blondie?"

Lancelot's brow furrowed at the old man's mocking tone for, as Arthur's champion and the best swordsman in the warlord's army, he wasn't used to being made fun of. The smiles of Bedwyr and Arthur were infectious, however, and he found himself accepting the decurion's banter as the foibles of an old soldier. "Well, then, baldy," he retorted good-naturedly. "Let's see what you've been teaching them. Let us see what you think will be able to stop a charging line of Saxon spearmen."

"Baldy, eh? Oh, that hurts, I've never been called that before." Sulinus said with a sardonic shake of his head. "Very well, you want to see something impressive?" He turned his attention to Aesibuas, shouting, "Duplicarius!" and gesturing for the men to bring their steeds to a halt. When they were at rest, the decurion called again to Aesibuas, "Testudo."

Lancelot, Bedwyr, Arthur, and Merlin looked at one another with great interest. They all knew of the testudo, or tortoise formation, but only in connection with infantry, where the troopers would hold their shields in such a way that every angle of the formation – front, back, sides, and even above – was protected, like the shell of the tortoise from which it took its name. Horsemen could not possibly do that. Could they?

Sulinus read their expressions and cackled. "Don't be foolish, it's not what you're imagining. Watch."

Leading from the front, Aesibuas called to Rianorix to raise the standard – Arthur's blue and white bears on a background of the same, contrasting colours of course – and called out the order. Behind him, riders lined up, their left sides facing the watching warlord and his companions. The horses moved close together, so close that the blue-painted shield of the man in front concealed the head of the animal behind.

"That's an impressive line," Lancelot admitted almost grudgingly. "The shields are even at the same level all the way along."

"Not by accident," Sulinus said. "The horses are chosen for their height, so the line not only looks imposing, but the shields properly cover each animal's head. From a distance, in battle, how many riders would you think are in the formation?"

The spectators took in the compact formation and understood Sulinus's point.

"With them packed so closely together it looks like there's half the numbers," Arthur said.

Sulinus nodded happily. "Exactly. It's not so impressive with only twenty or so in a single line, but imagine it with a larger unit, or even more than one. The enemy sees a small cavalry force and plans accordingly, getting a nasty shock once the fighting begins and they realise there's double the horses they expected and double the number of javelins flying through the air towards them." He was smiling like a boy carrying out a prank as he pictured past victories.

Sunlight glinted off the riders' spears, helmets, and shields, and two of the riders moved forward, out of the line. These were to be targets.

"You've made Rianorix your *signifer* then?" Arthur asked, but Sulinus waved the question away.

"Not exactly," he said. "There's not enough time to train a standard bearer properly, or any real need, given we've only one cavalry unit. Rianorix will carry it – he volunteered, even though he knows how dangerous a job it is – but he won't perform any of a signifer's other duties."

Aesibuas shouted and the line of horsemen began to move as one. The tight formation remained intact, offering a hugely impressive sight in itself. As Arthur and his friends knew, it took a lot of skill to ride horses this well, especially laden as they all were with arms and armour. The horses rode faster, around the *gyrus*, circling the two animals and their riders in the centre of the arena. These horses were visibly keyed up, eyes wide, nostrils flaring, but they remained steadfastly in position, suggesting to the onlookers that they were the cream of the crop, with the rock steady temperament required for success in battle.

"I'm amazed," Bedwyr said, staring in fascination at the scene before them. "You'd think those horses would have bolted back to the safety of the line by now."

"They're the best we have, in that regard," Sulinus confirmed. "Not just the horses, the riders as well. Those two are able to remain calm, and to impart that feeling to their mounts. They have extraordinary empathy with their horses. It's not that common a talent. Some riders have the opposite effect, stirring up even the most placid of beasts. But look, the best is yet to come."

Rianorix, standard held aloft, pulled slightly ahead of the formation now, and, behind him, Aesibuas galloped forward, right

222

hand drawing a javelin from a quiver on his horse. He leaned back against the horns of the cavalry saddle Sulinus had introduced to Arthur's army and, with a great shout, threw his missile.

It struck one of the shields of the two horsemen in the centre of the arena, its blunted head hitting home with a thump and bouncing off. Already the next man in line was charging forward, this time aiming at the other target horseman. Again, the javelin was released and struck the blue shield.

In this way all the riders charged and attacked with their javelins, and every one managed to hit the target. It was an astonishing display, and Arthur watched with his companions in amazement as the targets remained in position despite the missiles hammering against their shields, transferring the force through both horse and rider. The sounds of hooves pounding, men shouting and javelins crashing against wood made the whole thing even more remarkable and, when the line returned to their starting position, including the two target riders, there was a stunned silence from the onlookers.

And then Lancelot began to clap, grinning wildly. Arthur and Bedwyr joined in with the applause while Merlin, smiling, watched Sulinus's own happy expression widen.

"That was incredible," Lancelot said to the decurion. "I've never seen anything like it in all my years as a soldier."

Sulinus waved the praise away modestly. "Pah, that was nothing. In the legions we had bigger units – you should have seen that same thing with double or treble the numbers. Two lines, not one, all crossing over one another and attacking each other as well as just the targets. Now *that* was a thing of beauty." He turned away and saluted Aesibuas in the *gyrus* below their platform. "But it's a start. My men are getting better every day."

"Gods," Arthur said, gazing into the middle-distance as if dreaming of a future that might be. "The Saxons will truly not have a clue what's about to hit them when we face off against them in the coming battle."

Bedwyr agreed enthusiastically. "One of the things they like to do," he said, "is make a lot of noise as they charge. They're a wild, untamed lot, and they like to be heard. It usually frightens horses but…" He gazed at Sulinus. "These animals didn't seem bothered by all the noise. They remained calm throughout the exercise."

"They did," Sulinus replied. "We have times set aside where we specifically make as much noise as possible – hitting swords against shields, shouting, screaming, whatever we can think of – just to get the horses used to it. Of course, you might still get one or two panicking, for it's a frightening place, a battle, and if one loses heart the fear can spread quickly through the rest of the unit. But we're getting there with both horses and men, weeding out those that might break in the fighting."

"Damn it," Arthur shouted, but he was smiling. "I wish we had more time to let you train another unit. Two!" He stepped across the platform and, to the decurion's surprise, grasped Sulinus in a bear hug. "Thank you," he laughed. "You and your cavalry are going to win this war for us, I can feel it."

"One thing," Bedwyr said, and his expression had turned serious again. "I've noticed your best riders all seem to be above average height. I always thought smaller men made the best horsemen. Less weight for the animal to carry means more speed and manoeuvrability surely."

Sulinus gave Bedwyr a disgusted look. "Maybe in a race," he said, as if talking to an imbecile. "But longer legs are an advantage for a rider in most situations, especially here, where we have to use our whole bodies to control the animal and use our weapons and shields at the same time. Longer thighs give a rider a better seat on their mount." He gestured towards his unit, still silently lined up in their testudo line. "Many of these manoeuvres were borrowed from the Gauls and Britons – men who were, generally, taller than the Romans. They knew how to ride, those old countrymen of ours!"

"All right, decurion, you've impressed me," Lancelot admitted with good grace. "But the question is, will your horsemen actually work in battle, when they face the hordes of screaming Saxons?"

Sulinus frowned and looked down at his cavalrymen. "Only time will provide the answer to that, my lord," he said, with unusually thoughtful deference to the younger man's rank. "But I have faith in them – both horses and men. There's not many of them, but each one will prove to be worth three infantry troopers, I would stake my lands on that." His usual toothless grin reappeared as he turned back to the blond champion. "Besides, they've been trained by the very best. Carry on, duplicarius!" This last call was accompanied by a wave of his wiry, tanned arm and in the *gyrus*

Aesibuas led his riders away to rest and take on water, for the sunshine must be taking its toll on the armoured unit.

"We'd best let you get on with your work, decurion," said Arthur, becoming deadly serious again. "I don't know if you've heard the reports, but Hengist's army is moving out and their numbers are far greater than we'd expected." He met the old man's iron gaze. "Chances are, more of their kinsmen will join them as they travel. We could be facing an army of two or even three-hundred spears, something we've not encountered in this entire war so far. Your unit will be invaluable, I hope."

Sulinus gave a low whistle but seemed unperturbed by the bleak news. In fact, his grin never wavered as he ran his tongue across his lower gum and replied, "Don't worry, my lord. The more of the bastards there are, the easier it'll be for my riders to skewer them with their javelins." He nodded to Bedwyr. "Just you make sure, quartermaster, that there's plenty of those missiles ready for us, for it would be a shame to run out when there'll be so many targets for us to aim at."

They chatted for a little while longer, and then Arthur led his companions back to Caer Lerion with a spring in his step that hadn't been there before they watched Sulinus's display. They didn't say much as they walked, digesting what they'd seen and how this fantastic new unit could be best utilised. It was obvious that, although the cavalry would be an incredible secret weapon in the Britons' arsenal, without the right tactics, they could be nullified and thus rendered useless. That would make all this time, and all these resources they were funnelling into the training and kitting out of the riders, a complete waste.

Arthur did not believe that would be the case and, when he turned to see Merlin beaming back at him he knew the High Druid shared his enthusiasm. This coming battle would surely be decisive – a chance to finally destroy the Saxon threat forever. A chance to prove himself worthy of the epithet Bear of Britain.

Sulinus's cavalry, led by stern Aesibuas, would give Hengist the biggest shock of his life when the two armies clashed. Arthur just had to make sure that great battle took place in a location that was best suited to his purposes.

That would be their next tough decision, and one he wasn't particularly looking forward to.

CHAPTER TWENTY-SEVEN

"What about Nant Beac?" Bedwyr said, rubbing a hand across his face. It had been a long few days for the young nobleman-turned-quartermaster of Arthur's burgeoning army, and this discussion was one he'd rather have had when his mind wasn't quite so busy. The warlord and his other advisors had insisted it take place now, however, for their reports confirmed the Saxons were already closer than anticipated and also that their numbers had, so far, increased to almost three hundred. Where Arthur's forces met those inexorable sea-wolves was a critical decision and one that couldn't be taken without proper discussion, even if Bedwyr was exhausted.

"Where's that?" Lancelot asked in answer to the quartermaster's suggested battle site. "The name doesn't seem familiar."

Merlin was nodding thoughtfully as he pictured the place in his mind. "Two or three days march from here, and sixty-odd miles to the west of Garrianum," he said. "There's a large, flattish plain with higher ground on the northern side which is covered in trees. That would be the ideal place to conceal Sulinus's cavalry."

"If we halt the Saxons ahead of that raised ground," Bedwyr continued, "the horsemen can attack their line from behind, throwing their javelins before riding back up the slope and into the trees. If Hengist's men chase them they'll tire themselves out running up the slope with all their war-gear."

Lancelot still looked bemused, clearly not being familiar with the area they were speaking of. "Won't the cavalry get trapped if that happens? Charging a line of spearmen, even tired ones, would be certain death for them, surely."

"No," Merlin replied happily. "The ground slopes down again on the other side of the trees."

Arthur's eyes were shining with that familiar excitement he got when imagining a scene playing out in their favour. "This is good," he said. "We could even set up traps in those trees. Tie wires across them at neck height for the Saxon bastards to blunder into or something."

Lancelot was apparently not quite convinced, and, at Arthur's urging, he said, "Look, I know the Saxons generally like to just line up their spearmen in a shieldwall if they're being defensive, or mount a straightforward charge when they're on the attack but...They're not stupid. Brave, reckless, proud, aye. But Hengist isn't a fool. I'm not so sure he'll simply lead his men against us then be caught unawares when you unleash the cavalry."

Arthur greatly valued his champion's counsel but he felt sure Lancelot was wrong in this instance. "I suppose it's possible they'll have learned new tricks," he conceded. "But even the Romans, as Merlin taught me by making me read old texts by the likes of Tacitus , knew how the Saxons fought. Nothing's changed in generations as far as I can see. Every time we face them in battle it's that same old 'shieldwall into charge' tactic they employ."

Merlin nodded agreement. "They might have Hengist leading as their *bretwalda*, but they're too disorganised to pull off any complex strategies. That is, and always has been, their biggest weakness." He smiled at Lancelot. "Usually you're the one calling for more aggression and less thinking," the druid said. "What's made you fear this battle could be so different to any other?"

Running a hand through his blond hair, Lancelot shook his head. "I don't know. The fact they've gathered so many men into one vast army, perhaps. Will they really just throw all of their resources at us so recklessly? They must have spies amongst our people – they must know we have similar numbers, including a new cavalry unit. I don't trust the bastards."

They all sat in silence for a time, pondering their friend's words. Lancelot, Arthur and Bedwyr were all quite young considering their positions as war-leaders of the Britons, but they had much experience in battling the Saxons in recent years and Merlin, of course, was a near-bottomless well of knowledge. They always knew it would be a major undertaking trying to stop the Saxons spreading across the country and they respected the enemy's military prowess but...Even if Lancelot was right, there had to be a battle and Arthur decided Bedwyr's suggestion of Nant Beac was the best place they could have it.

"I understand your wariness," the warlord admitted, "but I think Hengist is simply going to try and smash us with sheer brute force. And, since he's apparently bringing every warrior he can muster to face us, that must mean he's left his own fortress practically undefended."

Bedwyr and Lancelot shared a glance. Neither man liked the sound of this, but Arthur had always seen it as his mission in life to destroy the invaders, even if it meant being reckless at times. Apparently, this would be one of those times.

"What, exactly, are you suggesting?" Bedwyr asked.

"We send a unit to the Saxon Shore," Arthur replied grimly, fist clenched. "And take their main fortress from them. Burn their ships, steal their grain, free their slaves, and then, when we destroy Hengist's army at Nant Beac and they retreat to Garrianum, they'll find no succour there, only more death! Listen, this is our chance. Our chance to wipe out the Saxon threat forever. We *must* take it." Again, his eyes were shining, and it was hard not to feel the force of his personality, of his vision; yet Lancelot and Bedwyr both wondered how the discussion had gone this way. From Lancelot voicing fears over Saxon weaknesses to a plan which completely disregarded those fears and, instead, would be even more aggressive than the original one.

Bedwyr remained silent, for he was Arthur's man and would follow him no matter what. Lancelot could only grin and say, "I think you might be mad, warlord, but you've never led us wrong so far. If you need someone to lead a raid on Garrianum, I'm yours to command."

"Yes!" Arthur jumped up from his camp stool and came across to grasp both Lancelot and Bedwyr's arms in the warrior's grip, smiling in almost beatific fervour. It was obvious his mind was already moving ahead, planning in intricate detail how the final battle with Hengist and his hordes might play out. There was almost a madness in his eyes, a single-minded desire to see as many of their enemies slaughtered as possible. Perhaps Arthur *was* mad, in a way.

Perhaps they all were.

"Here," said the warlord, releasing his captains' arms and turning back to Merlin. "I was going to wait until we faced Hengist but...You might as well have them now, my friends. Do you have the gifts, Merlin?"

The druid stood up and silently disappeared out of the tent, leaving Arthur grinning and Bedwyr and Lancelot wondering what was happening. Merlin returned moments later, carrying a bundle which he gave to the warlord.

Looking from one friend to another, Arthur unwrapped the package, peeling back the cloth to reveal a scabbard and a helmet. They all looked down on the pieces, marvelling at them, for these were no ordinary armaments as worn by those men in their army who were wealthy, or lucky enough, to own something similar.

"I may not be a king," Arthur said, "but I can give my loyal friends, captains, and counsellors, gifts. You two have certainly earned these. I asked Merlin to have them made." He lifted the scabbard on the left and handed it to Bedwyr, then took the helm and gave it to Lancelot. They were accepted with gratitude and some wonder, for they were truly marvellous examples of workmanship and beauty.

Bedwyr's scabbard had a poplar core covered with red leather embossed with a wonderfully detailed hunting scene. Throat and chape were both of highly polished bronze, which contrasted well with the leather.

The helmet given to Lancelot was made from two iron halves held together by a central ridge and decorated with gleaming, embossed brass plates. There were neck and cheek guards attached with straps and buckles and a leather liner to make the whole thing comfortable to wear.

"I've performed magical rites over both of these," Merlin said seriously but without going into any other detail, leaving the men to use their imaginations over what exactly the druid's spells might have entailed. "They'll bring you luck."

"By Cernunnos," Bedwyr exclaimed, eyeing the hunting scene embossed on his scabbard. "This is an incredible gift, Arthur."

"Aye," Lancelot agreed, similarly touched to receive something so wonderful. "They must have cost you a small fortune."

Arthur waved that away. "It's a leader's job to feed and clothe his men, but to also reward their courage and loyalty. You both deserve these, especially you Bedwyr. Look at the state of that!" He pointed at the scabbard hanging from the baldric slung over Bedwyr's shoulder, shaking his head at the worn and tattered brown leather.

Laughing, Bedwyr removed the baldric, took out his sword and slid it into his new scabbard. It fit perfectly, as he somehow knew it would. He looped the baldric through the red scabbard's burnished loops and placed it over his head again, peering down to see how it looked.

"Impressive," Arthur said, nodding in satisfaction and pleasure at his friend's happy acceptance of the gift.

Lancelot pulled back his long hair and put on the helmet, smiling at the feel but looking around in consternation.

"What's wrong?" Arthur asked, fearing the helm had been made too tight. He should have known what the problem was, though.

"Do you not have a mirror?" Lancelot asked. "How am I supposed to see what I look like?"

Bedwyr groaned and slapped the blond warrior on the arm. "You look delightful," he said sarcastically. "Like a god come from the Otherlands to walk among us mere mortals."

"I'm more interested in how well it can turn a sword," Arthur laughed, tapping the helmet with his knuckles. "But it does look very impressive, if you really must know."

Merlin watched them, a wise older figure enjoying the camaraderie of his younger companions, but their mirth eventually dampened as the seriousness of the coming days and weeks returned to the forefront of their minds.

"How many should I take to Garrianum?" Lancelot wondered. "Twenty? Thirty?"

Arthur thought about it then replied, "How about in the middle? Take twenty-five, including Cador, since he can speak the Saxon tongue. And Kay too, he looks a lot like a sea-wolf. You can travel with us until we get near the battle site, then head east while giving Hengist's oncoming army a very wide berth."

They spoke for a little longer, then Lancelot and Bedwyr bid warlord and druid farewell that they might return to their own duties.

As they came out through the tent flap, squinting against the bright sunshine, Bedwyr ran a finger along the brass throat on his new scabbard, marvelling at the way it caught the light and stood out so magnificently against the red leather. "I'd best go and see if the blacksmith is staying true to his word and making enough weapons for our men before we have to march east. What about you, Lancelot? You going to continue training the new spearmen?"

230

"I am", his friend replied, helmet in hand as he too examined the exquisite gift Arthur had bestowed upon him. "Not much time to get them into shape, eh? I'll see you later for an ale or three."

Nodding at one another, they headed in different directions, but Bedwyr was surprised for Lancelot was walking away from the training ground and the noise of the men being drilled by their leaders.

"Where are you going?" Bedwyr called, pointing back to the north of their camp. "Training ground's that way."

"I know," Lancelot shouted back, familiar grin in place, golden hair glowing like a halo in the sun as he passed a couple of servant women who gazed in open admiration as he went by. "But first I'm going to the old bathhouse in the town. It's got a great big bronze mirror I can use!"

* * *

Bellicus and Duro's mission was over, they'd visited every name on Merlin's list with varying degrees of success and had ridden hard, pushing their mounts through the night in hopes of joining Arthur's army before it met Hengist's Saxons in battle.

They needn't have worried, for Hengist and his *comitatus* had been forced to slow their pace as they marched westwards. Although he'd been leading the majority of the sea-wolves in Britain for a number of years he'd never before led an army of such a size and the logistics of the operation had proven unexpectedly difficult. In a country like Britain it wasn't too difficult to find drinking water, for it seemed to rain constantly and there were plenty of swollen streams and rivers to plunder even at the height of this summer, but finding nourishment was another matter.

The villages they passed by were forced to provide what food they had to Hengist's scavenging warriors. Sometimes the folk gave it up without argument, knowing they couldn't possibly withstand an attack from the invading army and, in those cases, Hengist was happy to move on without any trouble for, although his vicious brother, Horsa, might not agree, the *bretwalda* did not want to kill innocent villagers if he didn't have to. Someone would

231

be needed to farm the land, tend the cattle, maintain the roads, and so on, once the Saxons finally took control of the whole island.

Sometimes the locals did put up some meagre resistance however and, in those cases, the settlements would be left smouldering ruins filled with nothing but corpses, their livestock slaughtered or driven along with the Saxon army, and any stores of grain or other foodstuffs loaded onto the wagons which followed Hengist's troops.

This was the nightmare that Arthur had been recruited to stop. For some of his people, they would never awaken from it, but Hengist wouldn't have things his own way for much longer. And, with Lancelot already on his way to what was hopefully an abandoned Garrianum, the end was surely approaching for the Saxons.

As Darac carried Bellicus through the tired ranks of Arthur's spearmen, the druid could smell the sweat lifting from their toiling bodies, mingling with hot leather and the familiar, pleasant aroma of his own horse. He slowed the big black to a walk and gestured towards one of the warriors marching along the old Roman road.

"Recognise him?"

Duro took off his centurion's helmet and wiped sweat from his head before replacing the helm and frowning. "No," he replied. "Don't think I've ever seen him before."

"Really? Think back to the day we met the fool and his bishop in Cwrt Isel."

Duro scratched his head, trying to see if he did know the man who had, by now, noticed their scrutiny and was smiling at them. Still the centurion could not place him. Just one bearded young soldier amongst hundreds.

"Well, I remember him," Bellicus said, slowing Darac even further, to match the pace of the footmen. "You're from Cwrt Isel," he said to the smiling fellow, who bowed respectfully and confirmed that he did indeed hail from that unwelcoming village, as did the nearest three men marching behind him.

"Our lord decided it would be unwise to anger Arthur," the man told them. "And, he never admitted it to anyone, but he still fears the old gods and your calling down of the rain gave him a fright. You could see it in his face for a couple of days after you left, until he finally asked for volunteers to come and join this army."

"And you wanted to fight for the safety of your home? Admirable indeed," Duro said seriously.

"Not really," the man replied. "Cwrt Isel is a dump and most of the people there are arseholes. I just want to fight Saxons and maybe loot a silver arm-ring or two so I can buy some goods and become a trader." He shrugged and, despite his bleak words, seemed quite happy to be marching off to war. "Maybe this will finally let me see a bit of the world!"

He was a large man and Bellicus could see this was probably the only thing that kept his fellow villagers from murdering him and throwing him in a river, for they glared at him with open dislike as they marched. None of them looked like they really wanted to be here, but then, Bellicus mused, what sane man *did* want to face a field full of experienced warriors with nothing other than an axe better suited to chopping wood than cleaving skulls from shoulders?

"Well," Duro said gruffly, not too pleased at these new recruits' attitude but experienced enough to know the fact they were there was all that really mattered. "Arthur will be glad you came, and, when we win, you'll get your share of the plunder." He put on his best parade ground stare and swept it across the men from Cwrt Isel and anyone else marching nearby. "So, make bloody sure we beat these bastards, and you can all go home with pockets full of loot."

"That's the plan, my lord," said the big axeman cheerily. "That's the plan."

Bellicus rode on and Duro followed and soon enough they reached the front of the great column, where Sulinus, Bedwyr, Merlin, and Arthur led the way. There were greetings and thanks for their efforts in swelling the army's numbers and then the warlord remarked on Bellicus's continuing hirsute appearance.

"I thought you'd have shaved it all off by now," said Arthur. "It's strange to see you like that."

"He needs his hair longer so he can do like some other druids do before battle, and smear it all with cow shit then caper about before the Saxons." Duro spoke without laughing and it was obvious Arthur and Bedwyr couldn't tell whether he was joking or not. The thought of Bellicus behaving in such a manner would

233

certainly be unnerving. Or perhaps merely hysterically funny. Bizarre, for sure.

"The day I cover myself in shit is the day I become a Christian," the druid said. "No, I just haven't got around to shaving yet. Had other things to occupy my time. But I'll do it before the battle."

"Next you'll be looking for a mirror," Merlin said in amusement. "You're getting as vain as Lancelot."

"Where is Lancelot anyway?" Bellicus wondered, sitting up straighter and looking back at the marching ranks behind them, eventually spotting the blond warrior talking with Cador and Kay.

Arthur filled them in on his plans and watched their reaction as he did so. Of them all, Bellicus and Duro were the only ones who had been anywhere near Garrianum in the past year or two and he wondered what they'd think of the mission he'd given Lancelot.

"Makes sense," Duro said, which pleased the warlord who, although happy making tough decisions, always appreciated them being validated and supported by his officers and advisors. "Strategically, if we were to take control of the Saxon Shore forts, we might be in a position to stop future invaders from gaining a foothold on the lands to the east. If we can do it with just twenty-five or so men, even better."

"When the cat's away, the mouse will play," Bellicus muttered. "If Hengist has truly left his fortress with only a skeleton defence force Lancelot should have an easy task ahead of him."

No-one mentioned the possibility that Hengist would not have been so reckless, for it was too late for that. In war, fortune favoured the bold.

Sometimes.

"How far away is the location you've chosen for the battle?" Duro asked and was told they had only a couple hours more to march.

"And our scouts place the enemy army two days or so away?" said Bellicus, nodding thoughtfully. "That gives us some time to make things ready for their arrival."

"Assuming they meet us where we want." Bedwyr voiced everyone's concern, but they could only plan things up to a certain point. After that they were at the mercy of not only Hengist and his plans, but the weather as well. It was dry and fine just now, but if it rained, the cavalry might not be as effective, sliding in the mud that would undoubtedly be churned up by the passage of dozens of booted feet.

"They're Saxons," Arthur said, in the tone of a man who'd been reassuring himself for days. "They'll meet us wherever we form up. It would show cowardice if they were to refuse battle, and that's one thing we can't say about the sea-wolves."

"They're not stupid either, though," Duro put in, obviously unaware of the previous discussions between the warlord and his counsellors.

"No," Arthur agreed patiently. "But they do have a certain way of fighting and we must plan with that in mind. One day, I expect, they'll change their battle tactics but for now, we can only act with the knowledge we have."

"And how did you get on, decurion?" Bellicus asked, neatly drawing the conversation away in another direction. "Is your cavalry going to perform as we hoped?"

"Wait and see," Sulinus said, but he had a knowing look in his eye that suggested confidence and offered nothing more. In truth, he looked extremely tired, as if this journey, indeed the whole recent venture, was taking its toll. But that's what war did, the druid thought sadly, it chewed people up and spat them out when it was finished.

It also gave them a chance to earn glory and win their place in the Otherlands or perhaps their next life, he reminded himself, so Sulinus had certainly made the right decision in joining Arthur and his fellows.

"When we reach our destination," Arthur said to them. "We'll have the men set up camp and let them rest. It's been a fair walk carrying full gear and rations in this heat. Might as well let 'em rest for the one night, eh?"

No-one objected to this for there seemed no point in forcing the tired army to erect temporary fortifications when the only force big enough to be a threat was miles and miles away.

"They can rest, eat, drink, sing songs, play dice and tafl, and whatever else they want, as long as some kind of discipline is maintained. Duro, in Lancelot's absence I'd like you to take a more active role in the leadership of the army, all right?"

The centurion nodded silently. In truth, he was glad to be given the role and Bellicus could see as much written on his friend's hard features.

"So, you make sure each group of men knows what's expected of them. They all have an individual leader and any transgressions—violence against their comrades, or deserting for example—will result in severe repercussions."

Duro's jaw was firm as he nodded again and replied with a terse, business-like, "Aye, my lord," for he knew better than any man there how an army should work. The Romans had been famously strict with their own men after all and it had often fallen to him, as a young optio mainly, to mete out harsh justice for any unacceptable behaviour.

"Before that, however," the warlord continued, "while the men are setting up camp, we six shall ride on ahead and make a survey of our chosen battlefield. Sulinus can make certain the terrain's suitable for his riders and what we'll be asking from them. The rest of us can see where any problems might arise should Hengist prove more cunning than we expect."

"You'll be wanting our report on the settlements we visited, lord?" Bellicus asked, looking from Arthur to Merlin, who had been the one that drew up the list of destinations after all. "I could do that while Duro's out inspecting the men tonight."

Arthur agreed to this idea without hesitation, impressing the druid as he always did with his dedication to the role he held. Arthur had much to do in the coming hours and days but never betrayed any hint that he lacked the energy, interest, or inclination to make sure every task was given his full attention. Bellicus could see exactly why the warlord inspired the men who followed him, for he truly led from the front and offered an example to all.

Whether he would retain this enthusiasm over the next few years, Bellicus could not tell. Perhaps it didn't matter for, if they defeated the Saxons for good in this upcoming battle, Britain may not have any further need for a warlord.

Bellicus smiled sadly to himself at that, knowing it was idealistic nonsense. There would always be raiders to harass and harry the people of these lands, whether it be Saxons, Picts, Dalriadans or some hitherto unknown enemy from across the seas that surrounded Britain.

"What did you make of the men and women you met during your recent travels, Bel?"

The druid turned to see Merlin riding on his right side. "Some of them were all right, some of them complete fools. I was sad to see how many of the noblemen in these parts have become Christian." He shook his head angrily. "Our ways are being slowly pushed out. You would think the Christians, like Elffin, would be doing everything in their power, sending us as many men as they can spare, to defeat the Saxons, for the likes of Horsa won't take kindly to their new religion. We druids are tolerant but the *volur* of the Saxons will take great pleasure in eradicating the bishops and all who follow their nailed God."

"It's a pivotal point in our history, that's certain," Merlin replied grimly. "It'd be better if we didn't have to waste so much energy battling Hengist and Horsa for we could otherwise focus on bringing our own Order back to the prominence it once enjoyed."

Neither man said it, but they both feared that, by the time the war with the Saxons was over, it would be too late for the Old Ways. Christianity, despite its apparent dislike of violence and its teachings of love, was a surprisingly aggressive religion. Ironically, there might be no place for Bellicus and Merlin in the future Britain they were fighting for while the Christians seemed content to let the warring heathens battle it out amongst themselves.

Maybe the Christians had the right idea.

Bellicus pushed such bleak thoughts from his mind and reassured himself that Arthur's plan would work – they'd smash Hengist's men here, and Lancelot would take control of the Saxon Shore, and that would be the end of the tale. Britain would live in peace for a thousand years or more.

But, of course, he didn't need to be a druid to know such a prediction would be foolish.

* * *

That evening, before Lancelot, Cador and Kay travelled to Garrianum and the rest of Arthur's army marched to meet Hengist, they feasted. It would surely be their last chance to enjoy a civilised meal for some time and, for many of them, their final feast ever, as bleak as that was. Everyone was determined to enjoy it fully while being mindful of the fact that making a long journey was never pleasant with a thundering hangover.

Merlin and Bellicus told stories and led songs, games were played – dice and tafl as well as more physical ones like foot-races and wrestling – and those who were lucky enough to find company to share their bed with made the most of the time. Eburus and Velugna were among those, and none could grudge them spending the hours alone together for the next time they were so close to another human being they wouldn't be making love, they'd be fighting desperately for survival.

"You not following Eburus's lead tonight?" Bellicus asked Lancelot as they, along with Bedwyr, Kay and Duro downed ale together at a bench in the centre of camp, the setting sun still warm and making the sky look quite stunning.

"You mean, why am I not spending what might be my final hours in the company of a beautiful warrior-woman instead of with you ugly bastards?" He grinned as he spoke, white teeth gleaming in the fading light, blonde hair immaculate as ever. "I like to save my energy before a battle, let it build up for the fight. There'll be enough time for lovemaking in days to come when we've smashed the Saxons. Arthur says Britain will be a land of peace and plenty then."

"And you're hoping that means, 'plenty of willing women'," Duro said with a knowing smile.

"Life has many pleasures, centurion," the blond swordsman grinned, raising his cup in salute and swallowing a mouthful.

"Arthur seems convinced this coming battle will be decisive," Bellicus said, watching as two bare-chested, perspiring men ran past in a race, their friends cheering them on until they passed on and were lost amongst the forest of tents. "Whoever wins will take control of Britain eventually."

"That's what we're all hoping," Lancelot nodded. "Do you doubt it, druid?"

Bellicus let out a long, thoughtful breath. "I'm not sure," he admitted. "I don't know Arthur as well as you and Bedwyr. I've only seen him commanding his men a few times."

Bedwyr gave a low chuckle. "Have no fears on that score, Bel," he said confidently. "Arthur knows how to lead. If anyone can bring us victory over the sea-dogs, it's him. He's always had that air of command about him, hasn't he?"

Lancelot and Kay both nodded and Duro asked, "You three have known him for a long time then?"

"Oh aye," Kay said. In contrast to Lancelot his dark hair and beard were unkempt that night, but he smiled almost as much as his friend and was just as good company. "All our lives. Our fathers were all friends and we used to visit each other often, growing up."

"Merlin really took Arthur under his wing when we were just coming into manhood," Bedwyr said. "We saw the change in him almost immediately. He really started to become a warlord from that point on."

"At such a young age?" Duro asked. "Sometimes, in the legions, we had officers who were little more than boys, inexperienced and completely unsuited to the job. But, because their families were wealthy, they were given promotions and command of men who could have outfought and out-thought them in their sleep." He shook his head in disgust. "Even I was young to be a centurion, but I was at least a man at that stage."

Lancelot laughed and Kay joined in.

"Arthur was old beyond his years," Bedwyr said, and there was a touch of sadness in his voice. "At least the three of us were allowed to act like daft boys until we were ready to grow up. Arthur didn't have that luxury. He was always striving to become that *Bear of Britain* Merlin likes to call him."

There was a moment of almost morose silence and Bellicus, not wanting to encourage any gloominess on this, of all nights, said, "You four must have had some grand adventures."

His gentle encouragement had the desired effect, as even Bedwyr's expression lifted at thoughts of past escapades.

"Oh, aye," said Kay. "Plenty. Just like any group of youngsters who know they can handle themselves and have enough coin to be drinking in alehouses when they're far too young to deal with the effects of the cats' piss they call ale in places like that."

"Drunken fights, wild chases, broken bones…," said Bedwyr.

"And the women," Lancelot added with a faraway look in his eyes as he recalled those days learning how to be a man. "Oh, the women!"

"All good, clean fun," Kay avowed, although not entirely convincingly.

"Those days are far behind us now," Bedwyr sighed.

"Speak for yourself," Lancelot retorted, and the three friends laughed, truly enjoying one another's company in a way neither Duro nor Bellicus had seen before in their time with the army. It was a fine sight, thought the druid.

"What about the battles, though?" asked the centurion, eager to find out more about their warlord's experience. "What makes you all so sure Arthur is a better fit than any one of you to command this army?"

The three young companions looked at one another in thoughtful silence for just a moment, then Bedwyr shrugged. "He just has this ability to see one step ahead. To read what the enemy will do."

"Don't play tafl with him," Kay snorted. "You'll lose every time."

Lancelot was nodding agreement with them. "But," he said, "don't play him at dice either. He seems to have more than his fair share of luck."

They all sipped their drinks, gazing into the fire or off into the middle distance and then Kay, smiling again, said, "Remember that battle with the Frisian raiders west of Derventio? Bastards outnumbered us two to one!"

"Aye," Lancelot said. "We should have all been killed that day. Would have been if it wasn't for Arthur. None of us expected the enemy warband to be so big."

"What happened?" Duro demanded eagerly, leaning forward to hear better for the battle songs were in full flow around them now and growing in volume in direct correlation with the amount of ale being sunk.

Bedwyr took up the tale. "We'd heard reports of this group of Frisian raiders, sailing along the coast and attacking settlements at their leisure. Arthur decided that, since we were nearby, we'd put a stop to the raids."

"We had twenty men," Kay said, leaning forward to grasp the ale jug that he might tip some of the contents into his cup. "And the reports we'd heard all put the Frisians' numbers at a little less than that. So, we thought we'd have no trouble if we could surprise them. Easy, right?"

"Only, when Arthur sent a scout on ahead we realised another ship had joined the original group of raiders," Lancelot said, sucking air through his teeth at the memory of the consternation that revelation had caused within their ranks. "Should we retreat? Let the sea-wolves attack our people?"

"Of course not," Kay cried. "That wouldn't be Arthur's way."

"So, what did you do?" Duro asked impatiently.

"I was all for sending half our men around to the beach, to come at the Frisians from their rear when they started moving. The rest of us would attack them from the front."

"Classic pincer movement," Bedwyr said. "It's what most of us wanted to do, although we'd surely have lost the battle. There were simply too many of the enemy."

"You not joining in, lads?" a drunken soldier cried, stumbling across to their bench as a large number of the warriors started chanting the opening refrain of 'The Battle of Duncombe'.

"Not just now, friend," Bellicus said, firmly guiding the man away from their bench as Cai, never comfortable around excessively inebriated folk, growled deep in his chest.

"By Lug," Bedwyr muttered as the fellow, grinning inanely, made his way unsteadily back into the throng of revellers. "I hope that fool isn't in the shieldwall next to me tomorrow. He'll be so hungover he'll be more of a danger to his own comrades than Hengist's spears."

"Let him have his fun, he might be dead in a few hours." Lancelot laughed at his friend's dour look then continued with their tale. "Anyway, Arthur had spotted a steep gully to the north, so he rode along it, and came back with a plan already formed in his mind."

"A gully?" Bellicus asked, picturing the scene in his mind.

"Aye," Bedwyr confirmed. "Not a big one – the walls were steep, but only about the height of two men."

"Bedwyr and Kay took half the men apiece and set them up on the ridges of the gully," continued Lancelot. "Then I walked ahead with Arthur, without our weapons or armour, until the Frisians spotted us, and then we acted bloody *terrified*. Screaming as if we were frightened children, we pointed at them, and waved our arms about, then ran like idiots down into the gully."

"A realistic performance, I felt," Bedwyr noted dryly.

"They fell for it?" Bellicus laughed.

"Didn't even stop to think about it!" Kay shouted gleefully, slamming his cup down onto the bench.

"Practically their whole warband chased Arthur and Lancelot," Bedwyr said. "Only a handful of older, wiser souls came after them at a walk, looking about warily. Perhaps they feared they were walking into a trap, but they couldn't stop their comrades charging on ahead."

Duro was shaking his head in disbelief. "I'd have been reduced to the ranks if I'd let my men behave so rashly," he said. "What happened next?"

"We'd blocked off the end of the gully with fallen logs and boulders," Kay said. "We helped Arthur and Lancelot out with long branches and then..." He spread his hands wide and smirked malevolently.

"It wasn't a battle," Bedwyr said, and he didn't sound proud of their victory. "Not even a fight. They were trapped, with no way to strike back at us as we rained great stones and arrows down on them."

"The ones who hadn't run into the gully tried to stop us," Kay growled. "But Arthur had expected a few of them would hold back, and hidden some of our men to ambush them too."

"Outnumbered two to one," Lancelot reminded them. "Forty-odd battle-hardened Frisians, against our twenty." He leaned back, beaming like a cat fed a bowl of cream. "D'you know how many men we lost that day? Druid? Centurion? None! Not one. But we slaughtered those sea-wolves, and gave their ships to the people of Derventio."

"What a day," Kay said proudly.

Bellicus and Duro looked at one another and nodded happily. Such a victory was exceedingly rare, and probably had more to do with luck than anything else, but it was hugely impressive all the same. It certainly gave them faith in Arthur's suitability to command the Britons' army.

"We could tell you more tales like that," Lancelot said, standing up and draining his cup. "But I think it's time we joined in with the singing. I have a lovely voice, don't I, Kay?"

"I'd rather listen to two hogs rutting," replied the big warrior, but he too stood and placed an arm around Lancelot's shoulders just as the "Hoi! Ho!" refrain from 'The Battle of Duncombe' came back around and both men joined in with gusto.

"Come on, lads," Bellicus called, draining his own ale and grabbing Duro by the arm as he gestured to Bedwyr with his free hand. "Join in!"

"Hoi! Ho! Hoi! Ho!"

CHAPTER TWENTY-EIGHT

"Get down! Sentry ahead."

Lancelot's warning came just in time, for the Saxon standing on the hillock a little way ahead of them turned in their direction just as Budic dropped back into the foliage, concealing himself from the man's view.

"Well, at least we know Hengist didn't take *all* his men off with him," the blond captain hissed. "If there's sentries here, outside the main fortifications, there's going to be more inside."

"What now, my lord?" Budic asked. He was well known as a hunter, so he and Lancelot had come on ahead of the main body of their unit specifically to check for Saxon sentries, but he wasn't sure what their course would be next. "Do we take him out and risk alerting them when he doesn't return or his relief comes and finds him missing?"

Lancelot had already decided what they would do, of course. He was moving now, in fact, but held up a hand to make sure Budic didn't follow him. This would only need one man.

Budic watched as his captain soundlessly made his way forward, towards the oblivious Saxon. Clearly, the guard was an idiot – he should have known better than to stand with his body visible on the horizon, but it just showed how secure these invaders felt in the Britons' own lands. They might have posted sentries but those men, or this one at least, did not really believe they were in any danger.

More fool them.

Lancelot moved as silently as a fox, creeping up on the low hillock as the sentry leaned on his spear and yawned, not even looking outwards in the direction he was supposed to be watching. Budic felt his own blood beginning to pound in his veins, excitement building – and fear too – as Lancelot inched up the grassy mound.

The slope was not particularly high, and easy enough to climb so it barely impeded Lancelot, whose lithe, muscular legs powered him up the towards his daydreaming prey. Budic could see the dagger already drawn in his captain's hand, ready to strike down the Saxon and he grinned fiercely as Lancelot drew closer.

Just as the Briton was raising his left arm to grasp the guard around the neck, he must have stepped on a twig or made some other noise, for the Saxon spun, spear swivelling, and Budic felt his heart leap into his mouth.

He needn't have worried. At such close quarters a spear was not much use, especially against a soldier as skilled as Lancelot.

The spear shaft had little force behind it and Lancelot was easily able to absorb the blow with his right bicep before leaping forward and plunging the tip of his dagger into the Saxon's face. It wasn't a clean strike, for the man was desperately trying to move out of the way while simultaneously calling for help, but his cry was cut off before it began as the blade hit his cheekbone and slid upwards, into his eye. Using his entire bodyweight, Lancelot pressed ahead, ending the guard's life quietly and efficiently.

Budic let out a relieved sigh and ran forward to grasp the dead man's legs as Lancelot dragged him back down the hill. Together they carried their grisly cargo away before dumping the corpse unceremoniously onto the ground and shoving it amongst the very bushes they'd been using to hide themselves in moments before.

"Now," said Lancelot, who appeared barely out of breath after his deadly exertions. "Time to see if our disguises will work. Let's go."

They hurried back to join the rest of their warband – twenty-five spearmen, all clad in helmets and furs looted from the bodies of Saxon warriors killed in earlier battles. Lancelot had thought of leaving behind his own new helmet, but it was similar enough to those worn by many of the sea-wolves that he felt comfortable wearing it. He did not believe their disguises would fool someone like Hengist up close for, although similar, Saxon and Briton had slight differences in appearance: different ways of wearing their hair and beards; different average heights with the Saxons generally being a little taller; even slightly different facial characteristics which, in one man would not perhaps be remarked upon but, in a group, would certainly arouse suspicion.

From a distance, however, Lancelot's warband looked like Saxons, especially Kay with his light hair, darker beard, and blue eyes.

"I hope your fake accent fools them long enough to let us get inside the walls," Lancelot said to Cador as they made ready to march directly towards the boundary of Hengist's fortress where they would, all being well, simply walk straight in unchallenged. It was a bold, perhaps stupid, plan, but, as the lax attitude of the dispatched sentry suggested, the Saxons were not expecting to see Britons here, so far away from the battle Hengist was marching towards.

It had to work.

Cador gave a shrug. He was fidgeting in a way that showed how desperate he was to get in and start fighting the enemy. "Should be all right," he said. "The Saxons have a hundred different accents, just as we do. More! My bastardised hybrid version of Jutish and Alemannic shouldn't raise too many eyebrows, even amongst men from those places."

Lancelot gave a tight smile which betrayed his uncertainty, but they were there now and there was no going back. Today they would either seize control of Garrianum, or they would die. "The horses are well hidden?" he asked although he already knew they were.

Cador nodded and clapped the younger man on the shoulder in an almost fatherly manner. "Have faith in yourself, Lancelot," he said. "You're the greatest swordsman in all Britain. The Saxons are no match for you."

"It's not me I'm worried about," Arthur's champion replied but this was no arrogant statement, decrying his comrades' skill – rather it was a commander expressing his fears over leading his men into the very lion's den. He turned to the warband behind them, seeing grim, determined faces staring back at him from beneath their stolen Saxon helmets. Cador himself wore a fine piece looted from some Saxon jarl, which had a mask covering his entire face and a veil of chainmail covering the neck so only his eyes were visible. Lancelot would have hated trying to fight in something so restrictive, but Cador, older and slower than the blond warrior, had been glad to put it on.

"Remember," said Lancelot. "Only Cador speaks. If anyone else is addressed, you just give an exhausted grunt. We stay together unless I say otherwise. And if the Saxons want to run away, let them. We're here to take control of their fort first and foremost. Killing stragglers isn't important at this stage. All right?"

As if in response to his orders, the men responded with grunts, but Lancelot could see the excitement shining in their eyes. These men were volunteers, and they were here with him to win glory by finally sweeping the invaders from the fort that had originally been intended to stop them gaining a foothold in Britain.

"Let's go then. Cador, you lead. Kay, you look more like a Saxon than I do, so you walk with him. I'll hang back in the centre of the group." It was his turn to offer Cador a bolstering pat on the arm although, in truth, the older man was the type who seemed unflustered by most situations, and this was no different. His calm demeanour suggested he was simply heading out for a stroll on a fine evening rather than about to lead one of the most audacious raids in recent history. Lancelot was pleased to have the man with them for his influence served to keep everyone's nerves in check.

In an extremely convincing attempt at a Saxon accent, Cador called, "*Foreweard!*" and strode ahead, towards the high stone walls surrounding Garrianum.

Lancelot was glad his wasn't one of the more restrictive helmets to wear, for it was a warm day and already he could feel his scalp sweating. He felt sorry for Cador and the others whose faces were completely obscured, but they didn't have too far to travel before the massive walls opened out and the eastern entrance to Garrianum beckoned them in.

The fort was hugely impressive, with high, thick walls built mainly of a light-coloured stone and banded with red tile or brick. Towers so large they might once have contained Roman artillery were placed at intervals and there were two even taller gatehouses, one on the west, close to the shore, and the main one on the east which they were approaching. Once, in earlier times, there had been a settlement beside the fort, but it was long abandoned, and the timber buildings were nothing more than ruins now. The whole formation was positioned beside the waters of a great estuary on the northern and western sides, and this meant the place could only be approached on foot via the old road to the south.

Lancelot's party had been happy to find a ferry operated by Britons who were only too happy to take the 'Saxons' across the river though, meaning they didn't have to spend days walking all the way around.

As they marched towards the gatehouse another sentry watched from the circular tower ahead and Lancelot could see bemusement on his face even at this distance, but his suspicions were not sufficiently aroused to challenge them. He merely watched them, apparently weary from some long journey, striding through the fort's entrance which, to the Britons' surprise, no longer boasted an actual wooden gate. The Saxons must have been confident enough in their numbers and position that they believed replacing the original wooden barrier an unnecessary hassle.

"Halt!"

As they walked into the fort, past the guardhouse, a voice called out to them and it was a strong, Germanic voice which clearly belonged to someone used to command.

"Keep moving," Lancelot muttered. "Slowly. As if we belong here."

They did, but Cador turned to look at the burly warrior stepping out towards them. He was accompanied by two other men, although Lancelot was relieved to see hardly anyone else within the fort's walls. At least, hardly anyone visible at that time. He prayed to the gods that the various timber buildings scattered around weren't heaving with enemy warriors who'd stream out at any moment to see what was happening.

Most of the structures were in poor condition or even derelict – houses, shops, temples, brothels, baths, workshops...This fortress must have played host to a thriving community of more than just legionaries at one time. Workmen, women, traders, merchants, laughing children, barking dogs – all would have called Garrianum home, but now, with Rome's power and influence gone, the place was crumbling.

"I said, 'halt'!" the guard captain shouted, bringing Lancelot rudely back to the present, and this time Cador did stop moving, raising a hand for the rest of their men to follow suit.

"What is it, brother?" Cador asked, shoulders low as if he was bone-weary. "We've been marching for days. We just want to get to our tents, down some meat and ale, and sleep for a week." He smiled tightly at the Saxon whose eyes were narrowed suspiciously but still betrayed no sign of alarm.

Their disguises were working so far.

"Who in Thunor's name are you?" the guard demanded, striding right up and planting himself in front of Cador who was a little shorter and a little narrower in the shoulders. "You don't look familiar."

Cador hesitated for only a heartbeat. "Adelfryd," he replied, sighing as if he really couldn't be bothered dealing with this right now. "Son of Asmundr. From Storsted."

All three Saxons were before Lancelot's troops now but the Britons held their discipline despite the odds seemingly in their favour. There was a little shuffling, but for the most part Lancelot was happy that they remained silent and resisted the temptation to reach for their weapons in the face of this scrutiny.

"What are you doing here, Adelfryd?" the guard captain demanded. "The battle is many days' march to the west. You won't kill many Waelisc here."

"What?" Now Cador's head came up and he looked amazed. Lancelot was impressed with the man's acting, for, although his helmet's cheekpieces concealed most of his face, the surprise in his eyes appeared utterly genuine. "We heard Hengist's call to join his army, but I thought we were supposed to meet here! Didn't you, brother?"

He turned to Kay who, although not understanding the question, immediately nodded and said, "Ja!"

The captain stared at Cador, then at Kay, his expression changing from suspicion to amusement before finally settling on angry. "You *were* supposed to meet here you fools," he spat. "A week ago! The army's already marched. Hengist or Horsa will have your balls for your stupidity when they return."

Cador groaned and slapped the back of his helmet as if berating himself. "Oh shit," he said, before brightening again. "We'll catch them up! Aye, you heard me right." He was smiling fiercely as he spoke, the guard captain's head tilting to one side as he listened. "We'll rest first, for we've been marching hard to get here before the army left. But, at the first light of dawn, we'll be up, and on our way to join Hengist. All right?"

The guard hesitated for a few seconds which seemed like hours to the men ranged behind Cador but, at last, the Saxon relented and stood aside. "Stupid bastards," he growled, shaking his head and glaring at Cador as if he was an imbecile. "You'd better hope you do join the army in time for the battle, or you'll get none of the booty."

Cador looked down at the ground as if too exhausted to care about that for now, and led the Britons ahead again, towards the wooden buildings at the centre of Garrianum.

They'd made it safely inside! Lancelot heaved a sigh of relief, eyes casting all around to see where they might begin their attack and which positions they should aim to take control of first. But he was convinced the hard part was over and the small number of warriors left to guard this site would be easy enough to dispatch.

"Hey, Adelfryd."

Cador turned at the Saxon guard's shout, feigned exhaustion now mingled with genuine irritation. "What?"

The guard was smiling nastily, sending a shiver of fear down Lancelot's back as he asked, "Did you not know Adelfryd is a woman's name?" Then he looked directly at Lancelot and his smile fell away, replaced by a cold stare. "And you – don't you remember me?" the Saxon asked, in the Briton tongue now. "Leofdaeg, I am, son of Jarl Sæwine of Tornhem. Did you think me killed during the battle for Waithe?"

Lancelot had no idea what the man was talking about, but then he remembered the snowy night last winter, when he and Bellicus had raided the Saxon camp at Longhafan, killing the jarl there before slashing open the tent and escaping into the night. Now the jarl's son, who had sworn vengeance on Lancelot for his father's death, was looking at him the way a cat watches a mouse before it pounces.

"I escaped that fight, and I am a jarl myself these days," Leofdaeg said as he raised his hand and the unmistakeable sound of an ox-horn trumpet filled the air, reverberating against the stone walls and, to the Britons' dismay, pounding footsteps which must have belonged to dozens of men came from the direction of the nearby estuary. "And now I will avenge my father's death."

"Form up in a circle," Lancelot commanded, his mind racing. Their only chance now was to defeat the Saxons gathered here within the fortress, not by stealth as they'd planned, but in open battle. So be it, he thought. He'd already killed Jarl Sæwine, now he would deal with the son, and rid the lands of yet another sea-raider.

It mattered little but, as the first enemy soldiers appeared from around the sides of the buildings, they were not wearing armour. Instead, many were stripped to the waist and sweating, and Lancelot guessed they'd been at work building or repairing the ships that had carried their hordes to and from the various lands across the sea. That was something to thank the gods for, since at least his men were heavily armed and armoured.

Unfortunately, however, the Saxons outnumbered them at least two to one and there were a couple of archers running to take up positions on the walls above. One of those, eager to do his bit, loosed an arrow which ricocheted off Cador's facemask with a clatter.

So much for their hopes that this would be an easy mission; now it seemed like Lancelot and his men could not possibly win this fight, given the fact they didn't know the layout of the fort. He was not going to admit that to his warband, of course. If they were to die, they would take as many of the invaders with them as possible.

"Brace yourselves, lads," he roared, pushing through to stand at the front of the encircled men. "This is going to be messy."

CHAPTER TWENTY-NINE

Arthur shook his head in frustration as he spotted the Saxon jarl, Horsa, brother of Hengist, leading a man on a leash as if he was a dog. The warlord knew what was about to play out and he hated the fact there was nothing he could do to stop it. Hopefully the brutal ceremony would bolster the Britons for the coming fight and give them an added incentive to sweep the hated invaders into the sea for good.

"Thorbjorg." Bellicus's voice, dripping with venom, was a low rumble that reminded Arthur of approaching thunder. The giant druid certainly seemed more like his old self now that he'd shaved his head and growth of beard.

"Thorbjorg?" asked the warlord. "The *volva*?"

"Aye," Bellicus replied, and he was staring at the woman accompanying Horsa with such hatred that Arthur wouldn't have been too surprised if she'd fallen down dead under the force of his gaze. "The witch who tried to sacrifice Princess Catia to her twisted gods."

"Looks like those poor fellows are about to suffer that very fate," Merlin said. "It's a shame we didn't have some Saxon prisoners we could do the same to."

Sulinus was beside them, squinting at the party with Horsa – four more tall Saxon warriors, the *volva*, and two naked, filthy men who it seemed could barely walk. They were so thin it was a wonder they weren't already dead, but their whimpers of fear could be heard even at the distance separating the two armies. Undoubtedly, they were prisoners taken in one of the many raids on the villages hereabouts but deemed no longer strong enough to be of use as slaves. They would be more valuable as part of Thorbjorg's blood rites. "I could have my riders try and capture some of the Saxon scouts," said the decurion darkly.

Arthur shook his head. "I don't want them to know how good your unit is just yet," he said. "They may already know of your existence, of course, but there's no point showing them just how efficient your riders are at this point. The bastards will find out soon enough."

"Hey, Arthur!" The Saxon jarl shouted across the open meadow to the warlord of the Britons. "You and your pitiful army with your silly blue shields can watch as our wise-woman butchers two of your people. Their blood will bring the favour of our gods, while their souls will serve me when I reach the feasting halls of the afterlife." He laughed and the sound boomed out over the land although Arthur didn't find it sinister or even threatening, merely annoying.

"Gods, he really is a pain in the arse," Bellicus muttered. "I wish I could have cleaved his chest open the last time we met, rather than merely removing a few toes."

"Your powers are nothing," Horsa screamed, pointing now at Bellicus whom he despised for having bested him in that fight where he'd lost those toes. For a time after that he'd been reduced to a limping figure of amusement in his own army and it only added to his hatred for all Waelisc. "You and the white-bearded sorcerer cannot defeat the magic of mighty Thorbjorg."

"Thorbjorg is a used-up old sow," Merlin retorted. "Her powers are nothing in these lands. She's spent more time on her back being ridden by Hengist than she has honing her magic. If you weren't so ugly she'd let you hump her too, Horsa, but you've always been second-best to your brother, haven't you? And you always will be."

Roaring with fury, Horsa spun, drawing his sword as he did so, and plunged the tip into the stomach of the Briton he held on the leash. The steel tore through the skinny body and erupted out the back in a spray of blood which splattered on the other Saxons and the remaining slave.

Merlin looked on in satisfaction as Thorbjorg berated Horsa for wasting one of her precious sacrifices. She should have killed the man with her special knife, after the appropriate rites. Now they only had one man left and Horsa was an idiot.

Like the druids, the *volur* were trained to use their voices for maximum effect and Thorbjorg's angry tirade was heard by practically everyone gathered there, leaving the big Saxon jarl red-faced and looking like a fool. The *volva*'s display was not going at all as she'd planned. To make it worse for her, there were other *volur* – younger, lesser-ranked ones, Bellicus guessed – looking on from further back, and their amused or even downright joyful expressions served to anger Thorbjorg further. They would be seeking to impress Hengist, and perhaps supplant the older woman whose display was doing little so far to inspire the gathered warriors.

With a scream, Thorbjorg looked skywards, raised her hands, and then fell onto her knees, stone dagger in hand. Ferociously, yet with undeniable skill, she sliced open the torso of the man Horsa had killed and pulled out an armful of entrails. Even at that distance Bellicus could see them steaming and more than one man in the front rank of Arthur's army retched at the sight. It was never nice to see such a thing, and even more challenging when one was nursing a hangover from the previous night's carousing.

Thorbjorg, determined to make the most of her two victims, was touching and staring at the scattered, red mess of entrails like a Christian monk engrossed in a holy book. At last, she raised her hands up once more, blood running down them hideously, and cried, "Thunor has spoken. The omens are good. We shall be victorious this day!"

There were cheers from the men behind her, led, Bellicus noticed, by Hengist himself who was sitting astride a dappled grey horse. "What about the other sacrifice?" the *bretwalda* shouted once the noise had died down.

In response, Thorbjorg beckoned her helpers forward. Horsa, eager to make amends for his earlier over-exuberance, slapped the terrified man on the ear. It was a ringing blow, the report of which echoed even to the watching Britons, making some wince and ending the victim's hysterical begging for mercy. One of the Saxon warriors kicked the man's knees from behind and, when he fell forward Horsa held him down as the *volva* crouched above, muttering inaudible spells and incantations.

The poor man was either too senseless to fight for his freedom or had simply given himself up to the inevitable fate in store for him but still, as Thorbjorg's deadly grey knife came up to his throat, he tried to jerk away. It was no use, the muscular soldiers held him firmly in place as the stone weapon did its terrible work, drawing a line of scarlet across his grubby white neck and forever ending his fearful whimpers.

"One day battles will be fought without all this shit happening before it," Duro said dully as they watched the man expire.

"Perhaps," Merlin said. "But not this day. For now, we must let the Saxons perform their rituals, and then we'll have our turn."

Thorbjorg had stepped back to stare at the pattern of dripping blood coursing down her victim's chest, trying to make sense of the message it carried from the gods.

"Our turn?" Duro asked. "What are you planning?" He looked from Merlin to Bellicus, but his giant friend didn't appear to know any more than he did, and the High Druid would say no more, even to Bel. There was a glint in his eye that made everyone curious for it seemed even Arthur hadn't been told what Merlin had in store. Certainly, without any Saxon prisoners there could be no blood sacrifice to match the gory show being played out before them.

Thorbjorg was cackling maniacally now and it was a strange, guttural sound that raised the hairs on the arms and necks of all who heard it. If Bellicus had practised his piercing stare in a polished bronze mirror, honing it until it could turn even the hardest of men's gaze, Thorbjorg had surely spent hours working to make that laugh of hers as blood-curdling as possible.

"Thank Taranis we don't have to face her in battle," someone muttered, drawing a vicious growl from Duro.

"She's a hag," said the centurion. "I wish I *could* meet her in battle. I'd ram my spatha right down her fuc—"

"She's finished," Merlin said dryly, watching as the *volva* disappeared, still cackling, into the ranks of massed Saxon spearmen, followed by Horsa and the other warriors. "Our turn."

He rode forward, ahead of Arthur's army, white beard practically glowing in the sun, and raised his arms to the heavens. He began to chant, a weird refrain the words of which could not be made out by anyone except Bellicus who'd heard the spell before although he couldn't quite remember where. During his training, surely, but when, where, and in what context, he wasn't sure.

The High Druid looked down at the Saxon army, lip curled with disdain as he eyed the bloody corpses torn open so brutally on the grass between them. Then he looked to his left, past the very end of the Saxon line and pointed.

All eyes had been on Thorbjorg's display first, and then Merlin, but Bellicus had noticed movement at either side of the battle lines. What had originally appeared to be merely tall bushes, were now pulled away, by some means the druid was uncertain of – probably

255

hidden ropes – to reveal uncanny clay effigies of human figures. They were monstrous in both size and appearance and, as all eyes were focused on the one Merlin had pointed towards, realisation of who it was supposed to be struck the stunned audience.

"It's Hengist," Arthur muttered, amazed by the likeness to the enemy *bretwalda*.

Bellicus couldn't say exactly what made it so recognizable for it was not quite lifelike, rather it was stylized and undeniably eldritch in appearance. But it had the beard Hengist was so fond of stroking, and the eyes and nose were so similar that no-one could doubt who it represented.

The Saxons, especially Hengist himself, were wide-eyed and stunned by the sinister effigy, obviously wondering what it meant and what would happen next.

Merlin did not make them wait. He turned in his saddle and pointed again, drawing every eye in both armies to a spot off to the other, far side of the gathered spearmen.

Thorbjorg's hideous laughter could not be heard any more and Bellicus wished he could see her reaction to the second clay effigy. Like the other, it had been sculpted in a stylized manner but was immediately recognizable, this time as the long-legged Saxon *volva*.

Duro was smiling, as were many of Arthur's men – astonished at the skill of the artisan who'd crafted the sculptures which were at once terrifying yet humorous, although the Saxons did not seem to find them very funny.

"You!" Merlin roared, in a voice so loud and powerful that it had no right emanating from the white-bearded, seemingly elderly High Druid. He'd taken his oaken staff from its place on his saddle and directed it at Hengist who blanched visibly, even at this distance. Then Merlin cried, "And your witch!"

He lowered his staff, hooking it back into his saddle as if its job was done, and his shoulders were shaking.

"What's wrong with him?" Duro asked. "Is he having a seizure?"

Bellicus immediately put his friend's mind at ease. "No. Watch." He knew the centurion had suffered seizures himself after receiving a head injury in the legions. It had been the reason he'd had to leave his post those twenty-odd years before, and the experience had always terrified Duro who feared it might happen again at any moment without warning.

Merlin's shuddering shoulders did not presage any seizure however, as the centurion realised when the druid's rich, melodious laughter came back to them on a sudden westerly breeze. The amusement ended in an instant, though, when Merlin shouted, "Die!" and jerked both hands forward, as if striking those distant, brown figurines.

Already, fire arrows were streaking from the bows of archers hidden amongst the foliage bordering the site of the coming battle. There were six that Bellicus could see, three on either side – Merlin was not taking any chances with an archer missing the target but, as it turned out, those he'd chosen for this task were highly skilled and every one of the missiles thudded home in the clay effigies.

"My spies in your camp took strands of your hair, Hengist, and brought them to me," Merlin called to the *bretwalda*. "And your witch's too. She should really be more careful, since she knows very well how much power even a single strand of hair can hold." He laughed again, as if hearing the funniest joke in the world for the first time. "I used those hairs as I moulded my effigies of you. You will die, Hengist. You and your *volva*." The High Druid was laughing hysterically now, and he was forced to wipe tears from his beard before he could finish his speech but, as he ground out the final words through gritted teeth, his laughter evaporated. "You will die today, Hengist and so will your witch, and every last one of your men. Now…Burn!"

He pulled his horse's head around and kicked it into a canter back towards Arthur in the centre of the Britons' line as the fire arrows quickly did their work and turned the pristine brown clay into masses of scorching flame.

"Wooden frames," Merlin grinned as he rode up to Bellicus. "Clay moulded over it and smeared with animal fat. They'll be smouldering ruins in moments." He turned to Arthur. "I'd suggest we attack then."

The Bear of Britain threw his head back and laughed. The Saxons hadn't finished their pre-battle rituals, but the first blow belonged to Merlin, and Thorbjorg's powers were not so feared by the Britons for now at least, while the enemy spearmen were visibly unnerved by the sight of the burning effigies.

Hoping to regain some of the momentum, a massive warrior strode out from the massed Saxon ranks, banging the blade of his massive sword against a shield painted completely black. It was like a gaping hole in the sunlit scene and the man raised his weapon and pointed it at Arthur, calling in the Briton's own tongue if a little disjointedly.

"Where's your champion, warlord? The one named Lancelot? I would face him in single combat and show you weaklings how a real man fights."

"He's away visiting your sister," Duro called back, making an obscene gesture, knowing such a childish jibe was always good for a laugh. As expected, it did arouse much merriment, from Arthur's men at least. The giant warrior was not impressed, however, and spat on the ground.

"That wouldn't surprise me," the Saxon retorted, and his accent was harsh and almost impossible to understand. "It's well known your champion is better at bedding women than wielding a blade. My name is Hrothulf, son of Hrothgar - are none of your so-called men brave enough to face me then?"

This whole ritual had been expected, of course, for it happened before practically every battle.

Eburus, on foot beside Velugna who'd insisted on fighting with the army, looked up at Arthur and nodded. With a grin at Bellicus and Duro and a last kiss for the princess he walked forward, rolling his shoulders and moving with the assured gait of a man who knows how well he can fight. Still only in his early twenties, he was tall, broad of shoulder and knew himself how impressive he looked although Bellicus was happy to note that, in the past few months, the Votadini champion had lost most of his arrogant over-confidence. Experience had tempered him somewhat, although not enough to make him think twice about taking on a duel such as this one. Eburus lived to fight, and this was his chance to make a name for himself among more than just the peoples north of Hadrianus's wall.

"I've never heard of you, Hrothulf," shouted the Votadini while smoothly drawing his own sword from its sheath. "But my name is Eburus, and I'm going to kill you."

"By Taranis," someone in the ranks behind Bellicus muttered. "His accent is almost as hard to understand as the Saxon's."

"I can't make out a damn word either of them are saying," another agreed, laughing somewhat anxiously. "But who cares? As long as the big ginger lad kills the ugly Saxon twat, I'll be happy."

The enemy soldier must have done this sort of thing before and wanted to make the most of his moment in front of the gathered armies. He started calling out again, boasting of his prowess, rattling teeth – harvested from slain enemies and worn around his neck on a leather thong – and describing what he would do with his sword to Eburus.

The Votadini champion wasn't interested in boasts, however. As the Saxon lifted his black shield high in the air and, Bellicus believed, proclaimed its name for all the world to hear, Eburus bent down, lifted a small rock, and threw it.

There was a clatter as the stone struck the Saxon's helmet, making him jerk back in surprise but, before anything else could be said, Eburus was on him and the black shield was needed to stop the Votadini's blade carving deep into the Saxon's ribs.

To his credit, Hrothulf knew his business and, with the time for posturing over, batted aside Eburus's attacks and rammed the boss of his shield against the Votadini's shoulder, hurling him backwards. On came the Saxon, relentless and fierce yet cold and in control at the same time, using both his sword and shield as offensive weapons.

It was possible Eburus had never faced someone using this kind of technique before, and he seemed lost, without any idea how to do anything other than simply remain alive and out of reach of the vicious pattern-welded blade of his opponent. He could not find a chance to launch so much as a single thrust or slash of his own but, after a time his youthful stamina prevailed and the older Saxon's punishing attacks slowed.

The combatants circled one another warily as acrid, black smoke from the burning effigies swirled about them, making eyes and throats sting. Warriors on either side roared encouragement to their champions and now it seemed there was a shift in the tide of the battle. Hrothulf had tired himself in his attempts to wear down Eburus and find an opening for a killing blow, but it hadn't worked and, as the Saxon renewed his assault with rather less vigour,

Eburus found it easier to defend himself and even launch attacks of his own.

There was an oddly high-pitched scream of pain as the Votadini's blade tore open a ragged gash in Hrothulf's mail coat, drawing blood for the first time in the bout, along with a delirious roar of triumph from Arthur's army.

"He's faking," Duro growled, shaking his head at his brash young friend's inability to read what was happening.

Bellicus nodded. "Agreed. The Saxon moves like he's exhausted, but you can see by the way his head tracks Eburus's movements that he's as alert as ever. It's a ruse."

Eburus was roaring and shouting insults at his opponent now, confidence filling him with bravado as he sensed victory approaching. Then the Saxon took a blow on his black shield which dropped him onto one knee and Eburus instantly lashed out, rapping the pommel of his sword against Hrothulf's helmet.

The Saxon rocked back, still down on one knee and Eburus, glorying in the acclaim from Velugna and the rest of Arthur's massed ranks, moved forward for the killing blow.

"It's a trap!" screamed both Bellicus and Duro at the same time as Hrothulf, eyes blazing in triumph, lunged forward, the tip of his sword glinting in the sun.

Blood spurted and the fight was over in an instant.

There was silence for just a heartbeat and then roars of delight filled the air, leaving Duro staring at Bellicus.

The druid was grinning in relief. "He knew the Saxon was acting."

"What happened?" demanded the centurion. "Damn sun reflected off Hrothulf's helmet and blinded me. I couldn't see how it ended!" He too was smiling for he'd truly believed their headstrong Votadini friend was about to die.

"He was waiting for Hrothulf's attack and dodged out of the way. Then he pierced the Saxon's throat with his own blade, raised his arms in the air, and laughed at Hengist's army."

As they were talking, Eburus reached down to claim the dead man's gruesome necklace along with his sword and black shield. Some warriors would remove any valuables, such as gold or silver torcs and leave them with their companions before fighting a duel like this one, but Hrothulf, confident of winning as he was, had not taken such precautions. Eburus quickly divested the corpse of a gold arm-ring and other, smaller, less shiny items even Bellicus couldn't make out at this distance, before striding back towards Arthur's army like an avenging god.

As he reached the ranks, he turned to acknowledge the shouted congratulations from Arthur with a salute, then he called to Bellicus and Duro.

"Thanks for the warning, lads, but do you think I'm daft? I knew he was pretending the whole time. D'ye like my new black shield?"

And the cheering hordes of Arthur's army enfolded him, Velugna drawing him in and kissing him fiercely as druid, centurion, and warlord grinned like drunks in an untended alehouse.

CHAPTER THIRTY

The Saxon, Leofdaeg, was grinning as Lancelot's men locked shields together and lowered their spears towards the oncoming enemy warriors. "Did you fools think you could just walk in here and slit our throats as we slept?" he snorted.

"What are we going to do?" Kay asked in a voice tight with anxiety although he held his spear in an unwavering grasp.

Lancelot looked around, trying to count how many soldiers they faced and how best to take the battle to them. As he was thinking, more Saxons ran towards the gateway they'd just come through and drew across heavy wooden beams. These would not have been as effective as proper gates in a siege, but now, if the Britons attempted to fight their way back out that way they'd be forced to stop and move the beams while simultaneously fending off the Saxons.

"We only have two options," said Lancelot, loudly enough for all his warband to hear. "Either we make a break for the shore through the western gate and hope we can steal a ship big enough to carry us all to safety, or we kill every one of these whoresons and take the fort as we planned."

There were scattered cheers at that, but not enough to inspire confidence in Lancelot who knew himself both choices were poor.

"Why can't we try doing both?" Cador asked, speaking more urgently as the Saxons were almost ready to mount their attack. "I mean, move towards the western gate in formation, while killing the bastards as we go, rather than us all just making a run for it."

That suggestion did bring some enthusiastic cries of support from the men, so Lancelot agreed, glad to have the older man with them. "All right," he said, trying to ignore the urge to sprint out of the shieldwall and skewer the grinning Jarl Leofdaeg. "Start walking towards the far gatehouse and make sure your shield stays locked to the man beside you. We'll head for that warehouse there to start with," he pointed his sword at a squat stone structure without windows. "Use it for cover as we move. If any of these bastards get in range, gut them with your spears."

The Saxon jarl's grin had changed to a determined frown and he called out to his comrades, urging them to attack. Some of them were happy to oblige, despite the fact they were completely unarmoured, for bravery was something the Saxons did not lack.

Even when it was more akin to stupidity than courage.

Screaming war-cries, two men, stripped to the waist, hairy chests rippling as they raised hammers over their heads, charged Lancelot's shieldwall. The first, a youngster trying to impress his kinsmen no doubt, was killed before he even had a chance to bring down his hammer, as, despite dodging the spear directly in front of him, two others slid into his pale torso on either side.

The second attacker fared a little better, managing to slam his hammer down on the helmet of one of Lancelot's men, but, again, a spear tore into his body, then a shield battered against his face. When he fell, dazed, the booted feet of the moving shieldwall stamped him into the dirt, cutting off his cries and leaving him dead in their wake.

"Not like that, you fucking idiots," screamed Leofdaeg, who must have been the man left in charge of the fort in Hengist and Horsa's absence. "Don't get too close!" To demonstrate, he lifted the hammer dropped by one of the dead men and threw it with all his might. He must have trained hard with throwing axes, for the hammer flew as straight and true as any hunter's arrow and smashed directly into the face of one of the Briton warriors. Even had the man been wearing a face-mask like the one attached to Cador's helmet it would not have saved him. He fell and was left behind, for those who'd been flanking him knew such a blow must be fatal and, even if, by some miracle he was merely knocked unconscious, Lancelot's warband could not afford to carry him.

"Keep moving," bellowed Lancelot, throat dry, heart pounding, as much from having to leave behind one of his men as any fears for his own skin. "We're nearly at the building. Raise shields!"

The last was screamed as a volley of hammers – tools used for constructing and maintaining ships rather than instruments of war but no less deadly for it – flew towards them. There was a terrific clattering as they struck the linden-wood and iron of the warband's shields but, mercifully, no more of the men were injured.

"Hold!" shouted Cador. "Lift the hammers and throw them onto the roof of the building so the bastards can't throw them at us again!"

"Do it!" Lancelot commanded. "Don't try and hit any of the Saxons, it'll just be more ammunition for them. Do as Cador says and get them up onto the roof."

The formation paused and any man who was close to a spent missile reached down and lifted it. They were then hurled, with varying degrees of accuracy, onto the roof of the nearby structure. Unfortunately, the Saxons rarely fought as part of a trained unit, moving in unison on a command; instead, they tended to act as individuals and so it proved now as one man, not as hasty as his fellows, still held his hammer and decided this would be a good time to launch it.

The tool spun through the air unnoticed, until it smashed into the jaw of a man to Lancelot's right. The crack as the hammer struck home left the blond warrior in no doubt that the bone had shattered but, perhaps mercifully, it either killed him instantly or at least knocked him unconscious and he fell like a dropped sack of turnips.

"Shit," Lancelot roared. "Keep your eyes open, lads, shields up at all times. Let's move on!" As he gave the order, he stooped to pick up the hammer that had killed his spearman. Quickly, he grasped the blade of his drawn sword beneath his left bicep and, turning towards Leofdaeg, threw the hammer using his right hand.

The jarl was still grinning wickedly, certain that his warband was about to annihilate the Britons, but his expression changed in an instant as the hammer Lancelot had thrown battered into his arm. He let out a yelp and spun almost completely around, sword falling from limp fingers, face twisted in agony.

The Saxon glared at Lancelot, who laughed, knowing he'd snapped the bastard's arm, ruining his chances of ever wielding a sword effectively ever again, and then the Briton's formation was moving on again, behind the cover of the squat, stone building.

"Does anyone know how to sail a ship?"

Three or four of Lancelot's men replied to his question with shouts of "Aye," and "I do," and, gods be praised, the open western gate and the shore beyond it were now in sight, along with the ships they hoped to make their daring escape on. The Saxons were following them around the building, screaming in anger but knowing it would be folly to attack the heavily armoured Britons without so much as a leather cuirass of their own for protection.

None ran to the gatehouse, suggesting that one, like the other on the eastern wall, did not retain its old wooden gates either.

"We're almost there," Kay bellowed, triumph in his voice as their tight formation moved ever closer to safety. Even if only a couple of their men knew how to get a stolen ship moving, they'd at least be able to get clear of this place and make it into the estuary. As long as Arthur's army won the battle against Hengist's hordes it wouldn't matter that Lancelot's raid had been a failure. They could come back here at their leisure, with dozens more men, and wipe out the remaining Saxons.

"Keep your shields up!" Lancelot commanded, fearing there might be more defenders that they hadn't seen yet, although that seemed unlikely.

Unlikely, but not impossible.

As they came past the end of the low building they'd been using for cover, Lancelot's eyes were flicking back and forward between the bare-chested men following them, and the gatehouse he was heading towards. Now, his gaze was drawn by the edge of the warehouse they'd just passed, and his guts fell at what he saw there.

"Shields up!" he screamed. "Shields up!"

It didn't matter; twenty or so javelins of the barbed-tip kind known as *angons*, were already coursing through the air towards the Britons and, before Lancelot could take another breath, the missiles tore into his men. Some battered into the sturdy shields, but not all. There were screams all around Arthur's champion and he saw men killed or horrifically injured by the six-foot long *angons* which, with their vicious, barbed-points, could not be easily drawn either from shield or flesh. Cador was no longer on his feet, but neither were at least half of Lancelot's men.

"Brace!" Kay shouted. "They're charging!"

The unarmoured Saxons following them had taken heart at the sight of so many of Lancelot's warriors being felled and they were coming to finish off the rest now. Swords, hammers, and *seaxes* were raised by the bearded, screaming men racing towards them with death in their eyes.

The battle was over, Lancelot realised, and he was amazed at how calm he felt despite knowing his doom was upon him.

"Run for the gate!" he shouted. "Make for the nearest ship!" Perhaps if they could get on board some vessel they'd be able to defend it for a few moments, until…What? There would be no-one to push it from the shore into the water.

All this and more raced through his mind as he ran, knowing flight was futile, but unwilling to simply die on the end of a Saxon sword or spear.

He looked back over his shoulder as he sprinted and saw two more of his men cut down, one with the back of his skull shattered by a thrown axe, the second taken by another of those cursed javelins. He saw Cador lying, face down on the grass, unmoving, along with so many more men who had, just moments before, been full of life and promise, and tears filled his eyes as he ran, wondering why he was even bothering. There could be no possible escape from Garrianum now – he had failed utterly, and any tales told of bold Lancelot in times to come would mention this defeat and his ignominious death.

He'd always thought there would be more for him – a heroic place in the druids' tales – but then, so had all those brave men who lay dead behind him, surely. He was no more special than any of them. Less in fact, since he'd been the one in charge of this disastrous raid.

Another missile whistled past him and struck one of his men in the small of the back. It didn't penetrate the armour, but it must have hurt terribly, and the unfortunate warrior screamed as he fell forward, sobbing in terror, for he knew he was done for.

The others ran on, but guilt assailed Lancelot and he bent to try and help the fallen Briton, trying to use his shield to protect them both, and it was just as well, for yet another missile clattered against it.

He pushed damp blond hair away from his eyes and looked back to see Saxons charging towards them. A few of his men were through the open gateway and climbing aboard the nearest ship now but, leaderless and stranded, they could do nothing more than try to form another shieldwall on the deck of the grounded vessel which, Lancelot saw, didn't even have a mast. That was lying on the shore, apparently in the midst of being repaired or renewed when the fighting had started.

Laughing in black frustration, Lancelot finally admitted to himself that they were all about to die. He counted just seven of his men still alive on the ship, while the warrior on the ground next to him could not even struggle back to his feet and was crying pitifully, begging Lancelot to help him. Saxons streamed past him, towards the gatehouse and it seemed like there were hundreds of them.

Rising to his feet again, Arthur's champion lifted his shield and tossed his spear aside. "Who's first then?" he demanded, pulling out his sword and making sure the helmet gifted to him by Arthur mere days before was still securely fitted.

He was glad he'd turned to face the approaching sea-wolves, for the sounds of battle filled the air behind him and he knew the rest of his warband were being slaughtered. Twenty-five men, proud and filled with hope and vitality that morning, all dead or dying, leaving only him to face the dozens of Saxon killers now arrayed all around him.

"This," he said as he tapped his helmet with the flat of his blade, "was a gift from the Merlin. It's imbued with his druid magic." His voice was mercifully strong, not betraying the fear he felt as he eyed the accursed Jarl Leofdaeg who'd originally raised the alarm and sealed their fate. That man's arm hung limply, uselessly, at his side, and his sweating, pale face betrayed the pain his injury was causing him, but it hardly mattered. The rest of the enemy warriors stared at Lancelot with undisguised battle-lust, beards bristling, teeth bared in feral, lupine grins as they crowded around the buildings and tents and rubble dotted about the camp. "Merlin promised me I could not be killed as long as I wore this helmet," Lancelot finished and the words seemed ludicrous even to his own ears, but they somehow filled him with a strength he desperately needed at that moment.

He held his sword and shield higher and his expression mirrored that of the grinning, bloodthirsty enemies surrounding him on every side.

"By the time we've finished with you," said Jarl Leofdaeg in a voice gravid with venom, "you'll be wishing I *would* let you die, Waelisc scum. And I'll have that fucking helmet from you too."

267

With that, the Saxons, masters still of Garrianum, closed upon him and the short battle for the Saxon Shore came to a wretched end.

CHAPTER THIRTY-ONE

"Enough talk," Arthur said, eyes aglow with the wonderful success of their pre-battle rituals. The burning effigies of Hengist and Thorbjorg had collapsed upon themselves, their thin wooden frames consumed by the intense heat, but those, along with Erebus's victory, would live in the hearts of the Britons at least until the battle lines met and dozens of men were cut down, screaming, in the first clash.

The glory of war would not seem quite so enticing at that point, but at least Arthur's troopers had the early advantage – all the Saxons had was the knowledge their magicians were soundly beaten, and their whole army embarrassed. Even the floods of ale that would have been downed as part of yet another timeless wartime ritual would not do much to assuage their superstitious anxiety.

Sulinus nodded as Arthur's gaze fell upon him. "My men are in position, my lord," he said, and his usual sardonic expression was replaced with a grim determination. The old man would not be taking part in the fighting, but he believed his riders, and their leader, Aesibuas, had enough training and natural skill to perform their duties competently.

"Everyone else knows what to do," the warlord said, glancing along his line of captains and advisors. It was a statement, not a question, and the grim nods he received in reply were all he expected. "Then make ready," Arthur commanded, and the captains hurried off to join their units. He waited until all were in position, and then he looked up at the sky and raised his sword aloft, shouting as loudly as he could, hoping everyone gathered there would hear his words. "This is the day we smash the sea-wolves forever and retake our lands. One last battle, my friends, and then we can live in peace."

Bellicus stared at the warlord's oiled steel blade, noting its blue-grey sheen in the sunshine, and, although the hilt and pommel appeared the same, he knew it was a different sword to the one that had been miraculously drawn by Arthur from King Ceneu's floorboards not so long ago. That blade had been iron, the druid was certain of it. A copy. Merlin's forethought was impressive. His

269

thoughts quickly turned to the present, however, as Arthur's arm came down to point at the enemy line and the command issued from his throat in a harsh bellow.

"Attack!"

The Saxons started moving forward at the same moment.

Arthur, Merlin, Bellicus and Sulinus held their horses in position as their own spearmen marched past, the sounds of their feet and equipment thunderous and almost hypnotic in the morning air. The young hunter, Cocca, was in their ranks, and right beside him was Elpin, the farmer who'd almost killed Bellicus. Funny how enemies could become allies and even friends over time, thought the druid, saluting to them both, noting their pale, anxious expressions and appreciating their courage all the more for it.

Duro was, of course, at the very front of the Britons' formation, as he believed a centurion should be. Bellicus had tried to talk him out of it, but, in truth, if the leaders would not take part in the worst of fighting, at the most dangerous place, why should their underlings.

The likes of Merlin, Sulinus and Bellicus were exempt from taking part in the fighting on foot for various reasons, and Arthur, no coward by any stretch of the imagination, had decided to remain in the saddle for now in order to direct his forces and make changes should things not go quite to plan.

When they were within range, both sides hurled their javelins and throwing axes, wooden shafts and iron blades sailing through the air in a deadly black rain which battered against wooden shields, iron helms, and flesh and bone.

When the initial thuds of the weapons striking their targets ended, the inevitable, horrific screams and moans of pain and anguish rose up, but Duro and the other captains ordered the second, and final, round of missiles to be launched at the enemy who were copying their movements.

Again, the cloudless blue sky, so beautiful on any other day, was filled with the terrible instruments of death and again there was that clattering, thumping, and pitiful, sickening crying of those maimed by the missiles. Then came more thumping and cracking as men tried to dislodge javelins stuck into the faces of their shields, or at least shatter the shafts so they didn't weigh them down as badly.

Bellicus muttered a prayer to Dis Pater, begging the deity to accept the souls of his countrymen taken so early in the battle and to grant them a place at his side until their next incarnation in this cruel world of men.

Even from his lofty vantage point atop Darac he couldn't make out Duro, but he could hear the centurion roaring encouragement and commands and the druid was glad. His friend had survived the battle's opening but now the real fighting was about to begin and neither side seemed content to hold back.

The Saxons were charging towards Duro and the rest of Arthur's front rank of spearmen, faces twisted with battle-fury, weapons held before them ready to taste the blood and soft flesh of their enemies.

When the lines met there was almost a collective grunt as the wind was blasted from chests and the shock of the clash was felt in the shafts of spears and on shield-arms, and then the field became a maelstrom of flashing blades, glittering spearpoints, gouting blood and wild, violent movement.

Cai looked up at Bellicus, ears down, tail lowered, and the druid smiled reassuringly. "I know, lad. Good boy. It'll be over soon enough."

At least he'll be safe from the fighting, thought the druid. Unless the Saxons break through our lines.

"Damn," Arthur muttered as he watched the battle ebb and flow. "We're being pushed back. Hengist's men fight like demons."

No one said anything. Everyone knew how dangerous the Saxons were – they fought with a savagery that few armies could match, which was, after all, how they were slowly taking control of these lands.

"Sulinus, give the signal."

The decurion nodded and made a gesture to the trumpeter standing beside them. Raising the bronze instrument to his lips, the man blew long and hard. The clear tone pealed out across the land and was followed by two more, shorter, blasts. Although it had an entirely different timbre, Bellicus was reminded of the sound of the carnyx which had helped him rescue little Princess Catia from Thorbjorg's sacrificial ritual what seemed like a lifetime ago. So much had happened since that dark night at the Hanging Stones…

The men fighting and dying before them took little notice of the trumpet, but Arthur and his advisors watched the low, wooded rise to the left of the battlefield, hearts beating hard, blood pounding in their veins, waiting for the new cavalry unit to make its appearance. If something had happened to them – if Hengist had realised the hillock, with its stand of trees, was a likely hiding place for enemy soldiers and sent men of his own to clear it – all would likely be lost for Arthur's army. The Saxons were winning the battle at this moment and, without other reserves of spearmen to call upon, there would be no stopping Hengist's forces if they managed to break through Arthur's line and so attack from the rear as well as the front.

It would be a disaster, and undoubtedly mean the end for Britain as it existed now. Their way of life, their very culture, would be swept away, taken with the souls of the dead by Dis Pater, only there would be no hope of reincarnation for the Old Ways of the Britons. The Saxons would make sure of that. It was unthinkable to Bellicus – they were only just coming to terms with the departure of the Roman legions and moulding the country to suit their own needs rather than those of some distant emperor. To see it all taken away by bloodthirsty sea-wolves…

"There!"

The giant druid's eyes, and thoughts, were drawn to the top of the rise by Arthur's excited shout. There, he could make out movement, small figures on horseback, two or three abreast, moving out of the trees at a steady pace down the slope.

Either they were Sulinus's cavalrymen, or the Saxons had slaughtered them all and stolen their horses. Which was not only unlikely, but ludicrous, for, as his sight adjusted to the distance, Bellicus could tell these riders were moving in a skilled, controlled manner. There was no mad, wild rush of the kind the druid would expect from any other group of horsemen, be they Britons, Saxons, Dalriadans or anyone else.

Except Romans. Or those trained by them.

He looked at Sulinus and saw the old man's jaw clenched in trepidation as well as anticipation. For all his bluff manner, the decurion had come to like and respect the men he'd been training these past few weeks and, as much as he wanted them to win, he also feared them being killed in the action.

The Saxons had their backs to the approaching horsemen and were completely unprepared for the volley of javelins which tore into their rear ranks. There was confusion and disarray as the men who had been pushing forwards on their comrades' backs were suddenly cut down. The riders raced along the Saxon line, letting fly all three of the deadly missiles they carried in their saddle quivers, and, at this close range, and with such a tightly packed target, many of the javelins found their mark in an enemy or his shield.

"Yes. Yes!" Arthur ground out the word with savage glee as he watched the panic spread through the ranks of the Saxons, until even those fighting in the front row could tell something was wrong.

In the grand scheme of things, of course, the numbers killed by Arthur's cavalry were a fairly small proportion of Hengist's overall army, but it was a devastating and wholly unexpected blow, and it rocked the Saxons to their core.

"Will they take the bait?" Merlin wondered, as Aesibuas raised his spatha overhead, ready to lead his riders back up the shallow hill they'd originally came down from. "Will the bastards follow them into the trees, and onto our traps?"

They all stared, hearts in their mouths, wondering if the Saxons would do as they hoped. Had Hengist's men been part of a well-trained, drilled collection of units, this plan would likely be a total failure, for the commanders would likely recognise this for the trap it was. But, of course, the Saxon army did not work like that – at this stage of the battle, it was a large mass of mainly battle-crazed individuals, doing whatever they pleased.

Did it please them now to run up a hillock, chasing horses?

"Idiots," Arthur said, with no trace of the relief Bellicus knew must be filling him at that moment. "They've fallen for it. They're going after Aesibuas."

Only the rear rows – the ones which had taken the brunt of the javelins and seen their friends cut down by those wicked, iron tips – had taken the bait, but it was enough. The pressure was relieved on the front ranks and that meant Arthur's infantry were not so badly beset. In fact, with the uncertainty this shift had brought to Hengist's army it meant Duro and those beside him were able to push ahead once more, and force the enemy onto the back foot.

"It's all going as we hoped," Merlin muttered in satisfaction.

As he said the words, Bellicus watched, almost in slow motion, as a slinger's stone sailed up into the sky – a poorly aimed shot if ever there was one – and then come back down in a shallow arc before smashing straight into Aesibuas's helmet. Despair filled him as the cavalry officer pitched out of his saddle and was lost from sight, his riders racing past him as the screaming, vengeful Saxon footmen charged after them.

"Fuck! He's down," Bellicus exploded, turning to Sulinus. "Slinger took him out."

The decurion's rheumy eyes caught his and there was disbelief in them. "Are you sure?" he demanded. "I didn't see that."

It was on the tip of the druid's tongue to retort angrily, *you can barely see the horse you're sitting on, old man!* but he held his temper in check and nodded. "Believe me, Sulinus. The cavalry is leaderless." He could tell neither Arthur nor Merlin had seen Aesibuas fall either, they'd both been looking at different parts of the battle. They didn't question him though for his conviction was clear to all.

"Will your riders be able to function without Aesibuas?" Arthur asked, nerves making his voice harsher than usual. Sulinus was used to it, however, and, indeed, felt the same anxiety as his warlord.

"They'll get away from the spearmen chasing them," the decurion nodded thoughtfully, liver-spotted hands gripping his reins tighter. "That shouldn't be too hard, as long as they hold their discipline and keep moving through the trees as they were told."

"But will they be able to ride around the bluff and rejoin us here?" Arthur demanded. "We *need* them here to take full advantage of our current position on the front foot. It's not going to last forever, and I want their support here as soon as possible."

Sulinus stared ahead, straining to see his riders, who had performed so well until now, racing back up the low hill and into the welcoming, concealing trees. Their preparations had been rushed and he had done what he could to make his *turma* as strong and well trained as possible in the short time afforded him. Aesibuas had been a godsend, for he was a natural horseman and leader, and quickly understood what Sulinus wanted from him. He would have made an excellent decurion himself one day, if that

Saxon hadn't cut him down just as he was about to write his name in the druids' histories.

But there had been no other standout candidates for promotion – none who came close to Aesibuas at least – and, without time, Sulinus had decided instead to focus all his efforts on making Aesibuas the best leader he could be, and the riders the best unit they could be.

"Sulinus!"

Arthur's harsh voice stung the old decurion back to reality and he sighed heavily, thinking of his son, oblivious to all this and safely back at their stables near Luguvalium with Licinia. Sulinus had promised Rues that he'd be careful, and not put himself in any dangerous situations. So far, he'd stuck by that promise.

"Shit, the Saxons are starting to take control again," Bellicus cursed, shading his eyes with his hand as he watched the battle's ebb and flow. "They fight like madmen. I'm not sure even the Picts fight with such ferocity."

"We need your riders, Sulinus," Arthur said, but his voice was softer now as he recognised the agony the old decurion was suffering. Aesibuas had become a good friend to the decurion in their short time working together and the man's loss must have been a heavy blow to him.

"And you'll have 'em. Hold the line, Arthur, Bear of Britain, I'll be back soon!" With that, the craggy cavalryman saluted in the Roman fashion, kicked his heels into his mount's flanks and galloped away to the northwest.

CHAPTER THIRTY-TWO

Arthur and his two remaining advisors watched in silence as Sulinus disappeared around the side of the bluff, wondering if they'd ever see him again. His mind was sharp and he knew his business, but he'd shown over the past few weeks that his body was not up to it any more. He grew tired quickly and the sight of him limping around camp, grimacing and gurning at his men – who all loved him of course – was a familiar one.

"He's not coming back, is he?" Arthur asked sorrowfully.

"I wouldn't bet against him," Merlin replied somewhat reproachfully. "Us old men are still capable of mixing it with you youngsters, just wait and see."

Again, Bellicus wondered at this suggestion of Merlin's that he was somehow more ancient than those close to him knew him to be. Admittedly, a man in his early fifties was quite old, but nowhere near the level of decrepitude Merlin liked to portray himself as. Bellicus could only assume that his superior within the Druid Order believed the people expected the Merlin, their High Druid, to have many decades of learning and experience behind them and played the part even when he was with friends.

It was not important at that moment though, and Bellicus's thoughts quickly returned to the battle raging before them, wondering if he would be forced to take part in the fighting himself, even in his weakened state.

* * *

"Aesibuas is down!" Ruui was the son of a tanner in Caer Lerion but he, like his fallen duplicarius, had been drawn to horses since he was young. He was still only twenty, but, when not working at the family tannery, he'd helped out at the town stables, learning to care for the animals and then, eventually, to his delight, getting to ride them himself.

He'd been immensely proud when Decurion Sulinus had chosen him to be part of his new cavalry unit, but his pride had turned now to panic as he'd been riding close behind Aesibuas and seen the duplicarius struck by the solitary missile which seemed to appear from an empty blue sky. As if the maelstrom of battle wasn't terrifying enough!

Ruui expected – needed – to be told what to do. He had never given a command in his life, but he was good at following orders. As his mount galloped on, up the low hill, he looked back over his shoulder, hoping that either Aesibuas would somehow have miraculously survived the slinger's bolt and be riding along at his back, or that someone else within the unit would offer him guidance. He could see similar, anxious looks on the riders closest to him. The ones that had noticed their duplicarius's demise, at least.

There was nothing for it but to carry on with what they'd been told to do: Reach the top of the slope and ride carefully through the trees. At the far end, where the grove opened out, there were more javelins which they would use to refill their quivers before riding hard around the bottom of the hill's opposite side and back to rejoin Arthur.

A horseman to his right swore as a branch struck him across the face. It was only a slim branch, thankfully, not enough to knock him out of his saddle, but enough to hurt.

"Keep moving," Ruui said encouragingly, recognising the dark rider called Catti. "Go carefully, follow the line we were shown."

Catti cursed, rubbing the red weal on his cheek but making sure his mount stayed to the left of the trees. That was the safe path – the rest of the grove was primed with caltrops and pits for the enemy spearmen chasing after them to stumble into. There were some of Arthur's own warriors up in the trees as well, ready to fall upon the battle-crazed enemy pursuers although they were so well hidden even Ruui, who knew they were there, could barely see them.

They rode as quietly as possible, picking their way carefully while still moving at a decent pace. Ruui was near the very back of their line and he could hear the savage shouts and thundering feet of the Saxons coming after them and then, when he was about halfway through the grove, the noises behind changed.

The warcries and threats in the guttural tongue of their pursuers became shouts of surprise, then cries of pain and screams of agony, and Ruui grinned. He didn't risk a look back for their orders were to move forward as fast as was safely possible, but he knew the spearmen were falling prey to the carefully placed traps. Then there were other shouts, only this time he could understand them for they were in his own language. Shouts of triumph and the promise of death, as Arthur's warriors concealed in the trees dropped down and attacked the slowed or incapacitated Saxons.

Before he'd reached the top of the slope leading towards the grove Ruui had looked back and guessed at least twenty spearmen were chasing after the departing horsemen. They would all be dead by now, or soon would be. And that on top of the ones the cavalry's javelins had killed. It was a goodly number to remove from Hengist's army in such a short space of time.

When the pursuing spearmen failed to return to the rear of the Saxon army Hengist would know something had befallen them, and the fear and uncertainty would slowly pass through to the rest of the men. They would need to fight with one eye on their backs, fearful of another charge by the riders.

It would not come, for the cavalry would be on the opposite side of the field, ready to attack their left flank. Or was it the right. Ruui frowned, for he wasn't sure where he was supposed to go after they cleared the cover of the grove. He listened, praying to Sulis that he'd hear Aesibuas's powerful voice telling them what to do next.

No-one, either their fallen duplicarius or Rianorix with the standard, or anyone else, was offering the riders guidance however, and a cold thrill of uncertainty coursed through Ruui.

The trees suddenly opened out and he was clear of them, sunshine making the metal on his companions' armour and weapons glitter as he followed their lead. They were all turning to look back now, wondering where Aesibuas was. Some had even reined in their horses and sat staring at each other in trepidation.

"Aesibuas is dead," someone in front of Ruui shouted. "We need to get back to the rest of the army. Head around the hill to the left there, and then ride to the Saxons' faraway flank. Follow my banner!"

"That's not right, Rianorix," another rider shouted, shaking his helmeted head emphatically. "We were ordered to head straight to Arthur, in the centre of our line."

Ruui recognised the other rider as Catti, and he watched the two men bicker while more added their thoughts to the debate as they cleared the grove and refilled their saddle holsters with the javelins stuck into the ground. Catti even suggested they go back through the trees and attack the Saxon rearguard again, since it had worked so devastatingly the first time.

Ruui was amazed at how things were so confused without Aesibuas to lead them, but, since he himself wasn't even sure what their orders had been he couldn't blame his comrades. The thrill and fear of their attack and subsequent retreat had driven everything else from his mind.

"There's no point going back through the trees," he said. "The Saxons will be wary of another attack from that direction, and they'll be ready for us this time."

"Aye," Rianorix agreed, removing his helmet and shaking sweat from his ginger hair. "And we know our orders were to get back to the front, even if we can't agree where exactly."

Ruui nodded. "You can ride back through the trees if you want," he said to Catti. "But I'm going around the hill to rejoin Arthur."

"You do that," Catti retorted, puffing out his chest and patting the trio of javelins in his saddle. "I'll be going this way and killing more Saxons with these." He headed for the trees, shouting for the rest of the men to follow him and win even more glory by his side.

Some decided to do as Catti said, while others started moving in the opposite direction behind Rianorix whose blue and white bear standard seemed to offer some kind of authority.

It was clear the entire unit would be fragmented and lose its potency. Ruui hoped the rest of Arthur's army were winning, because the cavalry would play no further part in the battle.

"Where the *fuck* are you lack-wits going?"

A rider appeared, coming up the hill towards Ruui and a moment of cold fear soon gave way to immense relief. Aye, he might get a bollocking for not following their orders quickly enough, but at least now he had someone to look to for direction and leadership.

"Decurion," he said, blinking and smiling at the cranky old fellow riding past him with a face like thunder.

"Get ready to move, Ruui," Sulinus spat. "At least you and Rianorix were going in the right direction. Where in Hades are you going, though, Catti? And you idiots following him?"

Catti was just at the entrance to the grove, but he wheeled his mount around and saluted his decurion with complete submission. No-one in the unit would dare to question the experienced old man, it simply didn't happen, not after the first few days of training. They all learned soon enough to do as he told them.

"Sir, we, ah. Our attack on the Saxons was…"

"Shut up, Catti," the decurion broke in, shaking his head in disgust. "And get back into line. We're riding to Arthur's position at the rear of the army, all right? Everyone understand that? If I fall off my horse, or have a sudden heart attack and can't hold your damn hands to make sure you go in the right direction: *Follow Rianorix's standard back to Arthur in tight formation.* All right?"

"Yes, decurion!"

Ruui grinned at the sudden infusion of confidence Sulinus's appearance had brought to the entire unit and edged his horse alongside Rianorix. He also sat straighter in his saddle again, and looked calm and composed and ready to continue the fight, bear banner held proudly aloft.

Sulinus cantered past them and, without slowing, bellowed, "Forward," right hand raised in the air. The riders followed in perfect formation and soon they were galloping hard back towards their warlord, eager for the second phase of the battle.

* * *

"By the gods, Merlin. Where is that damned cavalry?" Arthur was alternating his view, from the main battle ahead of them, to the northwest, where he hoped to see his riders appearing from around the side of the low hill. The massed ranks of spearmen, many deep at first, was growing ever thinner as the warriors of Britain were cut down by their foes. They were giving their all, but the numbers were dwindling with every passing moment. Inspired tactics and clever planning were all well and good, but when it came to standing toe-to-toe with an enemy and wielding sword, spear, axe and shield, there were few more deadly than Hengist's Saxons. The sea-wolves fought with a ferocity and skill few in Arthur's ranks had come up against before, and it was a shock to them.

Hengist himself, and his massive, sneering brother Horsa, were in the very midst of the fighting, laying about themselves with abandon, cutting down Britons until there was a semi-circle of corpses around them. It inspired their soldiers to fight with ever more aggression, despite the fact they were tiring beneath the high sun.

"If we can attack one of their flanks, it might allow us to encircle them," Arthur muttered to himself.

"Which flank?" Bellicus asked, looking from one end of the warring sides to the other. "I'd suggest the southern end, my lord. The Saxons are down to only a few ranks there, it should be easier to smash them and throw them into disarray."

Arthur was looking in the direction indicated, nodding as he did so. "Agreed, Bel," he said. "We just need Sulinus to return with his horses. By Taranis, where is he?"

As if in reply, the decurion galloped into view, quickly followed by his standard bearer and then, to Arthur's immense relief, the rest of the cavalry.

"About time," the warlord cried, shaking his head and throwing up his hands in exasperation.

"I'll pass on your orders," Bellicus said, and kicked Darac into a canter. He soon closed with the galloping cavalry unit but, without the training they had, he knew he would never be able to turn Darac and join up with them. He would simply get in the way and slow their run, possibly even crash into one of them. So he rode towards Sulinus, making sure he caught the decurion's eye as he approached, and called, as loudly as he could, "Attack the southern flank. South!"

Sulinus nodded as the druid passed on his fine, black horse, and then the decurion pointed to the right, and the Saxon's southern flank, using his knees to guide his own mount in the indicated direction.

Bellicus brought Darac around in an arc, nowhere near as tightly as even the lowest ranked member of Sulinus's unit could do, but he was soon thundering back across the open field to rejoin Arthur.

"D'you think it'll be enough?" the druid asked, breathing heavily and wiping sweat from his shaved head.

"It'll need to be," Arthur replied quietly, eyes narrowed as he followed Sulinus's progress. "We don't have much left to throw at them."

They, with Merlin stroking his long beard in silence beside them, watched the cavalry unit as it raced towards the far edge of the battle. Sulinus kept them well out of range of any possible missile attacks although Bellicus thought the Saxons probably wouldn't even notice their approach and, if they did, had likely already sent their archers and slingers in to support the spearmen in the close combat, hand-to-hand struggle.

It felt like Bellicus's guts were turning to molten iron as the cavalry galloped past the battling sides and he waited for the worst to happen, but no missiles were launched towards them. At last, Sulinus brought them around in a stunningly co-ordinated turn which seemed to propel them directly towards the Saxons' flank without losing much speed.

"Surely he's not going to lead them himself?" Arthur said. "He's far too old for that!"

"Who else is going to do it, now that Aesibuas is dead?" Merlin replied.

"Well, pray to the gods, you two," the warlord commanded, turning from Merlin to Bellicus and back again. "Ask them to protect the cranky old sod. We'll need him to train more cavalry units after all this is over."

Silently, Bellicus did as he was bade, mouthing a silent imprecation to Sulis Minerva to protect the decurion and guide his men in this attack. Merlin followed suit and, together, they watched as the riders galloped ever closer to the Saxons until, at last, they saw the sky turn momentarily black in that one small section.

The javelins plunged down but Sulinus, crested helmet easily visible to Bellicus even at this distance, was already leading his riders away and around for another attack. A dozen shouts of pain were added to the already terrible sounds of the raging battle as the missiles did their brutal work.

"Yes," Arthur said in satisfaction. "That's it, decurion. Kill the bastards."

"But look." Bellicus pointed off to the left, and the hill the cavalry had launched their earlier attack from. "The Saxons who chased our riders up the bluff are returning to help their kinsmen!"

"So they are," Arthur agreed, lean face turning as he followed the druid's finger to see thirty or so spearmen running down the hill. "I expect Hengist will be happy to see them coming back…"

CHAPTER THIRTY-THREE

Hengist, and Horsa were no longer fighting at the front line of the battle. It was no cowardice that made them retreat to a place nearer the centre of their army, rather they needed to try and see the bigger picture. To gauge what was actually happening because, for some reason, their followers' greater numbers and legendary ferocity didn't seem to be pushing the damned Britons back very far. So the *bretwalda* had cut down one last enemy with a savage cut across the unfortunate fellow's face followed by a sword thrust directly to the guts and then called for his brother to move back with him.

Horsa, although covered in blood – none of which seemed to be his own – and relishing the chance to kill men, was tired and glad of the respite so he went with Hengist to find a position in the very middle of their massed ranks. Ranks which were quite noticeably thinner now. The battle was not going at all as the Saxon chiefs had envisaged, and they had nothing in reserve to bolster their flagging soldiers.

"Did you know the Waelisc whoresons had cavalry?" Horsa demanded as they stood catching their breath amidst their sweating countrymen and allies.

Hengist shook his head. He felt quite dazed, from the heat and exertions of the battle. He was never one to shirk combat but perhaps, he mused, it was time to let the younger men do the fighting from now on. He could see the enemy warlord, Arthur, sitting quite comfortably on the back of his horse, directing his men without ever coming under any personal threat himself. It seemed a craven's way to lead an army to the Saxon *bretwalda*, but he had to admit it made sense. "Our spies reported the presence of more riders than usual training within their camp," he told Horsa. "But I had no idea they would have something like this."

Horsa followed his brother's nod and saw a rider wearing a Roman-style crested helmet leading his horsemen at great speed towards the Saxon flank and directing them to unleash a devastating volley of javelins. He cursed, but knew they had nothing to counter the speed and obvious skill of the Britons' cavalry unit. "What are we going to do?" he demanded, and his tone was harsh, accusing. "You brought us here, my brother. Lead us!"

Hengist drew in a deep breath and, for the first time Horsa could remember, his sibling seemed completely lost.

"Look," said Horsa, wiping sweat from his forehead. The greasy sheen mixed with his enemies' blood and made him look even more savage than usual. "Arthur only has his druids as bodyguard. Why don't we try and kill him? If we cut off the head of the bear, the rest of the animal will die soon enough."

Hengist held a hand up to shade his eyes and tried to see Arthur in the distance. The shimmering heat made it hard to see much, especially surrounded by battling warriors, but he could just make out a trio of horsemen watching the fighting off to the west. It was tempting to try and do as Horsa advised, but he knew it would be a waste of time. Arthur and his pet druids would see any Saxon would-be killers approaching from a long way off and simply gallop away to a safer place.

"Waste of time, brother," said the *bretwalda*, but his face brightened as he gazed about them and noticed the return of their spearmen who'd chased the enemy cavalry up the hill what felt like æons ago. "Look, though! The horsemen might have escaped them, but there's twenty or so of our warriors coming to rejoin the fight. That should swing things back in our favour, eh?"

Horsa saw the men indicated and his smile mirrored his brothers. "Aye, and welcome they are. Damned fools should never have run off like that though."

"Ach, I don't blame them," Hengist said. "They watched their comrades cut down by cowards with missiles and sought to avenge them. Let's just be glad they're coming back, for those cavalrymen of Arthur's have shredded our flank over there and we need every man we can get! Look, they're eager to get amongst the fighting, watch them run…"

His voice trailed off and he stared, open mouthed, astonished, as the returning spearmen – his spearmen, for their helmets and armour were clearly Saxon – did not slow as they reached the rear ranks of Hengist's army. Instead, they seemed to pick up speed until, with sickening force, their charge hammered into the distant row of Saxons.

The deadly spears did their bloody work, downing a dozen men, before the polearms were dropped and swords drawn in their stead. Then the returning 'Saxons' laid about themselves with a savagery that, although it seemed to have been bred in Jutland or Frisia, was actually born in Lindum. Edern, son of King Caradoc, whose men performed so poorly during last winter's battle in Waithe and been criticised for it by Duro, had volunteered for this duty as a way of restoring their honour. They were certainly proving their courage and ferocity now.

The *bretwalda* and his brother cursed loudly at this strange turn before Horsa cried, "Those are no Saxons. They're Arthur's men, wearing our gear!"

"Thanks for pointing that out, brother," Hengist retorted sourly. "I would never have figured it out for myself."

"Well, what are you going to do about it, by Frigg?" Horsa said, voice cracking from dryness as he repeated his earlier question. "Look, their cavalry's coming back for another attack. We're done, *brother*. Done! You've led us to our people's greatest defeat in living memory."

Hengist was not a man to panic, and he took his time to look all around, taking in each area of the battle, before, finally, he conceded the truth of Horsa's words. They could not win and, if they continued to fight it was likely every man in his army would finish the day dead and burning on a funeral pyre built by the Britons.

"Retreat!" he screamed at the top of his lungs. "Retreat and reform at the—" he'd been about to say, 'at the burnt effigies' but quickly changed his mind. Why remind his exhausted forces of Merlin's earlier magical victory? "Reform over there!" he commanded, rather lamely gesturing with his drawn sword at an amorphous point on the shimmering horizon.

"Retreat, you goat fuckers!" Horsa's voice came out louder and stronger than his older brother's but even so, it took a few attempts before the command sunk into the battling Saxons' minds and they started to move back, westwards, to the point their chiefs and captains were indicating.

"Come on," Hengist growled, not hiding the irritation he felt at his brother's stinging commentary on his leadership. "Let's go.

Maybe we can get our lines sorted again over there and win this battle."

Horsa did not reply. He didn't need to, for his look of disgust said it all.

* * *

Sulinus's weather-beaten face bore the biggest smile Bellicus had so far seen as the wizened cavalry officer led his *turma* back towards Arthur and his advisors. And it was understandable, for the horsemen's javelins had been enough to break the right flank of the Saxon line, allowing Arthur's spearmen to take control of that side. Combined with Edern's men surprise attack on the rear of Hengist's army, it had been enough to force the enemy into retreat. The centre of their formation was moving back in a controlled manner, giving up ground at a steady pace, but some of the men on the periphery, far from the calming influence of Hengist, were running for their lives.

"What d'you want us to do, my lord?" Sulinus called to Arthur. "The bastards have given up. Now would be a good time for my riders to use their training and cut down the panicked enemy soldiers."

The warlord didn't answer immediately. He had thought of commanding the cavalry to wait until the fighting moved back and they could gather their spent javelins – use them to mount another attack like their previous ones and perhaps break Hengist's resolve for good. But Sulinus's question did give him pause, for hadn't his own inability to fight from horseback been the entire reason for his wanting a cavalry unit? This would be the perfect opportunity to give those riders valuable experience of such a tactic without placing them in too much danger. Many of the fleeing Saxons had dropped their heavy spears that they might run faster so…

"All right," he shouted, nodding to Sulinus. "Bring down as many as you can, decurion, but don't take risks. Your men have proved their worth, and I don't want to lose any of them."

Sulinus was already bringing his horse around, the excitement of battle apparently making him forget his usual aches and pains.

"He's going to feel it in the morning," Merlin laughed. "Old coot thinks he's twenty again!"

"Aye, it's a fine sight to see," Arthur said, joining in with the High Druid's mirth. "And I'll personally make sure there's enough ale in his cup all day tomorrow to make sure he can't feel the tiredness in his bones. Or anything else, for that matter!"

Their eyes traced the decurion's progress as he galloped gracefully back to rejoin his men and then, voice calling orders even over the continuing din of battle, led them after the retreating Saxons on the broken southern flank.

"I have to say, my lord," Bellicus said. "I wasn't sure you'd ever be able to defeat Hengist. No offence," he held up a hand, noticing Arthur's frown at the apparent insult. "I simply wasn't sure it would be possible for anyone to bring together all the petty chiefs and kings and form their soldiers into such a cohesive unit. Not to mention overseeing the formation of a cavalry unit that might have matched the Roman *turmae* of old."

Arthur waved a hand modestly, batting aside the compliments, but he looked pleased nonetheless. "I have good advisors, and the best men to train my soldiers. The ones who deserve the plaudits are out there – warriors like Edern and Eburus and Princess Velugna, spilling blood for their lands. I hope you druids will be coming up with some suitable songs to celebrate the bravery and skill on display here today. This battle should be remembered for generations to come."

Bellicus nodded but Merlin was stroking his beard thoughtfully.

"Songs can come later, Arthur," cautioned the High Druid. "And you can be sure they'll do our warriors justice. But the battle isn't over yet, and the war will *never* be won until Hengist and Horsa are food for the worms."

Merlin's phrase painted a stark image in Bellicus's mind and, despite their jubilation over the surely impending victory, the battle was moving away from their position and, in its wake were the bloody remnants of those who'd been killed in the fighting. It was a sobering sight to see so many mostly young men hacked apart in their prime, heads crushed, limbs sliced open or even completely off, sightless eyes staring up at the sky they would never see again...

Aye, the druid mused, their songs would celebrate the courage of their warriors, but, given the choice, he felt sure the slaughtered spearmen on both sides would prefer to be still breathing – to be

288

able to see their families tomorrow – than have their comrades sing drunken words of praise in their honour.

He looked down at Cai, lying contentedly on the grass by Darac's feet, and prayed with everything in him that Duro was not amongst the ranks of the fallen.

CHAPTER THIRTY-FOUR

"Move!" Duro pushed against the man on his right, just in time to save him from being spitted by a Saxon sword. "Shield up, soldier. Shield *up!*" To demonstrate his point, he raised his own and clattered it against the enemy warrior's chest. At this stage in the fighting they were all tired, and the lime planks with their rounded iron boss – heavy at the best of times – felt as though they had tripled in weight. It took great strength as well as steel will to keep that left arm up at all times, but Duro's shield had already saved him from being wounded or killed numerous times that day. Arthur had tasked him with leading the men he and Bellicus had brought down from the far north, and, with Eburus helping command slightly further along the front line, the Alt Clotans and Votadini were performing admirably.

Duro was right in the centre of the battle, where the fighting was still brutal, and he could see the tall shape of Horsa just a few ranks ahead of him. It drove the centurion on for he desperately wanted to feel the tip of his spatha sliding between the Saxon's ribs. That thought had kept him going when his wife's murder had been a fresh, open wound and now it was almost within touching distance.

"Their flanks have broken," he bellowed, seeing Sulinus away on the edge of the battle, charging along with his riders, swords just like Duro's in their hands, ready to slash at the backs and exposed necks and heads of the retreating enemy troopers. "Push forward, the battle will be over soon enough, lads."

The leaf-shaped blade of another spear was suddenly thrust towards them but this time Duro could not help the man on his left. The Saxon weapon tore straight into the chest of the Briton and then it drew back, covered in blood and leaving Duro's comrade gasping and staring at him with wide, horror-filled eyes. The man could not stand for long and there was nothing the centurion could do but let him fall, to be trampled beneath the boots of his own army as it continued to surge forward, the Saxons pulling back step by agonizing step.

Earlier, seeing that would have spurred Duro on, inspired him to fight with even more ferocity, but now he was too tired. Indeed, he was slashing and thrusting with his own spatha less often now that the battle was, it seemed, coming to an end. He was content to move forward, encourage his men, keep his shield up, and pray that someone didn't thrust a spear beneath it, into his legs or groin.

Another man had quickly taken the place of their fallen comrade, and Duro was glad because the lad was tall and powerfully built and seemed somehow fresher than the others around them. It would save the centurion looking out for him, as well as trying to keep his own hide intact.

The young warrior was not holding back, either, as he slashed his sword down, into the shield of a Saxon. The wood shuddered and dropped as its bearer felt the brunt of the blow all through his arm and, in the resulting gap, Duro thrust the point of his blade into the enemy's neck, opening it up in a terrible, raw wound. Blood spurted and Duro roared but it was all lost in the maelstrom and then the Saxon was gone and Duro was holding off another attack and kicking out at yet another long-haired, bellowing axeman just ahead of him.

The battle had found its rhythm by this stage, swords rising and falling, shields pushing and shoving, men screaming and shouting either war-cries or for their mothers to come to them as they lay dying on the blood-soaked ground.

Duro did not enjoy these kinds of skirmishes. They were too random. Even for the most skilled of fighters a chance spear thrust, or a stray sling bullet, or even a panicking comrade could mean a gruesome death with no chance to defend oneself. No, the fights he'd had at Bellicus's side, against just a handful of men, were a better test, and he always enjoyed the thrill of fear and excitement more when facing up to a single man with a sword.

This – chopping and parrying with a relentless, almost unthinking regularity – was not really the place for a warrior to show his skill. Courage, nerve, fitness, and luck were all more important than an individual's training or talent with a blade.

As if to emphasise his strangely detached musings one of his own men clattered into him, the boss of the man's shield thudding into his back and knocking him down onto one knee. He took the chance to lash out at the legs and feet moving in front of him, sharpened spatha blade leaving a bloody trail in skin and flesh and drawing yet more screams to add to those already filling the air.

A hand grasped the centurion beneath his sword arm and helped him stand up again. He grinned savagely at the agonized faces of those he'd just wounded so painfully and then returned to his earlier rhythm, chopping and thrusting and parrying with shield and blade until, at last, he realised the enemy ranks were much thinner than they'd been. At the same moment he noticed Horsa and Hengist were no longer visible and he couldn't even remember when he'd last seen them.

Had the Saxon *bretwalda* and his brother escaped?

He roared in frustration and then the idea struck him that perhaps both of them had been killed in the battle. Duro wanted to kill Horsa himself but...If the bastard was finally dead it could only be a good thing. He allowed himself to be overtaken by his men as the fighting continued ahead of them, the remaining Saxon ranks doing their best to stay alive until they could reach the trees in the middle-distance and escape into their cover.

"Where are you, Horsa?" he muttered, squinting in the sun as he tried to see some sign of his despised enemy. The Saxon was not as tall as Bellicus, but he was bigger than almost everyone else on the battlefield and Duro hoped to see his helmeted head towering above the rest of the sea-wolves.

Eventually, the centurion's eyes came back to Sulinus, still filled with an energy that belied his advanced age. The decurion was riding here and there, giving commands to his cavalrymen, directing them to chase down a couple of fleeing warriors one moment, then ordering them to return to formation in readiness for another charge.

The old man was completely in his element. Duro might not be enjoying the battle much, but Sulinus obviously was, and the centurion knew the riders, especially their leader, would enjoy great renown and fame once the fighting was done.

Good, Duro thought, the cranky old bastard had worked wonders in training the raw recruits and stepped in today when Aesibuas had been killed. The centurion hadn't seen that happening, but he knew something must have befallen the newly promoted cavalry officer to make the aged Sulinus take his place on the field.

"They're running!" Eburus's powerful voice carried along the line to him and the Votadini champion raised his new, black shield high in the air triumphantly. "Centurion, the bastards are running for it!"

Duro's attention snapped back to the scene before him and he mentally kicked himself for not noticing the ebb and flow of the battle. The men beside him were jubilant for, sure enough, having almost reached the woods behind them, the Saxons had decided it was time to give up the fight and sprint for the safety of those trees.

"Do we go after them?" More than one man was calling the same question and their voices, although tired, were expectant. Hopeful. They wanted to charge after the routed enemy and hunt them down like animals.

A trumpet sounded from the rear, however, and Duro recognised the signal: Hold your positions.

"Halt!" he shouted, emptying his lungs in a bellow that was probably heard all the way back at Arthur's position. "Hold the line, *do not go after them!*"

"Have we won, centurion?"

Duro recognised the voice and turned to see the farmer, Elpin, face caked in dry blood, standing in the rank behind him. Then he focused on the Saxons again, wondering if they really were giving up, or going to reform and return to the fray when their lines were settled again. The latter appeared unlikely, and he glanced to the right where the cavalry was finishing off a pocket of fleeing enemies.

"Aye, soldier," he said with a tired smile, speaking so everyone formed around him could hear. "It looks like we've won."

Lusty, relieved cheers rippled out from his position and, in that instant Sulinus looked over and their eyes met for just a moment. Duro raised his crimson-spattered blade and saluted the old man with it. The decurion's eyes were not what they'd been even a decade ago, but it must have been obvious who the warrior in the Roman helmet was in the front ranks and he too grinned, raising his own spatha to return the respectful greeting across the battlefield.

As they saluted one another, overjoyed by the great victory, a spear shaft lanced upwards and the blade on the end tore into Sulinus's neck and on through his jaw, and then Duro could see the decurion no more.

293

CHAPTER THIRTY-FIVE

"It's my fault."

Duro shook his head and rested a hand on Arthur's back. "You're wrong. It's mine, my lord."

They, alongside Bellicus, Bedwyr, and Merlin, were standing over the body of Sulinus and more than one of them had tears in their eyes at the pitiful sight of a man who was old enough to be Arthur's grandfather yet had acquitted himself so magnificently in the battle.

"I should never have ordered him to chase down the fleeing Saxons," Arthur insisted sadly. "I should have told him to gather the spent javelins and use them to mount more attacks from distance. He'd never have been close enough to let the spearman kill him then."

Duro felt sick. Even the decurion's beautiful warhorse had been killed by the Saxons. It lay beside Sulinus with multiple wounds in its sleek, muscular body. The sight of those great ribs, completely still now, unmoved by the breath of life, brought a lump to Duro's throat and he remained silent, not trusting himself to speak. He wanted to tell them all that he'd distracted the old man and, as a result, stopped him from spotting the spear thrust that had killed him.

"It's no-one's fault," Bellicus said, running a hand across his recently shaved head, the new bristles making a rasping sound. "Sulinus was a soldier and he died doing what he was born to do. He led from the front and helped bring us a great victory this day. He's a hero."

Merlin agreed with his fellow druid. "Bel's right. There'll be time to properly mourn and honour the dead later. For now, there are things to be done."

Despite his words, Merlin did not move from where he stood, and neither did anyone else. They stood with heads bowed, silent, and might have stood there forever had a warrior not stumbled past them and fallen to his knees by Sulinus side.

The man was crying openly but making very little sound, resting one hand on Sulinus's arm and the other on the fallen horse.

Duro could not bear it. Tears blurred his vision and he walked away, staring down so that no-one would see his face.

Bellicus watched his friend go but did not move to go after him. He knew Duro would prefer to be alone with his thoughts for now, and besides, he recognised the man with the dark moustache sobbing on the grass unashamedly before them.

"Aesibuas," said the druid in amazement. "We thought you were dead!"

"So did I," the kneeling man laughed, looking up at Bellicus and wiping his cheeks with the backs of his fingers. "One minute I was riding up the hill, the next I was waking up on my back with a pounding headache." He touched the back of his skull gingerly, wincing as he did so but, when he brought his fingers away there was no blood on them which could only be a good sign. "My helmet saved me." He looked back down to the man who'd trained him, promoted him, and been a friend to him. "If only his helmet could have saved him too, eh?"

Arthur squatted down on his haunches and grasped Aesibuas by the shoulder. They weren't that far apart in age, but Bellicus could see the cavalryman was amazed by his warlord's familiarity and respectful tone and it visibly helped to lift Aesibuas's mood.

"You led your unit superbly today, duplicarius," the warlord said. "And I'm overjoyed to see you're not dead after all."

"Thank you, my lord," Aesibuas mumbled, too overcome to speak clearly.

"The gods have called Sulinus to them," Arthur said to him. "But they saw fit to spare you. I think it's a sign."

Aesibuas gazed at him then wiped his nose. "A sign, lord?"

"We would have been lost if you and Sulinus had both been killed," Arthur said, nodding. "Our cavalry would have been completely leaderless, and we saw very clearly today just how much they need direction, as skilled as they are."

Aesibuas, of course, had not seen that at all, being unconscious, but he stayed silent as his warlord continued.

"You have been spared, however, and for that I'm grateful. My cavalry is *not* leaderless, but it does need a new decurion."

The tall rider's back straightened and he gaped at Arthur in shock. "Me? But I'm just—"

"You're a soldier," Arthur broke in, patting Aesibuas's arm and nodding reassuringly. Encouragingly. "You proved today, until you were, er, incapacitated, that you can lead from the front and remain calm under pressure. You shall be my decurion now." He rose but kept his gaze fixed on the new cavalry officer as he said somewhat sternly, "Make sure you live up to Sulinus's example though, all right?"

Mention of the old man's name brought fresh tears to Aesibuas's eyes, and it was all he could do to mumble, "Thank you, my lord. I'll try," before his head sagged and he looked down again.

"Come to my tent, Bedwyr," Merlin said as the quartermaster strode towards them, blood caked on his face, hands, arms and even his legs. "You need patching up."

Bedwyr gave a rueful shake of his head. "This *is* me patched up, Merlin," he said. "Hardly any of this blood is mine, but the cuts and injuries I did take have been looked at by our healers already." He raised an eyebrow and hesitated before deciding he held enough rank to say, "Perhaps you and Bel could go and help them? They could do with it. We have a lot of wounded, not to mention dying men who could do with some advice on how to pass into the Otherlands."

Merlin's head tilted back and Bellicus thought the High Druid might make an angry retort, but he simply peered at Bedwyr and seemed to accept the man spoke fairly and within his rights as a captain of the army. "Of course," he said. "We'll do what we can, eh, Bellicus?"

They hurried away, first to Merlin's tent to gather bandages and ready-mixed poultices and other healing supplies, and then to the battlefield, Cai trotting along with them to offer whatever comfort he may. It had not surprised Bellicus to discover that men about to pass into the Otherlands appeared to find great comfort in the dog's stoic presence.

The Saxons – those that remained alive at least – were gone, and, for now, Arthur was content to let them go, despite the fact Horsa, Hengist, and Thorbjorg had not been found amongst the dead. The battle had been won and the Britons had not suffered anything like as many casualties as their enemies. The cavalry, and the inspired idea to disguise men in Saxon armour and strike the rear ranks of their army had helped give Arthur's army a resounding victory so, when the defeated Saxons had made it to the woods in the west the warlord had allowed them to go.

Bellicus thought, with hindsight, that Arthur should have laid traps in those woods to kill even more of the sea-wolves, but they'd only had so much time and so many resources. The young commander had more than earned his position that day. Whether the gods had bestowed it upon him or not.

Besides, Lancelot and his warband would be in control of Garrianum by now. When Hengist stumbled back to their fortress with his survivors they'd be in for a shock. The thought made the druid smile although it quickly disappeared once he and Merlin began tending to the wounded and dying.

CHAPTER THIRTY-SIX

The victory feast was destined to be as legendary as the battle itself, with numerous gallons of ale being consumed, dozens of animals of all kinds slaughtered in sacrifice and for the table, and songs sung loudly enough to shake the very sky above them all.

It was a beautiful sky too, that night, with the setting sun covering everything in a red hue that mirrored the blood spilled on the ground earlier. Those of Arthur's warriors who'd been killed were burned on great pyres at the battlefield, the smoke rising to that red sky in thick, dark plumes as Merlin and Bellicus asked the gods to show the glorious dead favour in the next life.

The Saxons were, for now, left to the wild animals.

Although many of the surviving Britons had lost friends and kinsmen, and suffered wounds of their own, Bedwyr had been commanded by Arthur to see those Saxon bodies completely stripped of valuables and the booty then shared out fairly amongst his warriors.

Edern and his men from Lindum, now divested of their Saxon disguises, were rightly lauded and given an extra share of the battlefield spoils, although Edern himself had been happy just to receive a respectful salute from Duro in recognition of their valour.

So, it was a contented army that evening after the fighting had ended and Hengist's forces had disappeared into the west. They might not have killed the *bretwalda*, but it seemed like the war had been won for most of his followers had been killed and it would take perhaps a generation for enough fresh blood to sail across the sea and start the process again.

At least, that was what Merlin had said, and Arthur and Bellicus had agreed as they retired to sit around a small cooking fire of their own near the command tent.

"How many survived, do you think?" Arthur asked his scouts who had been sent out to watch the Saxon retreat. They suggested that half of Hengist's army had escaped and would reform on the road back to Garrianum. Maybe some of them would see the defeat as an indictment on Hengist's leadership and wander off in other directions, to look for new chiefs and new lands to settle here in

Britain, but, even so, it would be a fair number who went back to the Saxon Shore behind their *bretwalda*.

Too many for Lancelot to hold off within the unfamiliar fortress for long.

"If possible," Arthur told his captains. "Don't drink too much tonight. I know you've all earned it, but we'll have to lead a warband of our own towards Garrianum in the morning."

"We'll ask for volunteers once dawn approaches," Merlin said. "They'll be rewarded with extra booty. There should be plenty of it once we meet up with Lancelot and strip Garrianum of its treasures. Gods, there must be a fortune in stolen goods in that fortress."

Bedwyr, always thinking logically, wondered why they didn't choose the hundred men they'd need for the next day's mission now, and forbid them from drinking more than a cup or two of ale.

"After today's fighting," Arthur told him, "I'm not about to stop them from enjoying another night alive on this earth. They've earned it." He smiled placatingly. "Don't fret, old friend. Not everyone wants to get blind drunk tonight. There'll be enough sober, clear heads to get a warband together in the morning." He turned then to Aesibuas, frowning. "Although, we're going to need your cavalry, decurion. I know you've earned a rest after today's performance, but...Your unit will be invaluable in scouting and hunting down the Saxons in the coming days."

"What about supplies?" Bedwyr asked unhappily. "We should—"

"This is why I value your so much," Arthur laughed. "You deal with the things I wouldn't think so much about. Can you see to the preparations?"

Sighing, but not appearing too upset by this new duty, Bedwyr saluted somewhat ironically and left the fireside. It was not wholly unexpected, there'd always been a fair chance that the Saxons wouldn't be entirely wiped out and a force of Arthur's men would have to go after them. Everyone had hoped there would have been fewer survivors to go after, however.

There were speeches, by Arthur and Merlin, thanking the warriors for their service and praising their valour and skill, and promising them a time of peace now that the Saxons were finally beaten. And there were solemn speeches by men who had lost close friends and comrades. Men who were confident enough to stand before such a large gathering and speak which, as Bellicus knew, was a more terrifying thing to do than facing an enemy army for some people.

The ale flowed, and the meat was cooked by servants who brought it around on trenchers beside bread and cheese. And, for after, there were the ladies who had joined the army at every town it passed, knowing they would be well rewarded for offering particular services to the stressed men.

Life was cheap for a soldier and, once the eulogies had been spoken and the lays sung, laughter filled the warm night air and thoughts turned to the future.

"Even if Hengist is truly beaten, and we either annihilate his forces or send them back over the sea to their own lands," Arthur said, sipping contentedly from a cup of ale, "I still want more cavalry units."

Bellicus nodded. "It's a good idea, if you can find another man like Sulinus to train them. Any enemies that might raid our towns and villages won't know how to deal with them."

The warlord nodded and leaned back on his camp chair, staring into the flickering campfire as if looking into a time still to come. "I foresee a time of peace and plenty for us all, gentlemen," he said. "A golden era for Britain, now that we've shown we can come together as one to stand against our foes. Our people will no longer be bullied and pushed around by the likes of Horsa."

Duro's jaw clenched and he gripped the hilt of his sword at the mention of that hated name. It did not truly feel like a victory for him when his wife's murderer had escaped to carry out further evil deeds. The centurion would certainly be volunteering to go with Arthur's warband on the morrow.

"We'll train individual warbands," Arthur went on. "Each under my overall command, but based all around southern Britain so they can quickly react to threats from the likes of the Picts, Dalriadans and, should more return, Saxons." He had that familiar faraway look in his eyes as he imagined this wonderful new Britain, where raiders would trouble them no longer and his people could live long, fruitful lives without worrying about being cut down by some savage.

"Don't get carried away just yet," Merlin cautioned, wiping pork fat from his white beard as he chewed the succulent meat. "We still have to finish Hengist off completely."

"A formality," Arthur said, and Bellicus was surprised for the young warlord was not usually so bullish. Perhaps he was drunk, the druid thought. Well, why not? He'd earned the right more than anyone, even if he hadn't actually taken part in the fighting that day.

"Lancelot will have Garrianum sealed up tighter than a bard's drum," Arthur continued. "And we'll catch them there, between the hammer and the anvil. What could go wrong?"

Merlin did not answer, but he was staring westwards, towards the still-smoking funeral pyres of their own dead.

"What?" Arthur asked, just a touch of irritation creeping into his voice.

"I can't see clearly," the High Druid replied, still staring into the distance. "But I believe someone, or something, is coming towards us."

Arthur stood up, as did Bellicus, and the two men gazed out into the night. The sun had gone now, and there was only a thin sliver of moon to light the fields before them but, as they stood there, Bellicus cocked his head and said, "I think you're right, Merlin."

"How many?" Arthur muttered tightly, still trying to see any movement. The funeral pyres continued to burn, even so long after they'd been lit, but they didn't cast much light outwith their own radius.

"There," Bellicus said, pointing just as a lone horseman galloped past one of the pyres, the orange glow revealing him to them all.

"What does it mean?" Duro asked, coming to stand beside them. "An emissary from Hengist? A scout?"

"Maybe it's just a hunter from one of the surrounding villages," Bellicus suggested, but no-one believed that. The rider was pushing his horse despite the darkness and was making his way straight towards them, something no hunter was likely to do without good reason.

"Well, whoever it is," Arthur said, returning to his folding chair beside the fire and lifting his ale again, "they'll be here soon enough."

Bellicus and Duro didn't take their seats again, preferring to stand and watch as the rider grew ever closer. He was stopped at the outskirts of the army by the watchmen and must have offered them a legitimate reason for his presence for he was waved through and continued to ride hard, passing groups of men around their own little fires until, at last, he approached the command tent with its fluttering blue flag bearing a white bear.

"Where's Arthur?" they heard the rider calling, and his voice was filled with exhaustion and an anxiety that instantly spread to those who heard him. "Where's the warlord?"

"Who are you, and what's your business with the Lord Arthur," one of the guards at the tent's entrance replied in a professional, level tone.

"Send him around, Eiludd," Arthur called. "He hasn't ridden through the dark for miles without good reason."

"On you go then," Eiludd, said to the rider. "But I'll be watching you, lad."

Arthur rolled his eyes at his guard's over-protectiveness. "Does he not think we can defend ourselves against one man?" he muttered to Merlin who smirked in return. In truth, the High Druid had chosen Eiludd for this duty himself, knowing it would take a really determined would-be killer to get past the ever-alert guard.

The rider appeared around the side of the tent, and, despite his helmet and the shadows hiding his features, his exhaustion was plain for he was forced to rest against the leather structure just to keep himself upright. When he looked up and met Arthur's stare, though, the warlord suddenly jumped up, crying out, "Kay! Gods, someone get him a drink!"

The rider's shoulder's sagged and, with a shaking hand he tried to swallow some of the ale from the cup Bellicus pressed into his hand.

"What are you doing here, Kay?" Arthur demanded, stalking across to kneel beside the rider who was now, terrifyingly, almost sobbing as he tried to breathe. "Why aren't you at Garrianum with Lancelot? What's happened, Kay, speak to me!"

"They're dead, Arthur," the rider replied. "They're all dead."

302

"Who is?"

"All of them, lord," Kay said, and his shoulders were shaking as he cried, Arthur's wrathful glare only serving to make him even more emotional. It was a disturbing sight, given Kay's size and usual fierce demeanour.

"Lancelot?" Merlin asked in a kindlier tone.

"Lancelot too," Kay said, and now Arthur reeled back, stumbling against his camp chair before finally righting it, and himself, and dropping down onto it.

"Drink," Bellicus said to Kay. "It'll help steady your nerves. Go on, finish it." He took the empty cup and refilled it before handing it to Kay once more. Again, the man drained it and then he placed it on the grass, removed his helmet, and stared sadly at Arthur.

"I'm sorry, old friend. We failed you."

"How?" Arthur asked simply.

"They saw through our disguise as soon as we were inside the walls," Kay said. "Their jarl recognised Lancelot and raised the alarm. There were a lot of them still there instead of being off at the battle – all mending ships and the like. They attacked us and…" His voice trailed off before he took a deep, shuddering breath and finished, "killed everyone."

"Except you," Duro said, careful not to make his tone accusatory. "How did you get away?"

Kay looked sheepish, but Arthur barked at him to hurry up and tell his tale and, wringing his hands the rider said, "When the Saxons attacked, Lancelot ordered us to try and reach the shore. To capture one of their ships but..." he shook his head. "It was impossible. There were too many of them and, before we knew it, more than half of our lads were already down. We were sheltering from their missiles behind a low row of buildings, so, I jumped up onto the roof of one of them and hid. I know it wasn't brave, and I should have died beside my comrades but..."

"Enough of that talk," Merlin said sharply. "The gods spared you, Kay, that you might bring us this news. You did well. It was a bold plan, but one that was always going to be dangerous. No-one is to blame for what happened, least of all you. Everyone here knows you're no coward."

Kay's blue eyes were still downcast, avoiding looking at Arthur who seemed enraged by his bleak news, and he shook his head as he recalled the rest of that terrible, failed raid. "The Saxons stripped our dead of valuables, then dragged them outside the walls and dumped their bodies. Their..." He shuddered, choking on the words. "Their heads were taken and displayed on those walls for all to see."

There were cries of outrage at this, although Bellicus was not surprised for his own people followed similar gory traditions when they won a battle. It was a crude, but effective way of sending a warning to their enemies.

"Scum," Kay went on, his earlier sobs now turning to hard, cold anger. "Those scum cleared their camp, found our horses where we'd left them outside the fortress and brought them back for their own stables. Then they celebrated their victory with cask upon cask of ale. By the time night fell they were all singing and fighting amongst themselves, bloody barbarians, and I was able to climb down and slip out over a low section of the wall. I ran, practically without stopping, until I reached the nearest town and took a horse from there. They were Britons at those stables but, with this armour and stuff on they thought I was a Saxon. Didn't argue when I picked out their finest looking animal." He glanced across in the direction his mount had been taken to be fed and rubbed down and a small smile brightened his grubby features. "Fast as lightning it was, carried me all the way here."

"Did you not run into Hengist's forces on their way back to Garrianum today?" Duro asked.

"I passed some of them," Kay replied. "Scattered groups here and there mostly. They were in no mood to ask who I was or what I was about. I saw the main body of their army in plenty of time to give them a wide berth."

They all sat in silence for a long time after that, digesting the news, wondering what it would mean for their plans going forward, and mourning the death of their countrymen, including Cador and, of course, Lancelot. Bellicus pictured the handsome swordsman, smiling, blonde hair tumbling about his shoulders, and mouthed a prayer to Dis Pater. It was a hard blow to lose someone so vital, so full of life and energy, and he pitied Arthur who'd been friends with Lancelot for many years.

304

Many fine warriors had died that day, but few deaths would be felt as keenly as Arthur's popular champion.

"We'll come up with a ballad befitting one of his greatness," Bellicus said to Arthur, and Merlin nodded silent agreement. "His sacrifice, and his men's, won't be forgotten, depend on it, my lord. Lancelot's name will ring throughout the ages, for a thousand years or more."

Arthur appeared to take little comfort from the druid's words at that moment, and the men drank their ale down in silence as the fire burned low and the army camped around them raised their voices in triumphant songs and laughter long into the night.

The Bear of Britain had won a great victory that day, but the shine had been cruelly taken from it by Kay's news, and, as Bellicus walked tiredly towards his tent followed by Cai and Duro, he wondered what the morrow would bring.

* * *

It was a dull morning when Bellicus awoke, the sun not managing to break through the clouds that covered the sky from one end to the other. He felt rested and glad he hadn't downed too much victory ale the night before, although Duro was not so happy.

"Gods below," the centurion grunted, rubbing a hand over his eyes and squinting at the half-open tent flap as if the feeble light was blinding him. "It's times like this that you realise you're not twenty-five anymore."

"You need a drink of water?" Bellicus asked him sympathetically, filling a cup from the jug beside his own bed roll.

"Aye, thank you." Duro accepted the wooden cup and took a mouthful, swilling it around before swallowing with a sigh, licking his dry lips and teeth before downing the rest of the rather stagnant liquid. "My arms, shoulders, thighs…Mithras, my entire body aches."

Bellicus grinned and patted his friend none-too-gently on his tired shoulders. "That's how it always feels after a pitched battle, Centurion, you should remember that!"

"Didn't feel like this twenty years ago," Duro groused, shaking his head and rising to stretch out the kinks in his muscles as best he could. "At least I'm still here though, unlike old Sulinus and

Lancelot and the rest of the lads." He sighed again but set about shaving the stubble from his face before washing away the tiny hairs and putting on his Roman cuirass and the rest of his armour in preparation for whatever Arthur decided they would be doing that day.

"You think we'll still be heading for Garrianum?" Bellicus asked as he cleaned his teeth with a dried birch twig and watched from the tent flap as Cai wandered outside to empty his bladder and sniff about the place, enjoying pats and smiles from the soldiers camping nearest to them. "Knowing Hengist is still in possession of the fortress changes everything, doesn't it?"

Duro shrugged, then winced at the pain that flared across his neck. "Not really. We still need to finish the job we started yesterday. If we allow Hengist to retain control of the Saxon Shore he'll eventually bring more men over to replace the ones we killed yesterday. It will all start again, and our victory on the battlefield will mean nothing in the long run."

"I suppose so," the druid muttered, not relishing the thought of trying to storm the massive stone walls that had been built so well by the Romans at Garrianum. "But simply turning up and trying to take the place by force of numbers seems madness. We should have ladders at the very least."

"Aye," Duro replied almost wistfully. "A few catapults and ballistae would be useful but..." He finished buckling on his cuirass and stood up, placing his crested helmet beneath his arm. "I suspect Arthur'll be in no mood to do anything other than launch an all-out assault on Garrianum as soon as possible. It didn't take a druid's training to see he was devastated by the news of Lancelot's death."

Bellicus did not reply. Arthur was not a king, and should not abuse his powers by throwing men at a near-impregnable wall simply to avenge his friend's death. Lancelot might have been killed, but this was war, men died, and plenty of other Britons had lost loved ones yesterday. The druid truly hoped Arthur was sensible enough, wise enough, to act rationally. And, if not, Merlin at least should guide him.

"I'm ready to go and see what our warlord commands," Duro said, stretching again, head pressing into the roof of the tent but still managing to look every inch the experienced, tough centurion. "Coming?"

Bellicus, copying his friend, hefted his eagle-topped staff and rose to his full height, lifting the whole tent a foot or more off the ground. "Yes, sir," he said, smiling, happy that he and his friend had survived Britain's greatest battle for a generation mostly intact and would face whatever came next side by side. "Let's go."

They, like many others in the camp, had slept later than normal thanks to their exhaustion from the previous day's exertions – physical and mental – as well as, in some cases, thundering hangovers. When they reached Arthur's command tent the warlord was already there with Bedwyr, Merlin, Kay, and some of his other captains. Druid and centurion were greeted with nods and found a couple of empty stools to sit and listen to Arthur's plans. There was food and drink laid out on the big folding table and they helped themselves to bread, water, and even a ripe, red apple each as the council of war continued. It seemed everything had already been decided.

"Kay will lead us back to Garrianum," Arthur was saying. "We have one hundred men picked out and ready to move shortly, unless anyone has any objections? Or wishes to flag up something I might have missed?"

A plump, red-faced chieftain with an accent that marked him as being from the far west, said, "What if we get there and there's no way in?"

The man in the stool beside him, a kinsman undoubtedly from their similar looks and build, nodded agreement. "It's long been said that the Saxons didn't bother rebuilding those old forts to any great extent, because they knew they had the numbers to keep out any attackers. But what if we get there and it turns out to be wrong?"

Arthur shrugged. "Then we'll look for a way in and, if we can't find one that will cost us too many lives, we'll have to give up the siege before it begins." He steepled his fingers and looked directly at the men who'd asked the questions. "Trust me, my friends, I've no desire to lose any more brave warriors than we already have. This will hopefully be our best chance to sweep the sea-wolves from Britain for good but I'm not going to needlessly throw good men onto their spears to do it."

307

The westerners accepted this answer gladly, as did everyone else in the tent.

"All right then," said the warlord standing and clasping his hands behind his back as he looked around at them. "Ready your men to leave, and, gentlemen, thank you for volunteering for this. Yesterday was hard enough; what comes next could be even worse."

"I want to see those bastards dead," said a swarthy-looking middle-aged fellow who patted his sword hilt as he spoke. "Like you say, now's our chance. And besides," he gave a lopsided grin, "the chance to loot the Saxon fortress is too good to pass up."

The men filed out beneath the iron-grey sky, chatting quietly amongst themselves as they went, discussing what they might expect to find when they reached Hengist's stronghold, what their losses had been like yesterday, and what a shower of bastards the Saxons were.

"You two are coming with us?"

Bellicus nodded in reply to Arthur's question as the other captains headed back to their own units. "Aye, my lord. Why wouldn't we?"

Arthur held out his palms. "You're still not fully recovered from your injury, Bel, and Duro has already more than played his part in this war for now. Your advice is always welcome, both of you, but if you wanted to sit out this one, I'd understand. Some of your kinsmen from the north are coming with us anyway, led by your young friend Eburus."

"Why does that not surprise me?" Duro asked rhetorically. "If there's a fight to be had, Eburus will be there in the middle of it."

"Aye," Arthur laughed shortly. "He's a true warrior, that one. I wish we had a couple of hundred more like him. No-one would try to invade our lands then."

"One Eburus is more than enough," Bellicus said wryly. "As much as I like the big lad."

"It's settled then," Arthur said, and he was clearly pleased to know he could count on their continued presence. "Gather your things and be ready to leave when you hear the trumpet's call." He saluted in the Roman fashion, and Duro instantly returned the gesture with parade-ground precision. Bellicus merely nodded and led Cai and the centurion back to their tent to break camp.

They knew their business and it didn't take long to have the tent in pieces and stowed in its carry bag along with blankets, cooking utensils, supplies, and spare clothing. Their horses were readied, and laden with their packs, all well before Arthur's trumpeter sounded the advance.

"You think we'll finally end this war when we get to Garrianum?" Bellicus asked his friend. "I mean, we've been there, but it was night when we visited, remember?"

"How could I forget?" Duro replied, checking the buckles on his pack were firmly tightened and wouldn't come loose as they rode. "But I can't say if this will be it for Hengist or not. We were close to Garrianum once before, but, like you say, it was dark, and we were never inside the walls." He shook his head and looked to the east, where their destination lay. "I just pray to Mithras that I get a chance to face Horsa, man on man, blade on blade and, failing that, that I see his cold, lifeless body in the dirt before me."

The druid shared that hope, knowing that finally seeing his wife's killer dead would offer the centurion at least a little solace. A crumb of comfort that might allow him to move forward in his life.

The rest of the army around them were slowly dispersing, back to their own lands, laden with whatever booty Bedwyr had shared amongst them and tales of glory and valour to tell their people at home in their towns and villages. Bellicus and Duro jumped into their saddles and, with Cai an ever-present, comforting shadow, rode past the departing soldiers towards the head of the force Arthur was to lead eastwards.

"It's a pity about Lancelot," said Duro as they went, nodding and smiling at the happy warriors they passed. "I'd have liked to get to know him better. He could have done great things in this life."

"He had the skill with a blade, and the self-confidence to be a legend," Bellicus agreed sadly. "But the brightest flame burns quickest, and Lancelot was certainly a flaming brand in these dark times."

They soon reached the front of the line and joined up with Arthur and the other captains, then settled in for the journey, each wondering what they would find when they reached their destination.

309

CHAPTER THIRTY-SEVEN

The four-day march to Garrianum was uneventful and passed quickly enough. Since the men with them were volunteers there was little of the usual moaning about rations or sore feet or the speed their chiefs were pushing them at. Instead, the warriors seemed excited by the prospect of facing Hengist's followers once again and having a chance to take back whatever booty they could find. It had all been stolen from Britons after all, so liberating it seemed only fair to the marching soldiers.

Kay looked pained as they approached the towering walls of the Saxon fortress. "You better all prepare yourselves for the sight to come," he told them. "You might just see the severed head of a friend nailed up."

Bellicus noticed Arthur's face turn pale, but they did not slacken their pace and, at last, Garrianum, captured home to Hengist, *bretwalda* of the Saxons here in Britain, came into view. They'd not been accosted on the approach, although a large, bushy-bearded hunter, out searching for deer, or hares perhaps, had spotted them and immediately sprinted back to the safety of the walls. So, Hengist would know they were coming and be ready for them.

Garrianum's location on the estuary forced Arthur's warband to travel further south than they'd have liked, just as Lancelot's earlier group had done, before turning northeast once more. Unlike the previous force of Britons, however, Arthur's men found no ferries to cut short their journey, since the Saxons had sunk the boats and killed their owners after Lancelot's failed raid.

The great stone walls, as high as three men standing on top of one another, were intimidating as they came closer, and Bellicus tried to picture the fortress during the height of the Roman occupation. Ballistae on the towers and grim legionaries all along the walls, while smoke from cooking fires would rise up along with the sounds of smiths' hammers, barking dogs, merchants hawking their wares, and all the other bustle of a thriving settlement. The silence as Arthur's men marched towards them now was not quite as intimidating, but it was certainly unnerving.

"Why did the Roman's need such enormous forts to defend the sea?" Eburus demanded, staring at Bellicus as if he was personally responsible for Garrianum's construction. "They had the legions, after all. Wasn't that enough to deter pirates and raiders?"

"Who knows?" the druid replied, eyeing the impressive walls with some trepidation. "Maybe that wasn't the sites' purpose at all. Perhaps these fortresses were just built to house something? Food supplies, money from the trading ships, taxes…" He trailed off, shaking his head. "Could be they were never really supposed to stop the Saxons landing here. The Romans liked building walls; it kept their soldiers busy when they weren't killing people."

"How many of these places are there?" the Votadini warrior asked, using a hand to shade his eyes as he tried to see into the distance.

"Nine," Velugna said. "They must have been some sight when they were first constructed."

Rather to the druid's surprise, Velugna had accompanied Eburus here, after acquitting herself admirably in the earlier battle. Bellicus had warned the Votadini to be careful with the girl, who was, after all, a princess with a very protective king for a father, but Eburus assured him the two were just happy to enjoy one another's company while they could, with no hopes on either side of a more lasting relationship.

Duro nodded at the princess's comment. "Aye, but even I couldn't tell you exactly what these forts' purpose was. They were built long ago, well before my time in the army."

Eburus whistled and winked conspiratorially at Bellicus. "They must be ancient," he said, "if they're even older than you, Duro."

The centurion rolled his eyes as the Votadini chuckled at his own joke. "Just a bit, Eburus," he muttered. "Like a couple of hundred years or so. Even Sulinus wasn't around when these places were built."

There was nowhere to hide as they neared the main, eastern gatehouse. Figures were waiting atop the walls, watching as they marched closer.

"Oh, gods…" Arthur's voice trailed off painfully as he caught side of his foster-brother Cador's head, crudely severed and impaled on a spike atop Garrianum's wall. "I should never have sent you here," the warlord muttered and there were tears in his

311

eyes as memories of his childhood, of kindnesses the older Cador had shown him over the years, replayed in his mind.

"Arthur," a voice with a heavy Germanic accent called down to them happily when they were near enough to hear. "Good to see you, warlord. Leave your friends there and join me for a drink. We have much to discuss."

Mocking laughter followed his words and Bellicus could see the helmets and spears of men spread out all along the length of the fortifications. Wagons and rubble had been piled in front of the entrance, blocking it as effectively as any sturdy gates. It would take many men to clear a path through, all while being attacked from above by Saxon axes, stones, javelins and Taranis-knew what else.

"Aesibuas," Arthur said in a low voice to his cavalry commander. "Take a couple of your men and ride around the walls. See if there's another way in. Be sure and stay out of range of their archers and slingers, all right? You're far too valuable to lose."

The new decurion's back stiffened in pride at the warlord's words and he gave a crisp salute before riding off with a couple of his horsemen.

"Merlin," Hengist was shouting now. "Your effigy of me was very good. Looked a lot like me. Why don't you join Arthur and come in for a drink? You must be parched after riding all this way to see me. I'll have a rope let down for you both to climb up. Just be careful you don't dislodge any of the severed heads decorating my walls, eh?"

"We're not here to talk, you ugly bastard," Arthur shouted back furiously. "We're here to finish what we started on the battlefield. We're here to kill every last one of you, Hengist."

They were close enough that those with clear enough eyesight could see the *bretwalda* shaking his head as if saddened by his counterpart's threats. "Oh well. I suppose you might as well get on with it then. See you in a little while, eh?" With that, he wandered off to the right and was slowly lost from sight as he went down a flight of steps.

Arthur stared at the wall as if he might bring it down with the force of his gaze. The sight of Cador's and so many more of his own men's heads adorning the pale stone edifice was clearly affecting the warlord. Bellicus could tell by the tightness of his jaw and the way it twitched as he ground his teeth while trying to remain calm.

"How many of their soldiers are on the walls, do you think?" Merlin asked.

"Thirty," Bellicus and Duro said at the same time.

"And there's at least double that many inside," Arthur growled, "that we can't see from here."

"He's probably sent ships to the other forts the Saxons have occupied to ask for reinforcements," Bedwyr said dourly. "If we're going to attack them, we better do it soon, before their ships arrive from Branodunum and Othona."

Aesibuas's reconnaissance didn't take long. The trio of riders galloped along the walls unmolested by the enemy, probably because the Saxons wanted Arthur to know the size of the task he faced. Soon enough, Aesibuas returned, shaking his head.

"There's another entrance on the opposite side, my lord," he reported gloomily. "But, like the one here, it's blocked off." He didn't offer any opinion on how they might manage to get inside, but it was clear that would be incredibly difficult, if not impossible.

"Tell the men to rest awhile, Bedwyr," Arthur finally said in a resigned tone. "Eat something. Drink. And then we'll head back west. It would be madness to throw ourselves at those walls – we'd need to make ladders and Hengist will surely have cauldrons of burning hot oil and ashes ready to spill on us as we tried to make our way up."

Bedwyr nodded assent and rode back to spread the word among the ranks. Bellicus did not comment on Arthur's decision, and neither did anyone else. It was the only sensible option. Only Eburus seemed upset at missing out on another fight but even he knew better than to question Arthur.

"We should all rest and fill our bellies as well," Merlin said, sliding down from his horse's back and rummaging in his pack for a crust of bread. "We'll be wanting to put some distance between ourselves and Hengist during what's left of the day, in case he orders his men to follow, and attack us during the night."

The others followed his lead, dismounting and either getting something to eat or drink, or stretching tired legs after hours on horseback. Arthur remained alone, apart from the others as he paced, chewing dried meat and eyeing Garrianum as if he might spot some hitherto unnoticed entrance that would let his warband inside.

"Trust me," the warlord said, sensing Bellicus coming up behind him. "I'm as pissed off as any of you at simply riding away and letting Hengist escape so easily." He turned to look at the druid and, when he asked, "But what else can I do?" it didn't seem a rhetorical question.

Before Bellicus could reply, Eburus appeared.

"I've an idea," he said in his heavy northern accent. "Aye, we can't get in to kill the bastards behind their walls, but they can't get out to us either, unless they want to meet us in battle again. And we've already handed them their arses, so they'll not be wanting to fight us any time soon."

Arthur gazed at the slyly smiling Votadini champion and then he understood what Eburus was getting at.

"We can do what we like out here without any fear of attack," said the warlord.

Eburus grinned, white teeth flashing behind his ginger beard. "Exactly, my lord."

Arthur was nodding and Bellicus watched the pair, like naughty boys about to raid a farmer's orchard.

"Come on then, what are we waiting for?" Arthur led them back to the rest of the men and explained what he wanted from them. There was no shortage of volunteers to go with him, but he left half the warband, including Velugna, in the care of Bellicus, Duro and Merlin while he, Eburus and Kay took the rest off towards the shore which Garrianum had, supposedly, been built to defend.

314

CHAPTER THIRTY-EIGHT

The Great Estuary was well named, Arthur thought as they came to the end of the western wall of the fortress and the view opened out before them. The sea disappeared into the distance on the right but, ahead of them, far across the estuary on the land on the opposite side, the men could just make out a similar fortress to Garrianum.

"Is that another one?" Eburus asked in surprise.

"It is," Arthur confirmed. "Any Saxon pirates mad or stupid enough to come raiding here would've been attacked on two sides by the Roman ships in a pincer movement." He shook his head at the sheer scale and ambition of the legions' war machine. "Truly," he muttered, "the Romans have changed the world with their desire for conquest."

"Well," the Votadini replied, hearing Arthur's low words, "we're about to change the world for Hengist and his crowd of goat-shagging bastards. Look – their ships are all lined up and ready for us."

"Like whores in a brothel," someone said with a crude laugh.

"Aye," Eburus shouted, joining in with the merriment. "But we're going to hump them for free and leave Hengist to pay the bill!"

Arthur smiling, shook his head, well-used to the crude language of his men but not really one to join in with it. Eburus was right, though. Hengist was going to be left with quite a mess to clear up once the warriors of Britain were done here this day.

Only Kay was not laughing and joking as they approached the Saxons' ships on the beach and at the old ruined docks. He still felt guilty for surviving while Lancelot, Cador and the rest had been cut down, heads taken as gruesome ornaments for Hengist's pleasure. This was no substitute for sliding his blade deep into Jarl Leofdaeg's guts but destroying the row of ships would bring some measure of satisfaction. Everyone knew the Saxons loved their ships the way Sulinus's old cavalrymen loved their horses.

"There's not as many as I expected," Arthur said, counting ten large ships and a number of smaller vessels. "They must have feared we'd do this and taken some of them away with a skeleton crew."

"There's enough," Eburus growled, drawing out his flint and steel. "Enough for a fine bonfire."

"An offering to the gods, in thanks for our victory at Nant Beac," Arthur said. "Come on, let's get it done. Kay, you take ten men and start at the end, there. Eburus, you and your Votadini warriors do the ones nearest us. I'll take the centre, nearest the fortress's western gate. Stay alert," he called, so everyone could hear. "We're not too far from the walls. Their slingers might hit us with a lucky shot, so we do this as quickly as possible then get back to the others, all right?"

"Search each ship for anything of value before you set alight to it," Kay ordered. "They've probably been stripped of valuables but take a quick look anyway."

The guards on Garrianum's walls were watching in dismay, knowing exactly what the Britons were planning. Insults were called in their own harsh tongue and a handful of arrows were fired but fell well short of Arthur's men who had by now made it the first of the ships.

Arthur pulled himself on board the fourth large ship in the line and, with three of his men, hastily searched the vessel for any goods or valuables that might be useful. They found nothing and immediately all four set to the task of burning the ship, which proved more difficult than any of them expected. There were ropes on board, however, and these were formed into a pile which caught fire rather easier than the plain boards of the hull.

"That should do it," Arthur said to the warriors with him as, at last, the flames took hold. "Let's move on."

They jumped down onto the beach and hurried to the next ship in the line. Already, the first ship was burning nicely, as the pine tar the Saxon builders had used as waterproofing worked as an accelerant, spreading the conflagration quickly along the whole length of the vessel.

"Yes! This is fun!"

Arthur couldn't help laughing at Eburus's childish shout of triumph as his targeted ship also finally began to burn and he led his small group onto another one.

More arrows were being fired at them from the fortress's walls, and stones from slings too, but none had so far done any damage. Arthur could see Hengist and Horsa watching them now, and, even at this distance he could see they were arguing. No doubt the headstrong younger brother would be looking to come out and try to stop this destruction but Hengist, older and wiser, would see it as a wasted effort.

It took Kay's group longer to get their ship burning properly but, by the time he rejoined Arthur and Eburus half of the beached ships were ablaze, and their men were busily working on the remainder.

"We're going to have company soon," Eburus shouted over the crackling, hissing and shattering noises that accompanied a ship fire. "Look."

Arthur turned to see Saxons hurriedly clearing away the rubble they'd piled up in front of the western gates. "Aesibuas!" he shouted to the newly promoted decurion who was seated atop his mount back at the north-west corner of Garrianum's wall.

The rider could not have heard his call, but he saw Arthur's waving arm and immediately galloped out of sight.

"Keep setting fire to the ships," Arthur commanded his men. They were nervously watching the Saxons at the gate, noting the progress the sea-wolves were making in clearing a way through. Indeed, four or five of them were already outside and more were joining them with every passing heartbeat. "Eburus. Kay. With me." He looked along the line of ships and gestured for those who weren't actively setting fire to a ship to come and join him as he formed them all into a shieldwall.

"Shit, we've made them really angry," Eburus said and, although his words were fearful, he was laughing as he said them. "They really, *really,* love their boats, don't they?"

Arthur gritted his teeth and took his shield from his back, holding it up as the Saxons, having sufficient numbers at last, began charging towards them, faces twisted in rage and hatred.

"If they managed to fit through the gatehouse," Kay said to Arthur in a low, cold tone. "So can we."

The warlord shook his head emphatically. "No, Kay. They still have dozens of men on the walls to pick us off as we filed through. We defend ourselves here, then, once the ships are all burning, get back to the rest of the men. All right? All right?" He was forced to repeat the last as Kay ignored his question the first time it was asked, such was Kay's desire to make amends for the last time he'd faced the Saxons in battle.

The charging enemy was almost upon them now. Twenty, against the similar number in Arthur's line, as some of them continued their attempts to burn the ships.

"Brace!" roared the warlord, and then a snarling warrior smashed his axe down, clattering into Arthur's shield and the fight began in earnest.

"Waelisc bastards!" the tall, wild-bearded Saxon was screaming at him as they traded blows, and Arthur guessed he was the owner of one of the ships behind him. The man seemed enraged by the Britons' actions and wasn't just hammering his sword against Arthur's shield, but the two flanking the warlord as well. Until Arthur leaned to the right and thrust his long sword into the Saxon's chest.

There was no sense of triumph, only desperation to remain alive as another enemy axeman took the place of his fallen comrade and the force from yet another blow travelled through the wood of his shield and up into his aching left arm. He held it in place, teeth bared in a snarl, but the next attack did not hit his shield, it struck the front of his helmet and Arthur felt his legs give way. He slumped down, all the strength emptying from him beneath that single, terrible blow, and the enemy warrior that had struck him screamed in triumph and slashed his axe down again.

Another blue and white painted shield came out of nowhere and knocked the Saxon to one side, as Kay, roaring unintelligible, bitter words, attacked in a blur of motion and fury.

Pain filled Arthur's head and he was forced to look down to save from vomiting. When he looked up again Kay was standing over him like a guardian angel, sword, shield, legs all acting as weapons as he kept more attackers at bay until, mercifully, the nausea and confusion passed, and Arthur pushed himself back to his feet as the fight raged on.

Smoke filled the air, along with the sounds of the ships being destroyed by the raging fires and the outraged war-cries of the Saxons, but Eburus was shouting gleefully, "Ah, good sea air. Can't beat it, eh, lads?" as he smashed the pommel of his sword down on a man's skull.

318

The mad Votadini might be enjoying himself, but Arthur could focus only on the tiny part of the world that lay in front of him, as he was forced to defend himself with sword and shield over and over again, sometimes stabbing or slashing himself, but this continued for what seemed like an age. All was a blur of sound, and smells, and aching muscles, until, at last, the pressure in front of him gave way and reality seemed to rush in on him like a wave.

Aesibuas's cavalry had come, and rather than coming from the west, they rode all the way around the fortress's perimeter to the east. This meant their shields, held on the left, were able to protect them from any missiles launched from the walls, while using their javelins to attack those who'd sallied forth from the fortress to engage Arthur's shieldwall.

Sulinus might not have had much time to train his cavalry in as many things as he'd have liked, but he'd made sure they spent many hours honing their javelin throwing skills. It was worth it, as the enemy warriors engaging Arthur's pyromaniacs were almost completely wiped out in that first pass.

Aesibuas led his riders away to safety as the last of the Saxon's were finished off by Arthur's men, and the ships went up in flames.

"We're done here," Arthur bellowed, stooping to finish off an axeman who was trying to crawl back to the safety of Garrianum's gatehouse. "Keep your shields up and follow me."

At a steady pace the formation moved off, following the cavalry who were well in front of them by now, but Arthur was watching the gates and saw no more enemy warriors filtering through the narrow, cleared space in the rubble piled there. On top of the wall Horsa and Hengist had ceased their argument and simply watched the Britons as they made their way back around to the rest of their warband.

"How many have we lost?"

Eburus glanced back along their line and counted quickly, his face lighting up in astonishment as he looked back and met Arthur's eyes. "I don't think we lost a single man, my lord," said the Votadini champion.

"We almost lost one," Arthur said, removing his helmet and looking at the dent on the front. "You saved my life, Kay. Any guilt or remorse you felt about not dying beside Lancelot should be forgotten now. I'm forever in your debt, old friend."

Kay, utterly exhausted after his part in the fighting, smiled in reply and, when Aesibuas's riders escorted them safely back to Merlin, Bellicus and the rest of the warband, the cheers and joyful shouts at the success of their mission lifted everyone's spirits.

It might only be a few ships, and Hengist and Horsa might yet live while Lancelot's warband was lost, but, somehow, this small victory felt immensely important to them all. The Saxons had had things their own way for too long here in these eastern lands, but today, and the battle at Nant Beac, would show Hengist that times were changing.

This was the beginning of the end for the sea-wolves, Arthur vowed. The Bear of Britain had finally shown he was worthy of that extravagant appellation, and he wasn't about to take his foot from the Saxons' throat now that he had the advantage at last.

CHAPTER THIRTY-NINE

"What next for you, Duro, my friend?"

It was an hour after the ships had been set alight and the smoke was still lingering about the walls of Garrianum as Arthur's warband rested and gathered a breath before setting off on the road back to the west. The centurion was sitting enjoying some bread and beer beside Bellicus on the grass, and he looked up to see Arthur standing by his shoulder after spending a long time looking at the severed heads adorning the fortress's walls.

"You've sworn no oaths to me," the warlord said to him. "But I'd welcome you as a permanent member of my staff, if you were willing. I need men like you beside me."

The centurion rubbed a hand through his hair and thought for a moment. "I'm not sure," he replied eventually, glancing at Bellicus, as if his friend might offer some advice. "I've sworn to see Horsa dead, and he's still up there on the wall beside his brother, looking down on me. But…"

"You wish to remain with Bel," Arthur said, nodding, an understanding smile on his bearded face. "I appreciate that. It's not often one finds such a good friend in this life. Think on it, though, centurion. My offer will remain open." He walked off to speak with Merlin, leaving them sitting in thoughtful silence.

"What do you think?" Duro asked as they finished off the last of their short meal.

Bellicus stood up, rolling his head from side to side and grimacing at the cracks and pops he heard as a result. "I'd be sad to say goodbye to you," he said. "Of course. We've been through so much, and Cai would miss you too. But, like you say, you've sworn vengeance on Horsa and there's little chance of you getting that if you come back to Dun Breatann with me."

As Duro got to his feet they faced one another with serious expressions and the centurion opened his mouth to say something else. Bellicus could tell before the words were spoken that their time together was coming to an end and he felt a lump form in his throat.

"Bellicus! Bellicus of Dun Breatann!"

321

A voice came from behind them, calling the druid's name, and he turned, trying to see who was searching for him.

"Bellicus, Druid of Dun Breatann," the voice was shouting, more urgently now. "Where is he? Come on, he's hard to miss by Taranis, someone must know where he is!"

Someone must have given the hunter directions, for the thunder of hooves approached them and they reined in their mounts, loosening swords in their sheaths just in case the man searching for Bellicus was there to do him mischief, unlikely as it seemed surrounded by allies as they were.

When the rider came closer Bellicus felt a momentary surge of pleasure, for he recognised the man – he was one of Gavo's guards from Dun Breatann. Panic flared in the next instant though, as he wondered why the man was here. What could be important enough for the guard captain to send a messenger all the way to Garrianum from Dun Breatann? Something dire, for sure, but what? His imagination whirled as he thought of young Princess Catia, Narina, Gavo, his kith and kin back home, and the idea that something terrible had befallen one or all of them.

Duro too had recognised the rider by now and he was having similar thoughts to Bellicus. They shared worried frowns, and the druid forced himself to remain calm, using his training to slow his breathing and stave off the involuntary fight-or-flight response his body was instinctively slipping into.

"Beda!" the druid shouted, waving to the rider. "Beda, I'm here."

The man's head turned as he heard his name called and, with obvious relief, headed directly towards them.

"What's wrong?" Bellicus asked, before Beda – who should have been back in Dun Breatann teaching Catia how to use a sword among his other, usual duties – had even jumped down from his horse. "Why are you here?"

Cai, recognising the lean messenger, sidled up to Beda, pressing against him and receiving an absent pat in return.

"Bel, thank the gods you're here, I've been riding for bloody days. Thought my journey was finished when I met Arthur's army back in—"

"Why are you here?" the druid broke in. "What's happened?"

Beda took a deep breath, gathering himself and nodding a silent greeting to Duro. "It's Princess Catia," he said. "She's disappeared."

Bellicus blinked. Disappeared? From an impregnable fortress in a land that was at peace with its neighbours? "What are you talking about?" he demanded. "Disappeared how?"

"The Pictish woman," Beda replied. "Aife. We think she kidnapped the princess and is taking her back north to her father, King Drest, in Dunnottar."

"Shit," Duro exploded. "I knew it was a mistake having that swordswoman about. She was always going to be trouble. Too young, too full of life to be kept a prisoner in Dun Breatann for long."

Bellicus's mind was whirling. Not this again. Catia, his daughter although only Queen Narina and he knew it, had already been abducted once before in her young life. It had been a terrible experience that had changed the girl forever, and the thought of her suffering like that again was almost too much for the druid to take in.

And yet...Aife? Bellicus liked the young woman. Aye, she was that useless prick Drest's offspring, but she seemed an honourable girl, and a likeable one too. Would she really have kidnapped Catia? How? How would she even have managed it, if she'd decided to go through with it?

He couldn't make any sense of the report, but there would be plenty of time to think things over on the long ride north. Turning to Duro he grasped his friend by the arm and said, "Farewell then, centurion. I hope you find Horsa and kick his arse. I'd best be off. The sooner I leave, the sooner I can start hunting for Catia."

Duro's brows drew together and he didn't let go of Bellicus's arm as the druid tried to turn away and mount Darac. "Farewell?"

"Aye," Bellicus replied, irritated at being held up, fearing every moment wasted was vital. "I'm going back to Dun Breatann *now.*"

"And you think I'll let you go without me?" Duro demanded. "When Catia is in danger?" He released the druid's arm and headed for his own horse, buckling his pack and jumping into the saddle. "I didn't help you rescue her from the Saxons just to let the Picts take her, Bel. I'm coming with you."

Despite the peril of Catia's situation, Bellicus couldn't help the grin from spreading across his face. A tear even threatened to spill from the corner of an eye, and he turned away, saying gruffly to Beda, "Thank you, Beda, for delivering your message. Rest a while. You and your horse must be exhausted. Bedwyr will make sure you're taken care of. Then travel home with the rest of our men." He saluted the messenger then shouted, "Eburus! Mount up. We're riding northwards, right now."

"What the fu—"

Princess Velugna grabbed the Votadini champion and kissed him passionately, halting his expletive before he could finish it. "Go!" she said, eyes shining. "I've enjoyed our time together, but we'll meet again, my young warrior."

"I hope so, my lady," Eburus replied, returning her kisses but more than a little dazed by the speed of this unexpected farewell.

"Bellicus," Arthur called, striding back to look up at the druid on Darac's back as Eburus, shaking his head in consternation, ran past them to fetch his own horse. "What's the rush? Is everything all right?"

Quickly, the druid explained what was happening and Arthur reached out, clasping arms with Bellicus, Duro, and then Eburus, thanking them for their part in the recent victories over the Saxons.

"Go, my friends," said the warlord. "With my blessing, and the gratitude of everyone in these lands. I hope to see you all again though. Soon?"

"Count on it, Arthur," Duro said with a grim smile. "I still have a score to settle with that whoreson Horsa, and the best place to do it is by your side."

"I'm always glad to do my bit, kicking Saxon arse," Eburus said, "and I'll be back to see you, princess, as soon as I can." He was holding the reins tightly as he tried to turn his horse and it reared unexpectedly although serendipitously for it made him appear quite heroic and Velugna's smile reflected that.

"We'll meet again, my lord," Bellicus said with a wave to Arthur. "Farewell, Bear of Britain! And farewell to you, Merlin, my brother. Bedwyr. Princess." He nodded to the others and then impatience overcame his manners and he kicked Darac into a canter just as Arthur was ruffling Cai's ears one last time.

324

Very soon they were past the surprised warriors who'd come with them to Garrianum, and on the road back home.

"Why am I here?" Eburus asked, shouting to be heard over the wind rushing past them thanks to the swift pace Bellicus had set. "I'm not one of your Damnonii, or a Pict. Why didn't you leave me to come back north with the rest of our men?"

Bellicus looked across at him, ground passing in a blur beneath Darac's pounding hooves. "You're here because you're my friend, Eburus," he called. "And I want you with me as we try to sort out whatever's going on in Dun Breatann."

Eburus's face lit up in an almost boyish delight. He wasn't used to people wanting him around and this, along with his recent tryst with Velugna, made him feel happier than he could remember for a long time. "I'm glad to hear that, druid," he replied. "But did you see how happy Arthur was when you told him we were leaving? He seemed glad to see the back of us."

Duro laughed at that, and Eburus turned on him. "What's so funny, Roman?" he barked.

"He wasn't happy because we were leaving," the centurion replied. "Did you not see the severed heads on Hengist's wall?"

"Aye," Eburus shouted. "Why would that make Arthur happy?"

"Because," Bellicus broke into their back-and-forth. "Lancelot's wasn't amongst them. Now, shut up and ride, we've got a long way to go." With that, he led them onwards, three riders and one massive, loping dog.

The druid was going home. He dreaded to think what would greet him when they got there, but the gods were with him and, with his friends by his side and Melltgwyn in his hand, he would face it head on.

Dis Pater take any who tried to stand in their way...

TO BE CONTINUED

If you enjoyed *The Bear of Britain* please leave a rating and/or review. It's a huge help and is greatly appreciated!

Author's Note

Ah, the sword in the stone! An iconic Arthurian image – one which everyone knows, so it surely has to be included in any book mentioning the origins of our titular warlord, right? But *The Bear of Britain* is historical fiction, not fantasy so how can we explain what was clearly some kind of magical event? Well, that depends on what you call 'magic'. As readers of the earlier books in this series will know, the druids don't shoot blue fire from their fingers or levitate or ride dragons. Instead, Bellicus and Merlin use the power of suggestion, superstition, psychology, hidden knowledge, theatre, and even trickery to work their 'magic' on the world. With that in mind, I thought making Arthur's sword a crude magnet might work. Nowadays, electromagnets could very easily be used to perform this trick but I've probably stretched the truth a little in suggesting this as the explanation for the sword in the stone. As reported by Pliny the Elder, the shepherd, Magnes, was supposedly the first person to discover magnetism when the iron nails in his shoes stuck to piece of magnetite ore on a hillside. I doubt you could find such a naturally occurring magnet strong enough to hold a sword in place while a man tried to pull it free, but allied with the power of suggestion, and some pressure on the blade in a perpendicular direction, it might just be enough. I can see someone like British stage magician/mentalist Derren Brown pulling off a trick like this. It's certainly possible.

Next in our well-known list of Arthurian tropes is the character Lancelot. My editor asked me if there wasn't an older, Brittonic or Welsh, name for him. Well, yes, but Lanslod simply doesn't sound very nice! Some characters, like Bedwyr, appeared in the earliest of these legends, while others, like Guinevere/ Gwenhwyfar came later, but none of them were recorded in the fifth century when they're supposed to have lived. They are, most likely, all completely fictional so I feel quite justified in going with the name Lancelot simply because everyone knows it and it sounds pleasant.

Similarly, yeah, I know 'mirror' wasn't a word in the fifth-century, but I could hardly call a piece of polished metal a 'looking glass' and the old Roman word for it, *speculum,* means something quite different nowadays... Sometimes I just go with what fits the story best...

Now, onto book five, where we'll discover what happened to Catia and Lancelot. Your guesses are as good as mine, since I haven't really planned anything out yet. I hope you'll join me to find out!

Steven A. McKay,
Old Kilpatrick,
September 24th, 2021

Acknowledgements

Usually, this space is taken up by thanking editors, beta readers and the like, but this time I want to thank my readers Terry and Lauren Boodell. When Terry saw the shield on the cover for this novel he painted a full-size replica shield just like it, and actually sold it to me when I told him how awesome it looked! Lauren also sent me some really nice messages and I was quite moved by how much both of them enjoy my writing. It was a lovely reminder that my books mean a lot to some people, and it made me very happy.

Thanks must also go to my editor, Richenda, and Bernadette McDade who helped me polish the text before publishing. And, my designers at More Visual do a great job on my covers and social media images and I'm always very grateful for their excellent, timely work. For this particular novel I wanted to be sure I wasn't making huge mistakes describing the cavalry and horses so riders (and readers!) Leni McCormick and Jonathan Hopkins deserve a big shout-out for casting their expert eyes across a couple of advance copies and keeping me right.

I'd also like to thank *everyone* who's reviewed my books, but there's a couple of bloggers who've supported me from the start and still do, despite going through some hard times of their own recently. I greatly appreciate it, and wish both all the best. Cheers, guys!

ALSO BY STEVEN A. McKAY

The Forest Lord Series:
Wolf's Head
The Wolf and the Raven
Rise of the Wolf
Blood of the Wolf

The Warrior Druid of Britain Chronicles
The Druid
Song of the Centurion
The Northern Throne

LUCIA – A Roman Slave's Tale

Printed in Great Britain
by Amazon

84412910R00192